NO PORTRAIT IN THE GILDED FRAME

No Portrait in the Gilded Frame

Tudor Alexander

ISBN-13: 9781530623143
ISBN-10: 1530623146

ÍNDEX

For Vio

How beautiful you are, my darling!
Oh, how beautiful!
Your eyes behind your veil are doves.
Your hair is like a flock of goats
descending from the hills of Gilead.

(Song of Songs, 4.1, The Old Testament)

PROLOGUE

"Look how beautiful you are," he said to me. "Look at your long, black hair and your smooth, white skin. Look at the sky-deep color of your eyes and the delicate eyebrows arching like gateways into your soul. Look at your lips, red and sensuous, reminding me of sweet, freshly picked strawberries. Look at your nose and small, rounded chin that tell me about your playfulness and determination."

"Yeah," I said, wondering how much he loved me. "Look at me…"

We met at a difficult time in my life. He took me and cuddled me and asked me to follow him. In his company, I was as beautiful and uninhibited as I desired to be. When he told me his life story, I wanted to trust him, and I followed him the way my husky follows me today in the streets of Tel Aviv. Of course I had doubts. There were rumors and gestures and comments and fears and telltale signs.

He was over forty, I was twenty-two, and we only saw the blue sky ahead of us.

And now that I have retreated from the noise and the world, I have Bari and Yari with me.

PART 1

Chapter 1

CHILDHOOD

My name is Miriam, or *Miri* to those close to me. Miri, a diminutive like the purr of a cat, like a squirrel's dash through dry leaves. My surname is Sommer. It is pronounced with a *z* in the beginning, and it sounds foreign in Romania, the country where I was born.

I remember the balance of my early childhood in the mid-1950s: my mother and father; my older brother, Jacob, and younger sister, Adina; our three-room apartment in a building near the railway station; kids rolling hoops, jumping rope, or drawing with chalk on the sidewalk; the farmers' market at the outskirts of town; the sky; the river; the ruins; and the traveling circus that visited at the end of each summer.

We lived in a town called *Bistriţa*, in Northern Romania. My father, who worked for the government, told us that Bistriţa, thirty thousand strong, was the capital of Năsăud County, a place crucial in the struggle of the proletariat.

Horse-drawn carriages waited for passengers in front of the railway station. The horses were scary to me, huge, their tails constantly swooshing, and the air near them smelled of dung.

The tall Evangelical church stood in Main Square. A few hundred yards from there, on Victoria Street, was my maternal grandparents' apartment. We visited them often. Their apartment was old, spacious, and drafty; it stayed cool in the summer and had many dark places for me to hide in and disappear. It also had a fenced-in courtyard and a former stable.

A man and a woman lived in the former stable, I was told, because of the severe housing crisis. The woman's name was Ileana. When I visited her she treated me to freshly fried pumpkin seeds generously salted. We spat the shells on a newspaper spread out on the dirt floor and drank lemonade from a pitcher. In the fall, Ileana got sacks of corn from the farm cooperative and let me pull the husks off the ears and play with the soft brown silk. The man, who I assumed was Ileana's husband, had strong arms, wore torn undershirts, and was always tinkering. When he wasn't tinkering, he was drinking plum brandy. All of us, my grandparents included, called him Uncle Tokachi, even though he was no uncle of ours. To begin with, he was much younger than my grandparents, perhaps younger than my parents, and, besides, he was Hungarian.

We were Jewish, although in those times we weren't too vocal about it. Grandfather, especially, had this idea that being Jewish was a family secret. For a while I didn't understand his fears too well, and I surmised that as far as family secrets went, they were always complicated. I also figured out that my grandfather didn't like my father too much, but my mother loved him, and that was what mattered.

My grandparents' parents came to Romania from a city called Lvov in Galicia in the 1900s in search of a better life. After the Soviets took over Lvov and, as my grandfather put it, liberated Romania at the end of World War II, his being originally from a territory now belonging to the Soviet Union could have gotten him a ticket straight to Siberia. Even I knew Siberia was a dreaded destination. To ensure this didn't happen, my grandparents tried to disappear by settling in Bistrița, a sleepy town in the middle of nowhere, and by changing their last name from Levin, which was typical Jewish, to Levinescu, which sounded Romanian; then my grandfather joined the Communist Party. He was a doctor, for a time the chief cardiac surgeon for the County of Năsăud, and had to rush to the hospital each time there was an emergency. A black telephone mounted on a wall in my grandparents' bedroom alerted him with its shrieking ring, inevitably in the evenings. The phone didn't have a dial—just a cradle that supported the receiver—and to make a call you had to talk to an operator.

Whenever the phone rang, my grandmother answered. "Comrade Levinescu is resting," she pleaded with the caller. "The doctor is taking a nap after a long day," she argued in her slightly accented Romanian. "He has a weak heart as you know, and if you want him around, keep in mind he's no longer a spring chicken."

They wouldn't listen and would send an ambulance to pick him up, or an army truck, or a horse-drawn carriage. A black Volga sedan stopped in front of the building once or twice, and often my grandfather would be gone for the night and the morning after.

Before he left, grandmother made sure he had his nitroglycerine tablets.

He tried to calm her down. "Erica, this is my duty."

"Your duty is to your family," my grandmother countered, her accent amplified by frustration.

"The party is his new family," my father said when he happened to be present. "Comrade *Levinovich* yearns to be with his comrades. Together they constitute a dialectical unit that cannot be severed by our *petit bourgeois* sword."

I didn't understand all the words, but I knew my father was kidding, inserting humor into a tense situation. My grandfather didn't appreciate it. In particular, he was annoyed at my father's habit of russifying his last name after the trouble he had gone through to change it. But my father did that to everyone, as a joke or a term of endearment. He called me *Mirichka*, and my siblings *Jacobski* and *Adinka*. He was a member of the Communist Party as well, but he seemed to take his responsibilities less seriously. His demeanor was playful, and he didn't think everyone's purpose in life was to uncover my grandfather's history and deport him to Siberia.

"It's his youthful inexperience," my grandfather would say.

Except that my father was anything but inexperienced. After serving in a labor camp for Jewish youth during the war, he joined the Soviets and marched with them all the way to Berlin, possessed by a silent determination for survival. Upon his return he found out that his parents had perished in the concentration camps, as had his older brother. He settled in Bistriţa, his hometown, and dedicated his efforts to reconstruction. At the beginning of the war he had studied engineering in Cluj, but he had never graduated. After the war he became an administrator with the county—part of the new dictatorship of the proletariat. His government-issued apartment was not as nice as Grandfather's, but my father wasn't envious. And he wasn't afraid. He refused to deny his heritage and didn't change his name, thus causing his children to end up with the surname that sounded like a false note in Romania.

While my father didn't hide his Jewishness, he didn't promote it either. He hoped the country was entering a new era of equality in which religion and ethnicity would lose their significance. His sense of humor and, taking into account his war experiences, his surprising and uncanny optimism gave him an aura that women found hard to resist. My mother told me how she fell in love with him within five minutes of their first encounter. I was convinced that my father antagonized my grandparents without malice. I also knew that he changed his mind often and always defended vehemently his newest conviction.

The Perlmans lived for a while in the two rooms on the first floor of my grandparents' house. The rooms were not connected, and they opened into the fenced-in courtyard. The family had five members, including an aunt and two boys, named Ezra and Mordechai, too young for me to play with. The boys were wild, often running through the courtyard in the rain buck naked, always fighting, throwing rocks, or chasing small animals. They were short and chubby, round almost, and both had heads full of very curly hair. Romulus and Remus, my father nicknamed them. As far as I could see, the family didn't do anything to hide *their* Jewishness. They kept the required holidays, went to the synagogue, and taught Ezra and Mordechai Hebrew. At Purim the boys' aunt brought Grandmother platefuls of *hamantaschen*. It was, she told me, their way of showing gratitude to my grandfather for having arranged for them to live in the two rooms downstairs.

One year before my parents separated, the Perlmans packed their belongings and left for Israel.

When my father decided to divorce my mother, he took me aside. "I'm sorry," he said, "but I don't know how to handle your mother. I wish she'd scream at me, scratch my eyes out. I wish she'd be angry, but no, she's forgiven me. I don't want her forgiveness, Miri. I love you and I'll miss you, but at this point all I want is to get the hell out of here."

I was nine years old, and I understood that my father was furious. He didn't use words like *hell* in my presence. Until that moment the mother-father union had seemed monolithic to me. Their love could only be for each other and for us—my brother, my sister, and me.

With time, I intuited both my parents were at fault, and I was angry with them both, yet I mostly blamed my mother. It was easier to blame her. She was the one always there, always providing opportunities to disobey, to talk back to her, or to make faces when she looked away. By disappearing from our lives, my father acquired imaginary qualities. I soon realized he had left for another woman, and even that seemed excusable to me, since he really didn't leave me; he left my mother. He left her nagging habit of always trying to smooth things over, to make them proper. He left her for not being spontaneous. He cheated on her, and she begged him to reconsider for the sake of not breaking up the family. She humiliated herself, and she forgave him.

Could you beg to be loved? I didn't think so, and over time I resolved not to be like my mother.

Before he left, my father gave me a black-and-white photograph of the two of us standing on a wave breaker in Eforie, a Black Sea resort: a skinny little girl holding tight to a tall man with youthful features and eyes as gray and restless as the sea in the background. Growing up, I looked at that photograph many times with nostalgia, wishing that I would inherit my father's bright personality and his ability to always land on his feet.

Even though my father contributed financially and my mother worked, she still needed help, and after the separation we moved in with her parents.

I was in fourth grade when Jacob's math teacher suggested that Jacob change his name.

"Change it how?" my mother asked.

"To Levinescu," Jacob said.

"Because your father moved out?"

"I don't know." Jacob looked confused. He had the long Levin, or Levinescu, face and the aquiline nose. The pale shade of a mustache was taking form over his upper lip. "The teacher laughed," Jacob added. "He said Sommer is German and Levinescu sounds better in Romanian, unless I preferred Somerescu, which would be the best of all worlds."

"*Sommer* means summer in German," I said.

"Everybody knows *that*," Jacob said.

"This has nothing to do with your father," my mother said and got red in the face. "This is chauvinistic."

"It's because we are Jewish," my grandmother said.

My mother decided to call my father. He and the other woman were in the process of moving to Bucharest, but they were still in the area. My mother used the phone in my grandparents' bedroom, and we listened to her voice, which penetrated through the wall and at times rose to a shrill.

"He wasn't joking," my mother said to my father, obviously referring to the math teacher. "I'm sure of it." She continued after a brief silence, during which she listened to my father speak. "Yes, I know there are Germans in town, and Hungarians and Romanians and Gypsies and Poles. You're such an idealist, Rudy, really." My father's name was Rudolph, and my mother used to call him Rudy at home. "Yes, because we are Jewish," she yelled a little later. "Listen, I don't care what world you believe in! You need to speak to the principal, that's what you need to do. You're still Jacob's father, and you still have some pull in this town."

Perhaps my father spoke to the principal, or maybe he spoke to somebody else or to nobody at all. My mother never brought up the subject again, but I began feeling conflicted by a self-awareness I didn't invite. Many people changed their names in those years. I wanted my father, not my grandfather, to be right, and for us to live in a new and perfect society where religion didn't matter. I didn't want to stand out on account of my Jewishness, or my surname, and at the time I didn't know you could be hated for it. All I wanted was to be like the rest of the children, at least like the majority of them, and I slowly worked my way back into believing that I was like them, especially since nothing indicated the contrary.

Jacob started high school, which was in a building adjacent to the middle school, and got a slew of new teachers. My parents' divorce was finalized, and we, the children, kept our surnames, while my mother casually changed hers back to Levinescu.

In middle school the girls had PE class together with the boys. Some girls were precocious, and on certain days they didn't feel like PE. The teachers understood, while the boys were always quick to comment and make it unpleasant for the girls.

My friend Claudia asked to be excused from PE one day, and I decided to join her even though I didn't have a good reason. When, an hour later, we returned to normal class, a bunch of boys blocked our way. Ricu, a new classmate, seemed in charge. His father was a member of a patriotic guard that traveled from major construction site to major construction site throughout the country, at the direction of the party. At the time they were building a new road from Cluj to Vatra Dornei and farther through the Carpathians all the way to Suceava. Bistrița was on the way. Ricu's father, a hero of the regime, and his family, along with the families of other workers like him, were temporarily housed in barracks along the route. Their children attended local schools for the duration of each assignment.

"Girls, not feeling that well today?" Ricu asked in a piercing voice, mockingly looking at us and at the sneering boys gathered around him.

"None of your business," Claudia said.

"C'mon, don't be shy. We know what your monthly problem is." He pronounced *problem* with peculiar emphasis, as if forced to acknowledge an unpleasant fact of life and imitating the cold and realistic tone he might have heard adults use when discussing the subject.

"Maybe you have a problem in your head," Claudia responded, not very inspired.

The boys whistled and laughed.

"Go back to your barracks," I said.

Ricu laughed with the other boys, but when he looked at me, I realized he was sad.

Later he ambushed us again.

"How you doing, *Spring Sommer?*" he addressed me.

The boys chanted, "Spring Sommer! Spring Sommer!" and started making faces.

"You're all stupid," Claudia said, clenching her fists.

They weren't just stupid. They were mean, and even though their meanness was only clumsily expressed by their words, I could read it in their faces.

"Call her *Winter*," one boy suggested. "Look at her snowy-white skin."

"Snowflake," another boy said.

I liked that nickname and surprised myself by bowing in his direction, smiling and extending my thanks.

The boy changed his tune. "Blob of slob," he uttered.

"Marshmallow," Ricu said.

"Marshmallow, marshmallow!" the boys chanted.

"So white because all she does is read the Torah," Ricu said.

The next day Claudia and I were summoned to the principal's office. My mother, Ricu, and Ricu's father were there. Ricu kept his eyes to the ground. His hair was disheveled, his face flushed, and I saw finger marks on his jaw and the back of his neck. I couldn't be sure, but I guessed his father had slapped him.

The principal asked me to recall the events of the previous day, and asked Claudia to confirm. He seemed mostly intrigued over Ricu's comment regarding the Torah. "Do you read at the synagogue?" he asked me.

"I don't."

"I didn't think so. Women are not allowed to read the Torah, and you're a woman—well, not a woman, a girl."

"I've never been to the synagogue," I said.

Ricu glanced at me sideways.

"Does the family belong to the synagogue?" Ricu's father asked.

"No," my mother quickly said.

"In our country, the government and the party ensure that people don't discriminate on the basis of religion," the principal said.

As bland as the statement was, it was meant as a peace offering, and we all relaxed.

"OK, Ricu, what did we agree you do now?" Ricu's father nudged Ricu forward.

Ricu advanced a step and looked at me and then at Claudia. "I'm sorry," he said.

"Sorry and what?" Ricu's father insisted.

"I won't do it again."

"Ricu's moving on," the principal added, as if in Ricu's defense. "He'll attend a new school in Vatra Dornei, starting in a few days."

"We will need his transfer papers," Ricu's father said, and the two men exchanged a glance like people who had talked before and understood each other.

The meeting ended. My mother went to work, and Claudia and I returned to class, but Ricu disappeared. I guessed he went back to his barracks. If any of the other boys knew what transpired, they didn't show.

On my way home from school, Ricu jumped out of a niche in the wall and blocked my path. There was nobody else on that sidewalk on Victoria Street, fifty paces from the Main Square. "Jew," he hissed in my face, exhaling rapidly, so much hate in that word that my knees buckled. I was afraid he would hit me, but he stepped sideways and dashed across the street into the square.

I watched him disappear, not sure of what had just happened. It was retaliation for that morning in the principal's office—just one word, yet why was it so hurtful? I wondered if his father had had a hand in it or if it had been Ricu's idea. I doubted he understood what he did or the pain he inflicted. He was a child, like me, acting under the influence of others. Unlike him, I was at the receiving end, and while I could deal with the hatred in his voice, the fear I could be pursued for who I was, well, that felt devastating. I was different, OK, but why, and how? I didn't want to be different. What could I do for myself? Complaining wasn't going to serve any purpose. Ricu was leaving town anyhow, and that word, *Jew*, extended beyond the present moment. The hate would live inside me forever. I would remember and revisit it again and again in the future. Silence seemed my best weapon.

I walked slowly home, resolved not to share my shame with anybody.

———— ✿✿✿ ————

I was fourteen when I went out with Jacob's classmate Mathew. *Going out* is, in fact, a misnomer, since people in their teens in our town could only walk through the streets under the gaze of adults, make out on the green benches by the soccer field when no one was watching, or go for a stroll in the nearby forest.

Rolling hills covered by woods surrounded the town. The Bistriţa River ran clear and fast through lush banks, with trout swimming against the current. We had a favorite spot by the river that we called "the waterfall." The river flowed in a thin, frosty layer over a natural dam topped by a platform of wooden planks, fell about five feet into a small but deep pool, and continued downstream. During the hot summer months, boys liked to dive from the platform into the pool. There was an abandoned flour mill on one side of the waterfall, its massive wheel fallen halfway into the water in a heap of rotting wood and rusted steel. The mill house itself was a moss-smelling ruin. It was rumored the former owner, the miller, had been arrested as an enemy of the people a decade earlier and had never been heard from again.

Mathew was tall and athletic. His blue eyes cut a sharp gaze under a head of blond hair that framed a face much like that of a true Adonis. We first spoke toward the end of the school year when I ran into him and Jacob on their way to the library. Jacob asked me to tell Mother he would be late for dinner, and then introduced me to Mathew. I was holding a worn-out copy of *How the Steel Was Tempered* by Nikolai Ostrovsky, and Mathew reached over to see it. When he took it from my hand, he touched my fingers, as if by accident.

"A little communist propaganda," he said, regarding me with indulgence.

I shrugged.

Next to him, Jacob looked small. Jacob rarely joined the boys in their noisy pursuits, spending most of his time reading or doing other things that were tame or useful. I was surprised to see the two of them together, and I had the feeling that Jacob was trying to ingratiate himself with Mathew. Boys followed Mathew, who was a good student—his strong suits were math and biology—and a little bit of a prankster. Every time he walked by, girls giggled and threw meaningful glances. They liked him, and so did I.

During the summer vacation, I saw him a few times at the waterfall with his friends, but he ignored me. Then we bumped into each other at the circus fairgrounds. I was in front of the merry-go-round, eating ice cream with Claudia and Adina. Mathew came over to ask me if I wanted to go on the big wheel with him. I did. He paid for the tickets, which I thought was very elegant, and when we reached the top, he took my hand and held it. The steeple of the Evangelical church in the center of Bistriţa seemed to be very near. Back on the ground, he asked me to go out with him. I was giddy from the ride, and I agreed too quickly. A few evenings later, we kissed on a bench by the soccer field.

I could still feel his lips on mine the next morning while sunning myself on the bank of the Bistriţa River. The air was clear, carrying waves of refreshing night coolness while the dew slowly evaporated off the green blades of grass.

Nearby, my brother was reading.

Mathew led a procession of boys to the wooden platform. He didn't look at me. Two boys dove into the water. When they came to the surface, one of them yelled over the sound of the falls.

"Hey, I saw you with Miriam last night. Taking good care of her, huh?"

"What's it to you?" Mathew answered, stretching on the platform. A small golden cross dangled on a chain around his neck.

"You guys looked pretty hot," the boy hollered.

"You need glasses," Mathew said, before jumping in the water.

It felt strange to be suddenly the subject of interest of boys, and I was glad that Mathew had deflected the provocation. I would have liked for him to come to me and say good morning. We would lie in the sun for a few minutes together, only a few, and then he could go back to his friends. I understood him wanting to be with them. I didn't mind it; we had our evenings. When we parted the night before, we had agreed we would see each other in the morning at the waterfall. I wanted to talk to him about things, about everything...

When Mathew came out of the water, the boys gathered back on the plat-form. This time they spoke in lower voices that I couldn't hear, looked in my direction, and laughed. The one who had started the conversation earlier leaned into Mathew and whispered to him.

Mathew thought for a second, waved to me, and announced at the top of his lungs, "If you want, I'll ask her to go out with you. She could use the expe-rience." Then he added something that got lost in the noise of the waterfall, and the boy who had whispered to him stuck his tongue out. The boy stood on the wooden platform looking directly at me, his naked back slightly arched, his arms to his sides, his tongue lashing in and out of his mouth in a primitive reptilian movement.

I was wondering how to react, when my brother got up. He advanced calmly toward the platform as if he were just going somewhere, into the shade perhaps, to continue his reading. In fact, I barely noticed his movement, a slight silhouette against the sun, repositioning itself in a larger world. Then he was on the platform, looking Mathew straight in the eye, surrounded by the boys, who stopped laughing. Jacob was a good two inches shorter than Mathew and thinner.

He said something I couldn't hear, and Mathew screamed, "Get the hell out of my face. Are you kidding?"

"No," Jacob said. "You apologize at once."

"Fuck off," Mathew said.

"Make him apologize!" the boys yelled, amused, and they started jumping up and down on the platform.

Jacob punched Mathew in the stomach. Mathew doubled over and fell to one knee. The cross at his neck shone. I was sure the water would push him over into the basin below, but Mathew held on and got back on his feet. He looked surprised by what had just happened. Jacob started retreating toward the shore where the wrecked flour mill stood.

He wants to be on dry land, I thought, where there is room to maneuver, to run or to fend. Two of the boys had already moved onto the grass, but the others were still on the platform, blocking Jacob. This was unfair: he was fight-ing for me. Suddenly I felt as daring as any of the boys, and as I got up and ran toward them, I saw Mathew punch Jacob in the face. Jacob's head jolted, and a thin stream of blood appeared under his nose. He spat.

"Stop it!" I screamed and tried to get near my brother.

The boys laughed in my face, and one of them grabbed me by my arm. I tried to punch him, but he ducked. I pirouetted around and slid on the wet grass. At first he didn't let go. Then he did, with a healthy push. The ground spun. I tripped, flew backward against the wall of the flour mill, and fell onto the old broken wheel. The place where I landed seemed softer than I would have guessed.

I saw the blood. It was bright red, covering the entire inside of my upper left leg, from the knee to the crotch, dripping onto the pile of rot under me and disappearing rapidly through its porous surface. The funny thing was, it didn't hurt. Angrily, I gathered my strength and charged. Behind me, little droplets of blood shone on the ground like rubies.

I didn't get far.

When I came to, I was in the open bed of a pickup truck, shaking on an unpaved forest road. My head was resting in Jacob's lap. His belt was wound tightly around my left thigh, fashioned into a tourniquet. Blood dripped continuously from the long cut onto the soaked burlap sacks that supported my leg.

"Hey," Jacob said. "Does it hurt?"

"No."

He smiled.

I didn't have the strength to ask any questions.

At the hospital I fainted again, and then I opened my eyes, and my mother was there.

"Darling, baby," she said. "We almost lost you."

Jacob was sitting near her, his lip swollen.

"What happened?" I asked him.

"Jacob rescued you," my mother said. "He carried you through the woods and hailed the truck. You were lucky. Grandpa said you arrived in the nick of time. A few more minutes and you'd have bled to death. They gave you two pints of blood on arrival."

Dust particles danced in the light that fell through the window and landed in a rectangular spot on the floor. I was wearing a hospital gown, and my left thigh was freshly bandaged. The pain was sharp.

I looked at my brother. "Mathew, what did he say at the waterfall? I couldn't hear everything."

"It was nothing important."

"Did he apologize afterward? Did he say he was sorry?"

"He didn't."

He's embarrassed, I thought.

That afternoon and later while I lay in the hospital bed convalescing, I kept my eyes on the door, hoping to see Mathew walk through it. He liked me, or maybe he loved me, I thought, because he had told me so when we had kissed in the park, and he knew that I loved him also. I was sure he had wanted to help Jacob carry me to the hospital, but somehow he hadn't known how to offer. Boys were boys—I'd seen it myself many times. Mathew was a good person. What he had done was all peer pressure; that's why in the beginning he had stood up for me, but after his friends teased him and pushed him a little, his attitude had changed. Like all of them, he'd do anything to be liked by his buddies, but sooner or later he would conquer his pride or fear or shyness or whatever was causing him to stay away, and show up.

Every day I waited for the visiting hours to start, and I dreamed that Mathew came into my room, timid and uncertain, his face in a regretful grimace, sullen. I could see his blue eyes turn gray with remorse, his blond curls falling in disarray on his forehead.

"I'm sorry, Miriam," he'd say, handing me three red carnations with stems bent from the grip of his fingers, or a popular book like *The Catcher in the Rye* or, better yet, one with a love story in it, like *Shannon's Way*, or a box of bonbons with fondant from Cassata, the only candy store in town.

"Call me Miri," I'd tell him.

"Miri, please don't hate me," he'd say.

"I don't hate you. It wasn't your fault I got injured, and I know that what you did was because of those other boys. Boys tend to have a bad influence on each other."

"I love you."

"Do you really, a little, perhaps? Or did I allow you to kiss me too soon, and you didn't like it? I didn't kiss you the right way, did I?"

"Oh, Miri, don't talk like that. Please, I'm so sorry, and I don't know what to say."

"Nothing, darling. Don't worry. I know you're sorry, and I'm happy you came."

He'd lean over my bed and kiss me on my dry lips, and goose bumps would form on my arms and the back of my thigh where the cut was still raw.

But during visiting hours my mother was always there, and a kiss from Mathew was too farfetched of a dream.

❦

The windows of my grandparents' apartment faced Victoria Street. Cars were almost nonexistent, and on sunny weekends people dressed in their Sunday best strolled leisurely up and down the street in front of our row house. Tucked back from the sidewalk, the entrance was through a carriage gate under my grandparents' bedroom. A red wooden door located to one side of the passage opened into a drafty, two-story foyer with a large cracked skylight and a white marble staircase with a wrought-iron railing. The stone bust of a very young woman rested on a pedestal at the base of the stairs.

Lying in my bed at night, I often envisioned the wealthy original owners of the house arriving, many, many years ago, in their fancy horse-drawn carriage. Servants would open the red door, and the owners would walk into the foyer, noisy and happy, basking in the light thrown by hundreds of white candles. There would be no bust at the base of the stairs, since their beautiful teenage daughter would be alive. She would be there with them.

After my accident, I imagined the unexpected death of the daughter and the pain of her parents, who, overcome with grief, commissioned that lifeless bust in a vain attempt to immortalize her.

At the top of the stairs, a door opened into a large living room while a cantilevered passage led to the one and only bathroom in the house. After we moved into my grandparents' apartment, the living room doubled by night as a bedroom. My mother and Jacob slept there on convertible sofas placed on opposite walls. A black table located between the sofas was surrounded by eight sturdy chairs, with the seats and backs recently reupholstered in green damask.

Every Sunday afternoon my grandfather played chess on that table with Mr. Moisil, who was not Jewish and was never too vocal about the new world order. The only person Mr. Moisil talked about was chess grandmaster Mikhail Moiseyevich Botvinnik. In silent delight, my grandmother watched him try to outmaneuver my grandfather at chess and served them Russian tea in Japanese Satsuma porcelain cups with fierce gold worriers around the rim. She also gave them butter cookies, and baklava drenched in honey, prepared fresh by Pani, our cook of many years.

Pani, too, was from Galicia. She was of Polish origin, had settled in Bistrița after the war, and spoke German and Romanian with a soft Slavic accent. Despite the oppressive heat of her wood-burning stove, in the kitchen she wore starched white aprons over sleeveless tops, displaying arms as round as the lion's paws supporting our tub in the bathroom. Her girth approached the width of our table. When she laughed, which was often, Pani's body shook as rivulets of sweat traveled downward from her double chin to her belly and hips. Dry, hissing air, like the helpless cough of a person suffering from a sore throat, escaped through her full lips. Besides our family she claimed she didn't have a soul in this world, and she slept alone on a cot near the stove in the kitchen. A flight of service stairs allowed her access to the backyard, where she shared an outhouse with Ileana and Uncle Tokachi.

To serve her Sunday-afternoon cookies, Pani had to pass through a narrow connecting room that was windowless, except for two panes of glass opening toward the foyer. On sunny days they allowed the few rays penetrating through the skylight to illuminate the gloomy interior.

I shared that room with my younger sister, Adina. We slept in the same bed, side by side when we were little and later with our heads on opposite ends, like queens in a deck of playing cards. A table and a lamp stood by the glass panes, and we both did our homework there. Grandmother would wheel in her Singer sewing machine and teach me how to sew blouses, long skirts that hid scars, and fancy shawls and sashes. She showed me how to choose colors and fabric as we flipped through fashion magazines for inspiration.

On the Sundays Mr. Moisil couldn't make it, my mother invited Miss Diddieny to join us for a game of canasta. Miss Diddieny was a dentist. She was slim and very proper, her thin brown hair always tightly held by a headband. Her unadorned dresses elongated her body, making it look emaciated. I often thought that if people's sizes were arranged in ascending or descending order, Pani and Miss Diddieny would place at the extremes of that continuum. I liked Miss Diddieny's demeanor and the musical rhythmicity of her name, and I repeated her name to myself on sleepless nights, like a nursery rhyme, like a poem. The old walls creaked, the wind howled, and Pani snored in the kitchen. I sought the warmth of my sister's body under the blanket while the bust of the young woman in the foyer grew and came alive, haunting my imagination.

Diddi-eny, Diddi-eny, Diddi-eny…

To the left of the living room was the door to my grandparents' bedroom. The old receiver on the wall was eventually replaced, in the early sixties, with a regular black ebonite telephone placed on a shelf between grandfather's side of the bed and the window. Next to the telephone my grandfather kept his reading glasses, a small metal box containing his nitroglycerine tablets, and his cigarettes. Despite being a cardiologist, or maybe because of it, Grandfather was a double-heart-attack survivor. His doctor had told him long ago to quit smoking. My grandfather considered it seriously, and after deciding he couldn't comply, he began cutting each cigarette into three pieces and smoking one-third at a time.

To give me more space when I returned from the hospital, Adina slept for a while on the floor in the living room with Mother and Jacob. The pain from my injury had subsided, and I was alone for long periods of time. At night, I continued to think about Mathew, more than ever before, my dreams taking a course of their own. My mother and Mathew's mother were acquainted, and in our small town my injury couldn't remain a secret for long. I dreamed that Mathew's mother took him aside and told him that I was out of the hospital and he'd better pay me a visit at home and apologize. She wouldn't be able to face my mother if he didn't do so. In my dream Mathew agreed, now that he had the perfect excuse to do something he had secretly wanted to do all along.

But Mathew never came, and when I woke up, I felt irascible and melancholy at the same time.

I was also upset with my mother, as much as I could be upset with her. She had called my father several times and begged him to come back. She was failing at raising her children, she had said. What happened to me was proof. She needed him. We all did. I needed my mother to be strong, and I didn't like that she was using me as an excuse, causing him to reject us again.

He was in Bucharest with his new wife and child. How could he come back?

✇

At the end of the summer, I was able to walk without limping.

After the Perlmans had left for Israel, Ileana and Uncle Tokachi had moved from the stable into the two vacated rooms. I found Ileana in a good mood, frying pumpkin seeds on a tin plate. I lifted the dress that my grandmother had helped me make and showed her my scar, long and ragged.

"It's ugly," I said.

"Nonsense," Ileana said.

"How will I ever be able to wear a miniskirt?"

"It's really not that ugly. Besides, it will heal. Give it a little more time. And men will find it appealing, you'll see. They'll find it interesting. Sexy. Some men, at least."

Which men exactly, I wanted to know. The odd ones, I feared. Better not to think about them. Ileana knew, since she seemed to know a lot about men, but I didn't have the courage to ask her. After all, she was right: my scar would pale and look better, and I could wear long skirts. What men, under which circumstances, would lift my skirt to look at my scar? No one. It wasn't such a big deal, and I wouldn't return to the waterfall anymore, or the beach, and I wouldn't stay in the sun. My skin was too white anyway.

That was it. Boys made me unhappy, and there was something *limiting* and strange about them.

Ileana must have sensed my discomfort, and she changed the subject. "We bought a young breeding bull who lives now in our old place," she said with a smile that signified a reversal of fortunes. "I mean, in the stable where we lived before. He's a real beauty. Uncle Tokachi is with him right now. He's in love with that bull, I swear, as if the bull were his child. You should go over there and see."

It was cool in the stable, and it smelled of manure and animal sweat. I could distinguish the rump of the bull, who sensed my presence and bellowed. His back arched, and his big eyes rolled in their sockets. His young short horns curved slightly backward.

Tokachi was tinkering, sitting on a bucket. He stood up. "Easy, boy, easy."

I came closer, not feeling too comfortable.

"I see you are well, Mademoiselle Miriam."

I nodded. "Your bull is stronger than a horse," I said.

Sunshine fell through the door and on Uncle Tokachi. His eye gleamed. "He certainly is. Like you, he's still very young, but he'll grow up, and when he does, he'll enjoy a good life. And so will you."

The house Miss Diddieny lived in had been built at the end of the fifteenth century. It was located behind the Evangelical church, in the middle of a row of thirteen similar two-story houses called the Sugalete Row. Like old men bent from the waist and leaning on their crutches, each house had its second floor arching over the sidewalk and leaning on massive quadrilateral pilasters. There was a constant draft on the Sugalete sidewalk, caused, in the summer, by the cool air escaping from below the stone walls and, in the winter, by the wind squeezed between the pilasters and the front of the buildings.

Miss Diddieny raised her hands to her narrow chest as if to defend against the cold. "One day I'll be out of here," she sighed.

I walked along looking for cracks in the walls, for heavy cast-iron gutters shaped like lizards, and for the remnants of the old coat of arms still carved above certain doorways. Roaches scuttled through the weeds and the moss growing in dark places. I followed Miss Diddieny up a narrow stairway into her room and hopped onto her deep windowsill. Miss Diddieny served me sugar cookies and gave me pencils and a few sheets of paper so I could draw. Outside, the tower of the Evangelical church threw a long shadow across the pavement.

"The market was held here in the Middle Ages," Miss Diddieny told me.

I tried to draw the market with its merchants and colorful wares, the little children playing in the gutter, the small animals, and the old walls and their dark shadows on my white paper.

After my accident, the merchants I drew on Miss Diddieny's paper became recognizable. Their faces reappeared in sketch after sketch, and one day Miss Diddieny exclaimed in intrigued wonder, "Wow, Miriam, this boy reminds me of your friend Mathew."

Maybe she didn't know the whole story, or maybe she was holding back. The truth was Mathew was still on my mind.

Another time she said, "This boy over here is your brother, Jacob!"

I had no special reason to spend hours perched high on Miss Diddieny's windowsill sketching, except that I felt comfortable there, away from the children in school, and that I was able to think. It was surprising I didn't run into Mathew anywhere in the streets, and for sure I'd be seeing him sooner or later in school. But maybe he was avoiding me, and, who knew, maybe he had stopped thinking of me. I hated that thought because I wanted to be the first to forget. Sometimes I wanted to show him my scar. Look what you've done to me, bastard! I wanted to say. I wanted to see what he'd do. Would he dismiss me with a wave of his hand, turn red in his face, or run away? Would he ask for forgiveness? If he'd really forgotten me, then he'd managed to hurt me twice—in a physical sense, and by taking advantage of my feelings. Maybe I had been too eager, and maybe he didn't like me because I was Jewish. Drawing was healing of sorts, because I could draw him when I wanted and in the way I wanted. The way I imagined him. The way I felt: tall or short, thin or fat, his eyes, his thick lips that I kissed, his full face, his big hands, his body, blood dripping out of his nose, an arrow piercing his chest, cold and slippery like a fish, low as a snake, large like a horse. I drew him sad, and I drew him happy, and most of my drawings of him ended up in Miss Diddieny's wastebasket. Drawing him, and drawing in general, helped me heal. With every sketch I made, I got over him a little, and I felt a little less pain.

At home, I was guarded, and I didn't draw. There I did my homework, I improved my sewing skills with Grandmother, I talked to Adina and Pani, and I read. I was in my early phase of discovering the prose of Irving Stone and through it the works and lives of artists such as Michelangelo and Van Gogh.

Once or twice a week, on my way home from school, I stopped at Miss Diddieny's. When she wasn't home, I fished the large metal key from its hiding place in a crack behind the doorframe and entered her room.

I stopped in the middle of the room, lowered my backpack to the floor, and looked around for minutes on end immobilized by the solitude of the place, by its sternness, and by the smell of wet stone. There were the four walls covered in white plaster, the deep recess that formed the windowsill, a narrow bed, a massive armoire, a mirror, and a table with two chairs. Miss Diddieny shared a bathroom at the end of the stair landing with her neighbors, and she had no kitchen. Plates, pots, and cutlery were stacked on a shelf to one side of the windowsill, near a washbasin and a portable gas stove with two burners.

I went to her armoire and reached up to its two finials pointed like the horns of Uncle Tokachi's bull. Inside I raffled through Miss Diddieny's skirts and dresses. I pulled out the drawers and touched her silks and underwear. I wore her jewelry in front of her mirror. In a corner I found a medical kit in a leather pouch that contained gauze, two empty medicine bottles with red caps, tweezers, a syringe, a scalpel, and a few loose syringe needles. After my accident, these simple objects exerted a strange fascination over me. Again and again, I spread them on the table, felt their textures and surfaces, inhaled their mild medicinal scent, lined them up or piled them on top of each other, and drew them. The life of a single woman appeared as sterile to me as those objects were. Yet I drew them again and again as if in search of an answer.

I had no reason to think Miss Diddieny was sad, but I didn't think she was happy either. She, too, was looking for something.

Once she came home as I was taking her cigarettes from a pack and building a pyramid out of them on her bedcover.

"Would you like to try one?" She surprised me.

I accepted, and I smoked my first cigarette with Miss Diddieny, sitting on her windowsill blinking nervously, coughing, and sending streams of blue smoke to the white and cracked ceiling.

Chapter 2

GABRIEL

One day I drew a merchant family clad in elaborate medieval garments like those I had seen in my history books. The man's face was rough and dour, resembling Uncle Tokachi's. The woman, soft and plentiful, was modeled after Ileana, and the young girl near them displayed an unmistakable similarity to the sculpture in our foyer. Miss Diddieny showed it to my grandfather, and together they contacted Gabriel Gelb, the young art teacher at a neighboring high school, who, for a fee, agreed to come to our house and tutor me in drawing and painting.

Gabriel held a degree from the Fine Arts Institute of Bucharest, played guitar in a rock and roll band, and was a minor local celebrity. He was twenty-three years old, had a steady girlfriend he was supposed to marry, and rode a motorcycle. Taking private lessons with him was exciting and scary. He had apprenticed with accomplished artists of the Painting Colony in Baia Mare. He had spent six months studying sculpture and architecture in Budapest on a scholarship. His blond hair grew over his ears in a new style that originated with the Beatles.

At my request, Miss Diddieny stayed with me throughout our entire first lesson. At the end of the hour, Gabriel looked at Miss Diddieny with his penetrating blue eyes enlarged by thick glasses and said, "Young artists are shy in the very beginning. They should be. But give us some time together, and she'll open up." He turned to me. "And you, please call me Gabriel, not Mr. Gelb, and not Comrade Teacher."

In our early lessons, Gabriel talked to me about perspective. "When your space is a sheet of paper, the object of your creation tends to be flat, two-dimensional. This is why you need to master the art of illusion. When you draw, you simulate. You create the impression of reality with angles and shadows. You tell your viewers a story. Think about literature."

I didn't know what to say, and he continued.

"To develop a three-dimensional character in literature, the author delves into the character's history. He tells us about his childhood, relatives, boyfriends, and girlfriends. This helps the reader identify with the character, and the author's deception begins. The same is true with visual arts. When you know your subjects, your public will end up trusting you and accepting your perspective. But you need to really understand your subjects. You need to dissect them and study them."

Gabriel took off his glasses and massaged the thin bridge of his nose. His face was handsome, with a smooth forehead, high cheekbones, and full lips. He lit a cigarette.

I tightened the grip on my pencil, and my lines came out broken, unsure. They looked like those of a child. Instead of focusing on the drawing in front of me, I was thinking of Gabriel. I was thinking of what he said. His words blew over me like the drafts sweeping Sugalete Row.

Gabriel placed his cigarette in the ashtray, stood up, and walked behind me. He leaned over and took my hand in his. As he moved my hand and pencil, the lines became firm again.

"Let's go," he said.

I didn't know where he wanted to go, but I gathered my stuff, and without questioning him, I followed him outside and walked with him the one hundred yards to the Evangelical church in the Main Square. We crossed a patch of grass at the church entrance and passed the white statue of the Holy Virgin with Child. Inside we sat on a wooden pew, polished by those who had sat on it before me.

"This church was built in the fifteenth century by Transylvanian Saxons," Gabriel whispered to me. "What you see is mostly Gothic in style, but there are Renaissance elements everywhere. Petrus Italus de Lugano, who was Italian, finished the church a hundred years later. Go to the library and read about it, but right now let's draw something we like."

"Can we sit here and draw?"

"We can do what we want."

I noted his confidence and wondered if his words extended to more than just drawing in churches. I had never dared set foot in a church before. Gabriel was Jewish like me. I didn't bring up our religion, but I figured that if he didn't hesitate, I didn't have to hesitate either.

As if to add credence to my thoughts and to what he had said, Gabriel took out his pad and started drawing. His hand moved fast. The nails on two of his fingers were long and looked like bird claws. To pluck the strings of his guitar, I guessed.

The air in the church was celestial. Light fell softly through a series of small windows, and a hollow echo accompanied our whispers and movement.

That afternoon we drew sketches of the altar, the icons, the pews, the windows, and the doors. I drew a sketch of the girders supporting the steeple as seen from below, and Gabriel told me this was the tallest stone church tower in Romania. A young minister walked over to us and looked silently at our work. He wore a dark cloak, and his blond hair was tied in a small bun. A peasant woman came in, lit a candle by the altar, kneeled, crossed herself, and left. Two schoolchildren stopped by.

When we finished, I was surprised to see rows of small electric bulbs illuminating the nave. We had been there much longer than the one hour Gabriel was supposed to work with me, but he didn't seem to mind. I was exhausted and felt that time had expanded into an undefined entity filled by our desire to draw.

Gabriel insisted on walking me home. It was dark. We arrived at the red door under the carriage gate and stopped. He lit a cigarette. I felt daring and asked him for one. He looked around to make sure no one was there to see us and then handed me his cigarette pack. We smoked quietly, facing each other, for what seemed a long time. A little unsure, I puffed and flicked the ashes too often, while he took long drags and inhaled deeply. The amber at the end of his cigarette illuminated his pouted lips. When the tip of his cigarette burned his fingers, he said, "It was a good afternoon." I nodded. He let his cigarette fall to the ground and crushed it under his shoe.

With Gabriel's guidance I made sketches of the Evangelical church again and again. I drew its beautiful interior in great detail and its facade as well. I drew the garden, the large portal, and the statue of the Holy Virgin with Child. From the vantage point of the church, I sketched the Sugalete Row in its entirety, and then I sketched it up close. In my drawings the walkway under the arches looked like a tunnel of light. I came to know each of the thirteen houses in the row, including the one in the middle where Miss Diddieny lived and the one with the old coat of arms on the wall, worn and chipped: a stork with a horseshoe in its beak.

I sketched my grandparents' house on Victory Street with its tall carriage gate. I sketched the main bridge over River Bistriţa and the ruins of the old city walls destroyed in the sixteenth century by Austrian soldiers.

I went out with my easel, and the people of our small town started greeting me, sometimes with a condescending smile, but mostly encouragingly, stopping to contemplate my work and to comment. Some of them offered to pose for me, which in the beginning took me by surprise, but which I accepted eventually. I started sketching faces, trying to capture the essence of my subjects the way Gabriel had taught me, and aspiring to identify that unique feature, that crease on the forehead or that spark in the eye, that told me the story of the person.

I took my sketchbook home and assaulted the members of my family with constant requests to pose. My favorite model was Pani, with her voluminous body and expressive face. She was always willing, as if I was doing her a favor. My charcoals showed my feelings for her, and we met in a spiritual realm that was only ours. I drew Pani cooking by the stove with her blackened pots and pans. I drew her splitting wood in the yard and sitting on her cot with a Bible in her hands. I drew her sleeping with a newspaper over her face and ironing with a heavy iron that let out puffs of steam. I tried to capture her hearty laughter, but, despite portraying her with her head tilted backward and her mouth fully opened, I never succeeded.

I went downstairs and drew Ileana doing her laundry in an oversized tub. I drew Uncle Tokachi and his bull both inside and outside the stable, and I never knew which of the two, man or animal, was a more convincing symbol of virility. I sketched my mother, my brother and sister, and my grandparents. From my old photograph, I reconstructed my father's narrow and gentle face. When I finished drawing my father, I cried.

With every line I drew, with every shadow and every hatch, with every new subject, I hoped to impress those who paid attention to me: the people in the street, my family, and our neighbors and friends. I was eager to solicit their comments and hear their compliments. I wanted to shock them, provoke them with my genius. I didn't realize it at the time, but that's why I liked to draw Pani so much: she would always compliment me for my sketches and always tell me how great I was.

"Oh, Mademoiselle Miriam, where did you find all this talent? Don't tell me it grows on trees."

Mathew was long gone from my mind. I didn't know when I stopped thinking of him. Jacob said Mathew had a girlfriend, and it didn't matter to me. I saw him in school. He saw me also. We didn't talk. He was a jerk, as far as I was concerned. I valued only my art, and the man who helped me nurture it. I yearned for praise from him. Gabriel was the person capable of making or breaking me. His voice hurt me most or caused me to feel the happiest, depending on content or inflection, or on a fleeting movement of his eyebrows.

"Do you like my work?" I asked him, with butterflies in my belly. "Is it any good?"

"It's better."

"Better? Better than what?"

"You're making progress. You have to work hard and be patient."

"I *am* working hard."

"Let's try again, in a different fashion."

"You don't like it," I exclaimed, walking away.

"Miri, where're you going?" he said.

I turned back. "Why don't you tell me? Just tell me straight to my face. Do you think I don't get it? You can't say that I'm good, that I'm making progress, and then, in the same breath, tell me to do it all over again. That doesn't make any sense."

"But, Miri, it really does. Come here." He raised his arms and gently pulled me into a close hug. My body, tense as a strung wire a second before, grew heavy and soft. Through his shirt I felt the flatness of his chest. I felt his warmth and the strength of his arms protecting me.

"Miri, you have what it takes," he whispered reassuringly, and in that moment I loved him.

Soon we started working with oils and watercolors. This was more difficult than drawing, and finishing a painting took much longer. Applying gentle strokes of paint added challenge and complexity to my work. I listened to Gabriel's explanation of how the different techniques combine to shape space and form. He talked about paper, canvas, and other surfaces; about how they absorbed color and light differently; and about how mixing and associating colors could lead to dramatic results.

"It's like mixing words in a verse," he said. "You pair two words together, and suddenly they take on a new meaning."

"Is it possible," I asked, "for an artist to dedicate himself to more than one art form?"

"Do you mean like painting and music?"

"Yes."

"Of course. Think of Kandinsky—he was a great painter and a cellist."

"But he was better known as a painter than a musician, wasn't he?" I wasn't ready to accept anything less than absolute dedication to my art.

"It's not the degree of recognition that matters. It is the juxtaposition of feelings with the depth of experience in one's art. Creative people are creative in everything they do. That's why they dress differently, live differently, and measure everything by a different yardstick."

"Do they love differently?"

He looked me straight in the eye. "You're still very young."

Warmth overtook my entire body. I was almost sixteen.

"You know," I said, "I design most of my own clothes. I love fashion and consider it art, but I think I might be spending too much time doing something that is not as important as painting."

Gabriel knew about my interest in fashion, and he liked the clothes I had made for myself. Miss Diddieny had told him what a good seamstress I was when they spoke about him tutoring me. And yes, he said, fashion was definitely an art. He had been to Budapest and had seen a little bit of what the world of fashion had to offer. He had been on Váci Utca. The West with its modern, decadent styles had arrived there to meet Communism and gloat over its drabness. He would gladly live in the West, in Paris or London or New York. Talk about fashion, those were places where a girl like me would be happy.

I was happy. He liked the clothes I designed and the way I looked in them. I wanted to look beautiful for him. And I wasn't that young. I knew he said what he said to keep his distance from me. He was the teacher. I was the pupil. He had to do it, but we shared a passion that was bringing us close.

"I'm impressed that you're so accomplished both in painting *and* rock and roll," I said.

"I'm hardly accomplished in either."

"You are, because if you weren't, I'd be wasting my time."

He laughed.

"I'd like to see you in concert," I said.

"Come and see me," he said.

One day we rode on his motorcycle to the waterfall, the first time I went there after my accident. The memory caused me pain, but I did my best to control myself. Gabriel didn't sense anything, and I felt proud about keeping my secret. We spent a few silent hours in the sunshine, drawing the fast-moving river, the pond downstream of the dike, and the ruins of the flour mill. Riding the motorcycle on the way back, I leaned into his body, my arms wrapped around his middle and my face pressing against his shirt. The wind in my face made me think daring thoughts.

Gabriel's studio was in an industrial neighborhood not far from where I lived, and we walked there together. Gabriel pulled at the tin door, which opened with a long screech, and I entered a tall space with a cement floor and roughly finished brick walls, illuminated by a row of narrow windows located high on the same wall as the entrance. A woman stood in front of a makeshift stove at the far end of the studio, cooking. She looked a little perplexed when she saw me.

"Cecilia," Gabriel said, "you're here?"

"Surprise," Cecilia answered. "I thought you were free."

"I am. And this is Miriam, a student of mine." Gabriel paused and added with a coy smile, "She hopes to get a better sense of what an artist's life is all about."

"Then I am a part of that picture," Cecilia said. She took a few steps forward. "Hello, I'm Gabriel's girlfriend."

I nodded.

She was slim, in her twenties, with long hair as dark as mine and olive skin that glowed in the afternoon light. While keeping her big brown eyes on me, she hugged Gabriel and gave him a kiss on the lips that seemed long. "I was fixing us dinner," she said. "Gaby, do you think your guest would care to join us?"

"I don't know," Gabriel replied. "Miri?"

Given the way the invitation was made, I felt tempted to decline, but I decided to eat with them, mostly because I didn't think she wanted me there.

In the middle of the room was a large table crammed with paint cans, brushes, paper pads, stained rags, broken frames, and ashtrays filled with cigarette butts. Cecilia had cleared the corner closest to the stove and had covered it with a white tablecloth, on which she had placed silverware and two soup bowls.

Gabriel pulled out a chair for me and added a third table setting.

"It's not much," Cecilia said. "Just black bean soup and some bread and butter."

"Delicious," I said in a tone as uninterested as possible, and I started looking around the studio.

Large unframed paintings lined the walls. By the windows, where the light was stronger, there were three easels with three unfinished paintings representing parts of the female body in curvy lines and earthy colors. The anatomy was distorted, like in the albums of modern art I had seen, yet the attention to detail was painstaking, obsessive. I would have liked to know if Cecilia had modeled for Gabriel.

Near the front door stood Gabriel's motorcycle, supported by a kickstand. Leaning to one side, its handlebar turned, the bike seemed caged by the space around it, wounded.

In the back I saw a narrow bed—a cot, really—covered by a dark blanket, on top of which rested a guitar. The thought that two people couldn't possibly sleep on that cot was satisfying. A floor lamp with a white conical shade like a Chinese hat stood at one end of the cot. Next to it was the cast-iron stove, the floor blackened by soot, its flue running up at an angle and out through a hole in the ceiling. Books and art albums were spread on the floor among sheets of musical scores, shoes, and pieces of clothing.

A single lightbulb hung on a wire above the three easels.

The studio smelled of bean soup, paint, and rubber tires.

"Gabriel," I said when we finished eating, "those paintings are different than the ones I saw before." I turned my gaze to the three easels. "Are you trying something new, a new phase, perhaps?"

He scraped his bowl with his spoon, as if looking for a last drop of soup, and wiped his chin with the napkin. "Nothing is ever new. All that is in an artist's soul exists simultaneously. Phases are invented by critics."

"An artist has a hidden side, a black hole that's invisible to most people," Cecilia said. She smiled furtively and then got up and carried the bowls through a side door.

Gabriel got up also. "I'm not hiding anything from you, Miri."

It was a strange thing for him to say, and it sounded like an apology.

"We're out of coffee," Cecilia told Gabriel when she came back.

"Let's go to Cassata," he said.

"They don't sell coffee," I said, even though he wasn't talking to me.

"Oh, my mother works there, and she always has a little fresh coffee stashed aside for me. You know, from what they serve in the store." He winked. "Cecilia, let's take the motorcycle, and Miriam, we'll be right back, OK?"

I shrugged, and as soon as they left, I began exploring. I looked at the paintings that hung on the walls. Many depicted subjects familiar to me from the sketches Gabriel had done while tutoring me. I was glad to see his work in its final form, but nothing impressed me as unusually accomplished or interesting. I opened the door that Cecilia had gone through with the dishes and discovered a little bathroom. There were no cabinets or drawers for me to search. The soup bowls were drying on a shelf, and on the edge of the sink were Gabriel's shaving brush and soap. I smelled them and remembered the vague lingering scent on Gabriel's skin. I checked myself in the stained mirror mounted on the wall. My face was flushed and my eyes were alert, excited.

Back in the studio, I noticed a drawer built under the table. Inside was a pad with pencil sketches of body elements, some for the paintings on the three easels. They were provocative and revealing. I suspected Gabriel had done them for himself, not expecting viewers. A silent violence animated them, a repressed obsession. Some were downright repulsive—breasts with large nipples, erect penises and tight scrotums, plump female buttocks, and soft thighs opened or pressed together. I saw long dark hair let loose, women's subdued faces with closed eyes and parted lips, indulging, as the artist intended.

While I knew about sex, I possessed only a vague image of what men and women did to each other. Besides my brother, whose naked body I had seen when we were little children, the only naked men I had looked at had been on the pages of art albums. The image of a man overtaken by desire was new to me. That thing was huge and animalistic. The idea it had to somehow end inside me was shocking. And yet I felt excited. I could vividly recall the burning sensation in my belly and breasts when Mathew had kissed me the evening before my accident.

A page in my life was turning. I was growing up, getting on in the world, and the moment was defined by ambivalence. There were things in Gabriel's sketches I might never agree to, while others I would consider.

I was tempted to steal a few drawings, but I feared he'd figure it out and confront me. Even if I denied it, he'd know, and I would be terribly embarrassed.

I pushed in the drawer, paced the studio back and forth a few times, and opened the door to the street. There was nobody. My decision to leave was sudden. I knew where Cassata was, and, once outside, I walked in the opposite direction.

Gabriel called that evening. It was maybe the third time he had called me at home, the previous two to reschedule our lessons. I was in my room with Adina when Grandmother came to get me.

"Mr. Gelb, for you, on the phone," she told me.

She had a stern voice, and for a moment I panicked, afraid that somehow Gabriel had found out I had seen his sketches and had told my grandmother. I didn't get up right away, and I felt both my sister and grandmother watching me intently, so I dragged myself slowly to my grandparents' room and picked up the receiver.

Grandfather, at least, wasn't there.

"Miriam," Gabriel said, "what happened? Why did you leave?"

"I wasn't comfortable waiting."

"Are you upset?"

"No. Why?"

"I don't know, maybe because of Cecilia…"

There was nothing I could say to this, and I let the silence settle in, deep, full of meaning.

Listening to live Western music was a rare treat. I would be seeing Gabriel perform for the first time, and Claudia was coming with me. She knew how I felt. The two of us talked about everything, and she was the only one who understood the special relationship I enjoyed, in my mind at least, with my tutor. Like me, she liked art. I showed her all my paintings and craved her praise. We dreamed about going to Bucharest together to study fine arts in college. Her father had left her mother for another woman when Claudia was in kindergarten, but he lived nearby, and Claudia was able to spend time with him at his place or go hiking with him in the hills that surrounded Bistrița. I considered drawing for her from memory some of the anatomical details I had seen in Gabriel's sketches, but I hesitated, and when I described them to her, I exaggerated my outrage.

"This is normal for a guy," she responded expertly. "Oral sex is a part of the repertoire."

"Yuck," I said. "How disgusting."

"Not really," she said, and she burst into a nervous laughter.

The Youth Concert Hall, hailed as an accomplishment of the regime, was a modern structure in a neighborhood of new apartment buildings. When Miss Diddieny dreamed about moving out of her room in the old Sugalete

Row, she hoped for an apartment in that area. Wide steps led to a series of large entrance doors, guarded by two men in uniform. There was a small crowd of young men gathered on the steps. As Claudia and I went around them to talk to the guards, they whistled.

Gabriel was inside, and one of the door attendants went in to get him. There was a minimum-age requirement, and we needed an adult to accompany us.

Cecilia came out. "Gabriel sent me to meet you," she said and gave me a kiss on the cheek. It wasn't pleasant.

She looked prettier than I remembered, and we followed her to the second row of the auditorium.

"We reserved these seats for our friends, so you may sit here," she told us. "I'm heading backstage. Gaby gets nervous before every performance. I keep telling him it's not a big deal, but he doesn't listen. Maybe he'll come say hello, maybe not; I'm not sure."

As soon as she left, Claudia looked at me. "Gaby gets nervous. I'm telling him it's not a big deal, but he doesn't listen," she said, mimicking Cecilia.

I laughed.

"She thinks she's so special," Claudia added.

"He likes her."

"Are you sure? Maybe she gives him what he needs."

"She's pretty."

"So are you."

I took her hand and I squeezed it.

The concert started with obligatory local folk music that bored everybody, followed by an artist from Bucharest popular with an older audience. People applauded sporadically, some laughed aloud a few times during his performance, and some got up and walked out to the foyer. I had seen the singer on TV, and I had enjoyed some of his tunes, especially a love song about a couple breaking up, the young man thanking his girlfriend for everything they had experienced together—their first kiss, the times she said no, the times she said yes, and his hope for a future together.

I wondered what Gabriel would sing if I left him after becoming his girlfriend.

His band came on stage, five musicians, all skinny, dressed in jeans and tight flowery shirts, their hair combed over their foreheads and ears. Except for the drummer, who took his place at the back of the stage, they all started jumping, dancing, pumping their fists in the air, and talking to the audience. Gabriel grabbed the mike and announced the name of the first song. The audience broke into cheer. Claudia and I shot to our feet, clapping.

They performed a mix of American and French songs. Gabriel was the soloist. He accompanied himself on his guitar. His voice was deep and his stage presence commanding, but overall I found his singing a little bit like his paintings—good but predictable. I liked him best when he performed softer melodies with a story and a message, like *Donna, Donna,* by Joan Baez, or *Vous Permettez, Monsieur,* by Salvatore Adamo, rather than some of the Beatles' songs, like *Love Me Do* or *I Want to Hold Your Hand*, which required more rhythm and energy. Gabriel's voice was all honey, no vinegar, and as I was becoming more infatuated with him by the day, I was also uncovering the limits of his talent.

———— ∞ ————

I started working on a large oil painting of Pani using Gabriel's method with prep sketches. Like so many times before, I chased Pani around the house and drew her at every occasion, fleetingly, silently. She was so used to my following in her footsteps that she hardly even noticed. In my sketches I tried to capture the uniqueness of her expression and movement. I hoped to achieve something as big and as dear to me as Pani herself—a masterpiece.

I decided to draw her hanging laundry in the courtyard not too far from the stable. Pani would be standing there with sunlight exploding in her red face, her arms reaching the clothesline, hair tousled, head framed by colorful garments hung to dry. I considered a pale shadow of a bull in the background, but changed my mind. Just the essence of Pani needed to show on my canvas, her statuesque exterior revealing the depth of her inner world, tender and of an unflinching loyalty to us. Her voluminous belly, her massive bosom, and the rings of fat on her arms and neck would appear powerful in my painting, beautiful.

I took her outside and asked her to raise her arms above her head, as if hanging the laundry. I was aware the position would become painful after a while, but I thought that was a small sacrifice to ask in pursuit of my art. She reacted with the docility of a professional model. If her body hurt, I never knew it, since she looked at me lovingly, hiding her discomfort under a broad smile.

"You are a picturesque woman," I said.

"Oh, Mademoiselle Miriam, you're being too nice to me. I'm not picturesque." Her soft, Slavic accent dipped lower. "I'm a big, fat cow, and I know it."

"What are you talking about? You're a big woman, true, but you're not a cow, and your size shapes your personality. You're gentle and dedicated. Your white apron is always freshly starched. I wonder how you do it. How can you work as hard as you do and manage to look so neat?"

"Do you think I am neat?" Pani asked, lowering her arms just a little.

"Yes, Pani, you are, but keep your arms up until I'm done."

"That's me in your painting, Mademoiselle Miriam," she said later when she came near me and glanced at my work. "It's really me, like I see myself in the mirror."

"I hope you see more in my painting," I said. "I want your soul to come through, your goodness."

"Can you see my soul, Mademoiselle Miriam? Can you really?"

While I worked on Pani's painting, I kept it hidden. Then I took it to Gabriel. "Well," I said, "do you like it?"

"Yes," he said after looking at the painting for a long time. "I think I do. I think it's remarkable."

"You think, but you're not sure?"

"I'm sure, given your age and the difficulty of the subject matter."

"What's difficult with the subject matter? I've known this woman since I was a child. She's an open book to me. I know what she thinks, how she feels. If I can't paint her, how can I paint anybody?"

Gabriel sat down at the table and took off his glasses. He always did that.

"If you don't like it," I said, "just say so."

"That's not it," he answered. "I like it."

"Then what is it? I can take it. I invested myself into this piece, and I worked hard at it, but I guess nothing is good enough for you."

"Miri," he said.

"Miri what? Every time I talk to you, you give me this noncommittal response as if I'm missing something, as if there is something else, profound and hidden, that only you understand. Why don't you share this mystery with me? Why don't you explain it to me? Why not elevate me, your underling, your disciple, to your stratospheric levels?"

"Miri, get a hold of yourself."

"Oh, yeah? Well, I'm not going to. But here is what *you* should do. To start with, get rid of Cecilia. I can't stand her, and I don't want her around. Either her or me. You decide. And don't call my paintings *remarkable*. I know you want to keep getting paid, but I don't pay you to cover the truth from me."

Gabriel stood up and slowly walked out of the room.

<hr />

I spent the afternoon with Claudia, lamenting over Gabriel. She assured me I had done the right thing. My portrait of Pani was brilliant, and Gabriel was jealous.

I wasn't sure. I'd had no right to bring up Cecilia or the money for my lessons, but he had made me so mad.

My grandmother opened the door. "I need you to run to the pharmacy," she said.

"I'll go later," I said.

"I need you to go now."

"I'm busy. I have a visitor, don't you see?"

"Your grandfather's not feeling well."

"Let me finish talking to Claudia, and then I'll be on my way."

"Go now!"

I gave her a frustrated look. "OK," I said, but I took my time.

By the time Claudia left and I walked to the next block, where the pharmacy was, more than twenty minutes had passed. When I returned, my grandmother was in the bedroom, shouting into the phone, trying to reach my mother. She grabbed the nitroglycerine from my hands, dropped the receiver, and bent over my grandfather. The receiver fell off the nightstand.

Grandfather was on his back, his wide-open eyes fixated on the ceiling, lips parted, a thick, snorting sound escaping with his every breath.

Pani stood in a corner of the room, speechless.

"Here, take this," my grandmother said to my grandfather. "Open your mouth, now!"

"What's wrong?" I said.

"His heart. Call the ambulance, please!"

I heard noise in the phone, grabbed the receiver, and recognized my mother's voice. "Come home quickly," I said. "Grandpa is having a heart attack."

By the time she arrived, he was gone. It happened simply—he breathed one more time, deeply, and then snorted and grew silent.

My grandmother screamed.

I took a step forward and took her in my arms.

The doctor who arrived with the ambulance said there was nothing anybody could have done, but I knew differently.

After my brother and sister came home, the house filled with people. They talked quietly, hugging all of us, shaking their heads, and praising my grandfather's life. Some shed tears.

I ran out. It was already dark, and it took me only several minutes to reach Gabriel's studio and knock on his door. The lights were on. I didn't think of Cecilia, my heart pounding, torn by pain and guilt.

"Gabriel," I said when he opened the door, "Grandpa's dead."

He was barefoot. His face was drawn. Behind his glasses his blue eyes looked sad.

Perhaps everything looked sad to me that evening.

A cigarette, smoked halfway, was stuck between his lips. "Dr. Levinescu, dead?" he said. "Come in."

I followed him to the narrow cot. He sat on it and put out his cigarette in an ashtray on the floor. I sat near him.

There was no trace of Cecilia.

"What happened?" he asked.

"He's had a bad heart for years."

"But he was still working. He was a strong, active man."

"I know," I said, "and it's all my fault." I told him about Claudia's visit, and about Grandmother sending me to the pharmacy. "Had I hurried, I could have saved his life."

"That's not what the doctor told you."

"It's my fault," I said and burst into tears.

"Come here," he said.

I nestled against his chest, and he wrapped his arms tightly around me. I felt comforted by his embrace, sheltered, deriving strength from his body. His cheek, a little rough from the day's stubble, brushed my neck. My tears ran freely. As I turned my head to look at him, I found his mouth.

At first his lips were soft, tentative. I pressed, and we settled into the kiss, all my senses converging into it. My being became mouth, lips, tongue, teeth, all sweet and tender, and excitement moved through my body in a manner I'd had no idea existed. Our lips fitted perfectly, and my abandon was total, like plunging into a deep river when the water takes you instantaneously, when everything around you changes—texture, temperature, buoyancy. His hands were all over me, fingers exploring the contours of my body, hidden and unhidden, the soft and the bony parts. My guilt and sadness receded into a joy that started somewhere in my groin and quickly reached my heart, my soul, and my mind—and my breasts, my neck, my ears, my lips, my flaming cheeks. I liked his hands caressing me, his weight pressing down on me, his wet, hot breathing tickling my face, the strength of his limbs and muscles, and even the hard swelling below his waist. There was a slight bitterness in the air from his last cigarette, and I liked that, too.

When he went too far, I stopped him. "No," I said, and he pulled back. He took off his glasses, rubbed his nose, and looked at me with blue eyes that suddenly contained no trace of sadness. I realized we had crossed a bridge together. We were on the other side. One day I would have to say yes. There was only one way forward, and the decision was mine.

At our dinner table, my grandfather's chair was now empty. Sometimes it seemed he had just gone to his room and would be back in an instant, but he never came back. He was the first person in my life to die, and until his passing I had always thought that death was an impossible ending, not just for the one who had died but also for everybody involved, an ending that changed everything. I thought death would produce this unbearable break and the impossibility of simply going on as before, but it wasn't like that at all. Pani brought me my coffee with milk in the morning as she had always done. Mother rushed out the door grabbing her things at the last moment, stressed out that she might be late again for work, and Grandmother gave me my usual good-morning kiss. Jacob and Adina were there every morning, and the three of us joked and laughed and horsed around. Sadness was there mostly in the beginning, when the change was material, when Mom had to give his clothes away, rearrange the furniture, and do the paperwork for his pension to go to Grandmother. Slowly the reality of his death became acceptance, transparent like a layer of gauze that could be lifted by the lightest breeze.

Mother had a beautiful golden pendant, engraved with the Star of David, she had kept hidden in a drawer. Now she started wearing it, mostly at home on the weekends but once or twice when she went out with her lady friends.

Jacob studied for his baccalaureate and his admittance exam at the University of Cluj, where he wanted to pursue history and political science. At the same time he seemed to be reaffirming his Jewishness. In between his math and history books I saw a few on Jewish religion, and he befriended some of the few Jewish boys in Bistriţa and began spending his Saturdays at the synagogue.

My mother and my brother felt freed of the secrecy my grandfather had once imposed.

We didn't know, but Grandfather had a cousin by the name of Beatrice, who had sailed to Palestine during the British Mandate, and whose existence had been kept a secret. After he died, Grandmother wrote to her, and three weeks later we received an elongated Air Mail envelope containing a photograph and four thin pages covered by a nervous handwriting. She reintroduced herself to us as our *Tante* Beatrice. In the picture she looked like an effeminate and much younger version of Grandfather. Next to her stood *Onkel* Dagobert, a tall man with a dark moustache, a mathematician, and her husband of over forty years, dead several years earlier in a car accident. Their grown daughter, Ronit, was married but had no children. Later yet, we received a parcel postmarked Tel Aviv, full of silk scarves and stockings, silver bracelets, a flower shirt for Jacob, and Swiss chocolate.

"We live in a new world," I told Jacob. "Grandfather was old fashioned and afraid of his past. But in today's society people don't care about religion. Remember what Dad was saying. And I mean all religions…"

Jacob lifted his new flower shirt into the light. "We don't have to fear who we are, Miriam. Our religion is a part of us, whether we accept it or not. People care, some more than others, and it makes a difference."

"If they do, why don't I see more people go to church on Sundays?"

"Because it's illegal."

"It's not illegal," I said and filled my mouth with Swiss chocolate.

"Well, it's frowned upon."

"That's my point. Religion is less important, and there is a new type of universal person. You and I. We are equal to our friends. It doesn't matter if you are Romanian or Jewish or German. I don't feel any different from Claudia or Pani or Miss Diddieny. They are Christians, we're not, and nobody cares."

"And how do you feel at Christmas, when everyone is celebrating with their families and getting gifts?"

"Just a silly tradition."

"It's not silly. I mean, honestly, wouldn't it be nice to have a Christmas tree in our house?"

"No," I said. "I don't need any gimmicks."

He had hit a nerve and he knew it, but I wasn't going to admit it. I was talking about friends I felt equal to, while in reality, besides Claudia I didn't have any. Ileana, Pani, and Miss Diddieny weren't my generation. People my age were going to parties that didn't interest me and to which I wasn't invited. Never mind what had happened three years ago with Ricu (a fact I never discussed with Jacob or anybody), or maybe because of it, I had already convinced myself that every time I felt left out, it wasn't because I was Jewish but because I was an artist. Maybe I expected too much from people.

"Gabriel is Jewish," Jacob said. "That's why you're going out with him, isn't it?"

"Let's not drag Gabriel into this," I said. "And I'm not going out with anybody."

My mother talked to me about Gabriel. "Now that your grandfather is gone," she said, "we won't be able to afford paying for your painting lessons."

I didn't tell her I loved him. I said I understood, but I continued seeing Gabriel more often than before. He, of course, knew that our paid lessons were over. We still painted together and discussed our art, because we enjoyed it and also for appearance's sake, but we spent most time cuddling in his studio on his cot or looking for secluded places in the fields and the woods. He was the adult. If he worried that people would see us and judge us, he denied it. I was happy just being with him. When I was alone, I thought about him continuously. My grandfather's death had become for me such an unexpected and beautiful beginning. It was spring. Nature was in full bloom, and everything around us was bursting with life.

Each time he wanted to go all the way, I said no. It was hard, and many times I wished he were more assertive.

Chapter 3

BUCHAREST

I n July I went to Bucharest to see my father. He invited all three of us to visit him in an attempt to ease our pain over the loss of Grandfather, but Jacob couldn't make it because of his college admittance exams, and Adina simply refused.

"Why should I go?" she said. "I don't miss him."

"You don't?" I asked. "He's your father."

"Yeah, some father. And where was he for the last ten years to show that he loves us?"

"Six years. Only six years have passed since he divorced our mother."

"OK, six years. You go. After all, *you* used to be his favorite."

"He has Elise now," I said, understanding there was no point in arguing. Elise was our half sister, and no matter how much I insisted, it was clear Adina would remain Adina. We shared a bed, complained to each other about our mother, and talked about everything under the sun, but the differences between us were growing. Adina was not interested in painting or fashion (except to the extent she was borrowing my dresses and shoes without asking me), she didn't read anything unless required in school, and she changed her opinions with a frequency and ease that reminded me of our father.

I, on the other hand, was excited about the trip, and my mother was also, and I spotted a subdued longing in my mother's eyes. "Go, spend time with your father. He loves you," she said, as if hoping again for the miracle of reconciliation, as if my father would suddenly recognize in me something he had missed all along, abandon his new life, and return to Bistrița.

Gabriel came with me to the railway station. He gave me a book about Modigliani to read on the train and a bunch of wildflowers. I boarded the commuter to Sărățel, a small village where the express train to Bucharest stopped for a few minutes.

An hour later in Sărățel, I found a water fountain on the wall of the station and sprinkled my flowers, but they wilted as I held them in my hand during the long ride to Bucharest.

I was seated in a second-class compartment together with seven other people, four, including myself, facing in the direction of travel, and four sitting backward. It was warm inside the compartment, and the gentle and monotonous rocking of the train made me sleepy. I tried to read, and then I closed my eyes and dozed off. When I woke up, I had the unpleasant feeling of being watched. The man seated across from me was staring at me. I met his gaze, and his eyes slid away. He was in his thirties, shabbily dressed. On his ring finger he had a wedding band. A few seconds later I felt his eyes again, and when I looked at him he smiled. It was a sleazy smile, as if he wanted to tell me he had protected my sleep and now he was welcoming me back into his world.

I stood up, placed my book and the small, wilting bouquet onto the luggage rack above my seat, and walked into the corridor.

He came after me.

I lit a cigarette.

"Smoking, Miss, at such a young age?" he said. "This is a sign of sophistication."

"It's a sign I don't want to be bothered."

"I understand what you're saying, Miss, but all I'm after is a bit of small talk between fellow travelers. We have a few hours to kill, that's all."

"There are six other fellow travelers in our compartment. Talk to them." I turned my back and took a long drag from my cigarette.

"The other people don't interest me, but you do. We have similar tastes. I like Modigliani. Here, I have this great American cigarette for you, Miss. Why don't you throw away yours and give my cigarette a try?"

He grabbed my arm and spun me toward him. With his other hand, he extended a shiny pack of Kent superlongs to me, the cellophane torn, the tip ripped open, several white cigarette filters sticking out.

There were other people in the corridor, smoking, stretching their legs, or looking outside.

I freed myself from his hold. "No," I said as loud as I could, and I blew smoke straight into his face.

He remained motionless for a few seconds. Then he pushed the cigarettes back inside their pack, placed the pack in his pocket, and went into the compartment.

I smoked the rest of my cigarette and thought I would stand in the corridor until we got to Bucharest, but my feet hurt and that guy was nothing I couldn't handle, not with all those other people around. As I entered the compartment, I deliberately avoided looking at anybody. I took my book and my flowers, sat down, and closed my eyes. Thoughts swirled in my mind.

Gabriel's flowers were wilting, and there was nothing I could do.

If my father were here, he'd punch the guy in the nose.

The sun was shining onto the window, and when I opened my eyes, I could see the window mirror the interior of our compartment every time we passed a building or trees.

If my father were here, I'd ask him for something to drink. I was thirsty.

In the last three years, I had seen my father only once, and I wondered if he missed me as much as I missed him. I was sure he'd find me grown up. Adults didn't change a lot in three years, but children did. I was going on seventeen now, almost a woman. I was taller, my hair was longer, and I had a boyfriend, an artist, a painter known all over Bistrița, more or less. My father appreciated art—he had to. I realized I was happy I was going to see him alone. I would meet his wife and my half sister for the first time. Strange as this was, I was ready for them, mature enough, even though my half sister might be jealous of me. I wondered what my father would like to know about Gabriel, and whether I was still his favorite child, and I cried without tears and without making a sound.

Time stopped and I lost track of my immediate surroundings. Perhaps I dozed off again. When I opened my eyes, the outskirts of a city were flying by the window. It had to be Bucharest. The train was slowing down, and the man with the Kent cigarettes was nowhere to be seen. Gabriel's flowers were on the floor. My palms got sweaty at the thought of what would happen to me if I didn't find my father at the station, but as soon as the train stopped and I looked out the window, I saw him in the midst of the waiting crowd.

I grabbed my luggage, stepped off the train, and ran to him, yet his embrace seemed strangely foreign.

<hr />

Laura, my father's wife, treated me with polite detachment, and I believe that Elise, only six years old, didn't grasp the significance of us being half sisters. In the evening I played a few board games with her, but there was no emotional connection. The next day, my father suggested he and I take a drive through the city.

His car was a dusty, white Wartburg that shook and sputtered. We stopped at a traffic light downtown. I could see the exhaust fumes of the cars in front of us, the brown trunk of a tree on the sidewalk, and a tall rectangular stone pedestal of what had to be a sculpture.

Bucharest was like that—crowded, stony, and gray.

"Look up," my father said. "The Capitoline Wolf."

I leaned forward. On the pedestal stood a bronze she-wolf. Under her belly were two tiny human babies, their hands raised and their heads turned up to the heavy udders of the animal. Had I made that statue, the she-wolf would have been larger. She deserved to be bigger than life.

"Romulus and Remus," I said. "We must be in Romana Square."

"Actually we are in Floreasca. They moved the statue over here to appease the Soviets and deny our Latin heritage. They're trying to emphasize the Slavic influence over our nation."

"That doesn't make sense."

"Many things don't make sense."

The light changed, and we drove across a small square.

"Remember Ezra and Mordechai?" I asked.

"The two Jewish boys who lived downstairs from your grandparents? They left for Israel, didn't they?"

"Yeah, but why did you call them Romulus and Remus?"

"I don't know. I thought they were twins."

"They were Jewish. You could have called them Cain and Abel," I said.

"Romulus and Remus was funny," he said.

"You're always trying to be funny."

"What else is there?"

"I don't know. Jacob is finding his Jewishness. Do you think *that* is funny? He's working really hard at it, reading books, and going to the synagogue every Saturday. I guess he's always wanted to do it, but it started after Grandfather died."

We were on a wide street with red electric trams occupying the center lane.

"It's exciting to explore your heritage," my father said.

"As long as it's Russian."

"Now you're trying to be funny, aren't you?"

We stopped at another traffic light.

"I remember you debating with Grandfather," I said. "Getting on his nerves."

"I really didn't mean to," my father said.

"I know you didn't. But I also understand why my grandfather was nervous. Religion, you were arguing, was a thing of the past."

"Did I ever say that?"

"Of course you did. And I believed you, and I was proud of you. And I hope you still feel that way." Unlike when I was a little girl, I now comprehended much more. I had learned about the Holocaust and how my father's parents and brother had died during the war. I understood my grandfather's fears. The names people called other people in order to hurt them—much worse than simply calling me *Jew*—had been revealed to me. My own experience and feelings shaped me. And I wondered how my father responded to boys like Ricu in his life. No doubt he had dealt with a few. Had he told them we lived in a new society, or had he jumped at them with his fists?

I pondered telling my father all this, but I didn't, and the traffic light changed. My father switched lanes and turned onto a side street. To my surprise, he stopped at the curb and looked straight ahead through the windshield.

"*Mirichka*," he said, "I need to tell you something."

I waited.

"Laura, Elise, and I have been granted permission to immigrate to West Germany. We'll be leaving in September. Laura has an aunt over there who'll help us get settled, and, with a name like Sommer, we'll fit right in. I only hope our departure won't cause any problems for any of you. They can't hold you responsible for what *we* have decided to do."

I didn't say anything.

"Tell your mother this wasn't an easy decision. We thought about it long and hard. And it's the right thing to do, for us and, maybe, for you. From over there, we'll be able to help you."

"We won't need your help."

"I hope we'll be seeing each other more often once we settle in Germany," my father continued. "Traveling there will not be more difficult than coming to Bucharest, and it will be more fun."

"They won't let us," I said.

"They will. Why shouldn't they?"

"You know, they'll never give us a passport. What happened, Dad? I thought you loved Romania and were working hard for our new communist future."

"I stopped believing in it."

"You mean you were pretending with Grandpa? Were you deceiving us all along?"

"No. I dedicated myself to communism for a long time. Many people did. It wasn't a lie. Don't forget, your grandfather joined the Communist Party also. But over time I came to understand that the dream wasn't real. It wasn't achievable, because its entire foundation is built on a wrong premise, and the people at the top want everything for themselves. What can I tell you? I changed my mind."

I felt angry with him. That was it? And in changing his mind, he decided to leave me behind? And Adina and Jacob, all of us? Was that why he had invited me to Bucharest, to tell me this? Couldn't he have come to Bistriţa and faced us? The invitation had had nothing to do with Grandfather's death. Worse, he was among those who had started Communism in this country, and now that things had turned out harder than he had anticipated, he was packing his stuff and taking off. Unlike other people, because he was Jewish, he could do it. I wanted to ask him if he'd understand those tempted to call him a traitor, and worse, a *typical* Jew, but I didn't, and I mumbled something instead. "Did you change your mind just like that?"

"No, Miriam, it's been two decades—two decades of racking my brains. Besides, only fools never change their minds."

For my trip back, my father upgraded my ticket to first class. I traveled at night and slept almost all the way. Dawn was breaking when I changed trains in Sărăţel. I was thirsty, and I went to the fountain and remembered Gabriel's wildflowers.

Only fools never change their minds, my father had said.

I suggested to Gabriel we go to the waterfall. We could have gone to his studio, but I wanted the moment to have significance.

The sun was low on the horizon. He parked his motorcycle near the dam, and we walked upstream holding hands. The water shone like silver. We started kissing, lowered ourselves to the ground, and rolled in the grass. I took my sandals off and dipped my feet in the water. The long shadow of the surrounding forest was spreading over the meadow. A slight breeze rustled the trees. It was a warm evening, and the chill of the wind and the water rose through my body, tempting my desire.

"Follow me," I whispered.

I took his hand and led him to the abandoned flour mill. He didn't ask any questions. We walked inside through an opening that had to have been a door and found a flat area covered by moss, and he spread his leather jacket over it. A wall leaned inward, and a portion of violet sky was visible through a long crack in the ceiling. Weeds and wildflowers hung from the rafters. Nobody could see us. I felt sheltered, while the slice of sky above us gave me a sense of freedom.

We kissed again and went through our familiar moves, which started with him taking off my blouse, undoing the clasp on my bra, and pulling the zipper at the back of my skirt. His hands caressed my bare skin, and his lips burned my neck and my nipples. Like always, his fingers reached down to my underwear.

I didn't stop him.

He did.

I moved to the side and took my undies off.

"Are you sure?"

"I am."

I ran into Miss Diddieny.

"You look good," she told me. "The trip to Bucharest must have agreed with you."

"It was a good trip. My dad's leaving for Germany."

"Your mother told me," Miss Diddieny said, and she evaluated me one more time, top to bottom. "Something is different about you, I swear. I don't exactly know what, a glow, a light on your face."

"Well, I'm growing up," I said.

"You definitely are. Still seeing Gabriel?"

"I am."

Miss Diddieny waited a second. "Are you sleeping with him?"

The question was unexpected, but I couldn't lie. "Yes," I said.

She looked over her shoulder. Only the two of us were in the street.

"What do you do for protection?" she whispered.

"What can we do? The usual."

"That means nothing, and that's not acceptable." Miss Diddieny seemed concerned, not judgmental. "Tomorrow at four, come by the dental office."

When I arrived the next day, Miss Diddieny was alone. She gave me a small bag with fifteen contraceptive suppositories. They were half an inch in diameter, smelled like coconut, and melted between my fingers.

"Put one in moments before intercourse," she said. "They melt inside you and form a light froth. But don't tell anybody about this, not even your mother. Miri, you know it's illegal? People end up in prison for this."

"I do."

"One more thing. This batch is my gift, but you'll have to pay in the future."

When Pani left, it was a surprise to all of us.

"Mademoiselle Miriam," she said, "imagine how I felt when I discovered her. Here I was, alone in the world, not a relative to my heart besides you, and the entire Levinescu family, of course. You've all been so nice and kind to me. But I found her, my cousin in flesh and blood. She and I, we grew up together, Mademoiselle Miriam. How can I put it? Like you and Claudia, you know. Our fathers were brothers, and our families lived on the same block. I was your age when we lost touch with each other during the war, and I thought they all died, Mademoiselle Miriam, and here she is, alive and well and married with children."

"And you'll leave us and move in with her, right?" I asked, hoping that somehow, maybe, that was not what she intended to do.

"I will, Mademoiselle Miriam, of course I will. I will live with my cousin in Vama, quite far from here. I know. It pains me, but what can I do? Blood is thicker than water, you know?"

"Yes," I said, heartbroken, determined not to spoil Pani's happiness with my own sadness. "But, Pani, if for any reason you'd like to come back, our door is open to you. Always."

"Oh, Mademoiselle Miriam."

And so it went. We cried; we hugged. Pani packed her belongings, hung her aprons on the hook on the back of the kitchen door, and disappeared.

A few days later, my mother discovered that her Star of David was missing.

"You know, Miri," Gabriel said, trying in his way to console me. "There is a reliquary inside the Saint Stephen Basilica in Budapest. I spent hours engulfed in its beauty. The mummified fist of the incorruptible Stephen the First is kept there. That's what we need in this country—a fist, a dictatorship."

"Don't we have a dictatorship?"

"We do, and you know what I mean. We need to rid ourselves of petty thieves and people without any backbone."

I didn't know what he meant. It was typical Gabriel to go on a tangent and leave me on my own with my questions and worries. He was my boyfriend, but he missed the whole point. I couldn't care less about Stephen the First or the fact that Pani had left with a piece of my mother's jewelry—a week or so later, my mother actually found her Star of David in one of her purses. And Pani wasn't lacking backbone—she was lonely. She felt that way no matter how much love and attention I thought I had given her, how many times I had drawn her portrait, and how eagerly I had absorbed every word of her stories about her life. She was going *home* now, really home. It was painful to see Pani leave, but I was in love with Gabriel, and that love somehow gave me the wisdom to understand that it was right to support Pani in her decision because that's what she wanted to do.

I wondered if in Pani's place I would have been as resilient.

After Pani left, I hid the large painting I had done of her at the bottom of the closet. It didn't matter how good it was. She was gone. Life was full of twists and turns—my desire to become a painter, my grandfather's death, Gabriel, my dad's departure, and now her. Things jumped at me all the time; nothing happened as planned; in fact, there was no plan whatsoever.

I was proud of myself—not even seventeen and in a full-fledged sexual relationship with the man I loved. The fact that he was experienced helped, especially in the beginning. Where I was tentative, he was sure.

I understood how patient he had been and how he had waited for me to be ready. I was thankful for that. My previous hesitations had come from insecurity, because our relationship had grown and evolved so quickly, not from any kind of social or family pressure. To quote my father, I decided to change my mind. *I* became sure.

The concept that a young woman needed to remain untouched until marriage was silly and old fashioned. Some adults still clung to it, I knew, but in my generation most people in their right mind didn't believe in it. My mother, who, like me, lived in her own world, didn't know about Gabriel. Paid or not, she still regarded him as my art teacher. Sooner or later she would find out, but I didn't think she cared. At best she would ask me to be careful. The greatest fear women my age had—all women—was of becoming pregnant. There was no protection of any kind on the market, and abortions were illegal. Thanks to Miss Diddieny, I didn't have to worry. I wanted to make it up to Gabriel and push the limits with him. Make him happy. Be worthy.

"Where are those sketches?" I asked him.

"What sketches?"

"You know, the erotic ones you keep in your drawer."

"How do you know about them?"

"I saw them."

"Did you go through my stuff?"

"So what if I did? Are you hiding anything from me?"

He looked at me with innocent eyes.

"I didn't like the way you dissected Cecilia's body," I said. "You exposed her every nook and cranny."

"I broke up with Cecilia. For you."

"Did you really?"

"Yes, really."

"I bet you're still dreaming of her."

"I dream of you. I love you. The woman in those sketches is not Cecilia but a product of my imagination."

"Then show me. Display your imagination."

We placed a mattress on the floor in his studio, and I sat on the mattress, naked, in the lotus position. He cradled his guitar near me and sang a ballad in his voice without vinegar.

"Why do you love me?" I asked when he finished.

"You're beautiful."

"There're many beautiful women in this world."

"Yes, but you're special."

"I'm clumsy and inexperienced, and I don't have many friends," I said.

"You have me."

I closed my eyes and kept quiet.

"Your skin is cool and smooth," he said when I opened my eyes.

"I use creams and lotions."

"I love how you feel, how you smell."

"The lotions are very expensive. You'll have to give me some money."

"I can give you my love."

"Do you think that's enough?" I answered.

He knew I was joking.

I giggled.

He got up, and I lay on my stomach and covered myself with a light blanket. I closed my eyes again and tried to think about nothing. He tiptoed back, sat near me, and uncovered the back of my legs.

"I'm cold," I said.

"I love your scar."

"It's ugly."

"It's intriguing." He leaned forward and kissed the low end of the scar at the back of my knee. "You never told me what happened."

"I told you a million times. I was little. We played in the barn, and I fell and cut myself open. When I saw all the blood, I fainted."

"Last time you told me you were playing in the courtyard."

"It's pretty much the same thing, isn't it?"

"I'm not sure. Where was your mom?"

"At work."

"And your dad?"

"You know where my dad was."

"I don't know. Tell me."

I told him.

He kissed the back of my thigh up the length of the scar, flooding me with desire.

———⊶⊷———

We were painting at the top of the ruins of Bistrița's medieval ramparts. The day was hot, and the sun was beating down on us, relentlessly.

"I can't do it," I said, taking a step away from the easel.

"Keep trying."

The canvas shone as if it were on fire.

"Love is art," I told him. "Loving you fulfills me like painting. I'm at peace with myself, and I don't need anything else. I don't need to paint anymore."

He continued to work.

"Do you like me?" I asked.

"I do."

"Then make love to me."

We lived in a small town where everybody knew everybody, and we tried to ignore the fact that people were talking. One evening we made out in the shadow of the Evangelical church, behind the rectangular columns of the Sugalete Row. I looked around; nobody saw us. In the dead of winter, he walked me home and followed me inside the foyer. It was late, and the house was dark and silent. Upstairs, people were sleeping. The moon peeked through the skylight. We were frozen, and we warmed up by holding each other under the indifferent eye of the stone maiden.

———⊶⊷———

We went to Cassata, and I met Gabriel's mother. I had seen her many times before at the coffee shop, but we had never been introduced officially. As soon as Gabriel opened the door, she left her customers with an attendant and came over to greet us. Her hair was held back with a white kerchief, and she looked older than my mother.

"Hi, Mom," Gabriel said. "This is Miriam."

"Miriam," she said, and she shook my hand. "I know you. I remember every child who ever came to Cassata."

"I'm no longer a child, Mrs. Gelb," I said.

"Sure you are. And Gaby tells me you're very talented."

A sweet cocoa-powder aroma floated through the store. I looked sideways at Gabriel, who shrugged his shoulders.

"Sit down," Mrs. Gelb said. "Would you like some tea with a few lemon tarts or some ice cream?"

"Miriam likes pistachio ice cream," Gabriel said.

"I'm afraid we're out of pistachio."

While we ate she went behind the counter, but then she came back again and sat at our table. "So, how are you, children? Are you behaving?"

I blushed. I didn't know her, and this seemed very direct to me. The way I saw it, this was code for fear of pregnancy.

"Mom..." Gabriel said.

"You don't joke with those people."

"I'm not joking. I'm annoyed, and I don't want to talk about it."

Mrs. Gelb leaned back in her chair and looked around, as if fearing they had spoken too loudly. Slowly, she removed her glasses, and while she massaged the arch of her nose, I noticed that her eyes were the same blue as Gabriel's. "Tell him," she said, looking at me. "They summoned him to the party cell for indecent behavior."

It was clear I had misunderstood her. She wasn't talking of pregnancies. What idiots had accused Gabriel of indecent behavior?

"Mom," Gabriel said, "leave her alone. I'm the adult in this relationship, and I know what I'm doing."

"You're a nice couple," Mrs. Gelb said. "People are watching you and are jealous. If only *your* father were here..."

Gabriel's father was dead, and his mother was struggling.

"Miri, let's go," Gabriel said abruptly, and he got up from the table.

"Wait." Mrs. Gelb looked around one more time. "I have some coffee stashed aside for the studio," she whispered as if pleading. "Stop after seven when the store closes and knock three times so I know it's you, and I'll have it ready."

"What was this all about?" I asked Gabriel as soon as we were in the street. "Party cell? Indecent behavior?"

"Nonsense," Gabriel said.

Clearly he didn't want to talk about it, but I wouldn't have it. "Gaby, you have to tell me."

"I guess somebody saw us kissing or something in broad daylight and complained, so they called me the other day and gave me a warning. I told them it was none of their business. Miri, I'm not going to lose you over this. I'll handle it. A warning doesn't mean anything."

We walked for a few minutes in silence. I shared his indignation but understood that we had to change our ways. Be more prudent. I had pushed him in my desire to be wild and spontaneous. He was a man. He had responded.

"Why didn't they call *me*?" I asked. "Don't I have my share of responsibility?"

"Miri, you're underage, and you don't want to be there."

"Why? What can they do to me? Nothing. But you can lose your teaching position, and they can expel you from the party."

"I don't care," he said. "I can live from my music and my art. You know I always wanted to leave Romania. All they're doing is pushing me in that direction."

"You're not alone anymore."

"I know, Miri."

"They can take your studio."

"If they do, it's *arrivederci* forever."

Our downstairs neighbor, Ileana, moved out. Uncle Tokachi sold his stud bull and relocated a few weeks later. They didn't say good-bye to us, and we had no idea where they went, or if they went together.

That was the story of my life—people who disappeared.

I told Gabriel about them. We were walking behind the soccer field, in the park with the green benches. It was getting dark, leaves were falling, and a light fog was enveloping us.

"Sorry to see them go after all these years," I said. "I liked Ileana, and I liked Uncle Tokachi, as weird as he was. And I painted them both many times."

"When I was in Budapest..." Gabriel started.

"Give me a break with your Budapest stories."

He stopped.

I kept going.

"I was trying to help," he said, a few paces behind me. His voice sounded as if it came from a tunnel.

"I know, but sometimes all I need is for you to listen."

He came near me and took my hand. "I'll listen, OK? I'm sorry."

"You don't have to be sorry."

"OK."

"And you don't have to agree with me all the time."

We walked side by side, in silence. It was annoying—Gabriel always afraid to upset me, always following my lead, holding back, and apologizing. He reminded me of my mother.

You know, I wanted to tell him, if you don't ever pour gasoline on the fire, the flames die. There'll be nothing left except ashes.

I led him to a bench tucked behind a few bushes. He sat near me, silent. I kissed him, and I kissed him again.

"I might lose my job over this, but what the heck," he said and started responding.

I fished a coconut suppository out of my purse, turned away from him, and inserted it.

Chapter 4

DEPARTURES

I t was a cold and wet April at the end of my eleventh grade when it happened. "Miri," he said, "I'm going to Bucharest for two or three days with a guy from the band, Alex. You know him. We have to discuss some music engagements, and I'm riding the motorcycle." He seemed preoccupied, but I didn't think twice about it.

Later I did—his deadpan words like rainwater.

When I didn't hear from him in a week, I went to his studio. A heavy padlock hung on his door, which surprised me.

"Did Mr. Gelb call for me yesterday or this morning?" I asked my grandmother.

"No," she answered.

"Are you sure?" I didn't have a reason to doubt her, but I didn't want to take any chances.

A few days later, I walked by the studio again, and from there I went to Cassata. Behind her counter, Mrs. Gelb gave me a blank stare. The cocoa aroma seemed an illusion. I waited in line, and when my turn came, I asked her in a low voice, "Where's Gaby?"

"We don't have what you want," she said loudly, "but we're expecting a delivery today. I suggest you check with me later."

I returned at 7:05 p.m. that evening and knocked three times on the shop window. I was still in my school uniform. Mrs. Gelb cracked the door open and handed me an envelope. I would have liked to talk to her, but she quickly retreated, leaving me in the empty street. The envelope had no stamps and no postmarks. Maybe he had sent it to his mother in another envelope, or maybe he was in town, couldn't see me for some reason, and had asked her for a favor. But then why wouldn't she talk to me? Why the secrecy?

I resisted my impulse to rip the envelope open on the spot and walked away. By the time I reached home, my patience had run out, and instead of going upstairs, I sat on the lowest step in the foyer, at the base of the statue. A bulb shone above the entrance.

Miri, I read. *I'm so sorry.*

Believe me, I'm crying as I'm writing this letter, and I can only imagine your sadness in reading it, and maybe your anger. My dear, don't be angry with me. Please forgive me.

A while ago, Alex found out that if we traveled to Hungary, we might be able to cross into Austria on certain national holidays when they don't require a visa. We don't know if it's true, but we both agreed that an attempt to cross over on May 1 is worth the effort.

Miri, it shouldn't be a surprise to you that I can't stand the way I live now. I'm not allowed to paint what I want, and I cannot perform my music. I am constantly coached on how to speak in class, how to grade my pupils, which artists to promote, and how to rein-terpret history. My money doesn't last from paycheck to paycheck, and at age twenty-five, I still rely on financial help from my mother. I am being criticized for the way I behave, and if I didn't possess a certain stature, I think they would have thrown me out already. Often I think I am being followed. Perhaps I am paranoid. When we are together, I don't want to worry you, so I don't talk about these things. I'm in love with you, and you are the only bright spot in my life—my joy, Miri, my beautiful wildflower.

Six months ago I applied to travel to Hungary. Alex and I wanted to try crossing into Austria at New Year's, but it took a long time to get my passport. Perhaps the delay had something to do with our relationship and the so-called "indecent behavior" that was raised with the party; I'm not sure. And it might be better this way, because the weather is warm now, the days are longer, and we can travel by motorcycle. A week ago we got our passports. If we succeed, in several days we'll be in Vienna, and we'll ask for political asylum.

I'm leaving this letter with my mother. I've asked her to wait for one week or longer before giving it to you because if we fail, I'll be back and the letter would not serve any purpose. Of course, if I return, I'll be very disappointed, but I'll be happy to be with you again. Also, if we are unsuccessful, I hope that our attempts at the Austrian border will not be reported back home and lead to repercussions. Silly of me to write these last lines because, my dear Miri, if you're reading this letter, I have succeeded.

I don't know how my future will unfold in the free world, with my degree in fine arts and passion for music. I hope I'll find a way of making ends meet and one day, soon perhaps, I'll be able to ask you to join me. I'll keep writing to you, through my mother first, and later, if you agree, we'll start corresponding directly.

Miri, believe me, I have to do this.

And I have to explain to you why I kept my plans secret. This is the most difficult part of my letter. Of course, I can come up with a million trivial excuses, like I didn't want you to be implicated for your own protection or I was concerned you'd insist on coming along, and while I'm ready to risk my life and my future, I have no right to risk yours. I know you oppose the idea of leaving the country, from the way you reacted when your father decided to go to Germany, and I thought you might try to stop me. But none of these explanations are real. The truth is, I was convinced that if I shared my plans with you, if I placed my cards facing up on the table, I would break down and be unable to leave you. I love you that much, Miri.

Last summer you returned from Bucharest a different person. You were angry with your father for leaving for Germany, while I understood him perfectly and envied him. Of course, I never said anything to you in his defense. Because suddenly you knew what you wanted more than ever before. And you gave yourself to me, and you made me happy.

You are a remarkable woman, Miriam. You are sensitive, compassionate, and intelligent. You are beautiful. But more than anything, you are a talented artist. Your artwork is magnificent, and I'm sure that a great career and recognition await you. Continue painting, my dear. Trust me. Soon you will turn eighteen and be able to decide for yourself. Finish high school and go study fine arts with Claudia in Bucharest. In the meantime, I hope we will write to each other, and as soon as I stand on my two feet again, I will ask you to join me.

I will never again in my life do anything secretly, never ever again. I promise.

Loving you more than you know,

Gabriel.

I read his letter again and began reading it for a third time, but when I reached the place where he called me his beautiful wildflower, I let the pages fall on the marble steps and rushed outside. It was cold and drafty under the carriage gate. I walked on to Victoria Street and took a right. The towers of the Evangelical church rose against a darkening blue sky, and I saw heavy rain clouds gathering in the distance.

I was his wildflower, and like weeds in the wild, I was being left on my own. He loved me more than I knew, but he had decided to leave me. He loved me so much that he didn't trust himself to share his plans with me. Yet he acted on them.

I couldn't go home and face my family. What would I tell them? That all things were totally peachy? That I had found out that Mr. Gelb had defected? Should I tell them I was devastated or ask what's for dinner? He had lied to me for six months straight, day in and day out, while we painted, walked hand in hand, and made love to each other. Should I tell my mother I had made love to Mr. Gabriel Gelb, my teacher, and watch her succumb into that unbelievable stupor that overtook her each time she was caught off guard and didn't know what to do to make things proper? Tell my grandmother?

I crossed the street and walked as fast as I could through the tunnel at Sugalete Row to the house where Miss Diddieny lived. She was my confidante, but I couldn't go talk to her. First I needed to cry and recover.

An empty taxicab was waiting at the corner. I walked around it and took a left in the direction of the old defensive wall. Yellow dandelions grew between the large stones of the ruins. Wildflowers! Another few days and the air would be dotted with their white umbrella puffs. We had spent so many hours in that area of town, painting. I knew every facade, every doorway, every dislocated stone, and every zinc gutter. He wrote that my art was magnificent. Of course it was! I knew I had talent, and it took him a long time to acknowledge it. Magnificent! I was going to prove it, to him and the world. I'd exceed his expectations. I'd outshine him, and everyone else in our town, and would study at the Fine Arts Institute in Bucharest and be the best student. I felt determined and excited by these thoughts, and I walked faster and faster. He would hear about me from other artists and read about me in international newspapers. He would try to take credit for my work, but I would dismiss his influence and treat his teachings as minor in my formative years.

I started to run, and I passed the bare lot where the circus pitched its tent at the end of summer, now deserted, wind blowing across, moving dust, cigarette butts, and pieces of torn paper.

Rain began falling, a few drops in the beginning, and then harder and harder.

The stone bridge arched over Bistriţa, and I ran across the swirling river, not sure of where I was going.

The forest.

How little we knew about each other. I had thought he was closer to me than to anyone else. I had been sure I understood his innermost feelings, his mind, and his passions. We had worked together, eaten together, slept together, and discussed and debated many subjects. And yet, while doing all this, while seeming to be offering himself to me, legible and transparent, on the inside he had conceived and nourished a new plan for himself in a world without me. He had looked at me with the trustworthy eyes of a puppy while plotting behind my back and leading a double life to perfection. How could I trust him? How could I trust anybody? Did anybody understand anyone at any time? He told me he loved me, but he had deceived me for six months, or even longer.

The raindrops found their way through the cover of fresh leaves in the forest. My hair got wet, as did my uniform. The path turned muddy and slippery, and I couldn't run any longer. It was colder than it had been in the streets, and it was getting darker. The waterfall was about two kilometers away. I found a fallen tree trunk at the edge of the clearing and sat on it to catch my breath. My feet were covered in mud to my ankles. Splashes of mud dotted my knees and the front of my pinafore. I began shivering, and I hugged my chest with my arms and brought my knees to my chin.

In his letter he had asked for forgiveness. With him next to me, my life seemed purposeful and appealing. Art made sense. There was a starting point, a reference, and a progression. He was my art teacher, and he was my colleague. Together we were different. We stood out in a crowd. We were artists. Without him I was a leaf in the wind—there were a million leaves in the forest. Suddenly I felt I had no friends and no sense of direction. My life held no special meaning. I wasn't better than anybody else, just vulnerable and insecure. Scared. Sad.

Mud got on my hands and my hair. On my face, tears mixed with rainwater.

Of course, he wasn't perfect either. Over the months and years we had been together, he had annoyed me on many occasions. His talent, I thought a few times, was mediocre. Yet he had been my man, my *raison d'être*.

I was sure he had gone through a number of drafts in composing his letter. Maybe he had suffered a little. Had cried. But writing was easy. In the end, he had betrayed me.

It was dark when I left the woods. In town, the sidewalks were deserted, and the rain was coming down like a curtain. Around each streetlamp, the water formed a halo. From the cold, I couldn't feel my toes or my fingers, and my lips were trembling. Yet I wasn't ready to face my folks, and instead of going home, I entered the Evangelical church. It was empty, and the air was warm and smelled of incense. I sat on a pew and looked around, as if seeing everything for the first time in the light of the myriad of electric bulbs, as if I had never sketched and drawn the details of that interior, alone or together with Gabriel. An unexpected sense of peace befell me, and I closed my eyes. When I opened them, an elderly minister stood in the aisle, looking at me intently.

"What's the matter, child?" he asked. "Are you lost? You look cold. You seem wet to the skin, and you're dirty."

Even in my terrible state, I realized I had never seen him before, and I hesitated.

"Nicolai," the minister yelled, his voice reverberating. "Grab me a heavy blanket."

I closed my eyes, and when I opened them again, the minister was unfolding a dark piece of fabric that looked like a tablecloth or a bedcover, while Nicolai, the younger minister I knew from the times I had painted inside the church, was looking at me curiously.

"This is Miriam, Mrs. Levinescu's daughter," Nicolai whispered.

"Do you know where they live?" the older minister asked.

"Not too far. Just around the corner."

"Then run over there and tell her mother to come quickly."

I started to object, but the minister took one step forward and covered me with the blanket.

"Do not worry, child," he uttered, and he made the sign of the cross over my head.

My high fever lasted three days. On the fourth, when I opened my eyes, I saw my mother sitting at the edge of my bed.

"Hi," she said, and she touched my forehead as if feeling my temperature.

"You're not working today," I said.

"I took the day off. You've been pretty sick, you know. Good thing Jacob's in college and Adina slept in his bed to give you space to recover."

I looked around. Adina's side of the bed was empty. Things were stashed away. My school uniform, washed and pressed, rested on the back of a chair. On my nightstand a vase held three red carnations.

"Who brought me flowers?" I asked.

"I did," my mother said. "You poor thing. I put his letter on your desk over there."

I looked again. My notebooks were neatly stacked, and next to them was the white envelope Mrs. Gelb had given me.

My mother knew. She had read his letter, and for now no explanation was necessary.

I spent the day and the rest of that week in bed, reading, crying, and talking to myself. Daydreaming. Adina slept in the other room with my mother. Jacob called and promised he'd visit during his summer break. My grandmother brought me tea and baked me cookies. She brought me a stack of fashion magazines and a newly translated novel by A. J. Cronin.

Adina came to talk to me.

"They believe he escaped to Austria," she whispered.

"He got there through Hungary."

"Did you know he was planning it?"

"Yes," I said without batting an eye.

"You are such a nice person, so much better than I would ever be."

The following week I went back to school. Gabriel had never taught in our school, but everybody seemed to have heard of him and of the fact that he had defected.

"Are you going to join him?" Claudia asked me one day.

"He needs to establish himself," I said. "He needs time. But maybe."

"He was Jewish. Why didn't he go to Israel?"

"This way the entire world is his playground."

I was making things up to block the pain I was feeling. Yet the question about Israel was reasonable. "Going to Israel" entailed legal emigration. There was a process in place in Romania, long and tedious, but less risky than illegally crossing the border. In the early seventies, people unhappy with their lives talked about wanting to live in the West. This had been going on for many years, even though I had ignored it until my father left and the trend had become painfully obvious to me. With my classmates it was always an exhilarating topic of conversation, never mind that even in our midst, in high school, there were government snitches. But I kept to myself, busy making up for lost time and getting an early start in preparing myself for the exams we had to take at the end of the next year.

Summer vacation came and brought with it a lot of free time that I thought I would be dedicating to painting. But painting without Gabriel was a waste. I couldn't do it. Art is love, I had told him at one point, trying to be interesting, and now my own statement blocked me like a boulder. Instead of helping me forget, the way it had helped with Mathew, painting reminded me of Gabriel every time and everywhere. What I needed was a real change—a change in life *and* in scenery.

Mrs. Gelb bumped into me while I was walking with my easel. "I have a letter for you," she whispered. I would have stopped and talked to her, but like the last time, she handed me the envelope and quickly walked away.

Gabriel was in Germany, in a city called Duisburg. His hair was now shoulder long. *I could braid it*, he wrote in his letter. *With the money they're giving us, I bought myself an electric guitar, and every day I write music. Sometimes I go to the*

Hauptbahnhof. *There is an underground there, and I play in there for people. I think they like it. Alex is in Hamburg. He's trying to resettle to Sweden. I miss him.*

Gabriel promised to continue to send me letters at his mother's house, but he gave me the address of his refugee hotel, hoping I'd write back.

I love you—he ended his letter.

I tried answering him, but I couldn't. *Dear Gabriel*, I started each time, and I couldn't continue. I was sad, heartbroken, and still very angry. Putting my true feelings into words would be offensive and wouldn't serve any purpose. The rest was trivial. *It's hot outside. My family's doing well. Bistriţa is a boring place. Yesterday they sold apricots at the market.*

I threw crumpled sheet after crumpled sheet into the wastebasket.

Claudia invited me to a party. "Don't be alone all the time, and don't fool yourself."

I didn't want to go, but Claudia insisted.

"What are you waiting for? He's a man. Even if he loves you as he says in his letters, I'm sure he's looking around. Don't you think so?"

"I don't care," I said to Claudia, but in the end I decided to join her.

There were about thirty people at the party, mostly from the two high schools in Bistriţa, and a few college guys who were home on their summer vacation. I drank a sweet Martini and Rossi on ice with a slice of lemon and listened to French and American music played on a Grundig tape player. Somebody dimmed the lights, and people started dancing, which was enjoyable. At the end of the party, Claudia left with Victor, a classmate she'd been on a few dates with. Two college students I didn't know from before, Radu and Mircea, walked me home. I felt comfortable in their presence. Mircea talked about the privileged son of a Romanian ambassador who had gone on a ski trip to France and had smoked marijuana.

"We're missing out on so much," he said after he made sure nobody was following us. "What kills me are the people who can leave the country. You know, the Germans going to West Germany and the Jews to Israel. Even some of the Hungarians are leaving. But we, the Romanians, we stand no chance. Things are bad here, and we are imprisoned. This is our country, we're told, and this is where we have to live and build our multilateral socialist future."

The scorn in his voice was obvious.

I had heard people say this before, and what stuck in my mind was that "Jews went to Israel." It wasn't something I didn't know, and yet the way Mircea said it made that possibility clear. It was an opportunity I had, unlike him, unlike many others. And it suddenly became the right path, illuminated by the spark of his words, like a trail lost and found in a forest.

It took me a long time to fall asleep that night, excited by my thoughts, twisting and turning while half dreaming in my bed near Adina. In my dreams I was walking though Tel Aviv under the shade of old sycamores, my white dress shining in the crisp morning light. A red carnation was pinned to my lapel. My black hair was gathered in a bun under my hat. In my gloved hands I was carrying a portfolio containing several of my most recent abstract paintings. I was the new me, my reinvented persona, going to meet a gallery owner on Dizengoff Street. I knew all about Dizengoff and its fashionable boutiques from Tante Beatrice's letters. My new lover was a Jew from Morocco, or from Marseille, or from Southern Italy. He had smooth olive skin, and his name was Mario. He was a muscular sculptor and a disciple of Brâncuşi, at the time working in bronze and in marble.

In my dreams I was an art student. I could be anywhere, in Haifa, Tel Aviv, or Beersheba. I was working part time in a bookstore and living in a very small and very modern whitewashed apartment. I had my own bed that I didn't have to share with my sister.

⸻ ✣ ⸻

Mircea called and asked me out on a date. Intrigued about what he had said the previous evening, I agreed even though I wasn't that interested. He held my hand as we walked, but when he tried to kiss me and I said no, he acted annoyed, disappointed. Yet Claudia was right. Not every man I met had to be like Gabriel, and there was an entire world out there. I could play and experiment a little, especially now that I knew I was leaving.

⸻ ✣ ⸻

"I've decided to go to Israel," I told Jacob when he came to visit. "For good. I'm emigrating."

It was just the two of us, in the afternoon, on the bank of Bistriţa.

"I think we should all go," he said. "Eventually."

"No, I want to go now. As soon as I turn eighteen, in three months, I'm applying."

"Miri, do you know what you're saying?"

"Of course I do. I'm determined. I'm sick and tired of this place, and I want to be free. I want to read any book I like and paint any subject that inspires me."

"You cannot paint what you want?"

"I can't paint at all," I said. I picked up a small stone and threw it toward the river in frustration.

"Does Gabriel have anything to do with this?"

"It's because of him and because of many other reasons. It doesn't really matter, and I don't think I need to explain to you the advantages of being Jewish and living in Israel."

"Have you discussed it with Mother?"

"I haven't."

Jacob broke a thin tree branch with bright pink flowers and gave it to me. "Here," he said. "Take these flowers. They're beautiful." Then he added, "I think you should talk to Mother. You'll need her permission."

"I'm waiting until I'm eighteen."

"It won't matter. *They* want to make it as hard as possible on you, and as long as you live in your parents' house, you'll need your parents' consent. Obviously our father is away, but Mother will have to sign your application and actually state that she agrees with your decision to leave Romania. You know, this process is difficult."

"Mother will sign the papers."

"I hope so, for your sake. But be prepared for a fight with the authorities, and know that it will take a while. At least a year, if you're lucky."

"I have it all figured out," I said. "And anyway, I need the time to graduate from high school and get my baccalaureate."

"And if it takes longer?"

"I'll wait."

"Forever?"

"Why would it be forever?"

"You never know, but once you apply you are compromised, and you cannot take it back. Aren't you going to college?"

"No," I said.

"Wow, I think you'd better talk to Mother."

"I'll tell her after I apply."

"Miri, if you have the guts to do it alone, do it. Good luck and more power to you."

What could I say? I had the guts. I had what it took, and I *was* determined.

Next to us, the river was flowing forward, green shadows forming a dancing mosaic on its lazy surface.

In my dreams, I would be this successful person, and several years after my arrival in Israel, sooner than anybody had dared hope, my mother, my grandmother, Jacob, and Adina would join me. In my dreams, I would welcome them at the Tel Aviv airport, guide them, and help them resettle. I would have a huge apartment and host a welcoming party for them and invite all my friends and fellow artists. Or maybe Jacob would come first, and the three of them later.

One day I approached Grandmother. "With your help, I would like to sew a few things for myself. Maybe you could ask Tante Beatrice to send us some fabrics."

I walked through the streets of Bistriţa and thought about my future. In the free world, I would be unencumbered and allowed to think, to explore, and to travel. I could visit my father in Germany—not that I necessarily longed to see him, but it might be rewarding and interesting. And I could travel to France, to Italy, or even to the United States of America. I would be able to go to Jerusalem and experience history.

I could listen to the Rolling Stones, or Bob Dylan.

Israel was a country at war, but the war wouldn't touch me. Who knows, maybe I would have to serve in the military. I'd become a war reporter and go everywhere with my camera, and with my shades and protective headgear to shield myself from the relentless sun because I burned so easily. But before going to the military, I would study photography, in addition to fine arts.

In the Israeli streets, I would always smile to Arabs and speak to them with respect. I would purchase their freshly squeezed orange juice and bags of pistachios and always leave a nice tip because I knew how it felt to be a minority in your own country. There would be less rain than in Bistriţa and no snow in the winter. Sandstorms would be rolling in from the desert. I'd be wearing the clothes I had sewn with my grandmother from Tante Beatrice's fabrics—those beautiful, multicolored chiffons, silks, crepes, velvets, and cottons—and not just dresses and blouses and skirts, but scarves, sashes, and silky underwear. Getting the right shoes would be a problem, and I might have to buy those in Bucharest before my departure. And I would create my new persona: elegant, but also daring and friendly.

School started again in September. Somehow, my world was divided. I was there, doing what I was expected to do, studying, preparing my homework, and acting engaged with and friendly to my classmates; but my thoughts were far away, in a fantasy space I didn't share with anybody. Often enough I myself wasn't sure which of the two sides was more real.

In my thoughts, I was learning Hebrew at the synagogue, where I actually never went. But I spent a lot of time perfecting my English, which I spoke pretty well after eight years of studying.

In my fantasy world, I found a new friend in Tante Beatrice's daughter, Ronit. She was older than I, but that didn't matter, and I imagined that the two of us clicked almost instantly. She, being a figment of my imagination, understood me perfectly and surprised me by intuiting my deepest feelings and responding to them. She became my new sister, with the vehemence that I had only seen in Pani when she rediscovered her cousin missing since the Second World War.

In my real world, I started getting invited to parties and being courted by young men. I was amused and flattered even though I didn't take any of these men seriously, knowing that none of them would hold the key to my heart. My reputation of having dated an art teacher who had defected to the West preceded me. It added mystique and possibly caused some to think I was easy. Yet every time I heard the gossip, it was coupled with flattering statements about my looks and the way I dressed. I allowed some men to kiss me, but my rule was no action below the waist. After what Gabriel had done to me, it felt as good as payback. Those young men all wanted the same thing—it was easy.

With Lucian it was a misunderstanding, but luckily only for a few days. We went to a party the week before Christmas. I was wearing a silky long gown I had sewed myself that covered the scar at the back of my leg and made me look slim and attractive. Smoke rose from the ivory cigarette holder I held between my fingers. I was roaming around while Lucian sat on a couch. Suddenly I saw Mathew. He must have come home from college for his winter break. When our eyes met, he started in my direction.

"Miriam," he said. "Nice to see you."

"Really?" I asked and blew smoke toward him.

"*Really*. I'm here for a few weeks, and maybe we could get together. Catch up." He seemed very sure of himself.

"One moment," I said, and I turned to the sofa. "Lucian, come over here, please!"

Lucian got up.

"Mathew, meet Lucian, my boyfriend."

The surprise on Mathew's face was obvious. He was still very handsome. "Miriam, I didn't mean it that way."

"You didn't, really? I think you'd better fuck off, Mathew."

That evening Lucian walked me home. "Can I kiss you good night?" he asked when we stopped by the red door.

"You want to kiss me?"

"I'm your boyfriend," he said.

It was freezing outside. I led him inside the foyer, where we kissed for a long time.

In my dreams I figured that in Israel I would do something about my scar. There were doctors in Israel who specialized in cosmetic surgery, and my scar could be gone from one day to the next. Good riddance, Mathew, forever.

That December I received two more letters from Gabriel. His mother gave them to me in the same reserved, almost disapproving manner in which she had always treated me. Gabriel was still in Duisburg, and he was still waiting for his situation to be resolved by the authorities. I didn't write back, but I copied his address into the notebook I intended to take with me to Israel.

Lucian invited me to Cassata. It was the first time I went in there since Gabriel defected. His mother brought us the tea and cookies we ordered, and she spoke to us as if she didn't know who I was.

I deliberately sat very close to Lucian and held his hand on the table.

Gabriel stopped writing to me.

PART 2

Chapter 1

ISRAEL

I arrived in Israel on November 7, 1972, a day remembered in the Soviet Union and the Eastern Bloc countries as the anniversary of the Bolshevik October Revolution. I was amused by the coincidence and took it as a good omen, since we celebrated this event every school year, and since I had always been intrigued by the fact that the October Revolution had actually started in November.

In my possession I had two large suitcases, some hand luggage, a box of chocolates from Jacob, and a brown Romanian-issued passport for people without citizenship. My relatives didn't meet me at the airport in Tel Aviv. Tante Beatrice had been rushed to the hospital the week before, and Ronit, who lived in Beersheba and didn't have a car, announced via an agitated phone call on the eve of my departure that she was in the midst of a messy divorce and in no shape to welcome a newcomer to *Eretz Israel*.

The weather was picture perfect. As I deplaned and waited to get into the bus that would take us to the terminal, I was glad I had my hat on to protect me from the merciless sun. The air was diaphanous, different from the wet and fragrant air of Bistrița, and I knew right away that I was in a foreign land. I was curious about what was to come, and a little anxious. The passengers filled two shiny, spotless buses, and when we got inside the building, we split into two groups, a large one, consisting of regular travelers, and a much smaller one, the immigrants. Representatives from the *Sochnut*, the Jewish Agency responsible for newcomers, met us. My turn came at the end, after the others, all families, had presented their papers. I entered a brightly lit, windowless room and was met by a dark-haired woman in her midforties and a female soldier about my age. Both seemed relaxed and friendly. An armed security guard stayed outside.

"*Baruch ha ba la Aretz*," the female soldier said.

I looked at her, confused.

"Welcome to Israel," she translated into English, and she smiled. "Now that you're here, you'll have to learn Hebrew."

"I will," I said.

"*Roumanit?*" she asked.

That much I understood, and I nodded.

"Your passport," the older, dark-haired woman said in English. "And please, sit down."

There were three chairs on my side of the table, I guessed for people who arrived in family groups, and I chose the one in the middle. The dark-haired woman was seated on the other side, while the female soldier stood. Several empty plastic cups littered the table next to a stack of files and a sheet of paper that seemed to contain a list of names.

I handed her the passport; then I took off my hat and put it on the chair next to me, together with my white overcoat, my hand luggage, my purse, and the box of chocolates I had from Jacob.

"Nice hat," the female soldier observed.

"Thank you."

"Miriam Sommer?" the older woman said.

"Yes."

She found me on the list and made a check mark next to my name with her pen.

"Anybody waiting for you?"

"My cousin was supposed to meet me, but something happened and she couldn't come."

"That's OK," the older woman said. "From here you'll go to an absorption center or *ulpan*. Do you have a geographical preference? There are a few choices." She handed me a list typed in English, but the names didn't mean anything to me. "Where does your cousin live?" she asked.

"Beersheba."

"There are spots closer to Beersheba, but they're not as nice as the one in Netanya. Go to Netanya if you can."

"I'll go," I said.

"You're twenty years old, correct?"

"Yes," I said.

"And you came without family, all alone. You're very gutsy," the young soldier said.

I smiled.

"*Kol ha kavot*," she said, and then she translated. "More power to you."

They had me sign my *teudat ole*, which was my temporary new identity card, and gave me back my passport. "Show this teudat at the ulpan," the older woman said. "This will give you all your rights as an *olah hadashah*."

"As a newcomer," the female soldier said.

They told me I would share a cab with other immigrants once I retrieved my suitcases and passed customs. Just follow the signs.

"*Bună seara*," the female soldier said in accented Romanian, smiling broadly one last time as I was getting ready to leave.

"Good night to you, too," I said.

The taxi ride took about an hour. I expected to see some of the people from my plane, but instead I rode with a large family from Portugal. They spoke Portuguese among themselves, constantly, and besides a hello when I entered the cab and a few back-and-forth curious glances and polite smiles, there were no exchanges between us. The radio blasted rock and roll music interrupted by bouts of static and by commentary barked in a language I guessed was Hebrew. The driver chain-smoked. His window was lowered halfway, and waves of hot air mixed with a sharp tobacco smell reached my side of the cabin. I placed my hat in my lap, smoked one cigarette, and then a second, and looked out the window. We drove through city streets, in some places flanked by white stone houses and palm trees. Then we got on a highway such as I had never seen before, with two lanes in each direction and large green traffic signs. Cars and buses were zooming by, and from time to time, our driver would get very close to the car in front of him, utter a few angry words under his breath, and blow his horn. The landscape was mostly arid, brown and yellow, but we passed a few lush areas with pine trees and orchards. We sped by more clusters of white houses, with flat roofs and water cisterns heated by the sun, that were *kibbutzim* and Arab villages. Billboards stood on the side of the highway, and colorful flower beds decorated the intersections.

To my left I saw the Mediterranean, appearing and disappearing behind soft hills and houses, the sun shining directly over it, the blue of the water stretching far out to the horizon. Everything felt fresh and immediate, new, an attack on all my senses, like a bite from a succulent exotic fruit that overfills your mouth with juices, in stark contrast with the melancholy of the Romanian November. Only four hours ago, I was in another world and another season, with my mother, grandmother, brother, and sister, who had all come to the airport to bid me good-bye, grave and concerned, weary, worn out by the long train ride from Bistriţa to Bucharest, and burdened by the knowledge that my departure into the unknown could be a separation forever. I had to give it to my mother. During these last days she had been strong. Optimistic. It seemed that it was she and I who kept up the appearances and helped everyone move through sadness and gloom. My mother, because she knew she was the backbone of the family, and I, because I had the future, unpredictable as it was, ahead of me. They all felt so much closer to me now, so much more significant than before, when I took their presence for granted and noticed them only when they annoyed me. I would write to them, long letters, describing my new life in as many and as vivid details as I would be able to provide. Maybe I would draw and paint scenes from my new life for them, as I used to do before Gabriel left me. I might write to Gabriel as well. As that thought crossed my mind, I turned my face to the window, afraid I was blushing. But I didn't have any reason to be blushing right now, because I had left Romania and we were both on our separate ways.

The ulpan was a refurbished hostel, and the guy at the reception desk spoke Romanian. He checked my name on the list and gave me a room.

"We'll bring you the luggage in a few minutes, but let us first take care of the Portuguese family," he told me and winked. "Dinner is between six and seven thirty in the dining hall."

My room was sparsely furnished but very clean and bright. The floor was tiled. I had a small bathroom and a balcony. I unpacked a few things as soon as they brought me the suitcases, changed into a lighter outfit, and drank a glass of tap water that tasted different from back home. On the table was a bowl of oranges, and I grabbed one of them and weighed it in my hand. Then I walked onto the balcony and lit a cigarette. To the west, over red rooftops and palm trees, unmistakable, I sensed the breath of the Mediterranean. If I was tired, I didn't feel it. There was another hour till dinner, and I decided to go out into the streets and to the shore.

———— ✽ ————

I stayed at the ulpan in Netanya for only five days. That meant lonely early morning strolls through city streets and late afternoon walks on the beach. It meant a two-hour Hebrew session in a classroom. It meant breakfasts, lunches, and dinners in the cafeteria at a small table for two, where I sat alone each time, except once, when the table was occupied and I joined an elderly couple from Romania. They had already spent two months in the ulpan. They complained about their young Hebrew teacher, who introduced new words much too quickly, and the Sochnut representative, who wasn't able to explain anything properly to them. I was glad to be talking to them, and also glad when our meal was over.

My daily walks followed the same route, again and again, until the newness of it disappeared and I was able to move without thought of where I was or where I needed to return. I liked the sparkling windows of the shops I didn't dare enter for lack of money, crammed full of merchandise, and the flower beds at street crossings, at the edge of the many city parks, and in front of the white stone houses and small apartment buildings. The flowers were always opulent, magnanimous in the richness of their colors, surprising, bursting with life as if to compensate for the many parcels of dry and parched soil, yellow, reddish, or brown. Everywhere there were flowers, there were sprinklers as well, their life support, tracing the air with rainbows fresh against the morning or the afternoon sun. On the beach I took my shoes off, stepped on the warm sand, and advanced to the water and the gently crashing waves, sparkling in the shimmering light, back and forth, back and forth. I watched the expanse of the sea and pictured it on the other shore, where it washed the warm hills of Anatolia. In my mind I followed the water's edge as it merged with the Aegean Sea and the Sea of Marmara and, through the Strait of Bosporus, the Black Sea; and I remembered the shore of the Black Sea and that lost-to-the-world little place called Eforie, where a young skinny girl was once photographed with her father, and I thought of my father in Germany, hopefully in the embrace of his new loving family.

Every day for my strolls I wore a new outfit I created in Bistriţa with my grandmother's help, and I could sense people watching me, following me with their gaze, and commenting behind my back. Men at a bus stop whistled as I walked by on the opposite side of the street, and one morning a young man approached me.

"*Sliha*," he said.

"Sorry, I don't speak Hebrew," I said.

"But I speak English. You're obviously not from around here," he said.

Like many youngsters he wore a pair of faded blue jeans, a loose flowery shirt, and a peace pendant on a leather necklace. On his feet he had dusty Roman sandals. I realized how different I looked: my clothes, perfectly color coordinated in earthy tones, fluttered on me; my skirt reached to my ankles; my blouse had long, narrow sleeves; my hands were gloved; I wore dark sunglasses and a wide-brimmed white hat. I was hidden, covered like a Bedouin woman, elegant, striking, and odd. That was me at my best that morning, and I didn't want to speak to him in English or otherwise.

I turned away. He allowed a short distance to separate us and started following me. At once, I felt threatened and amused. I started walking faster, and the distance between us increased. Clearly I looked different in a way that reflected my personality but also protected the silence inside me and around me, pulsing with the rhythm of the sea. When I looked back again, he was gone.

In my loneliness I started talking to myself and pondering my every gesture, projecting ahead, and moving slowly because I had all the time in the world. I wasn't answering to anybody, depending on anybody, or following anyone's steps.

I was telling myself that I was doing exactly what I wanted to do.

In Bistriţa when I informed my mother of my decision to immigrate to Israel, she didn't oppose it, and she signed the passport application with a resignation that surprised me. She didn't ask whether I was afraid to go, the way Jacob did. There was no hint of her trying to understand my desire to leave because of Gabriel or any other reason. The future and the unknown were mine to worry about, and of course I would do very well. If she admired my desire to stand on my own two feet, she didn't show it at all.

"You're abandoning me," she stated instead. "Did you think at all about me?"

No, Mother, I didn't, I thought about saying, and I kept my mouth shut. Imagine, I didn't think about you.

In Bistriţa it was always about somebody else. I didn't have many intimate friends, but people existed around me, people who mattered and had roles to play. They told me what to do. When I felt suffocated in their presence, I evaded them in the privacy of painting or wandered on secluded streets or to the forest. And every time I did that, in the end I returned. In the evenings, my mother and grandmother waited for me with dinner. In the mornings, I woke up with Adina sleeping next to me in the bed.

Here, for the first time in my life, I was totally by myself. Even when surrounded by people, I was alone. I would go eat and go walk and come back to my room. All impressions, the newness, I took in by myself.

During my five days in the ulpan, I learned a few things, trivial as they might be, crucial to the way I organized my future. I could stay in the ulpan and receive financial aid from Sochnut until I graduated from language school, but then I would need to find a job and move out. Or, if I chose to become a full-time student, I could get a scholarship and live in a student hostel with people my own age. There was no admission exam, like there was in Romania, as long as I had my high school diploma and the baccalaureate. In fact, I could sign up for *mehina* (preparatory language classes) at the college I wanted to attend and start my life as a student right away. Since twenty was the cut-off age for military service for young women, I didn't have to worry about the military, but I was advised to visit the recruitment center to get my deferral papers if I wanted to travel abroad. And I wanted to travel to Bistriţa. I had dreamed about it since the day I arrived.

I tried painting, twice. I took time selecting the spot in my room and arranging my pencils, my brushes, my colors, and my sketchpad. I lit a cigarette. I put it out. Both times, I gave up.

On the second day of ulpan, I talked by phone to Ronit. She called. She was apologetic for not coming to see me, and she complained about her former husband, who continued to make her life hell. We agreed we would get together, maybe for a cup of coffee, very soon. Somehow I would get to Beersheba by bus. Tante Beatrice was still in the hospital and not doing too well. Ronit said I should go study at the University of Haifa, which was beautiful and calm. Beersheba was not a good place.

On the fourth day, I ran out of the cigarettes I had brought with me from Romania, and made my first purchase from the money I had from Sochnut.

I shared a two-bedroom apartment with three other young women at the *maon* (student hostel) in Romema. My roommate was Rita, from Portugal.

"It's funny," I told her in English the day we met. "I traveled in a taxi to the ulpan with a Portuguese family, the mother, the father, and their children." I gave her the name.

She shrugged. Of course she had no clue who they were.

Rita had immigrated years ago, spoke Hebrew like a *sabra*, and was up to her neck in her studies. She barely had time for her own family, never mind knowing who the newcomers from Portugal might be. People were arriving in Israel from all over the world. Rita was nice to me, and I was nice to her, and after a while I started feeling almost as comfortable with her as I had been with Adina in Bistriţa.

Vivette, from Istanbul, and Odette, from Bucharest, were the other two women in the apartment. We had different classes and little time to chat, except on the weekends and sometimes when we shared each other's food from the refrigerator. Young men lived in the building, too, on separate floors, and they showed up in our apartment for all kinds of reasons all the time. They started paying attention to me, but I was very reserved.

I was changing one day when Vivette noticed the scar on my thigh.

"How did you get it?" she asked.

I didn't want to go into the whole complicated story of Mathew, so I told her the tale about me falling on a nail in the barn.

"Wow," Vivette said. "Quite a long cut from a nail."

"I almost bled to death. And don't tell anybody, please."

"I won't, although you have nothing to hide."

"Maybe," I said, thinking that she might be right and that Gabriel had loved me in spite of my scar, if he had ever loved me at all. I had already altered my wardrobe some and bought one pair of jeans and a few casual tops, even though I didn't dare expose myself in shorts or in a miniskirt.

Through Odette, I met an entire group of young men and women from Romania; some of them lived at the hostel, and others in rented apartments. United by their common language, they gathered often and went to parties, movies, or the beach, or simply strolled on Herzl and HeHaluts, an area not too far from Romema, full of stores, movie houses, ice cream parlors, and falafel stands.

⸺∞⸺

"I've seen you before," Lydia said the first time we met. "We came on the same plane from Bucharest."

"November seventh, the date of the Bolshevik Revolution."

"Yep," she said. "I came here with my family."

I didn't remember her from the plane or from the airport when we waited for our Israeli papers, but I befriended her immediately.

She was from Bucharest and lived at the hostel on a lower floor. Like me, she was taking Hebrew prep classes, and we started traveling by bus or hitch-hiking together to and from the university.

"I have a boyfriend in Bucharest," she told me. "Nick. He's not Jewish. I didn't want to leave him, but we are too young, and I didn't have a choice with my family. We write to each other every day, and after we finish our studies, we hope to get married."

"That's going to take a few years," I said.

"It will be hard, but I love him."

The melancholy in her voice, and her conviction that her long wait would be worth it, touched me. I didn't say anything, though I thought she was dreaming.

In my room I retrieved Gabriel's address, looked at it, and read it aloud. It had been over two years. The address would no longer be current. I ripped the page from my notebook and threw it away.

After six months of Hebrew language classes, it was time to choose my major, and I opted for art history. It wasn't fine arts, but it was the field of study they offered at the University of Haifa closest to my interests, and I needed to be a full-time student. Lydia decided to pursue a double major in French and English literature. At first we attended a few electives together.

I worked at the university library and cleaned hoses, but that was hardly enough to save for a trip to Bistrița. My supervisor at the library was an older man by the name of Alan. I told him I missed Romania.

"Go back once," he said, "and your longing will disappear."

Adrian also belonged to our Romanian group of friends. One day, he showed up at the maon with a new car, a black Audi, elegant and low to the ground, with doors that closed with an airtight thud. Newcomers to Israel would typically buy Ford Escorts or French-made Peugeots. Not many could afford an Audi, especially not a student. Lydia said Adrian had an uncle who had come to Israel in the fifties, had made it big, and had bought him the car as a gift, to win him over and show him that he cared. I would have liked being cared for like that. I enjoyed things elegant and low to the ground. And I was tired of working odd and demeaning jobs. Working fulfilled some vague sense of responsibility, but it was dull, and it left me with no free time. I wanted to paint again and felt I couldn't. All I did was learn Hebrew, pay bills, and clean houses.

Tante Beatrice died that summer. I didn't know her personally, but I felt I had to go to the funeral. It was a long trip. The desert heat exhausted me at the cemetery, after which I spent a mostly sleepless night on a mattress in Ronit's apartment. In the morning we had the cup of coffee she had promised me since my arrival in Israel. We both cried. As I was getting ready to leave, she handed me seven hundred dollars in cash, my share of Tante Beatrice's modest inheritance.

Somebody did care for me, and I used a part of that money for a round trip to Romania.

Alan, the librarian, was right. My longing ceased. The train ride to Bistriţa was dusty and long. I was tired when I arrived. It was rainy and dark. The cheap gifts I brought everybody were received with fake enthusiasm. Many of my schoolmates were in college, including Claudia. Adina didn't seem too interested in what I had to say. As for sleeping arrangements, I slept in Jacob's bed in the living room with my mother. Jacob, who came to Bistriţa to see me for only two days, slept downstairs in one of the rooms formerly occupied by Ileana and Uncle Tokachi. Miss Diddieny was in the midst of setting up a new dental office and visited once. Mr. Moisil happened to be away for two weeks at a mountain resort. Neighbors came and left. They complained about the general state of affairs in Bistriţa and told me I looked great. They seemed provincial. Dull. My grandmother had an issue with some of the outfits I wore, but otherwise she kept to herself. My mother was upset I wasn't painting. She had rarely shown an interest in my art before, but now I was throwing my talent away.

On Iom Kipur, during the second week of my visit, Egypt and Syria attacked Israel. I landed in a Tel Aviv under blackout, in total darkness. Suddenly I felt a strong bond with my friends in Romema, and with all the people of Israel, with its openness, with its colors and smells. It felt like I closed a book forever and opened another one—my new country, at war.

Lydia's mother was a doctor at Rambam, a hospital in the Bat Galim neighborhood of Haifa. From her I learned of a reputable cosmetic surgeon from South Africa who ran his own private practice associated with the hospital. I still had a little money left over from Tante Beatrice.

The surgery lasted over an hour.

Several weeks later I returned for a follow-up visit. The nurse had me lie on my stomach, and the doctor took out the stitches, and touched the scar with his fingers. "It's healing nicely," he said.

I pulled my jeans back on and tucked in my T-shirt.

He caught up with me as I was leaving. "I'm taking a break. Join me for a cup of coffee in the cafeteria."

"Sure," I said surprised, thinking I had nothing pressing to do that afternoon.

He was young and dark skinned like Mario, my imaginary sculptor. But he was a doctor, *my* doctor—such a noble and reliable profession. His name was Zvi Rave.

"When it heals completely, it will barely be a line, hard to see unless you know it is there," he told me as we sat down at a table. "Don't be impatient. It will take up to a year to completely disappear."

"Thank you, Zvi," I said. "I'm glad I summoned the courage to do it."

"I'm glad also." He leaned back in his chair and gave me a broad smile, his white teeth shining in the neon light of the cafeteria. His white coat opened at the chest. At least he didn't have a stethoscope around his neck. "You never told me," he added, "how you got that scar in the first place."

I found the question amusing and gave him my sanitized version, the one without Mathew.

"Wow," he said. "Miriam, you're a student, yes?"

"I am."

"And you like the fine arts, and you'd love to be painting."

I was surprised. "How do you know?"

He smiled again. "I have my ways, and I check on some of my more challenging patients."

His tone was enigmatic and a little patronizing, as if he always knew more than he let on, but it also sounded as if he wanted to let me know that he had checked me out because he was interested in me.

"Do you find me *challenging*?" I said, emphasizing the words in a manner that begged for a compliment.

"Charming," he answered. "And you should know that I also like art, and a few years ago I took some art classes at the university. Now I spend most of my free time sailing."

I looked around the cafeteria—all the tables were empty at that hour, except one where several nurses, perhaps at the end of their shift, were eating out of plastic containers. My gaze returned to Zvi, and he held it, until I lowered my eyes to his hands with their long fingers, the ones on the left coiled around his white coffee cup.

"You have miraculous hands," I said, not sure where I found the audacity. "Like a pianist's."

He placed his cup in its saucer and spread out his fingers on the tabletop. "Listen," he said while examining his hands. "I have to go back to work, but would you consider going out with me? Say dinner, at seven o'clock the day after tomorrow?"

A dinner seemed much to me. "I'm not sure," I said. "How about a movie?"

"Movie? Yes. Have you seen *Doctor Zhivago*?"

As I left the hospital, I felt healed physically and spiritually. My scar would be gone, true, but the equilibrium had been restored by the unexpected appearance of this man in my life. It seemed he was all I needed. That's how lonely and vulnerable I really was. My exhilaration came from within, so intense I could hardly contain it, and when I arrived at the dorm, instead of going to my small room and possibly facing Rita and the others, I rode the elevator to the last floor and took the stairs to the roof. I had been there before to watch sunsets over treetops and buildings. Now I wanted to be alone.

The roof was a flat, industrial type place with gravel littered by cigarette butts over a tar-like base with vents, clotheslines, and TV antennas. A concrete wall, waist high, surrounded its perimeter. I walked to the edge and lowered myself onto the gravel with my back against the wall, its asperities clinging to the fabric of my T-shirt. The wind howled above. Sheltered by the wall, I lit a cigarette. The sun fell obliquely, throwing elongated shadows on the roof.

If I ever told my friends about Zvi, how would I do it? Hey, I met somebody this afternoon. Who's he? my friends would ask. My doctor, my cosmetic surgeon, you know. That wouldn't sound right. I could still feel his fingers on my thigh. He had seen me half naked, splayed on his table, and had touched me right there, at the top of my scar. Our relationship, if one were to develop, would be sexual, no doubt. I would have to visit my gynecologist and get on the pill. Tingling traveled through my body, and I closed my eyes and then opened them and extinguished my cigarette on the wall.

The next day, when I returned from class, I found a message Odette had taken for me. *Miriam, your doctor's office called. Your appointment tomorrow is canceled because of an emergency. Call to reschedule,* her message said.

We met several days later at the café on Yefe Nof, and we briefly held hands before being seated. I ordered a banana split and he an espresso and a *Calvados*. When he brought the cup to his lips, I noticed his wedding band.

"You're married," I said.

"Don't let that bother you," he said.

I felt dizzy. Blood left my face. "You didn't have the ring on at the hospital."

He laughed. "I can't wear jewelry when I work."

"Do you have children?"

"I do, a boy and a girl."

I pushed my dessert aside. "I have to go."

"Wait," he said. "Miriam, I didn't try to deceive you, and I like you a lot. You are the person I want to be with, beautiful, smart, and talented."

"Zvi," I mumbled, "I can't get involved with a married man."

"Why not? You wouldn't be the first or the last to do it. People do it all the time, everywhere."

"I don't care what other people do."

"Miriam, it just so happened that I met my wife before I met you."

"Zvi, what are you saying?" I asked.

He looked straight at me. "Do you like me?"

I didn't answer, and I lowered my eyes.

"Tell me, do you like me at least a little bit?"

"I do."

"Listen, I know you're confused, and I understand. But I have money and stamina, and I want us to be together. Trust me, you won't regret it. I'll make it worth your while."

⸙

It was difficult for me at first, but somehow I allowed myself to follow his lead. I couldn't resist. He helped me rent a one-bedroom apartment on Carmel—a desirable neighborhood—and paid for it in full. He covered my expenses. I thought it was a temporary arrangement until we figured it out. Eventually we could date openly, after he left his wife.

He brought me flowers and jewelry. Later he brought beer with him. He liked beer a lot.

He showed up with *Playboy* magazines rolled up in his pocket. "For inspiration," he said.

I thought I was inspiration enough.

He had come to Israel fifteen years earlier, had changed his name, and had blended in. He bragged about being an old-timer, proud of his years in Israel and of what he had accomplished and accumulated. Others, he claimed, were too quick to give in.

His time in Israel seemed an eternity compared to mine. After a while it didn't matter where you came from. He had built a reputation as a physician, bought a house, and started a family.

Painting was my calling in life. Like him, I wanted to be exceptional. I wanted to quiet down, settle down, and start painting again. Now I could do it, if only I had a studio, even only part-time.

His sailboat was anchored at a marina north of Haifa, but we never went sailing together. In fact, we hardly went out. We didn't go to see *Doctor Zhivago*. We had to be prudent. His wife cared for him. He was a good-looking man with enough stamina to have a thing on the side with me.

Before showing up at my place, he always called. That was nice. Given the circumstances, I ended up sharing the need for discretion with him.

Chapter 2

JONATHAN

I went on my second yearly trip to Romania to see my folks. Zvi Rave paid for the ticket. I really didn't have a choice, even though I considered going back to cleaning houses, and when I accepted his money, I wasn't too happy with myself. Of course, to him I showed gratitude, which he mistook for affection.

Lydia accompanied me to the airport.

My flight had a layover in Athens, and that detail alone made me feel excited and a little lightheaded, as if I was embarking on an international adventure.

At the security checkpoint, Lydia gave me a hug and left, while I stood there and watched her move through the airport crowd, slender and determined, until she disappeared. We were friends, but we were different. For a while, before both of us moved out of the student hostel in Romema, we had talked about sharing a room. Even now I regretted that we never did it. With Lydia close to me, I would have been more secure and focused. I would have started painting again, and Zvi Rave would have never happened. Perhaps. When I moved to Carmel, Lydia went to live with her family in their new apartment in Neve Sha'anan. Now we were together mostly at the university. She continued her studies and kept writing to Nick, her boyfriend in Bucharest, while I began to drift, jumping from painting classes to classical literature and languages and photography, complaining it was boring and hard and feeling sorry for myself.

When planning my trip home, I decided to spend the first night with Claudia in Bucharest so I could ask for her advice. Had I not left for Israel, we would have studied fine arts together. I wanted my childhood friend to listen to me and tell me what I needed to do. Where I went wrong. I wrote her a letter, and even though her response was reserved, I convinced myself that it was still a good idea to see her. If nothing else, it would be a break before my long train ride to Bistrița.

Lydia brought me a small package for Nick. "It's a pair of blue jeans, nothing fancy. He'll meet you at the airport with his dad's car and take you wherever you need to go," she said.

I had never told Lydia about my relationship with Zvi Rave. I should have told her, I think. But I had not told Rita either, or Odette, or Ronit. Maybe they wondered where I suddenly found the money to move out. But each one of us, the students in Romema, sooner or later followed our own path.

My relationship with Zvi wasn't leading anywhere, yet, strangely, I started enjoying it, while being ashamed of it. I valued the financial help, the fact I didn't have to fight for everyday stuff. An artist needed a *Mecéna*—this was the way of the world. But maybe I wasn't really an artist, or maybe *ashamed* was not the right word.

I compared myself to Nick, Lydia's boyfriend whom she loved so much. Nick enjoyed hiking. He considered *that* the good life. He would hike for days, just him and the beautiful Carpathian Mountains, carrying all his belongings in his backpack. "He despises material things," Lydia had said of Nick. Of course he did—he could afford to, and so could I, as long as I had Zvi Rave. Nick lived with his parents in a nice apartment, and except for Lydia, he didn't miss anything. His father was a doctor. He could borrow his parents' car to meet me at the airport, not an Audi, but a car good enough. He was studying engineering, he hiked, and generally he had no worries. He didn't have to work to support himself while he was a student.

That was the way it was over there. In Romania I would have lived like that, too.

———❦———

Past airport security, I bought a Coke and went to my gate. The area was crowded, and rather than look for a seat and get squeezed in by burly travelers and their luggage, I remained standing. I often did that, even though the eyes of men fell on me, invariably trying to engage me in some way or another. So I stood there feeling observed, taking long sips from my drink, and I must have emptied my cup without realizing it. The sudden slurping noise startled me, and when I raised my eyes in surprise, I saw Jonathan.

Sitting about eight feet away, in a chair to one side of the airline counter, near the door that led to the tarmac, he was clearly watching me. His brown hair was cropped and neatly combed, except for a strand that fell on his forehead, giving him a youthful appearance. I noted his beige linen slacks and his navy Polo shirt with a small monogram on the breast pocket. His hands were tanned and hairy, and on his wrist he wore a thin gold watch. It was October, and I found myself thinking that, dressed like that, he'd freeze in Romania. Then I thought he might be a Greek tycoon on his way to Athens—he had the aura of money. I looked straight at him, and his eyes did not turn away. He held a folded newspaper and a magazine in his hand, and he raised them to the middle of his chest in a silent greeting.

A young woman dressed in a blue El Al uniform approached him. He gathered his belongings, got up, and followed her through the door by the counter.

General boarding started ten minutes later. On the bus, I took my white hat and gloves from my carry-on luggage and put them on. I didn't want the sun on my skin. A line formed in front of the stairs leading to the plane. The jets were roaring, fumes danced above the hot tarmac, and the wind blew wet with the salty smell of the Mediterranean. I held the rim of my hat with one hand, allowing its shade to fall over my eyes and face. In my mind I was already at the end of my journey, after my conversation with Claudia and the tiring train ride, exhausted, being hugged by my family. Yet I was experiencing a trepidation, like a rendezvous with the future. I realized this had something to do with the man I had just exchanged glances with and the possibility we might meet again, even though I had no idea where he had disappeared. Passengers cut in front of me, but I was daydreaming, and I didn't care.

As soon as I boarded, I saw him. He was in first class, resting comfortably in a leather seat by the window, a drink on the wide armrest, near his newspaper and magazine. Except for him, the first-class cabin was empty. I advanced slowly, following the people in front of me, and as I passed him, I read in his eyes the spark of recognition.

⚬⚬⚬

We were far and high, flying northwest over the Mediterranean, when the stewardess came to me with a message. "Mr. Sommer would like to invite you for a drink in first class," she said.

The plane wasn't crowded.

I had a window seat, and the two seats next to me were empty. I lifted the armrest and turned to the stewardess with a confused look. It wasn't difficult to detect her amusement. Would I accept; would I not?

To be frank, I wasn't as surprised by the invitation as by the name.

"Mr. Sommer," I said. "Who is he?"

She blinked. "The passenger in first class. I presumed you knew him."

"I don't, but if Mr. Sommer knows me, and he thinks that I know him too, he should come here and reintroduce himself."

"Very well," the stewardess said.

As soon as she left, I tidied up the space around me, straightened my clothes, and took out my purse mirror. I looked good. The mascara was still on, and my black hair brushed. Calmly, I turned to the window.

White clouds floated between us and the sea.

"May I sit next to you?" he asked me in English. His voice sounded soft over the engines, yet it was masculine and inviting, meant to charm, to win over.

Saying no seemed out of the question. "Do I know you?"

"No, but I hope you will very soon."

I nodded. "You may sit if you wish. Nobody's sitting here."

"Thank you," he said, and he immediately beckoned the stewardess and asked for two glasses of champagne.

From up close I could see the fine wrinkles around his eyes, and, as he smiled, two short vertical lines formed at the corners of his mouth. His teeth were perfect. He was older than I had thought, but his age didn't bother me.

"I apologize if I'm intruding," he started. "Believe me, I usually don't do this type of thing."

"Nor do I."

"You looked charming back at the gate area standing there with your drink, clearly uncomfortable. I would have loved to invite you to join me when I boarded the plane early, but I didn't get the chance."

Even though English wasn't my native language, I realized he spoke with a strong accent. He had a heavy black-and-gold ring on his finger, but no wedding band, and the monogram on his shirt spelled JPS in a fine gold thread.

The stewardess brought the champagne, lowered the middle table, and placed the two glasses in front of us.

"We'll be landing in Athens in twenty minutes. This is our last call. Do you need anything else, Mr. Sommer?"

He looked at me, I shook my head, and he dismissed the stewardess.

"Tell me, is your last name really Sommer?" I asked.

"Sure," he said. "Oh, I'm sorry; I didn't introduce myself. My name is Jonathan Sommer."

"Jonathan," I said, "this is quite a coincidence. My last name is Sommer, too. Miriam Sommer. Maybe we're related."

"I don't think I'm your father," he said.

While his answer wasn't inspired, he had a nice and sincere smile.

"Is Sommer your married name?" he asked.

"I'm not married."

"Good. You're too young to be married."

The layover was supposed to last one hour or less. We remained on the plane and started talking about the origin of the name Sommer. He was from Turda, a small town not too far from Bistriţa. We concluded we weren't related, and he told me that his parents had perished during the Holocaust, just like my father's parents, and that he had left Romania in 1950.

I was born two years later, I thought.

The stewardess came. "We rearranged your seating the way you requested, Mr. Sommer," she said. "You're now both in first class, and I suggest you move before we let the other passengers in." She smiled and then cast me a quick disapproving look.

"I didn't ask to sit in first class," I whispered to Jonathan.

"I know, but *I'm* asking you," he said, and he grabbed my hand and squeezed it.

We moved, continuing to talk, and before I knew it, we were in the air again, and the stewardess brought us snacks, coffee, and more champagne.

"After the war I left Romania and went to live with an uncle in São Paulo," Jonathan said. "In Romania I didn't have anybody left. My older sister, Leah, had already immigrated to Palestine, and my brother, who is half paralyzed, had been taken in by a Christian family from Turda, due to their religious beliefs. To me, the fact that I didn't have to worry about my brother was a blessing. Samuel is my brother's name. Now that I live in the US and travel to Israel on business, I'm taking this opportunity to go to Romania and visit him. That's all I can do." He seemed thoughtful, apologetic, as if he regretted he wasn't doing more.

I said it was considerate of him to make the effort, and he shrugged and went on.

"I was seventeen when I left, and everybody says I couldn't have done anything for my brother. Maybe." Jonathan took a sip of champagne. "At any rate, to get to Brazil, I had to spend a few months in Rome waiting for my visa."

"Oh, Rome!" I exclaimed. "There is no place in this world I would rather visit than Rome, for sure."

"Honestly," Jonathan said, "Rome was not the highlight of my immigration experience."

"Rome," I sighed. "The city on the seven hills, the birthplace of Romulus and Remus." The champagne had gone to my head. "Isn't Rome the place where all of the world's art is gathered?"

Jonathan laughed. "Not all of the art," he said.

As we began our descent into Bucharest, Jonathan looked at me and shook his head. "Oh, my," he said, "I've been babbling for over an hour. I'm sorry."

"It was enjoyable," I said.

"You are too kind, but I didn't find out anything about you. You know, I want to know everything."

"Everything?" I asked.

"Yes."

"Well, there isn't that much to tell, but if you want to hear my life story, we'll need to go on another flight together."

"I have a limousine picking me up at the airport. Can I offer you a ride into town?" Jonathan asked.

"Thanks, but somebody's waiting for me, a young man, a friend of a friend. He has a car, and I have a package for him, from his girlfriend in Israel."

"You don't have to explain."

"I want to," I said, and then I told him I was catching the train to Bistrița the next morning, and we exchanged phone numbers.

Since Turda and Bistrița were close to each other, we thought we might be able to meet.

I recognized Nick right away. Lydia had shown me his photograph. He was waiting a few steps behind the crowd, distinctly different from almost everybody else in a way that was typical of Romania, where some people stood out. He was tall and nicely dressed. When our eyes met, we exchanged a simple nod, and I realized that he, too, knew it was me.

"Miriam," he said when I came closer, and he offered me a small bouquet of white carnations.

I was carrying my luggage, and we experienced a brief moment of awkwardness; then he smiled and grabbed my suitcases.

"Let's get out of here," I said, eager to leave the airport before Jonathan walked out of customs and saw us.

Traffic was light. We quickly arrived at *Kiseleff* Boulevard and drove toward the Triumphal Arch. On our left, the leaves in *Herăstrău* Park were turning. It was twilight, and everything around us seemed covered by a thin bluish layer of dust.

"Let me show you a little of Bucharest," Nick said, and he took *Ana Ipătescu* through *Romana* Square and *Magheru* Boulevard. As we passed in front of the Lido Hotel, I noticed a man in a navy Polo shirt stepping out of a black limousine. I couldn't be sure, but I thought that was Jonathan. Nick turned at the University Square, drove back to Romana Square, and swerved onto a narrow side street. On the right stood a stone building, somber and massive, the sidewalk crowded with young people. "The Trade Academy," Nick said. "And here, across the street, this is where Lydia used to live—in this apartment building on the second floor, where the balcony is."

The building was shabbier than the academy, and equally gray. The balcony seemed an appendage. It was getting dark, and as everywhere in the city, a persistent layer of dust clung to every horizontal and vertical surface, yellow streaks running out from each waterspout. The windows looked like black eyes.

"We celebrated New Year's once at Lydia's place," Nick added. His voice cracked. "We stepped out after midnight on that balcony to be alone. It was a mild winter, unusually quiet, and there were stars in the sky. The moon hung over the academy. That was our first kiss."

As I listened to Nick, I was unable to stop our drab surroundings from rearranging themselves in my mind to an old romantic setting in Verona.

<hr />

Claudia's dorm was on *Polizu* Street, a six-story brick building with a narrow front door. The paint on the doorframe was peeling. Only girls were allowed inside, so I suggested to Nick he go home, but he said he would wait to make sure Claudia was there. I left the suitcases in the car and went up the dirty staircase.

I found Claudia on the second floor in a room crammed with three sets of bunk beds, sitting at a small brown table and smoking. Two other girls were in the room, each on a lower bunk. When I walked in, they stopped talking.

"You're here already," Claudia said, as if disappointed.

"A friend gave me a ride from the airport."

She put out her cigarette in the ashtray and rose to greet me. The two girls stared at us. I placed the carnations on the little table. We hugged.

"You look good," I whispered, although I didn't think so. Her hair was in disarray. She was wearing a light-blue robe with a large stain at the hip, a frayed collar, and gaping pockets. On her feet she had gray woolen socks rolled at the ankles.

She didn't return the compliment.

I thought she would introduce me to the girls, but she didn't. As if on cue, they got up and left the room.

"Your roommates?" I asked.

"Yeah, they live here."

"And can I stay here, also?"

"If you wish. There is only one other girl in this room, so we're lucky. Choose one of the two free cots. It gets chilly at night, you should know. Very chilly."

I looked around the room. "Where can I put my luggage?"

"Oh, I'm sure we can shove it somewhere. How much do you have? Where is it?"

I told her it was in the car, and she said she'd put on a pair of slippers and come help me.

"Don't worry; I can manage," I said.

"The bathroom is off the hallway," she said. "But we don't have hot water tonight. Only on Tuesdays and Thursdays."

"Well," Nick said when I returned to the car, "how is it?"

I told him I didn't like it.

"You can come stay with us," he offered. "Take my room, and I'll sleep in the living room on the sofa. My parents won't mind, I assure you."

I didn't need to think. Suddenly there was nothing Claudia could tell me, about painting, career choice, love, or anything else. There was nothing I wanted to hear from her. I went upstairs and told Claudia I had changed my mind. She didn't blink. The carnations remained on the little table, forgotten like our past.

Nick's father was on duty at the hospital, but his mother and grandmother were home, and they fed me and took care of me as if I were their daughter. Nick tried on his new jeans. I took a shower. Nick's grandmother brushed my hair, and we smoked Bulgarian cigarettes together. She reminded me of my own grandmother. They were different, and yet something was the same, something that made me feel at home and taken care of in the way that only a true family can make you feel.

∞∞∞

Each time the phone rang in my grandmother's bedroom, I listened intently, hoping it was Jonathan and playing in my head the short and very polite exchange he might have with my mother or grandmother. Our own conversation would follow in a subdued tone, in code almost, both of us, but especially me, aware of others listening in, curiously, not that it was their business. The days passed and I realized that he wouldn't call, that his visit with his brother had most likely ended and that he had left the area, the country perhaps. I still hoped that maybe, just maybe, the phone would ring and it would be him, regretful, apologetic, with a totally reasonable explanation, something to do with emergencies, death, or poor and inadequate telephone service. And all that time, as I was talking to my family, eating Romanian dishes, and visiting old acquaintances and places, I would hear Jonathan's voice in my head, like a premonition of something I was meant to experience.

∞∞∞

When I returned to Israel, everything around me was fragrant and alive. The sunlight was sharp, the billboards vivid, and the flowers blooming. It was warm. The streets were bustling with people and honking cars. This was the third time I arrived in Israel and the third time I had the distinct feeling that I had escaped the gloomy cage of my childhood.

My apartment was close to *Merkaz HaCarmel*, on the second floor of a small limestone villa built during the *Fourth Aliyah* by settlers from Poland. The landlady was a heavyset older woman who vaguely resembled Pani. I knocked on her door to say hello, and she quickly wiped her hands on her apron and threw them around my neck in a strangling embrace.

"How was it?" she asked.

"Fine."

"Just fine, Miri? Tell me the truth. You've met someone! I can see it on your face."

"No, Mrs. Shames, just my relatives."

"Well, thank goodness for that. Family's important." In the shaded light of the hallway, her skin looked crinkled like an old sheet of paper. "You know, I opened your windows today to let in some fresh air for your return. Welcome home."

I suddenly felt more at home than I had felt during my entire week with my mother in the house where I grew up, and more than I had ever before felt in Haifa. Tears formed in the corners of my eyes, but I didn't want Mrs. Shames to see them, so I grabbed my suitcases and rushed up the steps.

A living room with a bay window connected to a small bedroom through a set of white French doors. There was a full bathroom and a kitchenette. The air was cooler than outside, and it smelled of pine. I dropped the suitcases on the floor, lowered myself onto my bed, and buried my face in the soft lavender spread. Then I turned on my back and looked at the spotless white ceiling. The gentle rustle of trees that surrounded the house and the familiar traffic noises from Merkaz HaCarmel reached me through the open bay window.

I wanted to call Jonathan. By now, he could be back in the States. There was a time difference, I was sure, but I didn't know what it was.

I got up, went to the bay window, and looked at the swaying trees and the flowers and, through the branches, at the blue glitter of the sea in the distance.

Jonathan, he should call me right now.

My phone was shiny and black, with a large round dial. Next to it on my desk was the charcoal sketch of a young man resting on a lounge chair. He was looking straight at me with dark, piercing eyes, strands of dark hair shading his forehead. He had long, bony features and a strong chin. His name was Daniel. We had gone out, strictly as friends, a few times before my trip. He, too, was a new immigrant from Romania, but unlike most of us who received money from the Sochnut, he had decided to work in a *kibbutz* and was waiting for a sponsorship letter from a relative to go to America.

I had paid him a visit once at his kibbutz, and he offered to pose for me. I had told him I used to paint. We were on the porch of his flat cinderblock house overlooking a meadow, the sun setting behind the trees. Daniel's roommates were still in the fields or at the dining hall eating dinner.

"I haven't done this in a long time," I told him.

"You can do it," he said. "I know you."

I looked at him. "You don't know me."

He smiled, a slightly crooked tooth under his upper lip softly shining.

The light was perfect.

He went inside the house and returned with a stack of drawing paper and charcoal. "While there's still light outside," he said. "Otherwise we'll go to the dining room, and you'll have to draw me in there."

"I'm not in the mood." I turned my back to him and descended the steps off the porch and into the meadow.

He was faster than I expected, and he grabbed me by my shoulders and turned me around. He was laughing, but his grip was determined, his fingers painfully pressing my skin. He led me back to the porch and softly pushed me against the railing. "Please do it," he said, giving me the sheets of paper.

I shrugged. I put one line on that paper, and then a second, a third. It was like a game, but before I knew it, his image was captured, his soul emerging from my drawing.

He asked me for the sketch, but I decided to keep it, and I took it home and placed it on my desk. Somehow, looking at it every day, retouching it here and there, changing its place in the room, and viewing it at different times of day and under different light, made the experience memorable, significant. It was the first and only drawing I had kept since coming to Israel, and through it I felt closer to Daniel.

I went to a jazz concert in Ein Hod, the artists' village not far from Haifa, with Daniel, Lydia, and Adrian. Rhododendron and bougainvillea grew between cypresses and pine trees in front of white stone houses with multicolored wooden doors. The old pavement was cracked and uneven in places. Mellow lights shone through the early evening from street poles, store windows, art galleries, and homes.

As we walked, I told Lydia about my encounter with Nick in Bucharest. She was pleased I had met his family. "Nick's grandmother's almost blind," she said when I finished. "She sees only a sliver of what's in front of her, like when you look into a room through a crack in the wall or a keyhole." It was a sad and strange detail she decided to share with me, but I didn't ask for a reason.

The jazz concert took place in the open amphitheater, where local musicians played Ella Fitzgerald songs from her Decca and Verve years. From the small bar behind the amphitheater, we bought beers, except Adrian, who insisted on drinking Coke. He took driving his Audi very seriously. During the concert Daniel caught my hand, and I let him hold it. The night was beautiful. When we returned to Haifa, he said he wanted to come upstairs and see his drawing. I knew what he had in mind.

The next morning I woke him up before seven. I didn't want Mrs. Shames or anybody else to see him. "Danny, you have to leave."

He seemed confused, but he didn't ask any questions, and he left right away.

———— ∞ ————

The phone rang a few hours later. It was Jonathan.

"I'm in Haifa," he said.

My heart pounded as I looked at my still-unmade bed. "I thought you forgot me," I said.

He hesitated. "I called you in Bistriţa, and I talked to your grandmother. Didn't she tell you? She wanted to know everything about me."

I let myself fall on a chair. "She didn't," I said.

We met in the afternoon at the Dan Carmel Hotel, a short stroll down from Merkaz. As I walked, my mind was abuzz with doubt and anticipation. Was Jonathan for real? And what about Zvi Rave? Did I have the right to hope, and why hadn't my grandmother told me? What if Jonathan was lying about talking to my grandmother, but how would he even know about her?

I stopped at the esplanade in front of the hotel and looked around. The view of the city and the bay always amazed me. Below me stretched the Baha'i Gardens and the beautiful Gulf of Haifa. Tourist buses were parked along the curb. The steep descent into German Colony started not far from the round café at the corner with Yefe Nof where I had had ice cream with Zvi. The hotel itself had always seemed intimidating to me, an establishment of unaffordable luxury. Tall cypresses grew around it. Ben-Gurion, I had heard, had stayed there.

Jonathan was standing in the reception area. When he saw me, he quickly stepped forward and took my hand. "I'm glad I found you," he said in Romanian.

He was wearing well-pressed navy slacks and a white short-sleeved shirt, and he looked young and very much at ease.

We advanced through the large hotel lobby, him leading the way.

"Good afternoon, Mr. Sommer," the two busboys waiting by the elevators said in English.

Jonathan answered jovially, as if speaking to friends. The bright afternoon sun trickled through large curtained glass panels and the sliding doors leading to the terrace and gardens.

"Let's have a drink outside," Jonathan said.

The lobby was nearly empty and sparsely furnished with green and gold couches and groups of tan leather armchairs around low tables with mosaic tops. When we reached the glass sliding door, the maître d' popped up from nowhere and opened it for us.

"Your table is ready, Mr. Sommer," he said. "Tea a l'anglaise, as you requested."

"Thank you, Andrew," Jonathan said.

"They all know you," I said after we sat down and the maître d' departed.

Shaded by a large blue umbrella, our table was covered in a white damask tablecloth. Coffee, tea, various glasses, and plates with scones and cucumber sandwiches waited for us. A bottle of champagne chilled in a silver ice bucket.

"I stay here when I come to Haifa," Jonathan offered as an explanation.

"Do you come often?"

"Mostly when I visit my sister in Tel Aviv and want to escape from her for a day or two." Jonathan smiled. "She can be quite possessive, you know. And when I come for business. But from now on I'll have a better reason to spend time here."

I ignored his last remark. "Business?" I said. "What exactly do you do, Jonathan?"

He raised his eyebrows. "It's not so easy to explain, exactly. You know, I do lots of things. For instance, I like to gamble, and I travel, and I collect art. But when I work, I mostly trade in agricultural products. I have a background in farming, since I worked as a farmhand when I was a young man."

"You? You worked on a farm?" I laughed.

"Why? Is that funny?"

"No, it's unusual. You know, for a good Jewish boy."

He threw me a confused look. "Let's change the subject and talk about you," he said.

"There is nothing interesting or unusual about me."

"There isn't? Oh, I'm sure there is. You're unusual *and* very beautiful, but right now I will start with a simple question. Tea or coffee, or shall we have champagne to celebrate?"

I chose tea.

The park that bordered the terrace dropped a few feet and continued to a large swimming pool surrounded by a patio with potted aloes and ficus spread between lounge chairs. Pines and cypresses screened us from the streets below, but the views of the bay and the harbor were unobstructed. The sun, still high in the sky, bounced off the swimming pool, the golden dome of the Baha'i temple, and the Mediterranean.

"Well," Jonathan said as he poured the hot water for my tea and as I helped myself to a cucumber sandwich, "tell me."

"Tell you what, Jonathan?"

"Tell me, why are you here?"

"Because you invited me."

"Touché, but no. I meant, what are you doing in Israel, and how long have you been here?"

"I came three years ago, and right now I take art history classes at the University of Haifa."

"Do you date anybody?"

He was quick, but there was no hesitation on my part. "No," I said, and I squinted at the pool.

"Good," he said.

I told him that my older brother and younger sister were still in Romania, that my parents were divorced, and that my mother had raised me.

"And your grandmother speaks with a slight Russian accent," Jonathan said.

"It's Polish." I smiled.

"I was on the phone with her for twenty minutes." The brilliant daylight caused his eyes to turn green. "She questioned me, and I was very truthful. I told her we met on the plane, and I explained why I was in the area. When I gave her my name, she thought I was kidding. I left my brother's phone number with her, and she promised to tell you."

"She never said a word, I swear."

"I believe you. I would have called you again in Bistriţa, and I would have come to see you, but my brother was rushed to the hospital. I think I don't have to tell you about Romania and medical care."

"You don't. My grandfather was a physician."

"By the time my brother got better, I had to hurry back. I simply ran out of time."

I finished my tea and agreed to have a glass of champagne with him.

He uncorked the bottle himself and filled the two flutes on the table. "*L'chaim*," he said.

As we sipped the champagne, he spoke about Leah, his sister; her two teen-age sons; and her husband, who was an engineer. They had a small house near the beach in Herzliyya, and Leah insisted he stay with them every time he came to Israel. He said he had helped them with the down payment. Her two boys had to share a room when he came, and the three of them hated the arrangement. But Leah wouldn't hear otherwise. He was stuck in a cubicle that contained a narrow bed, a desk cluttered with textbooks, and a small TV set.

"I'm not used to small spaces," he said. "You know, after so many years in America, I'm spoiled, and I have reached a point in my life when I have no problem paying for an excellent hotel, but I can't tell that to my sister. She'd get offended. Besides her and my brother, I have nobody else."

I told him that I understood and that in Israel I felt lonely sometimes. "I wish," I added, "I had a sister over here like you."

He lived in San Diego, a city like Haifa, hilly, with lush subtropical flowers and palm trees and sunsets over the water, only that the sea was the Pacific Ocean. From where he lived, he had magnificent views of that bay and a peninsula called Point Loma. His bedroom suite alone was larger than his sister's house, and it included a study and a sunroom. "But I'm rattling on about myself," he said. "Tell you what. I'll share one more story with you, and then it's your turn." He reached across the table and tried to caress my face. "OK?"

I moved back. "OK."

"Once I met an older gentleman in Guatemala. He dragged his left foot and walked with a cane. His white mustache was trimmed, and he wore gold spectacles. Sometimes he looked shabby, and other times he was dressed to the hilt. He was witty and ready to do damage in high society. But whether scrawny or spiffy, morning or afternoon, limping through a park or surrounded by friends and business acquaintances, this old man was always in the company of women—and not the same woman, mind you, but a different one every time, each one more beautiful than the last. It seemed women were drawn to him like birds in a flock. They swarmed around him like bees, illuminated him like summer light bugs. I was in a tough spot in my life, inexperienced and eager to establish myself. It was clear to me the man wasn't just having platonic relationships with these women. He seduced them. He dominated them and played them like an instrument with his fingers. One day I asked him his secret. 'Nothing special,' he said. 'I just *listen* to women.' So today I'll take the old man's cue, and I'll listen to you, Miriam Sommer. Go ahead and tell me your story."

"Why, Jonathan, do you want to seduce me?"

"I do," he said.

It sounded corny, and I rolled my eyes, but I liked it, and I laughed, and I started by describing for him our apartment in Bistriţa, with its grand carriage entrance and the young girl's bust at the bottom of the white marble stairs. I recounted the pain and terror I experienced as a girl when I fell on a rusty nail in the corner of our stable. I told him about Ileana and Uncle Tokachi, and the sorrow of losing Pani. I shared with him my passion for art and then told him how it all started with my drawings of the Evangelical church while waiting for Miss Diddieny and with Grandfather finding me an art tutor. I stopped short of saying that my tutor was young, handsome, and somewhat famous. I told him my father lived in West Germany with his new wife and my half sister. I mentioned my friendship with Claudia and my realization that we had nothing in common anymore when I saw her in Bucharest. He asked if I, too, had gone to an art school in Romania, and I said I had not, since by the time I had turned eighteen and graduated from high school, I had applied to immigrate to Israel, and no Romanian college would accept me.

When I finished, he looked at me as if I had just given him a great gift. The champagne bottle was empty.

"Will you have dinner with me tonight?"

"Not tonight. I'm sorry."

By now there were people at several tables near us and people at the pool, and the shadows of trees had moved over the terrace.

I had no other plans that night, yet I was sure I was doing the right thing. "Jonathan," I said, "I had no idea you'd be here tonight."

"Fair enough," he said, "but how about tomorrow? Dinner, please?"

I let a few seconds pass. "On one condition. Tomorrow is your turn to tell me about yourself."

⬦⬦⬦

Jonathan picked me up with his limousine in Merkaz, at the corner of my street and Moriya.

It was a warm afternoon and I was wearing a long flowery wrap skirt and a black blouse with small mother-of-pearl buttons. At my neck, on a delicate chain, I had my mother's gold Star of David. She had given it to me for good luck the day I left Romania.

- Where're we going? I asked him.

- You'll see, he said and took me to a part of town where I had never been before.

We entered a restaurant that looked very much like a private home from the street, and were seated in a garden set in a natural alcove carved into the steep Carmel mountain and shaded by countless old pine trees. A small waterfall trickled down the rocks right in front of our table.

"We are in a different world," I said marveling at the surrounding microcosm that was more evocative of lush temperate forests than Israeli landscapes.

"It's man made," Jonathan said.

I guessed he referred to the waterfall and I nodded in wonder. The stream flowed over a sunken bed of river rocks between the tables and filled a small pond surrounded by green ferns. Water lilies floated on the surface.

We ordered our appetizer of hummus and pita, pickled baby eggplant and cucumbers, red cabbage salad and lemony *tehina* sauce.

"Well," I said. "Jonathan, are you going to take me into *your* world?"

"I thought I just did," he answered filling his plate.

"You know what I mean. You promised. Tell me about your past."

Jonathan took a bite. He took a second bite, and a third one, and started slowly, his voice barely audible over the steady splash of the water.

"My Uncle Martin lived in Meoma, a fashionable district of São Paulo. He had three small children from two marriages, and he was a doctor with a very successful practice. I had never before set foot in an apartment as large and modern as Uncle Martin's, staffed by an army of domestics, with a bedroom all for myself and my own private bathroom. But the truth was I didn't crave luxuries, but love and acceptance, and I didn't received any when I came to Brazil. It was late spring and all Uncle Martin kept talking about was me going to the *Universidade* in the fall."

Jonathan used the Portuguese word, and pronounced it in a manner that gave it a somber distinction, cold and foreign.

I, at least, felt the chill.

He continued talking about the alienation he had felt in Brazil.

He had told Uncle Martin he had not yet graduated from high school, and he needed time to adjust and learn the language. São Paulo was larger than his native town of Turda, larger than Bucharest, larger than Rome, rough and beautiful, capable of swallowing him whole in a manner of minutes.

Nonsense, Uncle Martin had said. He, too, had come to Brazil as a young man, had studied hard, had worked hard, and had made something of himself. Nobody in Brazil would know Jonathan had not completed high school. Nobody would care. Jonathan had the age and the smarts, and he had done well leaving Romania. He should go to Campus Armando de Salles Oliveira and register for the *Vestibular*, the sooner the better. The Vestibular was the admittance exam. Jonathan had several months to prepare, and Uncle Martin insisted that, starting the next day, he would hire a tutor to help him.

The tutor was a woman named Consuela Martinez de Alcala, originally from Mexico. She had come to São Paulo eighteen years earlier at age eleven and had lived with her family in a *favela*. She was married to a Brazilian engineer who worked for a construction firm, and together they were saving for their first house. Pretty in a tame kind of way, Consuela kept her dark hair in a bun and wore no makeup. Her pale skin was freckled. She had a small nose and thin lips, which she squeezed together to form a straight line every time she was disappointed.

She was often disappointed in Jonathan, who didn't do his homework and who fell behind in history and Portuguese, both subjects of specific interest for the Vestibular. The more Consuela tried, the more Jonathan looked at her with empty eyes, seemingly in a state of constant daydreaming. On the day the two of them took the bus and went to visit the university campus, Jonathan acted so forlorn and so overwhelmed by his surroundings that Consuela pitied him and on several occasions grabbed his hand to pull him through traffic and throngs of pedestrians.

Back in the apartment, Jonathan fell to his knees in front of his tutor. He declared his love for her, his immeasurable grief for his deceased parents, and his inconsolable longing for home. Consuela lifted Jonathan by his arms, led him to his bed, and sat down next to him, allowing him to rest his head on her shoulder. She gave him a hug and caressed his face. Jonathan's tears rolled down his cheeks and dripped on the soft fabric of her blouse in a little wet stain. His sweaty hands squeezed hers. Then they moved up her arms, down her back, and around to the front of her blouse. She smelled of irises and rain and had the heart to understand Jonathan's turmoil as if it were her own. She also needed the money the job provided. Her breasts were small.

"Through her blouse, I felt her hard nipples," Jonathan said.

I brought my hands to my face.

He gave me a quick look. "I have to be honest."

I nodded.

By now, his voice was stronger, more self-assured, and his delivery took on a new tone, filled with the poetry of remembrance.

"Uncle Martin let Consuela go a few days later without as much as an explanation," Jonathan continued. "I was sure that one of the maids had seen us in our moment of weakness. But my mind was made up. I wasn't going to be afraid any longer; and I would leave Uncle Martin's home forever."

Jonathan met Consuela secretly behind the Monument to the Bandeiras in Ibirapuera Park. Her hair fluttered without restraint in the breeze, and, at that moment, in her fashionable yellow dress, Consuela was very beautiful. She gave Jonathan a letter addressed to her cousin in Mexico, Doña Alexandra Consuela Martinez Salina, recently widowed, who owned and lived on a fifteen-thousand-acre cattle ranch in the Papaloapán region of Oaxaca, near Tuxtepec, four to six hours by car from the Guatemalan border.

When Jonathan told Martin of his decision to leave, the doctor didn't seem to care. On Saturday they drove together to the São Paulo Israelite Congregation and prayed side by side for no longer than fifteen minutes. On the way back, Jonathan watched enviously as his uncle maneuvered without hesitation his Cadillac DeVille through the totally chaotic traffic.

Martin said, "Jonathan, I'm proud of you. Go into the world and become part of the diaspora that has shaped and strengthened our people for generations."

Jonathan understood it was time to stand on his own two feet.

On the nightstand in his bedroom, he found a one-way airline ticket to Mexico City, a silver cigarette case with the name of his great-grandfather inscribed on the inside of the lid, and two hundred American dollars.

Jonathan's journey lasted fifty-five hours, of which the first six were spent in the air, the next forty-two riding and sleeping on buses, and the rest walking along the eighteen-mile stretch of dirt road between the bus stop in Tuxtepec and his final destination.

Doña Alexandra had no idea Jonathan was coming. She was a tall woman in her midforties, with prominent features that overshadowed her severe attractiveness. Her beauty took some warming up to, a fact that Jonathan was not yet capable of appreciating. His eyes remained fixed on a portion of tanned skin on her forearm that reflected the healthy hue of a woman who favored the outdoors. With her wide-brimmed straw hat and her colorful and comfortable garments, she appeared to him like a queen of the prairie, the goddess of dust. The only item of clothing possibly evoking the memory of the loss of her departed husband was the silky black ribbon tied into her thick charcoal hair. She nodded at Jonathan when she finished reading Consuela's letter, rang for her maid, and asked her to escort him to the servants' quarters. As the tired young man dragged himself after the servant, he turned to Doña Alexandra who was watching him with the stern determination of a person whose life no longer held any surprises.

Jonathan washed at the well, ate a dinner of fresh vegetables and grilled steak, and slept for the next nine hours on a hammock stretched under the Mexican summer stars. In the morning he met Juarez Alvarez, the stable keeper; his wife, Maya, who tended to Doña Alexandra's vegetable patch; and their daughter, Chiquita, seventeen years old and lonely, who stared at Jonathan with an urgency that was almost alarming. He met some of the two dozen hired hands, who lived in the bunkhouse, and their boss, Roger, a sardonic American who oversaw everybody's daily activities on the ranch and spoke Spanish in dribs and drabs with a strong accent from north of the border.

After three days in Mexico, Jonathan realized that, given his knowledge of Romanian, a little Italian, and a little Portuguese, Spanish came easier to him than he had imagined. He couldn't say much, but he understood almost everything.

He certainly understood Doña Alexandra when she summoned him to her terrace overlooking the rose garden to inform him of his chores and of the small stipend she was prepared to pay him twice a month for as long as he worked there. Judging by the way she treated him, Doña Alexandra seemed convinced he would cut his losses and disappear before the summer was over. But Jonathan stuck around. He was there for the entire summer, the fall, the long winter that followed, and the next spring and summer. By the time fall came again, he could ride horses like a cowboy, milk the cows, fish in the pond, grill meat, pick mushrooms, sew, wash clothes, haggle at the Tuxtepec market, fix the roof of the main house, and be anywhere he was needed most. He learned how to drive the truck, the tractor, and Doña Alexandra's boxy black Oldsmobile. His skin thickened and darkened from the sun, and his face acquired wrinkles and furrows like those in the soil on the farm.

He enjoyed the hot days when red dust rose on the horizon and the cold mornings when the brownish grass turned to silver, each blade shining with a thin coating of frost. In the evenings he started smoking cigars. He learned to drink tequila with the men, and he memorized the words to the love songs they sang around the fire at the back of the stables. On occasion he would ride to the western edge of the property and spend hours watching in the distance the vaporous and mysterious outline of the Sierra Madres. He felt lonely then and pictured the hills around his hometown of Turda. He thought about his dead parents, his brother Samuel, and, sometimes, about Consuela. He had written to her in the beginning, but his last two letters had gone unanswered. He had also written to his uncle, who had responded by congratulating him on his newly found purpose in life, and he had written to his sister in a country that by then had changed its name from Palestine to Israel.

Most of all he liked counting the pesos that Doña Alexandra regularly paid him, even though all of it hardly amounted to much.

When Roger tendered his resignation, Jonathan asked Doña Alexandra for the job and got it. He bought himself a pair of shiny riding boots and a walnut-stock .38—55 high-powered Winchester rifle smuggled across the border from Texas.

He had changed. He was a man now, and nobody dared say otherwise.

Perhaps Doña Alexandra had seen the change in him as well. One morning she sent her maid to find Jonathan and invite him to a business meeting in her living room. They shared a cup of black coffee, after which she handed him two thick registers bound in leather containing the financial records of the ranch.

"Look through them, Jonathan," she said. "Study them. I think you could help me."

In high school Jonathan had enjoyed math. He could multiply and divide in his head. He remembered numbers, understood percentages and probabilities, and read the statements Doña Alexandra had given him with no difficulty. The ranch was losing money when it shouldn't have. The herds were smaller than economically feasible, and the dealers were paying them prices from years before. The property could easily sustain growth. There was work to be done.

Jonathan started meeting with Doña Alexandra, first once a month, and then twice, and then every week. When she took trips into town, Jonathan drove her. He told her what needed to be done on the ranch, she agreed with him, and he did it. In one year they painted the main house, fixed the road, rebuilt the stables, and dredged the pond. In two years they doubled the number of cattle and tripled the income. They hired a part-time veterinarian and an animal nutritionist from Argentina. By the time they made their first million, they were eating dinner together several times a week and meeting every day for breakfast.

Doña Alexandra had two grown children who lived in the United States. Her son, who was older, had settled in New York City and worked on Wall Street as a banker. Her daughter studied music at the Peabody Conservatory in Baltimore. Neither had shown an interest in the ranch or had visited their mother since Jonathan's arrival.

The more time Jonathan spent with Doña Alexandra, the more he learned to uncover the sadness in her intelligent eyes, the richness of her hair, the wine red of her lips, and the heart in her bosom. He became fond of her and often dared to wonder if the feelings were mutual or if the friendliness she displayed toward him was the pale echo of her misplaced motherly instinct.

Until the day she dropped the pomegranate from the breakfast table.

Instinctively, they both plunged to get it, and when their hands touched and their fingers linked over the glossy fruit, their breathing stopped, and their eyes became locked on each other. They rose in unison and remained standing, side by side, almost touching, enveloped in the mist of their desire. Then, slowly, Doña Alexandra brought his hand to her breast and pressed it.

Jonathan found the jungle between Doña Alexandra's thighs as mysterious as the remote outline of the Sierra Madres. Over time, he learned how to simultaneously be passionate and gentle, truthful yet manipulating. As they lay naked with each other in their postcoital bliss, he often peeked at the mellow curves of her body, the broad hips, the soft shoulders, the long black hair, and the brown skin that surrounded her large nipples.

One day, as he was walking out of the main house, Chiquita emerged from the shadow.

"You betrayed me," she hissed.

"I never promised you anything."

"I waited for you," she responded.

Chiquita disappeared from the ranch the next morning. Under her mattress Juarez discovered a love letter addressed to Jonathan that was never sent and a note informing her parents that she had left for Mexico City.

"It's not my fault," Jonathan told Juarez the first time they saw each other.

"If I find out you touched her, I'll cut off your balls," Juarez threatened.

Jonathan was half Juarez's age and twice his size, but the menace was downright painful, and he started carrying his Winchester with him everywhere. When he slept in the quarters, he kept it in his bed under the covers. When he was with Doña Alexandra, he propped it against the door on the inside of the antechamber. The rifle was designed for large game like boar, caribou, or bear, and he thought it should serve him well against a light assailant like Juarez.

Luckily he didn't have to use it. Juarez and Maya decided to follow their daughter to Mexico City.

Jonathan hired a new stable keeper and a new gardener.

Time passed. Doña Alexandra fell sick. She lost weight and became weak, her skin the color of beeswax. Jonathan took her to see a doctor in Tuxtepec. He took her to Oaxaca. When the local doctors couldn't figure out what the problem was, Jonathan and Doña Alexandra flew to Mexico City.

Doña Alexandra was diagnosed with a rare form of a lymphatic disease that had no clear cure. The doctors recommended a clinic in Tucson and suggested she would need care for the rest of her life and they should move there. Back home, Jonathan consulted the books and figured out they could sell the ranch for at least ten million dollars.

Doña Alexandra wouldn't have it. "I got married here, I raised my children here, and I buried my husband here. This is home. If I die, I want to die here, where perhaps, once, I was happy."

Even though he understood her, Jonathan was devastated.

For the next two nights, he slept alone in the servants' quarters. On the third day, Doña Alexandra sought him out. She asked for forgiveness. She said she'd cry with him if she could, but her eyes were dry of tears. There was white and gray in her hair, and from up close Jonathan could see the loose skin under her eyes and the bones in her shoulders. He returned to the house and continued tending to Doña Alexandra, cooking for her, bathing her, reading to her, and warming her by holding her in his arms at night, but her health deteriorated quickly.

He wrote to her children and suggested they pay their mother a visit. Felix, the son, turned out to be too busy with work, but his sister, Maria—or Mona, as she was known to everybody—broke free for a week and flew into Oaxaca. Jonathan met her at the airport and was shocked by Mona's resemblance to Doña Alexandra. Driving back to the ranch, he experienced the eerie feeling of being in the presence of one person and talking continuously to another. Even the mutual attraction that existed between him and Doña Alexandra seemed acutely present in the car.

For the seven nights that Mona stayed home, Jonathan slept with the workers. In Mona's presence, he and Doña Alexandra had agreed to maintain their distance.

On the eighth day, Jonathan drove Mona back to Oaxaca. She had to rush to Baltimore for a recital. She thanked Jonathan for inviting her to the ranch, kissed him on his cheek, and broke into sobs. "My mother's dying."

"I pray every day she is not," Jonathan answered.

Doña Alexandra passed a few weeks later. In her will she left two-thirds of the ranch to her children and one-third to Jonathan. Felix wanted his cut right away, but Mona agreed to allow her share to remain in the business and be managed by Jonathan. To make up for the financial hit, Jonathan had to borrow money and work hard, but that was exactly what he needed to do in order to get over the loss of Doña Alexandra.

Several years later, when the ranch was more prosperous than ever, Jonathan sold it, paid Mona off, and moved to Arizona. From there he moved to California and started a new business.

———— ∞∞∞ ————

Jonathan stopped talking, and we remained silent for a long time. He was a fascinating storyteller, and I wondered whether in sharing his past with me he had gotten carried away, or whether he had described those romantic moments on purpose. His story was the lure, and his raconteur's talent was the mythical spider's web he had woven before, trapping other women in it, many of them, no doubt. And I had just taken part in an exquisite performance, when the pomegranate of his past was cracked open to allow me a taste of its little sweet arils.

It was dark when the limo took us back to the Dan Carmel hotel.

"I have to be in Tiberias tomorrow for a business encounter," Jonathan said. "Can I see you again on Saturday? Will you come to Tel Aviv to meet me?"

"Tel Aviv?" I said.

"Yes. I have to be in Tel Aviv."

"I'm not sure. Maybe." I looked down.

"Listen," he said. "I don't want this evening to end. Stay with me for a few more minutes. Let's have another drink, just one more, shall we?"

"Let's go for a walk," I said.

We crossed the esplanade in front of the hotel, and turned left on Yefe Nof, in the direction of Stella Maris. We walked slowly and stopped a few times to admire the view of the city and the bay, aglow in a million lights. At the first crossing, Jonathan held my arm from below the elbow, protectively.

The wind swirled, pushing wisps of hair into my eyes. I raised my hand to protect my face and turned toward Jonathan and away from the breeze, laughing.

"I like your *Maghen David*," Jonathan said, using the Hebrew name for the Star of David.

"Thank you. I wear it as a good luck charm from my mother."

He hesitated, and then he took a small step forward and placed his open palms, fingers downward, on my hips. It was an unexpected gesture, awkward and intimate. Our eyes met. Our bodies faced each other, almost touching. I thought he would try to kiss me, but he didn't. Gently, I took his hands in mine and moved them away.

"Have you ever been married?" I asked when we resumed walking. "I mean, after Doña Alexandra."

"Yes," he said. "I moved to California and met a young woman who was Mexican and had relatives south of the border. Her family connected me back to my past and made me feel comfortable. I liked her. I didn't want to waste any time, so I proposed in a hurry. Her family insisted on a Catholic wedding, and she arranged for us to marry at Mission San Diego de Alcalá, a beautiful old church in Mission Bay."

"You got married in a Catholic church? You're Jewish."

"Jewish, Buddhist, Catholic, what's the difference? I had money."

His cynicism filled the space between us, and I felt the need to dispel it. "Do you believe in God?" I asked him.

"I believe in living life, Miriam."

The creamy stone wall of the Stella Maris Convent appeared on our right. A century-old oak tree shaded the sidewalk. Pink chrysanthemums bloomed in a flower bed bordered by a low wrought-iron fence.

"What happened?" I said, referring to his wife.

"Nothing. It was a mistake. She was only interested in my fortune, and the whole thing fell apart in less than two years."

He offered to walk me home, but I didn't want anybody who knew me to see us.

The next morning there was a knock on my door. When I opened it, I saw a teenage boy in a Dan Hotel uniform.

He handed me an envelope and a small gift box. "With compliments, from Jonathan Sommer."

The letter was hand written in Romanian on hotel stationery.

We've been apart for only a few hours, but I can't wait to see you again. Please come to Tel Aviv on Saturday. I'll have my driver pick you up at your house at three in the afternoon, and I'll reserve a room for you at the Savoy, off HaYarkon, right by the beach. If we meet at six for dinner, you'll have enough time to change, rest, and admire the view.

Believe me, I think of you constantly. You are around me, all the time.

Miriam, I'm happy. I hope you'll accept my invitation and my little present—a new good luck charm from your admirer.

From my heart,

Jonathan.

In the jewelry box was a golden Star of David, like the one I had from my mother, but with diamonds in each of its six corners. The diamonds shone like tears.

———

America could become my new dream.

I had no future with Zvi, and no past. We had never dated. We slept together, and he paid my bills. I had never truly recovered after Gabriel, no matter how far I had run. After almost four years, I continued to feel lonely and unbalanced. Searching still.

Tired of studying, I continued taking classes only for the meager scholarship I was getting from the Sochnut. I made some new friends, and I liked Israel, but something important was missing.

And I couldn't paint.

Lydia remained focused on studying and on her love for Nick. Why couldn't I find someone like Nick?

Since Gabriel left me, I had produced only one drawing. A sketch. One I reworked and retouched many times. Pathetic. The sketch of a man I hardly knew. In the end I became so attached to the sketch, so emotionally involved with it, that I slept with the man. Should I be ashamed? No, I shouldn't, and Jonathan was the one I wanted to trust.

———

Riding in the limousine and, later, receiving my key at the Savoy and having the bellboy bring my suitcase to my room on the fifteenth floor, I felt these men understood who I was and why Jonathan had me brought there. But I was at peace with the thought, and I gave the bellboy a good tip.

Through the window I could see the deep blue Mediterranean curving at the horizon.

I showered, I dried myself, and I looked at myself in the mirror. In the bright light, my white skin was pearly, and my hair looked silkier than ever. I used very little mascara.

Eagerness burned my soul.

We made love with the door to the balcony open. The sound of breaking waves floated fifteen stories up and accompanied us through the night, during repeated moments of quickening rush followed by slow breathing. Remote city noises reached us.

Sometimes we spoke, but mostly my thoughts roamed freely. I was glad he couldn't read them. Several times, he traced the scar on my thigh with his index finger.

I liked Jonathan, and his age didn't bother me. His body was fuller than those of the men before him, but nicely shaped and strong after years of physical work. When he pressed down on me, he did it with a heaviness that felt protective.

We spent the next day and the following night together. Nobody was waiting for me at home, and I didn't have to explain my absence to anybody.

On Monday he had to leave. I insisted on seeing him off to the airport. Girlfriends did that, and people who loved each other bid tender good-byes.

Jonathan warned me that Leah, his sister, would come to the airport as well. They were close, and she always came when he left. I said it was fine. If my brother or sister were here, I would want them to meet Jonathan.

Leah looked like her brother—the same brown, wavy hair and brown eyes, and the same polite and gentle demeanor. Her older teenage son was with her. She hugged Jonathan, who introduced me to Leah as "a friend." We shook hands. With her there, the two of us drew away from each other, displaying very little affection.

The fact that I was closer in age to her son than to her or to Jonathan must have crossed her mind. I wished she had not come.

———— ∞ ————

I called my mother in Bistriţa. Everything was OK; Jacob and Adina were away in college, and grandmother was reading.

"May I talk to her?" I asked.

"Sure," my mother said.

Grandmother came to the phone.

"Tell me," I said, "when I was home last month, a man, Jonathan Sommer, called for me. You two spoke for twenty minutes, but you didn't tell me anything. Why didn't you tell me he called, Grandma?"

She said she had forgotten, but I didn't think it was that simple.

My mother took the receiver.

"Did you hear what Grandmother said? Do you believe her?"

"Who's this man, and why is he important?" my mother asked.

"Because…" I said. "What's the matter with Grandma?"

"Welcome to my world," my mother said.

I imagined her on the edge of her sofa, in the same room that had served for years as a bedroom by night and a living room by day. It was the same convertible sofa she had slept in when we were little children, still missing her husband but not saying it anymore, perhaps missing life altogether and not knowing it. I pictured her graying hair, the circles under her eyes, her nervous hands pulling at the sleeves of her robe. My grandmother, her mother, stood next to her, an old woman now defining and completing my mother's world.

"Your world is what you make of it."

My mother sighed.

I heard voices.

"We don't need another Sommer in our life," my mother said. "One was more than enough."

———— ∞ ————

Jonathan called. He had arrived safely in the United States and wanted to hear my voice. One day apart was a day too many. He couldn't wait to come back to Israel, but for now he had to travel to South America on business for two or three weeks.

I had an idea. "Jonathan, please call me at the end of next week."

"I'll call you sooner."

"I have to move. You know, I was subletting this apartment from a friend of mine, but the lease is up, and I contacted the landlord, who wants too much money. I'm thinking about moving back to the dorm, you know, the one in Romema, where I lived before. I just want to make sure you have my new telephone number."

"Do you want to live in a dorm?"

I laughed. "I don't, of course not, but what can I do?"

"What kind of money are we talking about?"

I told him, and it was his turn to laugh. "Listen, sign the new lease, and don't worry," he said.

I rang Zvi's office. We had agreed I would use a code name. The receptionist said Dr. Rave was vacationing with his family in Eilat for a week, and I left a message for him. When he returned, he called, and then he came to see me. I had placed the *Playboy* magazines in a stack on the coffee table and two bottles of Maccabee beer in the refrigerator.

I was dressed as if ready to go out.

"You're all dressed up," he said, in the voice that meant I should have known better.

"Sit down," I said. "Have a beer."

He sat on the sofa. His tan was deep from the strong Eilat sun. "How was your trip to Romania?" he asked. "How's the family?"

I sat next to him. "Good," I said. Then I let it out, as directly as possible. "Zvi, it's over."

"What's over?" He took a drink from his beer.

"We're done. You and I, we're no longer an item. Not that we've ever been one in the true sense of the word. You should stop coming here."

His face twitched. "Why? Have you met somebody else?"

I was ready for his question, and I had decided it would be easier not to tell him the truth. "I did not," I said.

"Then what is it?"

"I'd rather not talk about it."

"I'm here. We have to talk about it." He placed his finger on the top *Playboy* and moved it up and down the magazine cover. "What about tonight? You and I, tonight, we can still do it?"

"No."

"What are you saying?" he asked.

"Zvi, I'm sorry."

He stood up, tall, sunburned, lust turning slowly to anger. "You're sorry? Don't say you're sorry! You're kicking me out!"

I didn't answer.

"Why did you ask me over?"

"I didn't. You returned from Eilat and wanted to see me. I agreed. I had to tell you in person."

"How noble of you." He opened the French doors to the bedroom and walked inside. "Come here," he said.

I didn't move but said to him through the doors, "Don't make this more difficult than it is."

"I'm not making it difficult. You are. Why don't you tell me the truth? Are you going somewhere tonight? Is that why you're dressed so nicely?"

"Zvi, we are through. It doesn't matter."

"Oh, but it does. I want to know what's happening. Why don't you want to make love to me? Am I no good all of a sudden? Am I not discreet enough? Don't I give you enough money?"

He came back and stared at me, his arms on his chest, challenging.

"I wish you wouldn't mention the money," I said. "I never asked you for anything, and this apartment and the money you gave me were your idea. You wanted me to live in a place that was convenient. Comfortable. *Discreet.*"

"You're right. This apartment and everything here is mine. The bed, the desk, the sofa, everything! You bought them with my money, and I should take them all back."

His hair was disheveled—he must have pulled at his hair when he was in the bedroom.

"You know what? Take them," I said in a very calm voice. "And then get the hell out of here."

The expression on his face changed from menacing to remorseful, and I thought he would start to cry.

"Miriam," he said, "I love you. You know I do. We had it so good together; why give it up? You are the jewel of my life, my secret jewel. You sparkle. You give me purpose and strength. Tell me, how can I change your mind? What can I do? You know I'll do anything for you. Anything. Just tell me. What do you want? Do you need more money? Do you want to start going out to restaurants with me? Do you want clothes, trips, a larger apartment?"

"No, Zvi, I want you to leave, and take these *Playboys* with you."

"I'm not leaving."

"Please don't force me to make a scene and involve your family."

The mention of his family had the desired effect. He picked up the almost full bottle of beer, and, while looking me straight in the eye, he poured it over the desk. He did it slowly, deliberately. The liquid foamed and gurgled and splashed over the black telephone, and the lower portion of Daniel's charcoal drawing. It ran to the edge of the desk and spilled onto the chair and the rug below.

He turned on his heels. Without uttering another word, he walked out of the apartment, slamming the door after him.

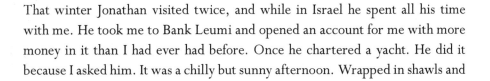

That winter Jonathan visited twice, and while in Israel he spent all his time with me. He took me to Bank Leumi and opened an account for me with more money in it than I had ever had before. Once he chartered a yacht. He did it because I asked him. It was a chilly but sunny afternoon. Wrapped in shawls and sweaters, we ate a light dinner on the deck and looked at old Acre and Haifa's hills from far out at sea. On the way back we passed a little marina. Our vessel was larger and more luxurious than any of the sailboats in it.

With the money I had from Jonathan, I started a class in photography and I learned how to drive.

Lydia received a letter from Nick in which he proposed. She had always thought they'd wait until his graduation, but here he was—in love, ready to tie the knot. She was surprised and happy, and also concerned. Now they had to go through the long and bureaucratic battle of getting their marriage approved by the authorities in Romania.

Daniel called to say his US visa had been issued and he was on his way to New York. We had a warm conversation. When I hung up, I noticed that the beer stains on his charcoal portrait were crisp and dry. I picked up the drawing, crumpled it, and threw it away.

Chapter 3

CONSTANTÍN

In the spring Jonathan invited me to go to Romania with him. Samuel's health had deteriorated, and he was again admitted to the hospital. Before traveling to Transylvania, we decided to spend a few days in Bucharest and booked a suite at the Lido Hotel.

Lydia had given me a gift for Nick. She was very meticulous that way.

I called Nick, and he asked us to dinner on Sunday. It was Orthodox Easter, and other guests would be there as well.

"My parents would love having you both," he said.

I wasn't sure. "You have friends coming over, and we don't want to impose."

"It's our tradition," Nick said. "Friends, a meal, maybe a song or two. You'll enjoy it. Besides, being friends of Lydia's, you are like family to us. Come, and we'll drink some wine together."

Sunday afternoon we stopped at the hotel gift shop. Only foreign visitors were allowed to shop there and pay in US dollars for imported cosmetics, liquor, and tobacco. The choices, so tempting for the locals, were actually limited, and we quickly selected a bottle of Johnny Walker and two cartons of Kent cigarettes, superlong. The saleslady placed them in two red and white plastic shopping bags.

The cab driver stared at them. "You've been to the tourist gift shop," he said.

"I'm from America," Jonathan said in Romanian, a big smile on his face.

"That's right," the cabby said. "That's why you're allowed to shop there while I drive like a maniac every day of the week, and at the end of each day, what do I get? Long lines for food and cigarettes made of straw. If I'm lucky, I find a pack of BT—Bulgarian Tobacco, that is."

I looked out the window and didn't say anything. It was a beautiful day. We were on March 6 Boulevard driving by the black equestrian statue of Michael the Brave. In front of a movie theater, the sidewalk was packed.

"American movie, *Love Story*," the cabby said, in a tone that implied he expected us to be pleased. "No wonder people are wrangling to get in."

A park surrounded by a black wrought-iron fence occupied an entire city block. Blooming crocuses and narcissus and bushes sprouting new leaves were everywhere. We drove by the Law School and the Opera House, and crossed a wide bridge. On the other side of the river stood an Orthodox church with green copper domes.

The cabby crossed himself. "This is Saint Elefterie," he said. "Last night I attended Easter Mass here, with my wife and daughter. When we came out into the street after midnight, everywhere we looked there were people holding burning candles in their hands. We were taking God's light back into our homes. Magnificent. No misery anymore—only the spring night and the miraculous light of the resurrection."

"Aren't you worried about consequences?" Jonathan asked.

"Consequences? No. Do you know how many we were, good Christian people? Thousands and thousands. What can they do to us all? Take away the BTs?" The cabby chuckled.

"That's it," I whispered to Jonathan in English. "That's why I hesitated going to Nick's. These people celebrated last night. They belong together. I don't. I'm alone here, the outsider, the Jew."

On the narrow bench in that taxicab, hugging my purse, next to the two bags from the tourist shop and the small parcel from Lydia, I felt caught in a bubble, encased in a shell of my own, traveling through a space that was very familiar and foreign at the same time.

Jonathan squeezed my hand. "You're not alone."

Suddenly he was closer to me than any other person on earth.

"This feeling of being an outsider has gotten stronger," I said. "When I lived here, I suppressed it, and now, in Israel, I am part of the majority."

Years ago I'd had a debate with Jacob, when I said that in postwar Romania religious holidays didn't matter. I was denying reality and pretending we were part of a new generation that smiled disdainfully at the story of God. I was under my father's influence, but then my father left for Germany. He had *changed his mind*.

"Growing up, how did you feel on Christmas and Easter?" I asked Jonathan.

"I was barely a teenager when I lived here, and it was during the war. What I remember is hiding. The Fascists were rounding up Jews, and Aunty was scavenging the neighborhood for food."

"How is it in America?"

"America's a melting pot. There are so many different people and religions that everyone celebrates their own. That's why I feel at home there."

The cab turned onto a narrow cobblestone street.

"Come to America with me," Jonathan said.

My heart leapt.

"Americans are cold people," the cabby said, switching to English, as if to prove he had understood all we had said. He pulled up at the curb.

I got out and waited on the sidewalk for Jonathan to pay for the ride.

His suggestion that I come with him to America surprised and pleased me to no end, and I tried to hide my elation by looking around with a newly found keenness.

A triangular courtyard was in front of the house, flanked by a concrete and wire fence that ran along the sidewalk and met at a sharp angle with a low brick wall. In the corner grew a tree covered in white flowers. The crowns of old oak and linden trees rustled behind the brick wall. The third side of the yard contained the actual house, a gray stone villa with tall, elongated windows and dark window frames, a pitched tin roof, several corner towers, balconies with potted geraniums, and a steel and glass awning that stretched over the front steps. Ivy draped the awning like a curtain above the front door and clung to the lower walls. Nick's family occupied the apartment on the second floor. Across the street were two apartment buildings, their gray facades stained and crumbling, and two huge poplar trees.

The last time I had been here, the place had looked different. Now it was spring, and all around me nature was ruling. Greenery was budding, growing, blossoming, filling in, and hiding decay and imperfections. In the middle of the yard, tulip shoots were sprouting around a rusty water spout. Fresh grass was trying to cover old car tracks leading from the double gate in the fence to the back of the house. Irises were blooming in a flower bed by the side of the front door. A rosebush was letting out new leaves and thorns as rough and light green as the skin of a lizard. Three tall lilac trees swayed their opulent flowers in the soft wind, over the fence and into the street. The lilac looked heavy against the pale blue sky, rich and sensuous. Tiny petals fluttered to the ground. Weeds grew in cracks between the concrete base of the fence and the sidewalk. Ants crossed the sidewalk and continued along the curb to a little white anthill. A tomcat dashed across the street and disappeared behind the poplars.

I hoped Jonathan's suggestion was serious and his words hadn't escaped him in the heat of the moment. With time things had changed between us. I had shaken off my past and accepted his financial help. We were traveling together. I was introducing him to Nick, my friend's fiancé, and to Nick's family. We were coming to Nick's house as a couple. We had never talked about it, but I thought that on this trip I would take him to meet my mother. When he said I should come to America, he crossed into uncharted territory. Did he mean I should come live with him, or just visit for a few days of pleasure and adventure? I needed to think. We needed to talk about it.

The cab drove off, and Jonathan took the shopping bags from my hands. He looked as fresh and solid as ever. I pushed the gate open, and we walked to the stairway, where I pressed the buzzer.

Nick opened the door. We exchanged greetings in a little foyer, and I gave him his present from Lydia.

"How is she?" he asked eagerly.

I told him she was OK.

"Promise we'll talk later," he said. "Now I'll go get my parents."

He returned with his father, who welcomed us warmly and extended his hand. "Dr. Bardu," he said.

"Miriam," I said when I shook his hand. "In Israel and America we call each other by our first name, even when not well acquainted," I said.

I read the surprise on Jonathan's face, but Nick's father smiled and said, "Certainly, call me Constantin."

He was a handsome man with blue eyes, a straight nose, and a full head of white, wavy hair, combed back over a wide and intelligent forehead. His hair was prematurely white, in contrast to his relatively young features.

"Here is a little something for you," Jonathan said, handing him the shopping bags.

"Oh, thank you. My wife will enjoy it." Without looking inside the bags, Constantin yelled, "Olga!"

As if waiting behind the door to be summoned, Olga appeared. I remembered her as welcoming and very motherly. She was radiant. Her brown hair was freshly coiffed, and her turquoise dress made her green eyes sparkle.

Nick had her eyes and warm smile.

"This is for you," Constantin said and gave her the presents, as if he were the one who had brought them.

"Thank you," Olga said and laughingly performed a deep bow that caused us all to relax. Holding the bags in one hand, she hugged me with the other, and then I introduced Jonathan to her.

"Please, come in," she said.

We walked into a large dining room, where another couple and Nick's grandmother were sitting at a fully set table surrounded by chairs of different shapes and styles. In the middle were platters with fresh lettuce, shiny red radishes, sliced green peppers, and green onions; two trays with sliced ham; several round loaves of Easter breads placed on thin wooden boards; and two oval crystal bowls with hard-boiled eggs colored in deep reds, blues, greens, and yellows. On a black credenza stood several pitchers of wine and a decanter containing a green-yellowish liquid that I soon learned was homemade lemon vodka. Above the chest, a narrow decorative shelf supported a row of Russian dolls and a small red vase with white daffodils that draped over its sides. Against the opposite wall was a walnut bookcase. Open shelves overflowing with photo albums and books of all shapes and colors ran along the top. The lower part had cabinets with doors. To the right of the bookcase hung a somber oil painting representing the barely illuminated profile of a man with sharp features wearing the armor of a gladiator. Wispy, white curtains covered the double doors that led to the balcony.

I went to greet Nick's grandmother. She seemed not to recognize me at first, but after Nick whispered something in her ear, she looked up, smiled, and motioned to me to sit next to her.

Olga opened the door to the credenza and tried to put the bags inside, but the chest was full. I could see stacks of American cigarettes and many bottles of liquor. She took the whiskey out of the bag and put it near the vodka. Then she walked around the table and shoved the cigarettes inside the bookcase.

"American cigarettes," said the man I didn't know. "Constantin, how about treating your less fortunate guests to some of this treasure?"

"Of course," Constantin said. "Olga, leave a few packs out."

Olga reached back inside the cabinet and took out a carton. She tore the cellophane wrapping, separated four packs, and slid them over the table.

The man grabbed one and shoved it in his pocket.

Constantin looked at Jonathan and shrugged. "Cigarettes move like currency around here. If you want something done, make sure to offer a pack of American cigarettes."

"And whiskey," the man said. He approached Jonathan and said quickly, "Hello, I'm Boris Vieru, and this is my wife, Tatiana. We live close by, practically neighbors."

"Nice to meet you," Jonathan said. "I'm Jonathan Sommer."

"And I'm Miriam Sommer," I said, without getting up from my place near Nick's grandmother.

"So you're Constantin's friends from America," Boris said with a booming yet pleasant voice. "We heard about you."

"I hope only good things," Jonathan answered.

I thought he'd explain that he alone was from America, whereas I lived in Israel, but he didn't, and he didn't mention that our last names were the same by coincidence.

"I understand you have a sick brother and came here to help him," Boris said approvingly. "Not many people would do that for their next of kin, travel all the way from America."

"It's the least I can do," said Jonathan.

"Oh, it's a lot. I know what it takes to go halfway around the world, and believe me, it isn't easy. I once went to Ulan Bator myself, the capital of Mongolia." Boris looked at Tatiana as if seeking approval. "I work for the Ministry of Agriculture, you see, and I was sent there in an official capacity. I remember dreading the flight to Moscow and the long train ride that followed. Good thing I speak a little Russian; otherwise it would have been a real nightmare."

"You speak Russian very well," Tatiana said.

"Not as well as our doctor here," Boris answered, throwing a sideways glance at Constantin.

"I've had more practice, that's all," Constantin said. "I, too, travel to Moscow on business." He walked to the chest and grabbed a wine pitcher. "Please, let me fill your glasses."

Boris pushed his glass forward, but seeing that Jonathan and I waited, he pulled it back.

"No, Mr. and Mrs. Jonathan, you go first. The wine is good and all natural."

"I got it through a friend of mine," Constantin offered, "from a local winery called *Pietroasele*."

"It helps being a doctor," Boris said. "You go to Moscow a lot, and every patient brings you gifts."

"Let's not exaggerate," Constantin said. "Not every patient."

"The peasants, who can't get you Kent cigarettes, deliver live fish and poultry to your door," continued Boris. "Some bring money."

"My dad never takes money," Nick protested.

"Yeah, right," said Boris. "Mr. Jonathan, the state of medical care in this country is awful. That's why you have to come from America and help your brother."

"He comes here because he wants to," Constantin said. "And our medical care is free for everyone. And it isn't that bad either."

Boris downed his wine, shook his head, and rolled his eyes. "It isn't bad? My goodness. Maybe it isn't for you, as chief surgeon at a premier Bucharest hospital, but go to the countryside."

"Boris, why don't you tell our guests how you slept in that Mongolian yurt and drank yak milk for breakfast?" Olga suggested.

But we didn't hear the details, as the doorbell rang and Constantin and Olga rushed to greet the new arrivals. There were two of them at first, and then four in short sequence, and another man later. The room became crowded and animated. Even Grandmother got up and started welcoming guests. I repeated my name and tried to memorize theirs. Sooner or later most of them told me they had heard about us, the Americans, and had looked forward to meeting us. By then I was aware that, besides knowing about Jonathan's brother, they didn't know anything else.

They were all originally from Bessarabia, that sliver of land that used to belong sequentially to Romania and Russia throughout history. They had Russian names and spoke Romanian and Russian fluently. The fact that they were refugees of sorts brought them close to my heart, as I saw in them my own grandparents.

A tall, handsome man, by the name of Igor, had brought his guitar. A beautiful woman, all mellow curves and light blond hair that was almost white, accompanied him. Her name was Albina.

Everyone took a seat around the table. I remained next to Nick's grandmother, while Jonathan sat to my right, and Nick on the other side of Jonathan. The more I looked at Albina, the more I found her name unusual yet fitting. In Romanian *albina* meant honeybee and was not commonly used as a name, but it sounded like *albino*, appropriately describing her striking lack of pigmentation. Constantin took the other end of the table, talkative and happy, standing one moment, sitting the next, barking jokes and laughter at his friends. He was proudly presiding at his table as a captain would steer his ship or a chief surgeon would lead his operating staff during surgery.

We started eating, and Igor lifted his empty glass. "Time for a little something!"

"*Davay!*" Constantin hollered, looking directly at Olga.

Even I understood, from the little Russian I knew. *Davay* meant, "Give us," or "Let's begin," or "Let's do it."

Nick grabbed the decanter, and vodka started flowing. It was a misty liquid, deceiving, its strength masked by lemon and sugar. We all had two rounds, and Nick poured the third. When he tried to fill Grandmother's glass, she objected.

"Mama, *pey do dna*," said Igor.

"Ma-ma, *pey do dna*; Ma-ma, *pey do dna!*" the men started chanting.

"Bottoms up," Nick translated for me.

"They're crazy," Nick's grandmother said to no one, obviously pleased by the attention she was getting and pronouncing the word *crazy* the way a proud parent would admonish a beloved child. "How much do they expect me to drink?" she added, and then she gave in. "OK, just a little, please—no more than the nail on my pinky."

I offered her a few slices of ham and a slice of Easter bread. "This vodka is different from what I am used to," I told her.

"It's homemade," she explained. "What they sell in stores is junk, but all you have to do is mix a liter of alcohol with half a liter of water, add some sugar and lemon peel to it, and let it sit for a few days."

"Hey, let's break some eggs," Boris said to Nick, and he grabbed a red one from the bowl closest to him. He cupped it.

Nick chose a green one and wrapped his fingers around it, letting only the tip of the egg show.

Boris lifted his elbow a little. "Christ has risen."

"Indeed he has," Nick said.

Boris pounded at the tip of Nick's egg with the tip of his own, and his egg cracked. He seemed disappointed. The ritual was in fact a childish game, the winner being the person whose egg didn't crack. Boris peeled and ate his egg, took another one, choosing carefully, and looked at Tatiana. "Your turn," he said.

They repeated the motions, unfortunately for Boris with the same result.

"Bad luck," he complained while eating his second egg. "I don't seem to find the right one. That's my problem."

"Your problem is with the hardness," Tatiana said.

There was laughter on our side of the table.

Boris ignored her. "I'll try one more time. Igor?"

"It's unhealthy to eat so many eggs," Igor said. "I'd rather arm wrestle."

"So you think you're strong?"

"No, but you're as pathetic as that gladiator," Igor said, laughing and pointing to the oil painting.

"Let's have a drink," Constantin shouted from the end of the table.

"Constantin dreams the gladiator's a Rembrandt," Boris said.

I guessed it was meant to be funny.

"And it isn't?" Constantin asked.

"Of course not. What are the chances?"

"I don't know. I got it from my uncle before he died. He told me it was, or if it wasn't, it could be by one of his pupils. They've had it in the family for generations."

"Let's ask Miriam. She's an art history major," Nick said.

I got up and walked around the table. The painting, hung low on the wall at my eye level, had no frame, and the canvas was folded over a wooden stretcher and tacked all around at the edges. Short threads were coming loose in the corners. The oil paint was thick and the brushstrokes visible, cracked in places, darkened by age and by dust and cigarette smoke.

"Igor, how do you know the man is a gladiator?" I asked.

"I don't know, but he looks like one, doesn't he?"

"This could be a fragment from a larger work by a Renaissance Italian master. Those people took their trade all over the place. Even in Bistriţa, where I grew up, the Evangelical church was painted by an Italian. What's remarkable here is the technique, the shadows, the *chiaroscuro*, first used by Caravaggio."

"Caravaggio's OK." Nick laughed. "I could live with a Caravaggio."

Nobody was following me too seriously, and I returned to my chair. Nick's grandmother offered me a BT. She lifted her lighter and tried to bring the flame to the tip of my cigarette, but she missed by a few inches. I guided her hand. The cigarette smoke was white-blue.

"You must be happy," I said to her.

"Happy? What would I be happy for?"

"You know, your grandson's approaching marriage."

"Oh, that. We're happy, of course. But we're also worried."

I had heard those words before from Lydia, and I thought that Nick's grandmother was referring to the long and arduous process of getting the marriage approved by the authorities. "Listen, they're in love," I said. "They had to take their chances."

She shook her head.

I was aware of Nick's presence, but I couldn't stop myself. "Don't you agree?" I asked, lowering my voice and hoping that the noise around the table would drown our conversation.

"They'll get their approvals, of that we are certain," she said. "Constantin knows people, and he'll help, but what next?"

"They'll be together, husband and wife," I said, suddenly understanding exactly what her concern was.

A stare burned through me. When I looked up, I saw Olga watching me attentively. I remembered my mother on the day she found out that I wanted to leave for Israel. It was Olga, not Nick, I should have protected from overhearing.

She got up and came over. "Once they marry, they'll leave," she said. She took another step and placed her hand, lovingly, on Nick's shoulder. "They'll go to Israel first, and from there, God only knows..."

"America, maybe," Jonathan suggested.

"Are you talking about me?" Nick asked, leaning into the table to look past Jonathan.

Olga let go of his shoulder.

"Do you want them to stay here?" I asked her.

"No, but I'll miss him terribly."

"I'll miss you too, Mom," Nick said.

Olga smiled and went to the kitchen. Nick's grandmother followed. Everybody else was talking, drinking, eating, and smoking.

Nick took his grandmother's place near me. "So how is she?" he asked.

"Lydia's fine," I said. "She sends you her love."

—⚭—

It was almost dark outside when later, glasses in hand, a few of us who needed a breath of fresh air stepped onto the balcony. The sky was violet, with a few little stars blinking in the distance. The wind was stronger than in the afternoon, causing the trees behind the brick wall to whisper.

"Beautiful," Igor said.

"Those trees are old," I said.

"They belong to the former royal palace," Igor said. "The king used to spend part of his summer here, before his exile. A decade ago they rededicated it as a youth club for schoolchildren. The *Pioneers' Palace*, they call it."

"Prime real estate," Jonathan said, "as we'd call it."

"Only party operatives and doctors can get their hands on homes in this area," Boris said.

Constantin stepped onto the balcony, carrying a vodka bottle. "Any refills?"

Glasses went up.

"So you grew up in Bistriţa?" Constantin asked me.

"I lived there until three years ago, when I left for Israel."

"I've been to Bistriţa at the end of the war, as a medic with the army. The Soviets were on our backs, and for the few days we were stationed there, Bistriţa seemed a small paradise. I remember the church you mentioned and the street next to it with the sidewalk covered by stone arches."

"Sugalete Row," I said.

"Yes," he agreed happily. "The peasants were selling fresh produce, and people were strolling up and down the street like in peacetime."

"On Victory Street."

"Maybe it's called that now, but not during the war. We didn't use such pompous names before the Soviets. Then the insurrection came, and when the army discharged me, I returned home to take my parents out of Kishinev and bring them to Bucharest."

"He didn't want to leave them behind in what had later become part of the Soviet Union," Igor said.

"Who would?" Constantin said.

I jumped in. "My grandfather feared the Soviets, too, and he came to Romania from the other direction. He was originally from Lvov, a doctor."

"A doctor? What was his name?" Constantin asked.

"Levinescu."

"I know him!" he exclaimed. "I met him in my last year of medical school as an intern at Năsăud Central Hospital. That was my second time in Bistriţa. He was chief cardiologist, a very nice man and very competent."

"He passed away of a heart attack about seven years ago."

"I'm sorry. I can still see him in his white scrubs standing in front of us, a bunch of rowdy Bucharest students. He was always calm when he talked to us, with the sort of authority that only a lifetime of knowledge and experience can give you. My God, it *was* like yesterday."

"His real name was Levin, not Levinescu," I said. "He was paranoid the Russians would find out that he came from Lvov and send him to Siberia."

"Not the Russians, the Soviets," Boris said.

"We were all paranoid," Igor said. "Changing names and hiding family history was as customary as snakes molting."

When we returned to the dining room, I noticed that Olga had started clearing the table, so I grabbed a few plates and took them to the kitchen. Jonathan followed me. Nick's grandmother was sitting in a corner smoking. Olga began scrubbing the plates, rinsing them with hot water, and placing them on a towel.

"What are you doing here?" she asked me. "You and Jonathan are our guests. Please go back and join the others."

Something made me want to stay. I sat down next to Nick's grandmother and bummed one of her cigarettes. Jonathan stood.

Olga said, "I don't want you to think for a minute that we are not happy for Nicki. Of course we are. We know how much he loves Lydia, and we love Lydia, too. They've been through a lot, and they've stayed together against all odds. We're not stupid. They're young, they're educated, and getting out of Romania is the best that can happen to them. But it hurts, nevertheless, and it hurts all of us, Constantin, too, perhaps more than you'd think. Every day that passes is a day less that we have with Nick, and the moment we dread is getting closer." She turned away from the sink and looked at me, watermarks staining her evening dress. "Why, you are so young!" she exclaimed, as if she saw me for the first time. "You must be Nick's age or just a bit older."

"I'm older," I said, although it wasn't true.

"Don't say that she could be my daughter," Jonathan joked.

"You men," Olga said. "Take good care of her. You have to promise me."

"I promise."

"Good, now get out of my kitchen and go have a drink."

"I can't drink any more," Jonathan said. "Your friends know no limits."

"Now that my son isn't here, let me tell *you* something," Nick's grandmother said. "The men you met in this house *have* limits. They are proud men who know what's acceptable."

"What's acceptable?" Igor said, walking into the kitchen. Then he added, "Ladies, Mr. Jonathan, I'm going to sing a few songs, so please, all of you join us in the dining room."

We found everybody at the table. Constantin was pouring a new round of drinks. The remaining plates were collected and stashed on the credenza. The tablecloth was littered with breadcrumbs and cigarette ash. Igor walked to the head of the table, propped one leg on the chair, and set his guitar on his knee, his left hand supporting its narrow neck. Constantin sat next to him. Nick put his arm around his father's shoulders. I found a spot near the bookcase and remained standing, my back close to the gladiator.

Boris suggested a song called *Defky'v les*, and someone translated, *Girls in the Woods*, and Igor started singing in a beautiful deep voice. It was a lively song clearly filled with sexual innuendoes. They all sang along and kept the beat by hitting the table with whatever utensils were still left, yelling from time to time to each other, winking and laughing. Then Igor sang *Katiusha*, a romantic Russian song made into a popular hit in French by Rika Zarai, the Israeli singer. I looked at Jonathan. He didn't know the words, but to my pleasant surprise, he was humming along. *Shalandi polnie kefalii* followed, and Albina told me it was an old song about the city of Odessa on the Black Sea and about a fisherman named Kostea, the Russian nickname for Constantin. Somebody added that *our* Constantin loved Odessa. The song was nostalgic and uplifting even though I didn't understand the words. When Igor got to *Y Constantin beriot gitaru, Y tihim golasom payot* ("And Constantin takes his guitar, and starts singing in a whisper," Albina said in my ear), I looked at Constantin and saw him raise his fist and open his fingers one by one in the slow rhythm of the song, and I saw tears streaming down his cheeks. These were tears of happiness, I thought. My back rested against the cold skin of the gladiator, and the ashes at the tip of my cigarette were just about to break loose and fall on the carpet. In spite of his impressive poise and stature, in spite of his striking features and oddly white hair, Constantin was a teddy bear at heart, and now, softened by alcohol and the melancholy of the Russian songs, he was crying for the inevitable departure of his one and only son. I thought of Gabriel years ago playing the guitar for me in his studio, and I compared his voice to Igor's less rehearsed but so deeply alive sound. And I thought that I felt comfortable in this house with proud men who had limits, on Easter and on any other day, that I was like them, and I was happy to be together with Jonathan, whom I loved.

———————— ❧ ————————

As we were leaving, in the little entrance hall, Constantin took Jonathan aside. "Your brother, Samuel, bring him to me. I'll take care of him like my own."

Chapter 4

MOTHER

The next morning while I slept, Jonathan and Constantin made a plan. Samuel would be discharged from the hospital, and an ambulance would bring him to Bucharest. The release papers had to be signed by next of kin. Jonathan wanted to go to Turda himself to see the Ionescus, the family that took care of Samuel, give them some much needed cash, and thank them again. Since he was already there, Constantin suggested, he should also "grease the wheels that needed greasing."

Leah and Samuel were all he had in the world, Jonathan kept repeating.

Now he also had me, I thought.

The concierge got us a limousine, a black Russian ZiL. The driver was a middle-aged Serb by the name of Bogdan, a discreet man, very experienced, the hotel manager assured us. He came from a village in Banat on the border with Yugoslavia. Years ago he had been one of Gheorghe Gheorghiu-Dej's personal bodyguards. In Turda Jonathan would stay with the Ionescus. He booked a room for me at a hotel nearby. The next day we would drive to Bistrița.

Jonathan filled his suitcases with whiskey and American cigarettes.

In Bistrița Bogdan dropped us off outside the carriage gate. The entrance door was still painted bright red, as it had always been. The marble steps seemed smaller now, and I winked as I walked past the statue of the young maiden.

Adina was home, but Jacob was in college, pursuing his PhD in history and political science at the university in Cluj. My mother was about to meet Jonathan, and I was happy for it.

Jonathan was charming that evening. He started by producing three little gifts from his luggage, all beautifully wrapped and kept hidden from me until that moment. There were two silk scarves, one for my mother and one for my grandmother, and a gold bracelet for Adina.

"When did you get them?" I whispered to him, and he grinned, enjoying my surprise.

My mother, too, rose to the occasion. She had the dining room table set with her good china, and, after a brief conversation by the living room window, she had us move over and served us baked trout, fresh from the Bistriţa River, a salad of tomatoes, lettuce, cucumbers, and radishes, and buttery new potatoes. A crisp white wine and sparkling water came with the fish. Jonathan looked happy, and only I knew how hard it must have been for my mother to get hold of all that fresh, beautiful produce. For dessert we ate blueberry blintzes, like in the good old times with Pani, Grandfather, and Mr. Moisil, and drank Russian black tea from the Japanese porcelain cups painted with gold designs.

The conversation ran effortlessly, with Jonathan doing most of the talking. He told us about Samuel, and then about his house in San Diego with the view of the bay, and finally about the wonderful coincidence of the two of us meeting on the plane. The wine did its trick, and he spoke about seeing me for the first time, describing with amazing accuracy what I had been wearing that day and what I had said, using a touch of humor and that unmistakable tone of a man in love. I worried he would mention his telephone call and the message he had left with my grandmother, but he didn't say anything about that.

Yet despite Jonathan's animated voice, despite the delicious dinner and everybody's cheerfulness, something felt wrong. I could see it in my mother's face and hear it in the high pitch of her voice, a fake exuberance that normally wasn't there. I saw it in Adina. She smiled a lot, yet every time I looked at her, her eyes darted away, avoiding mine like quicksilver. And I noticed it in my grandmother's wrinkles, more pronounced than before, and in her somehow shrunken presence. I was sure it had something to do with me, or with both of us and with our visit, and it started to bother me.

Jonathan didn't seem to have sensed it.

"What's wrong?" I whispered to my grandmother a few times during dinner. She took my hand every time and whispered back, "Nothing, don't worry."

When we finished eating, Jonathan asked to see the apartment. He wanted to discover as much of me in it as he could, he announced boyishly. We were standing by the table, and he pulled me close to his chest and hugged me.

We started in Grandmother's room, with the big bed in the middle and the black telephone on the nightstand; then we entered my former room, dark and narrow, leading to the kitchen. I noticed the unmade bed, Adina's suitcase half unpacked, and clothes cluttering the floor and the chairs. In the closet, I found my old sketches and paintings, and I spread them out for Jonathan to see on the narrow table by the inside window. A few stray rays of sun fell from the skylight in the foyer. Jonathan took his time and asked questions, and I answered them with the enthusiasm I used to possess when I painted.

My mother and grandmother came through carrying dishes. Soon we followed them into the kitchen and continued along the catwalk, down the stairs, and into the courtyard. The two rooms where Ileana and Uncle Tokachi had lived, refurbished and used for a while by Jacob, were now empty and locked. The stable had been converted into a storage area. We went out the backdoor and walked hand in hand through the carriage gate on to Victory Street. People were taking their evening stroll, back and forth by the Evangelical church and the Sugalete. I looked curiously into people's faces, hoping to run into somebody I knew, but the town was changing faster than I had thought. As we walked, I shared with Jonathan some of my memories. We turned back, and I stopped and gave Jonathan a long kiss at the bottom of the stairs, to chase away the old ghosts.

"I love you," I said.

I heard voices upstairs, but when we opened the door, the room fell silent. My mother and grandmother sat at the table, which was completely cleared. Adina was gone. My mother's bed was made for the night, and a pile of linens and two large pillows were waiting for me on the sofa on the opposite wall. We had planned the sleeping arrangements earlier. Jonathan was spending the night at the hotel, and I was too old to share a bed with my sister.

"What's going on?" I said again.

"Nothing," my grandmother said. "We're glad you're here."

"It's Adina," my mother said. "She quit college, you know, in her second year of study."

My grandmother looked the other way, as if she didn't want to discuss the subject.

"Did you talk to her?" I asked my mother, and I pulled up a chair.

Jonathan remained standing.

"Of course we did, both of us," my mother said. "She really doesn't have a good reason. She disliked her chemistry professor, or so she says. How many things have I disliked in life? But I didn't give up. You can't study biology without chemistry; that's a fact. All the sacrifices I made."

This was always the point with Mother—her sacrifices.

"Listen, I'll talk to her," I volunteered, not too concerned and emboldened by the fact that what I had sensed at dinner had nothing to do with Jonathan or me. "You know, there are things she might be reluctant to tell you, but I'm her sister."

"Don't," my mother said. "If you push her now, she'll withdraw. She'll close up like a clam. I know Adina."

"And I don't?"

"She has changed since you left us. It has been three full years." My mother looked up at Jonathan. "Do you understand? Miriam left for Israel. Jacob moved to Cluj and most likely will never come back to live in Bistriţa, and I'm here."

Jonathan didn't respond.

Suddenly the door to my old room opened, and Adina walked in, dressed to go out. "Hello, everybody," she said, smiling. In jeans and a lacy blouse, she looked pretty and self-assured. "I'm meeting some friends, and, Mama, don't wait for me. I'll let myself in through the back."

My mother nodded silently.

"It's late. I'll be leaving as well," Jonathan said. "Adina, if you wait a few minutes, I'll ask our chauffer to drive you."

Adina said no, thanks, and my mother sighed. "I don't want to lose you, too," she told her.

"I'll be here with you," Grandmother said and held my mother's hand the way she had held mine during dinner. "Even after they all leave, I'll be here."

Jonathan walked to the window, pulled a corner of the curtain aside, and looked into the street. Bogdan would be arriving anytime.

I had a hard time falling asleep. The streetlights were bothering me. There I was, my childhood home, feeling displaced and uncomfortable. I was physically tired and emotionally drained. I could hear my mother's light breathing in the bed across the room and could follow the shadow of the tree branches in front of the window moving on the ceiling. I had known that tree since I was a girl—a leafy old chestnut—and I had always been proud of it, as if it were mine, as if its beauty were proof that we were good people. Now that same chestnut tree seemed threatening. I had slept in that room before, and it occurred to me that the most familiar things could hide surprises. I missed Jonathan, and I hoped he missed me. He could be in some watering hole just then, sipping slivovitz with strangers, or with his chauffer. Was the chauffer's name really Bogdan, and was he as loyal and discreet as they said, or was he a scoundrel? As bodyguard to a person whose face I had seen only in the pages of newspapers, he had to have been on the payroll of the Secret Police, or *Securitate*. He had to be spying on us. The night before, when we got to the hotel in Turda, I had kept my distance from him. Jonathan had left Romania many years ago and might have forgotten how the Securitate spied on everybody. If he wanted to have a drink with someone, he might invite Bogdan without thinking twice about it. Would Jonathan do that? He had been polite and endearing tonight, generous with his stories, but did he leave because he was tired or because he was bored? Did he care for me? Did he really love me? And what if the two of them ran into Adina? She could be anywhere, my little sister. Somehow, tonight it ended up being all about her and about my mother's worries and loneliness.

The night before, falling asleep at the hotel had been easy. Tonight it was not. So many bad people! In a restaurant or a bar, somebody was bound to approach Jonathan and spill the beans about my past. About Gabriel or Mathew or worse. This was a town without secrets. When we walked in the street, how naïve of me to have wanted to meet any of my old acquaintances.

The next morning, as soon as we could, I thought we should leave. Bad enough our limo wouldn't make it through town unnoticed.

⸎

"How old is he?" my mother asked the next morning.

It was a reasonable question, but coming from her it annoyed me. There were so many other questions she could ask—good questions, like did I love him, or did he understand me, or what was his passion in life.

We were having coffee, just the two of us, on the sofa. I was still in my nightgown. Adina was asleep, and Grandmother was in her room.

"I don't know," I answered.

"You don't know his age?"

"No, not really. He's forty, maybe forty-one, I'm not sure."

"That's twice your age," my mother uttered.

The truth was I had a good idea about Jonathan's age, but the two of us had never discussed it explicitly. Every time our conversation skirted the subject, Jonathan found a way of avoiding it. He was skillful at that, and I never confronted him because it didn't feel right. To my mother, on the other hand, this was a line of attack. Jonathan had been pleasant the night before, polite, very polished. We looked good together, and he was a good-looking man. My mother didn't ask if he was wealthy. She must have figured out that he was. There was nothing for her to complain about except the obvious thing—his age. Somewhere in her little book of appearances, something didn't match up.

"Twice my age? Mother, I think you're doing your math wrong."

I adjusted a pillow to support my back. As I moved, the Star of David with the small diamonds in each corner sparkled over my nightgown.

My mother leaned toward me. She raised her hand and touched the pendant.

"It's from Jonathan," I said.

"I gave you mine when you left. Obviously it wasn't so expensive."

"I still have it," I said. "I wear them both, on different occasions, and I treasure them equally."

"You're wearing his now."

"I'm with him."

She gave me the resigned look I recognized from the times she had fought with my father. Then she got up, walked toward Adina's room, and stopped by the door.

"Mama," I said, "I came here for you to meet Jonathan. I love him, and I need your blessing. I understand you're upset over Adina's college, but this is *my* day. I'm here. Please, give me this moment. I don't have anybody else."

"He's taking my place," my mother answered.

When Jonathan arrived, my mother suggested we invite Bogdan in for breakfast, but Bogdan declined and waited downstairs. Jonathan called the hospital in Turda and was told they had sent the ambulance to Bucharest with his brother and a nurse.

We had a lengthy breakfast, very calm and polite. There were no passionate debates, no arguments, and no plans for the future. When we left, I hugged the three women in my family one after the other. It was good to be on our way.

At four in the afternoon, we arrived in Sibiu, a little less than half of our distance to Bucharest.

"Can we stay overnight?" I asked.

"Of course," Jonathan said.

After driving through a neighborhood of identical and decrepit buildings, we entered the medieval town. I got disoriented in the narrow cobblestone streets, flanked by sixteenth-century stone houses topped by red, tilted roofs. Oval windows running horizontally peeked through those roofs. Intricate wrought-iron lampposts stood at street corners. Statues decorated little squares. We drove by the Jesuit church and the Brukenthal Museum and stopped in front of the large white building of the Roman Emperor Hotel.

"I'm sorry we are delaying you," I told Bogdan. He had a family back home, and we were causing him to spend an extra night on the road.

"Don't worry," he said while unloading the trunk and carrying our suitcases into the lobby of the hotel.

"Before we left," Jonathan said, "we went to a dinner party, and we're still tired."

"Easter Sunday," Bogdan said, approvingly.

"With all this travel, we never recovered," I said. "I think we had had too much to drink."

"There is no such thing as too much to drink," Bogdan said and looked me straight in the eye. "Madam, where I come from, men know only two dignified ways to die: by the knife or by cirrhosis of the liver."

A shiver traveled down my spine.

⊙⊙⊙

I woke after an agitated nap, my eyelids heavy, my temple throbbing. The memory of the conversation with my mother was still bothering me. Stretched on the bed by my side, Jonathan was watching me, his head propped on his elbow.

"What are you looking at?" I asked.

"You. I'm looking at you."

"I feel awful and must be looking awful as well."

"You look good, and it's time to go downstairs for dinner."

I rolled onto my back. "I can't eat. I'm not hungry."

"Please. If you don't get up now, you won't sleep tonight."

A golden light was filling the room. I caught a glimpse of a late afternoon summer sky, puffy clouds moving fast in the wind. "Where are we?"

Jonathan laughed. "You know where we are." He jumped out of bed and disappeared into the bathroom.

I looked out the window again and around the hotel room at the old-fashioned armchairs and antique table, the huge armoire in polished oak with a full-length mirror mounted on one of its doors, and the TV set with a fully extended antenna on top and a piece of paper taped to the screen stating that it was out of service. Jonathan's jacket hung on the back of a chair. One open suitcase was on the floor.

It was time to decide what to wear. I got up and caught a glimpse of myself in the mirror. There were pillow marks on my face, and my hair was disheveled. I was wearing one of Jonathan's light-blue shirts, and I remembered that before falling asleep I had been too tired to look for my nightgown. The shirt reached all the way to my knees. The buttons were open to the top of my breasts. My eyes didn't reflect the turmoil inside me, and it suddenly occurred to me that my mother was right. Her question of Jonathan's age, which had annoyed me so much in the morning, was in fact only the first in a series of questions. Jonathan was very nice to me but too noncommittal.

I had a right to know.

I needed to know his age for sure and to understand his feelings for me and his intentions. He might think it was too early in our relationship to make commitments, but for me it wasn't, especially if he cared for me. I had kept the love letter he had sent me after our second date. There were gifts and the financial support he was providing and him saying that I should go to America with him. But I had changed my life to be with him, and my next steps depended on him, as I had to decide my future.

I turned away from the mirror, and I noticed the blue corner of Jonathan's passport sticking out of his jacket's breast pocket. I hesitated for a few seconds, and then I grabbed it. From the first page of the passport, a younger Jonathan smiled at me. I read his full name, Jonathan Peter Sommer, his place of birth, Turda, and his birthdate. The page for emergency contact was blank, and the rest contained border stamps from the countries he had traveled to—Mexico, Israel, Germany, Greece, Romania, and Venezuela.

Jonathan surprised me as I was standing in the middle of the room, staring at his passport. "What are you doing?" he said.

Born on September 9, 1933, he was forty-one years old, going on forty-two, my lover.

I blushed. "Me? Nothing."

"Miriam, you are looking through my passport."

"Yeah, I am. I've never seen one before, I mean an American passport, and I was curious."

"I'm curious about many things myself, but I don't rummage through your stuff, do I?" His question was delivered in a tone that was angrier than the words showed.

"I didn't rummage," I said and placed the passport back in the pocket of his jacket. "I just saw it there and looked through it. What's the big deal?"

"Did you look through my wallet as well?"

I made a long face. "You're being unpleasant."

"You're not to look through my stuff, ever again. Never."

Holding his gaze, I slowly unbuttoned the shirt and let it fall to the ground. I turned, walked naked into the bathroom, and locked the door. I washed my face, brushed my teeth, combed my hair, and put on lipstick. When I came out wrapped in a white hotel towel, I was ready for battle.

Fully dressed and wearing his jacket, Jonathan was waiting in one of the armchairs, smoking. He rarely smoked and didn't have his own cigarettes.

"You bummed one of my cigarettes," I told him. "Did you rummage through my stuff, or how did you find them, darling?"

He didn't answer.

"The truth is, I looked at your passport to find out how old you are."

"You should have asked me," he said, playing with the tip of his cigarette in the ashtray.

"Oh, yeah? And do you think it's that simple?"

"What's complicated?"

I wanted to be smart and win this argument. "Jonathan, I'll tell you what's complicated." I posted myself in front of him. "You have me at your feet, ready to be taken, but I'm not sure you want to."

"I do," he said.

"Then tell me so. Shower me with your words. Overwhelm me with your love, and persuade me. Protect me forever. Marry me. I didn't ask how old you were because I didn't want to dwell on our age difference and give you the impression that it might bother me or that I hold it against you."

"I see—you were being considerate."

"Yes, Jonathan, yes. I was being mindful of your feelings, which is more than I can say about you. Other men in your shoes would have said they didn't want to take advantage of my youth and inexperience. They would have made sure I understood. They would have told me they feared that in a few years I might wake up from this dream and regret it."

Jonathan stubbed his cigarette out and exhaled a long stream of smoke. He looked at me for the first time. "Tell me, how do you know what other men would say? Did your mother tell you?"

"Good try, Jonathan, but no. My mother has nothing to do with this. *I* need to know. Since we met, I've put my life in your hands, and I'm waiting. Tell me, what are your intentions?"

"Fair enough," Jonathan said. "Let me tell you." He rearranged himself in the armchair and combed his hair with his fingers. "I enjoy being with you, and I like your face, your style, the way you dress, the way you behave, and your laughter. I love the fact that you're young, and your youth gives me energy. I want you to come and live with me in America. Keep your apartment in Israel, at least for a while, because I'm not going to marry you—not now, maybe later. I've had marriages in my life that ended in disaster. For now, let's say I'm not the marrying type. But I am a very wealthy man, and I'll provide for you, I promise. Come with me. Trust me. I love you, and you will not lack for anything as long as you stay by my side. As for my age, that's for you to decide. I don't know how you'll feel in the future, and I can't sugarcoat it."

"You don't need to."

Chapter 5

SAN DIEGO

The visa application took several months to resolve. In fact, after visiting the US embassy in Tel Aviv a few times, filling out all the forms, and sitting through two interviews with a smiling and very presentable American consul, I got rejected. Then Jonathan contacted his attorney, who placed one phone call—only one—and the visa was issued.

"Take good care of my apartment," I told Mrs. Shames. "I'll be sending you a check every month."

"You'll be wasting your money."

"Why do you say this?"

"You'll never come back, Miri."

"And what if I do? Mrs. Shames, you should never say never."

"I've seen your Jonathan. The way he held your hand, the way he was looking at you. You'll be happy with him in America."

I was happy.

I hugged Mrs. Shames and waited for the driver to carry my suitcases to the car.

Jonathan greeted me at Kennedy Airport with one red rose, thorns removed, the end of the stem wrapped in cellophane. He had us booked at the Plaza. After a glimpse across the street at Central Park, I yawned and went to sleep for a few hours. Later we made love, and Jonathan presented me with his welcoming gift, an elegant gold and sapphire necklace.

In the afternoon we walked down Fifth Avenue holding hands, visited Saint Patrick's Cathedral, stopped at Rockefeller Center, turned east on Forty-Sixth Street, and entered Grand Central Station. I had never seen a city like New York.

We dined at Windows on the World, in the North Tower. The tablecloth felt cool under my fingertips, and in the distance I could admire the amazing skyline of Manhattan.

"You're on top of the world," Jonathan said, and I believed him.

The house in San Diego was an eighteen-thousand-square-foot mansion on a lot carved in the side of a mountain. It had a tall foyer with stained-glass skylights and a double staircase, a dining room with a table large enough to seat twenty-four, a living room, a library, a game room, and the main pantry and kitchen. Upstairs were the master suite with the sunroom Jonathan had described to me on our first date in Haifa, a guest suite, and six additional bedrooms, each with a separate bathroom. A petal-shaped swimming pool stretched in the shadow of a cliff at the far edge of the garden. Palm trees, pines, cacti, a mulberry tree, and purple bougainvillea sheltered the paved walkway from the back porch of the house to the swimming pool. The clubhouse, the six-car garage, and the servants' quarters were in separate structures. Marybeth was our housekeeper, Morris, the cook, and Juan, the gardener. When we arrived, they gathered on the front marble steps at the top of the semicircular driveway. It felt like the movies, and I was glad to be wearing my white gloves and wide-brimmed hat as I had seen women display in Hollywood productions.

The huge spaces, the dark-paneled walls, the classical furniture in the dining room and living room, the echo of my own steps on the bare hardwood floors in the hallways, the billiards table, the two Lincolns in the garage, and the security system gave me a feeling of unease bordering on anxiety. How much was too much? Did I deserve all this, and would I ever feel at home here?

I started doubting myself and fought back by concealing my insecurities, appearing aloof and irascible. I complained ceaselessly. Nothing was good enough. The weather was too perfect, and I longed for the cloudy and snowy days of my childhood. The air conditioning was too strong, and I had to wear sweaters everywhere in the house. The view from the sunroom was beautiful and reminded me of Haifa, but the bay in Haifa was busier somehow, more varied, and more alive. The grounds were too hilly. There were no pedestrians in the streets and almost no sidewalks. Why did we have to drive everywhere, and where was the city center I loved, with shops, crowds, noise, and exhaust fumes? Morris's cooking was predictable. The artwork on the walls reflected a taste that disagreed with my own. How could anybody like hunting scenes with horses, hounds, and bleeding deer, or nineteenth-century oils with mighty rivers, sunsets, scantily clad women, and plump Cupids floating on clouds?

I had to tell Jonathan how I felt. He listened. He became my refuge, and I clung to him day and night the way a toddler clings to the mother's dress. For a while he seemed to rejoice in my dependency.

We spent time together at home, talking, eating, drinking fine wines, and swimming in the pool. I complained about the kitchen. We made love. It was strange to wake up next to him in the middle of the night and to comprehend the permanence of his presence in my life.

When we went out, I needed him even more.

We visited boutiques in La Jolla and Carlsbad. We drove to LA, stayed overnight at the Bel Air in Beverly Hills, and went window-shopping on Rodeo Drive.

I didn't need to buy anything.

"Just wanted you to see these," Jonathan said, as if apologizing. "I wanted you to know these stores existed and you could shop here any time."

He belonged to a country club on Coronado Island and asked me if I wanted to go. I could meet new people, he said. I could get a personal trainer or join a class, learn how to play tennis and golf, or lie by the pool.

New people and new surroundings would have been too much for me. "We have a pool at home," I reminded him.

Jonathan kept horses at a stable in Rancho Santa Fe. I remembered the wind in my face on Gabriel's motorcycle and thought that riding horses might be fun. Jonathan's horses were beautiful from afar. Up close was a different story. They twitched. One of them whuffed and turned his head toward me. He had glossy, bloodshot eyes and looked fierce, like the horses in Jonathan's hunting scenes on the walls, like the ones harnessed to the carts in Bistrița when I was a child. The stable boy came to help me mount. I refused.

On Friday nights Jonathan had a standing reservation at a restaurant at the Dell. On the terrace one could hear and smell the ocean. Some of Jonathan's friends joined us for dinner. They were rowdy and outgoing, and I wanted to fit in. Jonathan ordered a martini for me. I tasted it, and I didn't like the gin in the drink, so he ordered me one with vodka. I didn't like it either. Carlos, who was seated next to me, suggested a Manhattan. He was younger than Jonathan and had black, wavy hair and dark skin, like a Mexican. His wife was the small woman at the other end of the table. The drink he recommended was sweet and more to my liking.

"I admire your husband," he whispered.

"He's my boyfriend," I said.

"Boyfriend, husband, who cares. He knows how to get the finest for himself."

I took it as a compliment.

The wind blew from the ocean, and I wrapped my white shawl tightly around me. It was August, but the breeze was cool.

"Here," Carlos said, taking off his jacket and placing it on my shoulders.

"Why, you'll be cold," I told him.

"Not to worry. I'm always hot."

He was wearing a white shirt and a red bow tie that looked pretentious.

Jonathan asked the waiter to bring a gas heater and place it near the table.

Carlos ordered another Manhattan for me, and soon my head started spinning, but I was having a good time, and when Jonathan had the valet bring the car, I reluctantly followed.

We went for a few days to Las Vegas, and Marybeth came with us. I didn't think we needed a maid, but Jonathan insisted. In the end it wasn't my call. She was a tall, attractive woman of about forty. Jonathan had access to a Learjet through his aviation club, and he chartered one for the trip. The view from the air was breathtaking—the deep ocean blue, the highway along the shore with little cars like beads on parallel strings, the soft hills with dry, mustard-yellow vegetation, and the gradual transition to sand. When we landed, the pilot told Jonathan to call him whenever we were ready to fly back. I had a lot of luggage. I wanted to be well protected against the harshness of the desert sand and heat. Two men carried my suitcases from the jet to the air-conditioned limousine.

At Caesar's Palace Jonathan had a suite that included two bedrooms, one for us and the other for Marybeth, connected by interior door to each other and a common living area. The bedrooms were identical. Each had a bathroom, a huge round bed covered with a heavy red spread, a round mirror on the ceiling above the bed, and a sunken area with a Jacuzzi. In the evening we went to see a show with lions, flamethrowers, and topless dancers. On the way, we stopped at the casino, and Jonathan tried to teach me how to play baccarat. It didn't excite me. Gambling wasn't my thing. We later dined on pulled pork and red wine at a Cuban restaurant. Through the huge restaurant windows, the strip looked very crowded.

∞∞∞

It was still dark when I woke up. I lay motionless on my side of the bed. The silence seemed overwhelming, as if something was missing, but slowly hotel noises started reaching me from afar. A door opened and closed somewhere, allowing the dull staccato from a TV to escape and then die away. Somebody used a sink or a shower for a minute or two. A gust of wind brushed the walls. I turned on my back. The mirror above the bed caught a part of the window and a sliver of light breaking at the horizon over the mountains. It also reflected the inside of the room, with the vague contour of the bed and that of my body under the cover. The other half of the bed was empty. Through the darkness I made out the bathroom door, which was half open. I panicked, got up, and took a few steps toward the bathroom, thinking he might be there. I didn't remember the sunken floor, and when I reached it, I lost my balance and came tumbling down. My hands caught the edge of the Jacuzzi, and my face hit the floor. Stars flashed behind my eyelids, but I didn't feel any pain. I was sure I didn't scream. I caught my breath, got up, checked the bathroom, and turned on a light. It was almost five in the morning. I went to Marybeth's door and stopped. This image, this idiotic idea of surprising Jonathan in her bed, crossed my mind. Why else would he want her with us on this trip? How stupid could he be? How stupid could men be, in general?

This was insane, only my insecurity speaking.

"Miss Miriam?" I heard a whisper. "Are you OK?"

"I'm OK," I said and opened the door. Marybeth stood in front of me in a hotel-issue bathrobe. Her brown hair was loose and looked black against the stark white of the robe.

"I heard something," she said.

"Oh." I smiled dismissively. "I fell. It was dark, and I didn't see the step in the floor. Did I disturb you?"

I backed away from the door, and Marybeth followed me. I sat on the bed.

"Never mind me," she said. "Are you hurt?"

"I'm not, but I have no idea where Jonathan is."

"He's out gambling."

"At this hour? What's the matter with him?"

"He loves it," she said. "That's why he comes to Las Vegas, and what he does every time—he gambles throughout the night. And that's why he asked me to come along—to be here with you."

"I had no idea," I said.

Marybeth walked to the middle of the room, picked up my high heels from where I had left them, and placed them neatly by my side of the bed. "Would you like anything to drink, Miss, a juice or a glass of warm milk? Shall I call room service for you?"

"No, thank you. I'll try to go back to sleep."

"Very good, but before you lie down, are you sure you're not hurt in any way?"

"I'm sure."

"Good night then," she said and tiptoed to the door.

"Marybeth," I called after her, "I take it you've been here before?"

"To Las Vegas?" she said.

I nodded.

"Yes, a few times."

"You and Jonathan alone?"

"I think you should ask Mr. Sommer," she said.

In the morning, while Jonathan slept, the hotel manager sent a bouquet of white gladiolas, an ice bucket with a bottle of champagne, and a box of chocolates with a thank-you note to Jonathan for being such a loyal customer. I took a few ice cubes from the bucket and pressed them to my cheek where it hurt. The skin burned a little. In the bathroom I applied foundation to the area.

Marybeth was up, and I asked her to join me for breakfast at a restaurant downstairs.

"It was nice of them to send us flowers and chocolates," I said.

"They do it every time."

"Why?"

"This is nothing, Miss Miriam," Marybeth said. "The amount of money Mr. Sommer gambles away pays for it a thousandfold."

After breakfast we went to the boutiques in the shopping mall below the main floor. I chose a few postcards to mail to Israel and Romania, and I bought a Gucci bag and several silk blouses for myself, and a belt, a silver bracelet, and some face creams for Marybeth.

She was ecstatic. "Thank you. You're being too kind."

"My pleasure," I said, and charged the purchases to the room.

"Mr. Sommer's a different person since you came," Marybeth said. "He's calmer, more content. I can feel the touch of the right woman in his life. All of us can."

I understood she referred to the staff.

"What do you think of Morris?" I asked.

"He's a good man."

We stepped out of the stores. "How long have you worked for Mr. Sommer?"

"Since he moved to Del Cerro. This spring it's been five years."

"Marybeth, will you help me understand him better?"

She kept her gaze straight ahead, but she didn't say no.

At the base of the escalators was a full-size replica of Michelangelo's David. Marybeth waited with the bags while I walked a few times around the statue. I found its location bizarre, but I understood that one didn't question taste in Las Vegas. As a former art student, I admired the accuracy of the replica in its minute details and the polished stone that reflected the light with a muted glow.

I was thankful Jonathan didn't have a job, at least not a regular one. This way, I told him, he could spend all his time with me.

He smiled.

We were lying by the pool in the garden—I, under the umbrella—and Marybeth brought us frozen margaritas on a tray. I noticed with pleasure she was wearing the bracelet I had bought her in Las Vegas.

"I like Marybeth," I told Jonathan after she left.

"I'm glad," he said.

"But I don't like Morris."

"What do you want me to do? Fire him?"

I sipped on my drink. Fleetingly, a cloud blocked the sun. From the corner of my eye I observed Juan walk in front of the triple garage door carrying an aluminum ladder and disappear behind the palm trees.

"Jonathan," I said, "I might want to start painting again."

"Do it," he said.

"I don't know if I'll be able to."

"You will. I've seen your work."

I told him I would need a studio, and we agreed that we would have the wall between two of our spare bedrooms torn down to create a larger space, raise the ceiling, and install a couple of skylights. We also agreed I would start buying modern art to display downstairs.

Jonathan put me in touch with a few interior decorators, opened a bank account in my name, and bought me a new car. It was a BMW 300 series, convertible, with white leather seats—a fabulous little toy.

Then he said I was ready. He looked satisfied. He said he had to go on a trip to South America, on business, nothing interesting, and for no longer than two or three weeks.

Before he left, he remembered to fire Morris.

———❦———

Morris was my casualty. He'd done nothing wrong, except that I had convinced myself I didn't like his cooking and he happened to be the cook. To be honest, I didn't want it to happen that way, and I didn't think of consequences. Until then, my world had revolved around art, around feelings and intuition—no wider circles, no cause and effect. Pani had left us even though my grandparents had treated her as a part of the family. It still hurt when I thought about her.

With Morris, I had the power. I was in control. For better or for worse, I was the one who made things happen.

My new car added to that feeling. Driving came easily and opened a new world for me. Distances that had seemed huge became manageable. Overtaken by the humming power of the engine, the serpentine roads alongside mountains and valleys stopped being an obstacle, adding a thrill to the beauty of the land. Vistas extended ahead of me with glimpses of the ocean, the long bridge over the bay, the harbor, the white downtown buildings, and the airport. My new world was designed for cars, not for walking. It *was* a new world.

I had a good sense of direction, and I quickly memorized the names of the main thoroughfares and roads. The fact that many were Spanish reminded me of Romanian and made them easier to pronounce and more exotic sounding at the same time. The house was in Del Cerro. The island I could see from my window across the bay was Coronado. To go to Balboa Park, I would start on El Cajon Boulevard, cross over Escondido Highway, and take a left on Cabrillo Freeway South. On the way back, if I reached Camino Del Rio, I had gone too far.

I drove to meet people at Contemporary Designs. I stopped at America's West and the Good Old Furniture Store. I spent hours at Pier 1. I perused department stores like Nordstrom and Bloomingdale's. I discovered little corner shops in quaint neighborhoods and art galleries on the north end of Mission

Bay. I visited the Museum of Contemporary Art in a downtown building and the Mingei International Museum in Balboa Park. I interviewed contractors. Some came to the house to take measurements. They remembered Jonathan when he first purchased the property. "What a gentleman," they all said. "He trusted people, and money was no object to him." I nodded and did things my own way. I decided my style would shine through everything I did. Jonathan entrusted me with the task, and this wasn't a game. I was determined. Uncompromising. I made sketches of the new studio and came up with an elaborate color scheme for the entire downstairs. The carpets would have abstract patterns like canvases by Miró. Light would bounce off the ceilings and penetrate the dark corners. I showed my ideas to the contractors and had them agree with me. They loved my creativity, or so they said.

I showed my plans to Marybeth. She was hesitant, but slowly she came around and became more comfortable in sharing her opinions. Our relationship was a little strange. She was shy, yet very direct. She could have been my mother. I thought of Pani again and reminded myself to be cautious. One could never expect unconditional loyalty. People did what was best for them, especially when in your employ. Jonathan paid Marybeth. *We* paid her.

Still, it was lonely at night. The Santa Ana wind came in from the east. It brought dry, hot air from the desert and hit the bedroom windows tangentially. It carried debris from the mountain—dust, branches, and leaves. When it blew, the entire upstairs creaked. The contractors removed a portion of the outside wall and covered it in black plastic. If burglars could get up that high, they could cut it easily with a knife. The wind caught in it like a sail. The plastic stretched and bounced back. When it did, it sounded like a machine gun.

The first night Jonathan left for South America, Morris was gone, too. The refrigerator and pantry were full, but no meal was cooked. I called Marybeth on the intercom and complained. She rushed through the yard. She didn't have her apron on, or her bonnet, but I didn't say anything. She served me a light dinner fixed on the fly. I ate alone in the formal dining room and felt out of place.

The next evening I ate together with Marybeth in the kitchen and asked her to move into the house with me. She had her own room in the servants' quarters, but that was at the other end of the garden, and I was lonely.

"There is plenty of room," I said. "Until Jonathan gets back, you can take any bedroom upstairs."

To my delight, she agreed.

We started shopping together for groceries, and sometimes we cooked side by side. She gave me the name of the employment agency that had put her in touch with Jonathan five years ago. She wasn't sure they were still in business, but if they were, they would recommend a new cook. We went on long walks all the way to Lake Murray, and around the lake as well. We watched television together and got hooked on *Starsky & Hutch*. I started thinking of her as a friend.

"Have you ever been married?" I asked her.

"Yes," she said. "But I wasn't too happy."

We left it at that.

I questioned her about Jonathan, and she made sure to stay neutral and reveal nothing at all.

I wanted to sew my own drapes for the studio and decided to buy a sewing machine. Marybeth told me to look in the Yellow Pages in order to find a store.

"Let your fingers do the walking," she said.

I was amazed by how well the telephones worked. Everybody in America had a telephone. I could see the endless black cables connecting us all over the world. They originated in my house, continued underground, merged, crossed each other, lay in parallel conduits on the bottom of the ocean, hid under roads, hung off electrical poles, rose, and penetrated through basements and walls like mysterious tentacles stretching to infinite ends.

I could call my father in Germany, if I wanted to, but I didn't. He knew I had moved to America, and for now I had nothing to say to him.

I could talk to my mother in Bistrița, and I did. I called her and found out that Adina had gone back to college.

"Good for her!" I exclaimed.

"She's missed a whole year," my mother complained, but I was used to her whining.

We talked about Grandmother, who was getting frail, and about Bistrița, where everything was always the same. I told her about our swimming pool and the plants in the garden. She sighed. I told her that Jonathan was away on business.

"Come visit me in America," I said.

"You're like your father," she said.

She was trying to make me see how self-centered I was. How, like my father, I had left her burdened and bound.

Jonathan called from Lima.

"I've started work on the studio," I said. "Progress is good."

He called a second time. The third time he called, he was on his way to Ecuador, the last stop before heading home. "I miss you," he said.

"I love you," I said.

Carlos called one afternoon. He knew Jonathan was traveling and was concerned about how I managed alone. His wife was visiting family in Kansas City. He had a babysitter at home. He was free that evening and thought we could dine together. A caring acquaintance, that's all. He knew of this place in La Jolla called the Brockton Villa, or this other French restaurant, Croce's, in the Gaslamp District, never mind the area's bad reputation since the food was so good.

"No, thank you," I said.

After hanging up, I realized I didn't know anybody in San Diego. I mean, besides Marybeth, and Juan, the gardener, and the contractors who now worked in the house, and perhaps the saleslady at Pier 1 who several days ago had been so nice to me. If I went there again, she'd recognize me, give me that friendly smile, and help me again. But she'd do that for anybody, wouldn't she?

In Bistriţa I had had relatives, friends, and acquaintances. As much as they had bored me sometimes, they had been there for me. And as much as I had thought I belonged someplace else, I had never been out of place with them. I had known people in school, at my grandfather's hospital, in the houses across the street. I had had neighbors who on occasion had seemed closer to me than my own family. Everything was close in Bistriţa. People lived on top of each other, and that proximity bred intimacy. That misery, that sweat and gossip, those people had been a part of me, woven within me without an effort, without me asking for it. They had formed the background that I carried with me and from which time had gradually disappeared. Everybody from my past was one now, like students in a black-and-white class photo. Mathew, the first boy to kiss me; Gabriel, who gave me art lessons, taught me to smoke, and took my virginity; Claudia, my best friend in high school; Jacob; Adina; my father, who left us; my mother; my grandparents; Pani; Mr. Moisil; Miss Diddieny.

What would they say if they saw me in my new BMW?

What would Gabriel say? Would he like my studio? Not now, when it wasn't ready, but later, once the roof got set in, the bay window installed, the curtains hung, the plumbing finished, the easels set up, and the canvases placed on the walls—the new canvases I would paint with Marybeth basking in the California sun, with Juan and his plants and the swimming pool as a backdrop. My new canvases with blue sky surrounding Mount Helix. Where was Gabriel now?

Lydia must be back in Romania, happily married. She must be living with Nick in his little room, sharing that bed that I had slept in on my way to Bistrița.

I picked up the phone.

"May I speak to Lydia?" I said.

"She's not here," answered a voice I didn't recognize.

"This is Miriam Sommer."

"Oh, from America, yes. I'm Boris Vieru."

"Mr. Vieru, hello. You are their friend who traveled to Ulan Bator."

"Yes," Mr. Vieru said.

"Well, are you visiting?"

"No, me and Tatiana are here to take care of the grandmother."

"And where is everybody else?"

"They're in Sinaia. The young ones are leaving for Israel. Their visas came through, and they went to the mountains for a week with Olga and Constantin, to be together as a family for the last time. To cry and to say their good-byes."

"For the last time as a family? They went there to cry? Mr. Vieru, what are you saying? This is cause for celebration, not tears."

"Maybe, but it's hard for the parents who are left behind."

I felt his sadness travel through the phone wire at the bottom of the ocean, and yet I felt good. Things would work out in the end for my friends.

—⊗∞⊗—

Jonathan called from the airport in Quito. They had just started boarding. He had a gift for me in a large box that was being loaded onto the plane at that moment. He hoped I would like it, but no, he wouldn't tell me over the phone what it was. It was a surprise, and he'd be home very soon.

Marybeth moved back to her room in the servants' quarters. I rang Remy, my new cook, and went over dinner arrangements with him. He was from Majorca, a short, burly man who suggested something Spanish—tapas for starters, followed by roasted pork tenderloin on a bed of saffron rice and mushrooms, a salad, iced sparkling water, and a red Rioja wine. For dessert he proposed a peach tart and a mango sorbet, coffee, and a sweet wine called Lastau, an East India sherry from Spain.

"With his sherry Mr. Sommer might enjoy a cigar," Remy added.

In my mind Spanish and Mexican dishes were more or less the same, and I hoped the food would remind Jonathan of his youth and the ranch near Oaxaca, take the edge off his travel fatigue, and make him feel happy to be home. What had Doña Alexandra served Jonathan before leading him to her four-poster bed?

I decided we would eat in the sunroom and had Remy reposition the armchair and love seat at the two adjacent sides of the table, as I had seen it in Ingmar Bergman's *Scenes from a Marriage*. Marybeth brought a white tablecloth, candles, decorative dishes, and table settings for us.

Jonathan came from the airport in a van. He and the van driver carried a large crate inside the house and placed it on the marble floor in the foyer. My name and our San Diego address were printed on three sides in indigo-colored letters. Juan brought tools from his shed and opened the crate. Set over a frame that looked like a side horse used in gymnastics was a riding saddle embellished with elaborate leatherwork and encrusted with silver ornaments.

I clasped my hands over my mouth.

"Do you like it?" Jonathan asked in an eager voice that sounded unsure.

"Yes," I said, not very convincingly. "What is it?"

"It's a real cowboy saddle," Jonathan said. "I bought it for you, and I hope when you go riding again you'll try it. Take a look at the tree base. They use synthetic materials these days to build the tree, but this one is wood lined with sheepskin on the underside to prevent chafing. It's the way they used to make them when I started riding in Mexico. The weight gets spread evenly on the back of the horse and gives you a large seat, big enough for two people. See the distance between the pommel and cantle?"

I must have seemed lost, because he pointed at the front and the back of the saddle.

"It comes with stirrups and fenders, but they are folded underneath for now. And you have to use this," he added, leaning into the crate and retrieving a dark-brown and white checkered blanket in a transparent plastic wrapping. "Well, do you like it?"

"I think so, Jonathan. It's beautiful." My eyes fell on a brown cylinder wrapped in dark leather with a rounded top rising at a slight incline from the part at the front of the saddle Jonathan had called the pommel. The cylinder was about one inch in diameter and five inches tall. "What's this?" I asked.

"It's the horn," Jonathan said, "mostly used to place a lariat for roping cattle. But you wouldn't be roping cattle, would you?"

"Of course not." I smiled and added in a whisper, "It looks like a penis."

Juan was standing across the foyer, seemingly lost in another world.

Jonathan recovered quickly. "Did you miss me that much? Wishful thinking?" He had an amused look on his face. His features were drawn, as if he had lost weight on his trip, and his eyes were darkened by shadows.

I blushed. "Let's go to the sunroom, where *I* have a surprise for you," I said, and I turned to Juan. "Call Remy, and the two of you move my gift to my studio."

"Who's Remy?" Jonathan asked.

"The new cook I hired while you were away," I said, proud of my role as the lady of the house.

I took Jonathan's hand and led him upstairs.

While we were admiring the saddle in the foyer, Remy had had the chance to plate the tapas on small serving dishes, between roses in porcelain bud vases and gold ball-shaped candles. At the last moment I had asked him to fix an ice-cold martini for Jonathan and a Manhattan for me, and our drinks were ready as well. The rest of the dishes and wines waited on a sideboard.

Against a lavender-blue sky, the sun was starting to set over Point Loma.

Jonathan took a sip of his drink. "Is all this Remy's doing?" he asked, visibly pleased and pointing at the table.

I nodded.

"I want to meet him."

"Sorry, I gave him the evening off. I'll serve you dinner, and you'll meet Remy tomorrow. Jonathan, I want us to be alone."

"Let me take a quick shower," he said. "Then we'll drink to being just the two of us, and to great things to come."

I found matches on the counter and lit the candles. The white dinner plates had gold circles around the rim, and the cutlery was silver and gold. They reminded me of my family's antique Japanese tea set with gold decorations, which we took out every time we had important guests. Now that seemed modest and far away.

While Jonathan showered, I changed into a gold sleeveless top that matched the gold accents on the table, a short black leather skirt, and black heels. I wore the Star of David I had from Jonathan, a gold watch, and a gold cuff bracelet with matching earrings.

The way I remembered it, in *Scenes from a Marriage*, the couple first ate a lavish meal; then they argued and then had makeup sex on the love seat. The difference was that Jonathan and I were not married, and instead of the bleak Swedish landscape, we were enjoying the warmth of the setting sun. I wondered if Jonathan would follow the script. He looked tired. Who knew what he had endured on his trip.

When he returned, his face was more relaxed, smoother, and more youthful. He was wearing a burgundy bathrobe with narrow white stripes along the lapels. A white towel was wrapped around his neck, his wet hair combed close to the skull. On his bare feet he had dark slippers. He lowered himself onto the love seat and crossed his legs.

I sat in the armchair. "Did you shave?" I asked him.

He rubbed his hand along his jaw. "No. It's sandpaper."

"That's OK. I like your rugged feel, very sexy."

"You do?" he asked and smiled. "When I put this robe on, I thought I looked like Hugh Hefner." He leaned forward, ate one tapa of lobster tail, and took a sip from his martini. The towel around his neck came undone, and he set it on the armrest.

"So, Hugh," I said, smiling in turn, "are you wearing anything underneath that bathrobe?"

"Come and check," Jonathan said, patting the space next to him on the love seat.

I moved over, slipped my hand under the flaps of his robe, and kissed him. He had just brushed his teeth, and his mouth smelled of mint and the ocean. He grew hard in my hand, and when I thought he was ready, I got up and started undressing. I could have done it quickly or partially, but I took my time and undressed all the way, enjoying the anticipation, the spectacle. I realized I should have arranged for music, but I hadn't, so I moved and danced in total silence.

We were surrounded by glass walls, and the light was crepuscular.

I untied my ponytail and shook my head, allowing my long hair to cascade on both sides of my face and flow freely, dark and shiny. My skirt came off and landed in a corner. I removed my top, my bra, my heels, my Star of David, my wristwatch, my earrings, and my bracelet. I wanted nothing to remain on me, nothing to separate me from him.

He watched.

My skin was white as milk. My nipples were hard. I felt moisture inside my panties, and slowly I rolled them down.

He took me on his lap, facing him, my legs wrapped around his middle. He kept my upper body at a small distance, his arms stretched, his palms touching my breasts. For as long as I could, I held his stare.

The sunset vanished.

"Let's eat," he said when we were done. "I'm hungry."

I walked to the side counter and grabbed the wine. Suddenly, moving naked through the sunroom felt wrong. It felt like swimming in a huge aquarium and being watched by people who walked by and looked through glass panels. It felt like being exposed. One window was slightly open, and on the table the candles flickered. By now, the sky was dark, and lights were being turned on in the city. Where the ocean had been, there was nothing at all but the reflections of the lights on the bridge and the ships. I could still distinguish the edge of our house and the plastic patch over the wall to my studio. The contractors were long gone for the day, and I knew that nobody could see us unless they climbed in a tree or used an airlift or scaffold. Yet the feeling was there, slightly awkward and slightly exciting. I don't know why I thought of my mother.

As I arranged the food on the table, I caught a reflection of myself thrown by the burning candles onto the window. I checked the outline of my body, brought a hand to one of my breasts, and touched it.

Jonathan caught my eye. "You look pretty."

"How was your trip?" I asked, wrapping his towel around me.

"Long," he answered.

We started eating.

"I know it was long. I waited for you."

He didn't say anything, and I continued, "Why did you have to go to South America? You never really told me."

"You know why. It was business."

"And what did you do there? Any interesting sightseeing?"

"Miriam, I've been enough times to South America not to have to play tourist. I had meetings. Business meetings. I trade and make deals with people."

"What kind of deals? Please tell me."

"There is nothing to tell, really. Let me put it this way—as a result of this trip, my bank account will do better."

"You mean our bank account?" I said softly.

"When I travel," he said, "I always keep an eye out for special bargains. That's how I found your saddle. I bought it from Peshea Calare, the master saddle maker. I have known him for at least twenty years. He lived in Mexico for a time and moved to Ecuador with his business. I couldn't say no when I had the opportunity."

"So my gift was a bargain."

"Yes, but a great one, a true collector's item. And I bought you something else." He took a small box wrapped in shiny red paper out of his bathrobe pocket and offered it to me.

Inside was a ring, a sapphire and platinum solitaire.

"For our engagement?" I said, hoping ever so slightly and knowing the answer.

"No, no engagement. Just something I liked and I thought would look nice on your finger."

I slipped it on and moved my hand to the candle. The stone caught the light. "Thank you," I said. "Delicate."

He nodded. "I got myself a gift, too, a gold pocket watch with rubies, on a heavy chain, beautiful and useless. I don't know if I'll ever wear it. A self-gratifying gift, pretty much like the ring on your finger."

I felt chilly.

My clothes were strewn all over the floor, but the evening was only beginning. I didn't want to get dressed, and there was no sense in showing I was disappointed. I didn't expect a ring at all, a gift I liked more than the saddle. And he had thought of me on his trip—that was obvious. I understood that both gifts were valuable.

"Jonathan, I'm glad you're back," I told him.

"I *always* come back," he said.

"With a saddle." I laughed.

"Sometimes with a saddle."

I allowed a short pause for effect. "Tonight I rode you quite well, without a saddle," I said.

Like a bear, he shuffled on the love seat, rearranging his bathrobe. "You did," he acknowledged. "You did, and I liked it."

He liked it. That's what I wanted—for him to be crazy over me and like it. I needed him to like it more than anything else, more than ever before, more than with any other woman. I needed him to never stop wanting me, always want more, and *always* come back. I loved him, and I didn't feel guilty. If there was even a hint of a quid pro quo in my thoughts, so be it. He was a businessman. Give love and get love in return—the ultimate deal. It wasn't unreasonable.

We had sex that evening again, and we did it again the next morning. We did it the following day, and the day after. I asked if he liked it every time, and he said yes to me, again and again, obsessively.

The cancer-research fundraiser was at the Getty Villa in Malibu. We stayed overnight in Beverly Hills. Jonathan wore his tux, and I wore a Carolina Herrera strapless black gown with pearl and gold beading around the bust. As soon as we entered the private dining room, my eyes fell on Carlos, who was talking to a small group of people.

"What's *he* doing here?" I whispered to Jonathan.

"Carlos? He's my lawyer."

I went straight to our table and sat down. Carlos came to say hi. I wasn't sure if he chose the moment because Jonathan was somewhere else. He pulled out Jonathan's chair and sat next to me.

"Miriam," he said, "you look ravishing."

His white dinner jacket contrasted with his dark skin and hair and his bright red bow tie.

"Thank you," I said. "You don't look too shabby yourself."

There were people at our table, and Carlos drew his chair closer and lowered his voice. "You know, that evening I ended up inviting another friend, and we had a good time. Too bad you couldn't make it. But Jonathan will be on travel again."

"Jonathan's not going anywhere," I said.

"Oh, he'll go somewhere, you'll see."

"How do you know?" I asked bitterly. "Is it because you're working for him?"

He picked a dessert fork from the table, and holding it with two fingers, he moved it from right to left and up and down through the air, like a child pretending the object he's holding is a plane. It was an odd gesture.

"I'm not working for your husband," he said, choosing his words. "But he's the most important client I have."

"He's not my husband," I said.

Carlos pierced me with his dark eyes. "And don't you think I know that?"

"Apparently not. But if you do, then maybe you're the one who told him not to marry me."

"Miriam, don't be silly. You bring value to him. You're his beautiful trophy, and your husband likes showing off."

My mother always said that a dog wouldn't bite the hand that feeds him, but Carlos seemed different. Maybe he couldn't help it, being a very peculiar dog.

"You know what?" I said. "Until now I didn't mention our phone conversation to *my husband*, but perhaps I should."

"You wouldn't want to do anything of the sort."

"I wouldn't? Excuse me, why not?"

"You are smarter than that."

I knew our conversation was very close to the edge. He was aggressive, yet I didn't feel threatened. On the contrary, I thought it was useful.

"Carlos," I whispered, "what's Jonathan's net worth?"

"What, don't you know?"

"I don't, and I would like you to tell me."

He looked pensive. "Of course you would, but you see, it is complicated."

"You're his lawyer, so simplify it for me. Does he have five million...ten... twenty?"

He shook his head. "My God, you truly have no idea...OK. Let me say it this way. If Jonathan wanted to spend ten million dollars a year, each year from now on for the rest of his life, he could do it without making a dent."

I wasn't a financial whiz, but I had read somewhere that well-invested money yielded a return, maybe 10 or 12 or 15 percent. I chose 10 percent because it was easy to calculate. So if Jonathan had $10 million a year in interest, his net worth could be as high as $100 million.

Carlos set the fork on the table, and I looked across the room, hoping not to show how perturbed I was. Then I heard Jonathan's voice.

We turned.

Jonathan was standing behind us, smiling, his tux jacket unbuttoned, champagne glass in his hand.

Carlos winked. "Hello, Jonathan."

"Carlos," Jonathan said.

During dinner Jonathan jumped to his feet to greet people, walked with them to other parts of the room, talked to them, smiled, and patted them on the back. A few times he introduced me to some of them, important contacts, I guessed.

Marina Carafolli was a slim, blond woman who sat with her husband across the table from us. The low-cut neckline of her silk dress displayed a bony, unadorned chest. First I thought she was my age, but we started talking, and I found out that she was in her thirties and had a five-year-old son.

Marina's husband, Tony, never left her side. He was a real-estate developer who knew Jonathan from political and charitable events. He didn't say much. Marina told me he was second-generation Italian, while she was a mixed breed—Hungarian on her mother's side, Dutch and Irish on her father's. It was the Hungarian heritage that attracted me to her. I told her I was from Transylvania, where many Hungarians lived. I'm not sure she cared, but I added that Jonathan spoke the language a little bit. She was a fine arts professor who had started her teaching career at UCLA, where she used to have a Romanian teaching assistant. His name was Nelu, and my accent reminded her of him. I thought of Gabriel and became curious, not that Nelu could be Gabriel, but that they might know of each other somehow.

"How old is Nelu?" I asked.

"He must be thirty-five."

That was close enough. I smiled, and she smiled in return.

"I am an artist, too," I said. "A painter. I'm having my studio built and intend to be painting a lot."

"That's very exciting. Did you know we're practically neighbors?" she asked.

"We are?"

"Yes. A few years ago Tony got a new job, and we moved from LA to San Diego. We settled in your area, on the other side of Lake Murray. I hated leaving UCLA, but when Bobby was born, I became a full-time mom. Eventually I found a part-time position at the University of San Diego, and I've worked there ever since. By the way, we have a Georgia O'Keeffe exhibit right now. Come and visit. I bet you would like it."

I had no idea who Georgia O'Keeffe was. "For sure," I said.

We exchanged phone numbers, and she talked to me about how interesting the Etruscan artifacts in the main Getty gallery were.

Jonathan and I must have missed them on the way in.

I complained as soon as we got in the limo. "You left me alone the whole evening," I said.

"Not entirely true," Jonathan said. "I introduced you to Billy Pratt, one of my accountants. I introduced you to my former real-estate broker and to his wife, and to Kenneth Antonio Topaz, my partner in one of my South American ventures. And you met the governor, too."

"The lieutenant governor," I said.

"You're an enigma, you know."

"Enigma?" It was an odd word.

We were on Pacific Coast Highway driving toward Santa Monica. Jonathan took a slim can of Coke from the car refrigerator and opened it with a fizz. A few drops spilled on the sleeve of his tux.

"Damn," he said. There were glasses on a tray, but he didn't use one. "I don't get you," he said. "One moment you complain you don't know what I do, and when I take you with me, you complain you are bored. I was working tonight, that's all."

"This was work? I thought we went because you wanted to contribute in memory of Doña Alexandra."

"That too," Jonathan said. "But it was also networking."

"If you paid a little attention to me while networking, I'd be happier."

"Miriam, I do pay attention to you. Tonight you wore a new elegant dress, had dinner at a fancy place, met the Carafollis, and spoke with Carlos. What was wrong with tonight?"

"Carlos makes me uncomfortable," I said. "And what's with his bow ties?"

"His trademark," Jonathan said.

"Whatever," I said. I shifted as far away from him as I could and looked out. There were lights shining on us from restaurants, hotels, and villas on the right. Jonathan could buy any of them with his money. The two of us were like characters from *Gatsby*, the movie. He even looked a little like Redford, I thought. He looked like a million bucks.

I could feel his gaze starting to explore my body.

"You're beautiful," he said.

He said that often.

"Did you like it?" I asked.

"I did."

He was on his back on the king-size hotel bed, his head on a large pillow, apparently trying to sleep. His tux and my Carolina Herrera gown were on the floor.

I pulled myself onto him.

"But did you *really* like it?"

"I really, really liked it."

"Tell me, which part was the best?"

"Oh, Miriam, I liked everything."

I made a long face he couldn't see. I stretched and turned on the light on my nightstand. "Open your eyes," I said.

He opened them.

"You're always like this. You never share your feelings. You don't tell me anything, and it makes me sad."

We were silent for a while, and I asked again. "Tell me, do you really think I am beautiful?"

"You are," he said in a whisper.

"Am I the most beautiful woman in your life?"

"Yes, Miriam, you're the most beautiful."

He seemed annoyed, just a little—like he'd done this before and he'd do it again, but only not to get me upset.

"You say so," I said, "but what do you like the most about me? Do you like my face?"

"I like your face."

"Do you like my eyes, my lips?"

"I like your lips."

"But you don't like my eyes."

"I like them."

"Then say it."

He did.

"Do you like my skin?"

"I like your skin."

"Don't you think it's too white? You know, people with a fair complexion like mine can't sunbathe. I can't go to the beach with you or to the pool because if I stayed in the sun for just a few minutes, I'd burn. I really would. And I wouldn't get a tan; I'd get freckles."

"I'd love your freckles," he said.

"Would you? Really? And how do you like my hair?"

He extended his arm and caressed my hair, thin strands floating through the air and cracking with static electricity. I climbed halfway over him, moved my head, and allowed my hair to cover his face, his neck, and his chest. Then I slid off and kneeled on the bed, exposing my upper body.

"Do you like my breasts?"

"Aha."

"Don't you think they're too small?" I pouted, looking down at my breasts—they were actually large—and pointing at them with my finger. "I don't like that they're so round. They look like two apples. And they are unequal. See, this one is smaller, and my areolae are pale. I'd like them to be more like pears, with dark, conical nipples."

"I like apples better than pears," he said.

"Do you?"

"I do."

"And how do you know?"

"Power of imagination," he said.

"Jonathan, you're making me jealous," I said.

"Don't be. I'll never betray you," he said.

I moved the pointing finger lower on my body. "Tell me, how do you like my stomach?" I asked.

"Sexy."

"And how about my belly button? You know, when I was a little girl, I used to pick my belly button. There was lint in there sometimes, and my mother would tell me it was a nasty habit."

"I love nasty habits," Jonathan said, by now alerted by the direction our game was taking.

My finger dropped to the dark pubic hair, but I didn't ask any questions, as if I had gone far enough, as if going further would be crossing a line I didn't want to cross.

Chapter 6

FLOWERS

After three months my studio was ready. All I needed were painting supplies, sketchpads, canvases, frames, and two or three easels. No artist in Romania had a studio like mine, no artist in America. It was spacious. The light was ideal. The ceiling was high, and the windows opened to a wide panorama. Two oversized vases—filled by Juan every morning with fresh irises, tulips, and roses from the greenhouse—occupied the low windowsill. I gave up the idea of hanging curtains, and stored the fabric away.

Before the contractors left, I had them build a stand for my saddle and place it in the studio. It turned out taller and sturdier than the original support, but not so tall as the pair of horses Jonathan kept at the ranch. A step covered in felt and a polished handrail assisted with mounting. I imagined myself riding on that saddle like Lady Godiva.

In one corner of the studio, the bathtub had been replaced by a Jacuzzi. White marble steps led to it. After soaking in the hot bubbly water, Jonathan and I would stumble out of it and collapse on the steps in a wicked embrace. I decided to place soft, colorful rugs over the steps and beyond, as in a sultan's harem. Persian rugs were embargoed, and I found hand-woven Romanian wool rugs that looked as good to my untrained eye. They reminded me of home, and they were cheap—not even twelve hundred apiece. I bought half a dozen of them.

Just like that, Jonathan said he had to go to Las Vegas. He didn't invite me and didn't say how long he'd be away. I resented that, but I told him I didn't mind, because I had to start painting. It was my feeble attempt to show him some spine.

Jonathan's departure gave me a good excuse to get in touch with Marina. She was glad to hear from me. We talked about her art students and the classes she taught and agreed to meet the next day on campus. I was hoping it would bring memories from my time at the University of Haifa.

That evening I had dinner with Marybeth, and I suggested she stay the night. "You'd be doing me a favor," I said.

I blamed myself for not having asked Jonathan to move her permanently into the house, and for possibly making her feel as if her place was with the servants.

"Soon," I said, "when my studio is ready, I'll ask you to pose for me."

We turned on the TV and watched *Starsky & Hutch*.

"You're anxious when Mr. Sommer's not here," she said when the show ended.

"A little," I said. "Maybe because he's not telling me much."

"Don't be. He loves to gamble. Miss Miriam, I'm not a nosy person, and it's none of my business, but I think you should know he's been married before. I'm not sure if he's divorced, and I heard that she lives in Lincoln, Nebraska."

I looked at her, surprised.

"The wife," she added.

I said, "That Mexican woman's no longer his wife. They'd been together less than two years, and their marriage was a mistake."

"Well then," she said, "you know more than I do."

The O'Keeffe exhibit occupied several rooms. Reproductions in simple black frames with nonglare glass hung on white walls illuminated by track lights, with printed captions pinned underneath. Not knowing what to expect, I started reading the captions and quickly got bored. There were bizarre desert scenes, bones, and flowers, some painted at close range and reminding me of the macro photography class I had taken at the University of Haifa. Marina, who obviously had seen the exhibit before, walked by my side and watched me. I thought she wanted me to comment, but I had little to say. Yet the more I allowed myself to linger, the more I sensed the surprising hand of the artist pulling me into the universe hidden beyond the innocent landscapes and luscious flowers. That hand was undeniably strong. It had meaning and purpose, and slowly I moved into a world of symbols, at once beautiful and odd.

In one room, two men and a woman, all young, stood talking. They were actually whispering, yet they seemed loud. The men shook with silent laughter until one pushed the other with a shriek. I looked at them with disdain.

"Children," Marina said when we left the room. "Most of them are reacting this way."

I shrugged.

"They're amused and intrigued," she continued. "They come because of what they heard. Flower petals like genitalia, you know."

"They have a point," I said.

"Do they? And do you think it is wrong?"

We were walking between buildings toward the cafeteria. The weather was mild.

"No," I said. "Nothing an artist does is wrong. I had a friend once who drew body parts—pages and pages of beautifully executed sexual organs, mostly aroused."

"And your friend was a man."

"He was."

"Georgia O'Keeffe is both subtle and bold," Marina said. "She's a great feminist, and her images stay with you."

At the university store, I bought supplies for my studio, several Georgia O'Keeffe albums, and one of her biographies. Later, as I read more about her, I became absorbed with her work and her life. My loneliness was reason to ponder. Like me, she had started painting early in life, and then she had given it up. She was uncomfortable in the mimetic tradition, I read. My reasons for giving up painting were less clear. Then O'Keeffe started painting again, which I was considering also. I was ready for it. She got involved with Alfred

Stieglitz, a married man twenty years her senior. At least Jonathan, as far as I hoped, was divorced. Stieglitz and O'Keeffe lived in Manhattan, where he had a well-known gallery. I surmised he was rich. They spent summers at Lake George. In her paintings of the place, I saw colors and hues that reminded me of Bistriţa. I could almost smell the air in her paintings—that's how good O'Keeffe was.

Living in New York, in that exciting environment, inspired her to start painting again. So could I, even without the external stimulus. I had strength.

I had fallen in love with her flowers and decided I could paint them myself. I had the bouquets Juan brought to my studio, but I didn't want to be an imitator. I could start with flowers until I regained my touch and then move to Gabriel's method with the human body. I could do Marybeth's ears, eyebrows, lips, and breasts, all as if seen through a magnifying glass. I had read *that* about Georgia O'Keeffe. I had memorized the names of some of her flowers and plants: calico, jack-in-the-pulpit, jimsonweed, amaryllis, morning glory, and bleeding hearts. Others I knew from before. I spent time studying her Black Irises, especially *Black Iris III*. It was a perfect representation of the center of an iris, the purity of it. I didn't think she intended for it to have a double meaning. She simply painted the way she saw. As Stieglitz had put it, her work was sincere, but the critics were hateful. They always found something to say. I, for one, preferred painting people to still life. O'Keeffe must have been very shy. Stieglitz had photographed her hundreds of times, and when I studied some of the photographs, I realized that she and I looked alike. A little. We shared those elongated features that people called elegant—long narrow faces, small chins, thin noses, long necks. We had charcoal hair. We were slim. I thought I was taller than she was but couldn't be sure. Her eyes seemed blue. My eyes were sky blue, but in a black-and-white photograph they would appear darker. Where we differed was the countenance. She seemed severe, profound. Unhappy, perhaps. Her skin had a grainy texture to it. I took her photographs to the mirror. My skin was white with slightly pink undertones. My lips were sensuous. I saw myself as playful, as healthy and warm.

A good thing, besides her success as an artist, was that Stieglitz had married her in the end. There was hope.

I read that their marriage had been *a collusion*, a system of deals and trade-offs. They avoided confrontation, and with Jonathan that's what I needed to do.

With Jonathan I needed to take it slow. I needed to understand him, to plan.

I went back to the exhibit and to see Marina at her house.

"O'Keeffe is the originator of female iconography," Marina said. "She has a place at *The Dinner Party* by Judy Chicago, near Virginia Woolf."

I felt as if I was coming from a different world.

"Feminist art in the Age of Revolution," Marina continued. "You know, there are many facets to feminism. It's so much more than free love, bra burning, or the right to vote."

In the world I came from, free love wasn't a concept. Women did it, if they did it, because it was in their genes. Ceaușescu had forbidden abortions. My mother had worked her entire life. She had raised three children on her own. There was nothing revolutionary about that. Had she had a choice, she'd have looked the other way when my father cheated on her. Forgiving him would have been the practical way out. I despised my mother for begging him to return, and now I also understood her. It wasn't about the equality of the sexes. As I saw it, it was normal that a woman wanted to be a pilot, or to fight in war side by side with the men. But deep inside, women were like O'Keeffe's flowers, and men had to treat them as such. A woman was delicate and fragrant and hidden by layer upon layer of petals. She needed to be tended to, nourished, moved away from the sun and the wind, dressed, undressed, caressed, spoken to, and told she was beautiful.

That's what I expected Jonathan to do.

I didn't have much to say to Marina.

I went to the university library and leafed through some books. I looked up Judy Chicago. I read about Mina Loy, her disenchantment with Giovanni Papini, and her *Songs to Joannes*. I read about Emma Goldman and discovered Erica Jong. On a shelf I found books on sexology, and I took out one of them. It was funny being at the university library behind a desk stacked with volumes and volumes, hiding and reading my book on sexology. The tone of the book was matter of fact, clinical, as if sex was only a series of positions and moves. Understanding anatomy seemed all that it took. I read about language during sex, dirty language, that is. I found some new tricks, but mostly it was stuff that I knew.

When O'Keeffe was younger, she, too, must have thought about sex. Like me, it had to have been on her mind. Critics said she adopted *precisionism* in her painting. Only by selection, they said, by elimination, could one get to the essence. I, too, needed to eliminate a few things. Like sand, my life was escaping me through my fingers. Here I was in my dreams, the way I wanted to be tomorrow, and here was tomorrow, my life turning out in a different way. Here I was later, thinking about my future again, my wishes altered, and my life taking another turn on its own.

When I was an adolescent, I thought I had found my life's calling. To paint I would sell my soul. I was convinced that by age twenty I would turn into this famous artist whom people traveled to see. My artwork would be expensive. It would be original yet rooted in tradition, abstract yet identifiable. I thought I would be Rembrandt and Van Gogh mixed in one, Picasso and Giacometti. Then I gave up because painting was exhausting and because when Gabriel left me I was drained of any creative energy. I decided to immigrate to Israel, to take life into my own hands. I thought people would admire me for my courage and independence, but I didn't know what I was getting myself into. Maybe I did it for the shock value of it. Except for my mother and grandmother, nobody really cared. Even my mother was more concerned about herself than about my future. I walked through the streets of Bistrița imagining a new world that was perfect, a world where I blossomed. Later I walked through the streets of Haifa finding signs of a new life here and there, not sad and not disappointing, but far from perfect. In Haifa I had to fend for myself—I was entirely on my own. Instead of a dream, my new life had become a string of prosaic activities: school, menial jobs, supermarket shopping, phone bills, my rent. Zvi Rave helped me out. I wasn't proud of my relationship with him, though I wasn't ashamed of it either. My strongest ties remained in my past. I thought of my father. He had *given me up* and moved away. He moved on and never looked back. I wondered if *his* life had escaped him through *his* fingers, and I swore I would never beg.

Then I met Jonathan and allowed myself to dream again.

Now, at age twenty-five, here I was. My studio was ready, a studio I had never expected to have. My life had taken over for me. The studio had materialized out of a passing comment over drinks by the pool—out of the whim of one moment. Out of too much money and nothing to do. But I didn't feel bad. I deserved to have my studio, along with my love and insecurities, my flowers, my Jacuzzi, and my mock oriental carpets. I had my new saddle, too. On it, I could spend hours riding my dreams.

I resolved to clasp my fingers and join my palms. My hands would form a perfect vessel without any cracks. The sand of my life would stop pouring away.

I was a woman, a flower, and I had a lot to give.

Suddenly I knew what awaited us.

Jonathan returned from Las Vegas and told me how much money he had lost—enough to buy a nice car.

"Why do you gamble?" I asked.

"I like it," he said.

He liked me also. Our marriage would be *a collusion*, but we had to get married, first.

We returned to some kind of a routine. Unlike before, he started spending time in his study, or office, as he called it when we talked about it. He was working; he made sure I knew. When his door was half open, I could hear him talk to people, sometimes barking into the phone. He had binders on shelves and dark-green manila folders hanging inside metal cabinets. I decided that one day, when he was traveling, I would look through his things. A pretty woman came to organize his paperwork and take dictation from time to time. His secretary, he said. I wasn't sure if I liked her or not.

When he worked, I *worked* also. I went to my studio and found things to do, drawing and painting a little bit. I was amazed by how much I remembered. After an interruption of seven years, it was as if I had stopped yesterday. And so I deluded myself back into liking to paint. I rediscovered that impression of self-fulfillment when something came out right, or at least when it seemed right to me. I was happy when people who looked at my doodles said something nice. I began with exercises such as copying from an album. Later, Juan brought me a wheelbarrow from his shed and a pair of old boots. I drew them. I tried a few watercolors—flowers, vases, and apples—still life. Marybeth posed for me a few times. Marina came to visit, and when she saw my beautiful studio, she gasped. Yet every time Jonathan wanted us to go somewhere, overnight or for lunch, I would happily lay down my pencils and brushes and jump at the opportunity.

Chapter 7

ISRAEL

Jonathan called me to his office and asked me to sit down.

"Miriam," he said, "we need to get you a permanent residence here, a green card." He had contacted an immigration attorney, through Carlos, and found out that the best way to do that was for me to return to Israel and apply from there. It would be an easy trip, and it wouldn't take long—a few weeks or a month, two months tops. I still had the apartment in Haifa. I could travel to the Negev and do some desert paintings, like Georgia O'Keeffe.

"I could paint in Temecula or Death Valley," I said.

"Your tourist visa will expire. You don't have a choice."

"How come you didn't think of this until now?"

"I did, but first I wanted to make sure you were comfortable here. How come *you* didn't think about it?"

He wasn't fair. "I wanted you to ask me to stay," I whispered. "I thought we would get married. Eventually. I could get the green card through marriage, you know."

"I'm not the marrying type."

"But, Jonathan, why not?"

"I told you from the very beginning I don't want to get married," he said. We fell silent for a very long time.

A framed black-and-white photograph of Jonathan on horseback stood on his huge desk, and a second one, in color, of the two of us on the Tel Aviv beach in front of the Savoy. I remembered the limousine driver who took that photograph, and the moment when I removed my hat to show my full face. Jonathan had sent a copy of that second photograph to Leah in Israel, as a memento.

Now I hoped Jonathan would speak first. When he didn't, I asked, "Do you love me?"

"I do."

"Will you come with me to Israel?"

"Not this time. It's a short trip, Miriam, but if it gets extended for any reason, I'll come."

"You promise?"

"I promise."

"And you can't arrange for the green card from here?"

"No, Miriam, I really can't. There are things money can't buy."

"But couldn't you try?" I insisted. "I love you, and I don't want to be without you, even for a short time."

He held my gaze.

"I love you," I said again.

"Look. I've already asked if we could get you the green card from here and was told it would be an uphill battle not worth the effort or time. Take the money you need, and have fun in Israel while we wait. You'd enjoy a short visit to Israel, wouldn't you?"

I had no reason to doubt him. If he didn't want me with him for the long run, he wouldn't have me apply for the green card. And even though parting with him even for a short time saddened me, he was right that I would enjoy the trip. The more the idea took shape in my mind, the more excited I got. It was time to be daring, I thought.

"Jonathan," I said, "how much money do you have?"

"What a question," he said.

I gave him a look. "You don't want to tell me. OK. But please tell me this: if I were naked, would you have enough to cover me in hundred-dollar bills head to toe?"

He laughed a nervous laugh, myriad small creases closing around his eyes. "I certainly would."

———❈———

On the eve of my departure, we were sitting together on the love seat in the sunroom. He caressed my hair and kissed me lightly on my lips.

"I want you to miss me, and think of me," I said.

"I'll think of you every day."

In the distance a ship was sailing across the bay.

"When I come back," I said, "even if we don't get married, could we live like husband and wife?"

"Don't we do that right now?"

"I want children," I said. "A little boy or a girl."

"It would make me so happy," he said.

———❈———

After five months in America, Israel seemed smaller and more *oriental* than I remembered, like a human anthill beaten down by the sun. People were everywhere, in the airport, in the streets, and in the little shops around Merkaz HaCarmel in Haifa. I had always enjoyed the bustle of crowds, but for the first time I felt that too many people in one place bothered me. That had to be the effect of my sheltered life in America.

In Israel, I felt aloof and detached, yet I enjoyed that everything around me was cozy and familiar. I was in the same time zone with Romania, and people spoke different languages everywhere, a fact that, strangely, made me feel comfortable.

Mrs. Shames was waiting for me.

"You said you'd be back, Miri."

"It's for a short while, Mrs. Shames."

I had called her beforehand, and she had promised to have my apartment dusted and aired.

The driver carried my luggage upstairs. Even though the windows were open, it felt stuffy inside, bearing no resemblance to the air-conditioned house in San Diego.

Early the next morning, in Tel Aviv, I met Ben Pinkas. He was my immigration attorney. He prepped me on the green card application process and assured me of his loyalty to Carlos, our mutual friend. We went to the American embassy, and I signed a few papers. The clerk said it might take a few months, but Ben assured me it would not be long.

We were sitting at her kitchen table.

"Typical Jonathan," Leah griped. "My brother, he'll always send you *alone* to deal with your problems."

I felt a need to defend him. "He's busy, Leah. You have no idea…Besides, I'm at home in Israel. I like being here."

"And how do you like the United States?"

"I like it there, too," I said. "Most of all I love being with Jonathan."

"We've been to the States only once," Leah said. "It's too big; you can't possibly visit the whole country. We've made it to both coasts—first New York, and then Yosemite, San Francisco, and San Diego."

"You've seen more than I've seen."

"Maybe, but we've seen it differently. The boys loved it, while I felt out of place, kind of. I missed the coziness of Israel, and the nuances."

"You think there are no *nuances* in America? Come and visit again. You'll stay with us, and we'll show you around. We have plenty of space."

"I know you do. I don't understand why people need such huge homes in America."

The first time I met Leah, I had felt scrutinized by her. This time was different. We were family now, and I saw no reason to hold back.

"Leah," I said, "Jonathan and I are planning to have children soon, and we'll put that big house of ours to good use."

My stay in Israel turned out to be a series of lazy, long, lingering days. I missed my BMW, so I rented the most expensive four-door sedan Avis had in stock on HaHistadrut Avenue. It was a Peugeot 505 station wagon that could easily hold six and was known, they told me, for its handling. It drove like a tank, which was a welcome feeling on the hilly and often congested streets of Haifa.

"You should have rented an Audi," my friend Adrian said when we met.

It was obvious he was still very proud of his own Audi, but I didn't mind. Our cars in America were at least as fancy.

"Do you have any news from Lydia?" I asked.

"You just missed her," he said. "She came back to Israel with Nick, and they stayed with her parents. They have always intended to go to America, so they didn't stay long. They're in Greece now, waiting for their visas."

"Like me," I said, venturing a happy comment.

"Not quite," Adrian said. "Unlike you, they're in a refugee camp near Athens. Write to them; they'll be glad to hear from you."

"I will," I promised, but with all the time in the world, writing a letter didn't come easily. In the end I bought a simple postcard, scribbled a few lines on it, and asked them for their telephone number. Calling would be better, I thought.

Those days I was calling everybody, just as I did in America. No sense of being intimidated by long-distance charges.

I took my telephone to my window facing the bay, placed it in my lap, and called Jonathan late in the afternoon. The sun was setting over the Mediterranean, but in San Diego it was lunchtime. "The view of the sea reminds me of our home," I said.

We talked until night surrounded me, and his voice became my anchor in a world sunk in darkness.

In the mornings I called Pinkas. I asked for news from the embassy and insisted he do more.

I called my mother several times a week, more often than ever before, feeling close to her and yet holding back, as if the two of us were following two paths that would never merge. One time she handed the receiver to Jacob, who was visiting during a break from his studies.

"Miriam," he said, "I'm finishing my PhD, and I have to get out of here."

I understood him right away even though he had been deliberately vague, since phones were tapped in Romania. Whoever listened wouldn't know if Jacob wanted to get out of his mother's house, out of Bistriţa, or out of the country. He had never said such a thing to me before, and his words filled me with unexpected sweet hope. Since the day at the waterfall, I had looked up to him and had considered him my silent guardian. Now it was my turn. I had always known that eventually I would bring my family out of Romania, but of the four of them, for him I was the happiest.

Jonathan was supportive.

"Get your green card and you'll be able to help them."

"I don't think they want to come to America. Israel might be more suitable," I said.

"Tell them we'll help them get settled," Jonathan said.

My new wheels made me restless. I had never driven through Israel before, and I decided it was time to explore the country. Day trips, I said to myself, nothing fancy.

Turning left on Moriya took me to Ahuza. Continuing on Abba Hushi Avenue, I made it to the university. Beyond the campus was an open area covered by Mediterranean pines and sprawling bushes. I carried my easel out of the car, found a clearing, and painted. Farther yet were Isfiya and Daliat el Carmel, two Druze villages with century-old stone houses, and streets lined with souvenir shops, and produce stalls.

At the university cafeteria, where I stopped for tea, I ran into Judith and Mike. She and I had attended a painting seminar together the year before. Mike was her husband and a fellow student. They had been married for less than six months, but she was talking as if marriage was this vast No Man's Land where people forwent their dreams and ambitions. I wished I could share her opinion or argue the opposite, but I couldn't. Marriage was something I was only hoping for, not yet within reach. Mike wanted to become a TV producer, and Judith an editor or literary critic. Their friend Peter, an American from the Pittsburgh area, stopped at our table and joined the conversation.

They seemed elated to hear that I had a rented car and planned to take short trips through Israel.

Together we drove to the beaches along the Mediterranean coast, north to Acre and Nahariya, south to Neve Yam and Zichron Yaakov, to Caesarea and Netanya. My friends lay in the sun and splashed in the waves while I carefully placed myself under an umbrella with my hat on and made charcoal drawings of the people around me.

We drove to Masada, parked in the scorched parking lot at the base of the mountain, and climbed to the top of the cliffs of the Judean Desert. We toured the ruins on the plateau and read about the siege of Masada two thousand years ago, when 960 Jewish men, women, and children committed mass suicide rather than surrender to the Roman soldiers. It was too hot to draw or paint, and I took a few photos, testing my new camera. The Dead Sea stretched below like a vast pool of shiny quicksilver with lacy white salt edges.

In the Galilee, we visited Safed and the springs at Sachne. There, in the shade of tall trees, I decided to put on my swimsuit and enjoy the clear water.

"You have a lovely body," Peter said when he saw me. "Wow! And all this time I thought you were hiding a flaw."

"I burn in the sun. That's my flaw," I told him.

Judith and Mike were sitting on a rock on the other shore.

"Maybe you burn," Peter said, "but don't be denying the world a hidden treasure."

His remark was direct, yet it didn't offend me.

"And you're a part of the world," I offered.

I took his hand, and we waded in together. The water was refreshing, a strong current moving us quickly. When we came out I shivered, and he put his towel over my shoulders.

As we walked to the car, he asked me to dinner.

"Peter, don't you know I am married?"

Later in the afternoon, I talked to Jonathan.

"This thing with the green card is taking too long," I told him.

"It's hardly been three weeks," he answered.

"That's almost a month, if you're counting."

"I told you from the beginning it might take longer than a month."

"Yes, and you said you'd come and wait with me. You promised."

"Miriam, I can't come right now. I'm traveling, moving from city to city. Tonight I'm in Kansas City."

"What are you doing there?"

"The usual. We are discussing the meat business."

"Speaking of meat," I said, "this afternoon Peter hit on me when we were in Sachne."

"What were you doing in Sachne?"

"We were sightseeing."

"Just the two of you?" asked Jonathan.

"No, we were with other friends. And I said no to him, not to worry. But to tell you the truth, I felt flattered."

"You're a beautiful woman."

"Then why don't you come and *reclaim* me? Prove you still love me."

"I love you, Miriam, and I'd love to come, but I can't. From here I have to go to Nebraska."

My heart sank. "Why Nebraska?"

"Why not? Why do I go anywhere?"

"I don't know," I said. "Where in Nebraska?"

"I'm going to Lincoln, if that matters."

I found the strength to respond, "It does. I want to look on a map and know where you are. It gives me a good feeling, like we are there together. I love you, Jonathan."

As soon as the conversation ended, I felt the urge to flee the apartment. I couldn't stand it. I slammed the door behind me, jumped in the car, drove on HaYam all the way down to Rehov Etzel, took the ramp to Tel Aviv, and pushed on the accelerator. I reached seventy, eighty, ninety miles per hour. There were no thoughts on my mind, only adrenaline. No destination or purpose. When I arrived at Neve Yam, I decided to stop. I left the car in the empty parking lot and found my way to the half-moon sand beach dotted with palm trees. To my right was a rocky L-shaped promontory, angled outward. There was nobody on the beach but a little girl who was playing with a red rubber ball and a man, most likely her father, who was watching over her. I walked straight to the promontory. The waves crashed over rocks, water coming and going, filling and emptying little pools in the stone, again and again, forever. A fine froth hung where the rocks met the sea. Crushed shells and sand moved with the water. A crab came out of a hole and crawled in my direction. I took a step, and the crab retreated. It was afraid. I was big, so much bigger. The sea, the sky, and the world around us were even bigger. This was life, a question of proportions. Of fear and survival. Whatever Marybeth had told me about Jonathan's wife in Nebraska didn't matter. Perhaps the wife was the Mexican woman I had known about. Perhaps she was somebody else, a new one. Who cared? I had to deal with her, with all of his women, and I was his love now, fair and square.

The little crab came out again and crawled to the water. He was persistent.

This was life, *my life*, and I was persistent.

By the time I returned to my car, it was dark. The little girl and her father had long since disappeared. I drove into Haifa, stopped at the *tahana merkazit*, and bought myself a falafel.

The phone was ringing when I entered my apartment.

Samuel had died a few hours earlier. They had just called Jonathan. The next day he had to fly to Romania, not Nebraska.

Life always took sudden turns.

We agreed I would meet him in Bucharest as soon as I could arrange for a ticket.

Chapter 8

SAMUEL

After the funeral Leah flew back to Israel, and Jonathan and I went to Bistrița and spent four days with my mother and grandmother. Adina and Jacob took a break from their studies and came to see us. We discussed the emigration of my family to Israel. Leaving the country was a foregone conclusion, yet the conversation was emotional and nerve racking. Romania was going downhill. Ceaușescu was repaying the country's deficit in hard currency through severe austerity, and everybody suffered. Jonathan was brave, calm, and reassuring.

On our drive back to Bucharest, we spent the night in Sibiu, at the Roman Emperor Hotel. Bogdan went to park the limo, and we told him to pick us up the next morning. It was springtime again, but the day was gloomy. The hotel restaurant was empty, and we walked through the room to a table we liked by the window. After a while a waiter wearing a stained apron showed up. We asked for menus, and he said they didn't have any. He recited the few available choices for the evening, and I ordered *papanași*, a Romanian dessert consisting of deep-fried beignets covered in powdered sugar and served with sour cream.

"Is that all?" asked the waiter.

"That's all," I said, smiling broadly. "I'm not very hungry, but I love *papanași*, and the only place I can get them is here. They don't have *papanași* in America." I thought my remark would make him feel special for serving me a dish that not even America could offer. And I wanted him to know we were from another country, used to superior service. "Perhaps you could bring us some mineral water," I added.

He acted annoyed. "We're out of mineral water."

Jonathan ordered a steak, fries, and a green salad.

They were out of green salad.

"Last time they *had* mineral water," I said after the waiter departed.

"You're a spoiled American now."

"After my folks leave, there'll be no more reason to come to Romania."

"My brother's gone," Jonathan answered.

At the funeral, he had not shed a tear. He had not lamented. He had kept everything going, taking care of business, buying the food, bribing the bureaucrats, and paying the gravediggers. In Bistriţa he had continued in that role, nudging and encouraging, listening, promising money.

The food came. Jonathan took a few bites and pushed his plate aside.

"Not hungry?"

"While my parents were alive," he said, "I played with the other children and did what children do, which is simply ignore a handicapped younger sibling. And after my parents perished, I was relieved when the Ionescus took my brother in, out of their religious convictions. You see, I wasn't responsible for him anymore."

"You were a child at the time," I answered.

"I was a teenager."

The light outside the window faded. The sidewalk was wet and cracked. The old buildings seemed props from a bygone era.

I took his hand. "Jonathan, you had your own future to worry about, and you left the country. But you did everything you could for your brother. You visited him and sent money."

"That's it!" he exclaimed and pulled his hand away. "I sent him money. That's what I do. That's what I promised your mother. Rich people do this all the time, because it is easy. But the Ionescus, these strangers, they did the hard thing. For thirty-some years they fed him every day, cleaned him, washed him, and took him to school and to see his doctors."

"They weren't strangers," I said.

"In the beginning they were."

"Yes, maybe, thirty years ago. But you treated them well and provided for them, most likely more than they had ever expected. And you're going to continue, won't you?"

"Money, that's all," Jonathan said.

"You arranged for his medical care through Constantin, the best in Romania."

"I should have brought him to live with me in America; that's what I should have done. He might have lived."

Rain and fog stayed like a fur hat over the Carpathians, but the next day, once we drove past Sinaia and into the plains, the sun pierced the clouds and evaporated the mist.

In Bucharest, we had reservations at the Lido. Amenities were better than at the hotel in Sibiu. It was an island in that decaying and deteriorating Romanian world. I tried to understand why, after such a short time away, I felt alienated, despite being with Jonathan, surrounded by family, and involved in very personal events.

Constantin insisted we pay them a visit right away. Constantin's home was a peaceful refuge. I recalled the Easter celebration there, the songs, and the faces. Jonathan was grateful to Constantin for taking care of his brother. After the initial treatment in Bucharest, Samuel had felt better, and Constantin had released him and monitored his medical condition through contacts at the hospital in Turda.

A richly set table awaited us on their terrace overlooking the garden. It was early afternoon, and the sun was warming the corner of the terrace where the table was, the carafe with homemade vodka aflame like an emerald vessel.

"*Davay!*" Constantin said as soon as we walked onto the terrace, and he offered us two shot glasses. He had his white doctor's coat on.

Jonathan pointed at it. "Are we taking you away from work?"

"Why, because of my coat? No, I'm having car problems."

"And you're fixing your car in this outfit?"

Constantin rolled his eyes. "Right now I'm fixing you drinks. I wouldn't know how to fix my car if I wanted to. My engine's *kaput*, and I need a new one. Someone has just given me a ride from the hospital, and I didn't have a minute to change."

His white coat looked becoming—the uniform that enhanced the rank.

"Friends, sit down," Olga said, while Jonathan gulped his first shot of vodka.

"Hear, hear," he said.

There were only four table settings, and I asked where Grandmother was.

"She's not feeling too well," Constantin said. He took off his white coat and handed it to Olga. "Put this somewhere," he requested.

Olga went inside, and I followed her. I really didn't want to be in the sun. "Could I say hello to Grandmother?"

She escorted me through the large room where we had had dinner a year ago and to a door off the hallway that led to the kitchen. "She's in here. Say hi while I grab some more food for the guys. They shouldn't be drinking on empty stomachs."

I knocked, but there was no answer, and I opened the door. I had not been in that room before. Heavy curtains covered the windows, and the room was dark. The air was full of smoke. Grandmother was sitting at the top of her bed, near an old Telefunken radio placed on a round glass-covered nightstand. She was leaning toward the radio, listening intently, her feet on the floor, her left hand on the round knob that controlled the backlit wavelength dial, her right hand holding a cigarette. The sound was full of static, a male voice reporting in Romanian on the Securitate's efforts to silence Romanian writer and dissident Paul Goma. She was listening to Radio Free Europe. Her peach housecoat was old, and her frizzy white hair was out of place.

"Hello," I said, but she didn't respond, and I took a few steps and stopped right in front of her. "Hello," I said again.

She looked up at me, and it was clear that she hadn't noticed me until that instant and she had no idea who I was.

"I'm Miriam," I said. "I'm Nick's friend, remember?"

"Is Nicki with you?"

"No, he's in Greece."

"In Greece," Grandmother repeated after me, and her cigarette ashes fell to the floor.

She could easily set the house on fire.

"When is he coming back?" she asked.

"He'll be back, but now he's in Greece with Lydia, on their way to America. They are waiting for their visas." I took a step closer, took the cigarette from her fingers, and extinguished it in the ashtray on the nightstand. The sound on the radio was annoying. "Are you still listening, or could I turn this off?"

"Turn it off," she said and let go of the knob. She raised her eyes to me. "You're very young."

I remembered Lydia telling me Grandmother could see only a slice of what was in front of her, and I wondered what she saw, if she saw me at all.

"I'm here with Jonathan," I said. "You met him last year. We live in America now."

"Do you have children?" she asked.

"Jonathan and I plan to have children."

"My great-grandchildren."

"No, Grandmother, we are not related. But Lydia and Nick will come to America, and maybe they'll live near us, and they'll have children, also." I pulled my Moore superlong cigarettes out of my purse. In Romania they were called Kojaks, after the TV series. I offered one to Grandmother, took one myself, and lit both with my gold lighter. "Let's see if you like them," I said.

"Is Nicki here with you?" Grandmother asked.

"No, Nicki's in Greece."

"I'm afraid of the Soviets."

"There is nothing to be afraid of. Greece is a civilized country."

"Is it?" she said. "You are so young. How old are you?"

"I am twenty-five."

"And are you staying long?"

"No, we came here to visit."

"Nicki will be home very soon," she said.

The cigarettes were thin and brown on the outside. We both smoked very fast. When we finished, I made sure to put out both cigarettes, arranged

Grandmother's pillows, and helped lift her legs onto the bed. My own grandmother was in much better shape.

"I'll see you later," I told her.

In the living room I stopped to look at the painting of the gladiator. In full daylight, the colors seemed faded, and the portrait was less enigmatic than I remembered.

Through the open door to the terrace, I overheard Constantin say to Jonathan, "We have an agreement, Nicki and I. We'll reunite in not more than five years. For sure, one way or another we'll get out of here and join them wherever they are. We decided this in Sinaia, the last day before they left—just the two of us, father and son."

"How sentimental," Olga said in a bittersweet voice.

"We called it 'the Sinaia accord,'" Constantin went on. "This way, when we write to each other, we know."

"And you want to give all this up," Olga said.

I couldn't see her, but I imagined her words being accompanied by a wide, sweeping move of her hand, indicating the table with vintage crystal glasses and antique silverware, the snacks she had brought from the kitchen, the ivy-covered walls, the garden and its delicate blooms, the tall trees that belonged to the former royal palace behind the brick wall at the far end of the garden, the street, the entire city.

"This is nothing," Constantin said. "Just things, material possessions."

"This is more than material possessions," Olga said. "This is our world. You're a doctor here. You have a career and patients you care for. You help people. You belong here, and this world fits you, whether you like it or not, like a glove. You are used to it, and you were shaped by this world. What will we do in America? Be alone and unhappy, have no friends? We hardly speak English. We'll become a burden to our son and his family."

"We won't be a burden to anybody, and his family is our family. We need to be together, that's all."

I had heard variations of this discussion before, for four days with my own folks in Bistriţa. Thank goodness, Jonathan had taken the lead role there, calming uncertainties, promising support. Now he was just a bystander. What could he say to Olga and Constantin? Nothing. I understood their fear and agony over having to abandon everything familiar and all they had acquired during a lifetime, for the promise of an uncertain future. The older you were, the more wrenching the decision was.

Yet Constantin seemed ready to sacrifice it all to be with his son.

I moved, and Olga noticed me through the thin curtains that hung in the doorway. She called out to me, "Come and sit with us. Tell us something nice, or funny. It's nonsense what we're discussing right now."

I stepped onto the terrace. "I don't want to sit in the sun," I said.

"We'll move the table," Constantin said, and he jumped to his feet. He seemed exceedingly eager, guilty somehow. Without his white doctor's coat, he looked ordinary in his street clothes, the soft, checkered shirt, the pants that didn't match, the worn belt.

Olga and Jonathan got up too. They all grabbed things off the table and slid it halfway into an area that was shaded by the roof. I watched.

"Please, sit down," Olga said to me.

"I didn't bring a hat," I mumbled as an excuse, and I sat in the shade. I turned to Constantin. "I'll drink to your confidence in the future."

"Please," Jonathan said, looking at them. "Both of you, don't be sad. Things will work themselves out."

"We're not sad," Constantin said. "If anything, we're disgusted. *I'm* disgusted. You know, this thing with my car. I need a new engine, so what's the big deal? But no matter what I do, who I talk to, I can't find one."

"Isn't this car engine a thing, a material possession?" Olga asked. "I thought they didn't matter to you."

Bogdan picked us up an hour later.

"My friend needs a new engine for his Dacia 1300," Jonathan said to him. "You know people, don't you? Money's no object, but we're leaving tomorrow."

"I'll see what I can do," Bogdan said.

We had supper at the Lido restaurant on the deck, overlooking the outdoor swimming pool. The pool was drained, its cracked concrete bottom painted blue.

"I keep thinking about Samuel and what his life might have been, had he been healthy," Jonathan said. "Do you know what Constantin told me? He thinks it's a miracle Samuel lived for as long as he did."

I nodded. It was closure of sorts.

Bogdan appeared from the kitchen, walking slowly between the tables. When he reached ours, he stopped as if by chance. "I found an engine for four thousand dollars in cash, plus a ten percent finder's fee," he whispered, looking away. "Brand new."

"Deal," Jonathan whispered back. "I can get you the money tomorrow when the bank opens, but can you deliver tonight?"

"I can."

Jonathan called Constantin from the room and asked for his mechanic's address. Constantin objected, of course. Jonathan insisted, got the address, and gave it to Bogdan.

I took a shower and changed into my nightgown. Jonathan went to shower also. We were beat.

The phone rang.

"It's delivered," Bogdan told me.

I lay down on the bed. Had I told Jonathan I admired him for what he did for Constantin, he'd have said it was only money. But I knew better.

Now I knew.

During these last days since his brother's death, I had observed him up close. He wanted to appear macho, a world traveler and a cool gambler, but I had seen him with his uniform off. I had managed a glimpse at what he was hiding inside, just a sliver, it's true, not more than what Nick's grandmother would see when she looked at a room, but more than enough. He was compassionate, a family man at heart, and I was so proud to be with him.

He came out of the bathroom wrapped in a towel, and I told him that Bogdan had called. He lay on the bed, and I crawled in to him, the warmth of his body spreading through me.

"Are you staying with me in Israel?" I asked.

"Only for a few days."

"Then what?"

"Then I go back to America. Business as usual." He shrugged.

"Do you love me?" I asked.

"I do."

"How much?"

"I don't know. I love you a lot."

"Let's get married," I said.

"Why, Miriam? Love and marriage have little in common."

"You're wrong. People who love each other want to spend their lives together."

"I want to spend my life with you."

"Then marry me."

"You're being old-fashioned."

"I love you, and there is no *old-fashioned* in love." I nuzzled my face in his shoulder. "Nebraska," I said.

"What about Nebraska?"

"Promise me not to go to Nebraska."

His body stiffened. "I can't promise you that."

He knew that I knew, so what choice did I have?

Chapter 9

BARI AND YARI

Morning sickness started while I was still in Israel. By the time I returned to the States, green card in hand, my pregnancy was well established. The life that I carried inside me was an extension of myself, a carbon copy of me, and no matter how small it was in the beginning, it made me feel fragile. I had the desire to be pampered, to linger in bed, to be picky. I didn't want the wind in my face, or the sun, or the spray of the ocean. Rotund bellies, swollen nipples, and tiny babies appeared in my sketchpad. I designed and sewed my own maternity clothes, but it got tiring, and I asked a seamstress to come to the house and take over. At six months I hired a nanny. It was premature, but I wanted to be safe. Marybeth moved into the house for good, to keep me company. Remy cooked dishes rich in vitamins for me. I ate cheese, polenta with sour cream, poached salmon, radishes, and white baby asparagus. I ate soft-boiled eggs, figs, and apricots. Carlos stopped by to see Jonathan, and when he ran into me, he winked happily. Good job, girl, he seemed to be saying.

Marina brought Nelu, her former Romanian TA, to my studio. I sat on pillows on the floor, my sketches and paintings arranged in a half circle around me. He had given up teaching and had become an art dealer. He appreciated my work and suggested that one day he might try to place some of it with the local galleries. Through him, I acquired my first Georgia O'Keeffe, an etching by

Picasso, a Jackson Pollock, two Marcel Iancos, and several pieces by San Diego artists. He came to visit me often, which I enjoyed not only because of his ties to the art world, but also because he was the only person besides Jonathan who spoke Romanian and understood my background. I told him about Gabriel, but he had never heard of him. When I found out he was planning a trip to Romania, I asked him to go visit my mother and rescue my canvases that she kept in my room in the closet. If he didn't, I said, my paintings would get lost when my family left for Israel. At that time crossing the border with almost anything that resembled artwork was forbidden. I was eager to recover my earlier work and especially the portrait of Pani. Nelu agreed and said he had a way to do it. I paid him good money, and he brought them to me in a leather portfolio.

I had seen my paintings two years ago in Bistriţa, and Jonathan had praised them. I looked at them now, silently, for a long time, and felt awful. What I remembered as really outstanding artwork appeared to me through the filter of time as barely mediocre. I had no doubt. The work screamed that word at me from every line, every shadow, and every blotch of paint on the canvas. There was no spark and no personality. No originality. Nothing I had painted as a teenager was special.

The more Nelu tried to encourage me, the worse it got.

I carried the disappointment with me for a few days and looked for excuses. I had been so young and passionate. My most recent hero, Georgia O'Keeffe, had also experienced setbacks.

Nelu had witnessed my embarrassment and had seen my pain. I avoided him, and when I resumed buying art, I contacted other dealers.

Our first son was born in February. Jonathan was traveling. He had asked me if he could go, and I had assured him I was fine. I didn't expect to be early. When my water broke, Marybeth came with me to the hospital. Remy drove us. There were several other pregnant women there, all with their husbands. I called Jonathan, and he said he'd get on a plane immediately. I missed him, and

I cried when the nurses weren't looking. It was painful and scary, but I didn't have a choice, and I convinced myself I could do this alone. I had done other things on my own, and this was no different. Labor lasted a full sixteen hours. Poor Marybeth. Remy went home, but she stayed. She held my hand, brought me water, and was the first to see my newborn son in the morning. Jonathan made it back that afternoon. He was all smiles and tears. We held the baby in our arms and named him Baruch.

I was still breastfeeding when I became pregnant again, and I told Jonathan he was very prolific. He said I was *his* fertile soil. He said I was a she-rabbit.

Yaron was born in May, the most beautiful month of all.

We gave them Jewish names, a nod to our ancestry. Their surname was Sommer. Nobody had ever asked us for a marriage license.

Our boys—we called them Bari and Yari—were two little angels with alabaster cheeks and curly brown hair. Their huge eyes sparkled like black onyx. We pointed to our children's this or that feature, and tried to attribute ownership, but in the end we decided they were simply adorable and looked like me *and* like Jonathan.

When they learned to walk, they started coming to our bed in the morning, Bari first and then his brother. They would crawl in between us sleepily, pushing us and pushing each other, reclaiming their right to snuggle. Their little fingers and toes were made for kissing, their tummies for tickling, and they smelled of milk and baby powder. They were like puffy clouds in the summer. At night they slept in the adjacent bedroom, first in their cribs and then in bunk beds, on the advice of our pediatrician. We installed a new door to connect our bedrooms, and after a while the nanny would knock on that door and come to get them ready for breakfast.

The boys took up all of my time and drained most of my energy. My priorities changed. First and foremost, there were Bari and Yari. If I took care of myself, it was for their benefit, and Marybeth and the nanny made it possible for me to get away. I didn't know how other mothers did it. In between time with my trainer and my hair appointments, which were necessary to regain as much as possible of my strength and physical appearance after childbirth, I made sure to hold my two boys in my arms and read to them from children's books that would shape their future. I did not believe in television. *Sesame Street* was all right, but only in small doses. At their age, a mother's influence was paramount. I played with them, and I told them stories about my life and about their daddy, who, in those days, was on the road very often. I'm not sure how much the boys understood my stories, but they always listened. Left to their own devices, which was rare, they fought and turned rambunctious, reminding me of Ezra and Mordechai in my childhood courtyard, except that those two had been little wild savages, whereas mine were porcelain bibelots thriving under the best conditions anybody could offer.

Except for my art purchases, I hardly had any time for shopping or visits with Marina and her friends. I placed painting on hold again, kept a corner for my easels and canvases, and converted my studio into a playroom. The flowers were raised off the windowsills, and the mock oriental rugs shoved into a closet. I had my beautiful saddle placed on a life-size wooden pony. A giant fish tank replaced the Jacuzzi.

Everywhere we went, Jonathan, the boys, and I, people greeted us with smiles on their faces. What a lovely family, they said. *Family* was the key word, and to me that was what mattered.

Even Carlos, when he stopped by the house, or if I ran into him at some event or dinner party, would salute me with newly gained respect, as if I had earned my place next to Jonathan. He talked to me like a friend, like we shared a history. He was going through his divorce, and I assumed that his own misfortune calmed his roving eye.

Then my mother and grandmother arrived in Israel. Being adults, my siblings had to apply for permission to immigrate to Israel separately, and their papers were not yet ready. Approvals generally took longer for young people. My mother and grandmother had to leave Romania without them. We asked Pinkas, the Tel Aviv attorney, to look into the matter, and he assured us that everything was OK and that Adina and Jacob would follow, but my mother and grandmother were distraught and nervous over the situation.

I flew to Israel to see them at their ulpan in Nahariya after their arrival. Their room had two metal beds, a bare tiled floor, a table, and two chairs. The door led to an inside courtyard. My small entourage seemed more disturbing than reassuring to my mother. Bari and Yari were with me, as well as Pinkas, Marybeth, and the nanny. We had no place to sit in the room. My mother hugged her grandchildren for the first time in her life and started weeping. We all walked into the courtyard. My grandmother remained on her bed, looking forlorn and tired.

I guess my mother and grandmother were so overwhelmed they forgot to ask me if I had finally gotten married to Jonathan. The truth was that I didn't want to discuss it. I had convinced myself that being officially married didn't matter. It was just a piece of paper, nothing more, nothing less, and who cared? We *were* a family, Mr. and Mrs. Sommer. Jonathan was traveling, but that was what he did, and we were intelligent and independent people. With his two babies in my arms, no longer was I afraid of betrayal. Jonathan owned land in Nebraska, had opened a new meat-processing plant in Oklahoma, had invested heavily in commercial real estate on both coasts, and sat on the board of directors of five multinational food corporations. I had everything I needed, and we all seemed to be safe and happy. He assured me he was making more money than ever before, doubling the family fortune, and if I couldn't paint as much as I wanted, I continued my investments in art. By the time Bari turned three, I had acquired thirty-two valuable paintings, and I promised myself to reach fifty by his next birthday.

—— ⊰⊱ ——

Weeks, months, years flew by. Everything was falling into place. My children grew. My siblings finally arrived in Israel. I visited them. Nick and Lydia came to the United States, lived first in New York City, then moved to Columbia, Maryland, the planned community between Baltimore and Washington, DC. Lydia got pregnant. Adina married a man she met in college. I would have loved to go to their wedding with Jonathan and watch his reaction, but we didn't get the opportunity because Adina eloped in her typical selfish fashion.

She beat me to it, my younger sister…

—— ⊰⊱ ——

I lay under the umbrella by the pool and read a new book about Modigliani's women. The sun was spreading a golden light over the garden.

Jonathan was in New York City.

Juan came running. "Baruch's sick. Marybeth is asking for you upstairs, please, quickly."

I found them in the children's bedroom, Bari in the lower bunk, crying and holding his stomach, and Yari standing by the little bookshelf sucking on his bib. Marybeth was wiping Bari's forehead with a wet washcloth. The smell of vomit was everywhere.

"My goodness," I said. "Marybeth, what happened?"

"He's a mess, poor baby," Marybeth said, looking worried. "He complained earlier that his tummy was aching, but he had eaten almost nothing at lunch, and I didn't think much of it. And then it started."

"Did you call Dr. Goldstrand?"

"I didn't have a chance. He threw up all over. If you watch the kids for a minute, I'll go clean up."

"Let me call the doctor first. Yari, come with Mama." I grabbed Yari's hand, but just at that moment Bari's body seized up, and a purge of vomit erupted from his mouth while his onyx eyes rolled in their sockets. Suddenly it seemed as if his pain gripped my body, and I felt fear and the need to kneel by the bed, take Bari into my arms, and hold him. I had heard parents say they wanted to trade places with their sick children and assume their suffering, and I had always thought it was just a nice turn of phrase, but now I understood it was real. Now I knew that if I could, I would gladly transfer Bari's pain on to me to relieve him of it. It was not about me anymore, as it had been in the past, but about him. About them. Yari's little hand was still in mine, and I forced myself to stay calm and maintain sanity. I reached for the box of wipes on top of the bookshelf and gave it to Marybeth. Bari started hiccuping. Marybeth cleaned his chin, his face, and his neck, and I went into my bedroom and called the pediatrician, who agreed to pay us a house call. I was grateful to the doctor, knowing that the norm was to bring the child in, and that he had offered this special accommodation because of his respect for us and especially for Jonathan, and for the status Jonathan had in the community. It occurred to me that perhaps it was because the doctor understood how critical Bari's sickness was, and I started shaking and needed to get a hold of myself and end the conversation with a proper, "We'll see you at five. Thank you, Doctor; we are very grateful." Yari stood next to me, watching me with a mixture of childish concern and annoyance.

"Bari wants to drink," Marybeth said when we returned.

"Bari, I'll get you a little water, but only to rinse your mouth. Don't swallow, or you'll throw up again. And the doctor said we should take your temperature." I sat on the bed and placed my hand on Bari's forehead. He was burning up.

Marybeth brought the thermometer, but Bari refused to open his mouth. I took both boys to my room while we waited for Marybeth to clean the floor and change the sheets in the nursery.

When Dr. Goldstrand arrived, Bari's temperature was 103, and the doctor said we should drive him to the hospital immediately. "I'm afraid it could be appendicitis, not very common with children as young as Bari, but possible. The temperature indicates an infection, his stomach hurts and feels hard, and I'd rather be safe than sorry."

By the time I called Jonathan, it was after 8:00 p.m. on the East Coast, and he promised to catch the first flight home and asked me to keep him posted.

That evening they decided to perform an appendectomy on Baruch. He cried when I let go of his hand and they rolled him into surgery.

The waiting room at the hospital was empty.

At home, despite the shock of seeing Bari so scared and in so much pain, and after talking to Dr. Goldstrand, I managed to take a hold of myself. I asked Marybeth to stay with Yari and go through his evening routine, and I changed into a sweat suit, ready for a night at the hospital. I felt in charge, my pain and my worry pushed away. I had to be there for Bari. The last thing I did was call Jonathan's hotel, and even though they weren't sure which flight he took, they said he was already in the air.

Then, in the eerie silence of the waiting room, I became aware of my sharp anxiety and remembered a story my grandfather had told us many years ago about a little boy, maybe a toddler, who had died of peritonitis in Bistrița. They had waited too long before they opened him up, and the infection had spread to the abdomen. The body of that little boy had been too weak and too small to fight, and he had died on the operating table. Peritonitis, the precipice at the edge of the cliff! How long had *we* waited?

All I could do was sit and keep hearing in my mind the sobs of my little boy on a stretcher disappearing through those double doors that closed behind him automatically. Trust the doctors!

I would have liked to ask Marybeth if she had heard Bari complain of any pain the day before, or in any of the previous days, but Marybeth was at home with Yari.

Marina came to the hospital, and later Remy showed up with some sandwiches in a paper bag, which I placed near me on the chair. "Remy, please, tell me," I asked him. "Baruch, did he tell you yesterday that his stomach hurt?"

"I don't think so, Miss Miriam. As far as I know, he's been fine."

"Then how could this happen? Perfectly healthy in the morning, and emergency surgery in the evening. Tell me."

"Miss Miriam, don't worry. Your son will be fine, and it's good to be rid of that stupid appendix."

I touched his arm, and for a few seconds, I rested my head on his shoulder.

Dr. Goldstrand came out of surgery in a little less than an hour. Everything was fine, and Bari was in recovery. They had performed a regular appendectomy with a two-inch incision that looked huge on his little tummy. But he was all right, and it was good they had done it, because his appendix had been inflamed and needed to come out. The procedure was timely. Bari would feel his normal self within the next twenty-four hours, and we would have to try to keep him restrained, prevent him from running and jumping.

Marina and I followed Dr. Goldstrand into the recovery room. Bari was sleeping on his back. An IV was hooked to his arm, and his body was tied to the gurney. Bari opened his eyes, and when he saw me he started to cry. I hushed him and gave him a kiss on the forehead. He wasn't feverish any longer. I wanted to take him into my arms and hold him, but I knew that was out of the question. Still I kept my arm on the gurney, my palm pressing lightly on his chest. All the time Marina held me.

A nurse came and said they'd be moving us into our room for the night, if we were ready. It was after ten, and Marina said she'd be going. We hugged. There was a medicinal smell in the air, and my eyes were itchy.

We were ushered into a private room, and they rolled in a cot for me. Bari woke up several times and went back to sleep right away. I sat on my cot so relieved that it took my breath away. I felt hungry and ate everything that Remy had brought me. Nurses came into the room all the time, making it almost impossible for me to fall asleep, while Bari did not seem bothered.

At about five in the morning, a shadow leaned over my cot. I opened my eyes. "Jonathan, you made it."

"Of course I did," he whispered.

"Bari's OK," I told him.

"I know. I spoke to the nurses."

The cot was narrow and low to the ground, and I lifted myself to a sitting position while he sat near me and placed his arm around my shoulders. I thought the cot would collapse, but it didn't.

"Let's look at him," he said, and he helped me get up and take the few steps through the dark room to where Bari was sleeping.

Light fell on us through the partially open door to the hallway. Under a white sheet, Bari's chest moved imperceptibly with the rhythm of his breathing. I couldn't see his hands, and I thought they might be still tied to the bed, to prevent him from trying to disturb his dressing over the incision. His face was serene. From time to time his closed eyelids were twitching.

"Our little angel," Jonathan said.

"He looks like you."

"I love you," he said.

In his presence, I allowed myself to let go. I felt happy and exhausted. Tears streamed down my face. I grabbed Jonathan's arm and leaned into him, seeking his steady support.

"Don't cry," he whispered. "I am here with you."

"I wish you were here all along," I said and tightened my grip on his arm. "Travel less if you can. It's hard without you."

Lydia called. Constantin was coming to visit, but without Olga, since the Romanians refused to allow married couples to travel together so they wouldn't defect. He wanted to see the country.

"Nick has a business meeting in Denver and plans to take his father along for a little sightseeing," Lydia told me.

"Maybe afterward you could all come and spend some time with us," I suggested. "Let me talk to Jonathan."

In the end, Lydia decided to stay home. They had two children, a boy and a girl, both toddlers. As a mother, I understood fully. Jonathan invited Nick and Constantin to spend a few days with us in Las Vegas. Nick had to go back to work, but Constantin would then join us for a week in San Diego.

We stayed at Caesar's and had one extra room added to our regular suite.

It was midafternoon. Bari and Yari were at the pool with Marybeth, and Jonathan was sleeping after a night of gambling. I was getting a facial in the living room. The receptionist called to tell me our guests had arrived, and I asked her to have the bellboy escort them upstairs.

I met them in the hallway.

"My goodness. How long has it been?"

"Four years," Constantin answered.

"Five," said Nick.

We hugged.

The bellboy placed their suitcases near the huge round bed in their room.

"Will you be OK sharing this bed?" I asked my visitors and looked at the ceiling. From the mirror above, our three pairs of eyes looked down on us.

"Are you kidding?" Constantin said quickly. "He's my son, and I am a surgeon and can sleep anywhere. How do you think I survive the long nights I'm on duty at the hospital?"

Nick seemed less sure but didn't say anything, and I felt disappointed in myself for not having thought of this earlier. I should have asked for a folding bed, but at least I'd had the foresight to order a cheese platter, a fruit basket, chocolates, and juices.

"You can nibble on those," I said, changing the subject. "Take your time, and relax a little. We have a full schedule for you later, but we're not in a hurry." I tipped the bellboy and asked him to unlock the inside door that connected their room to the rest of the suite.

Constantin looked around. "This is the trip of a lifetime. Who would have thought—Las Vegas!"

"What happens to your 'Sinaia accord,'" I asked daringly, "now that you're here?"

"This trip isn't it," answered Nick somewhat uncomfortably.

"But we're getting closer," Constantin added.

"So this is like a scouting trip," I said, and I sensed it would be a mistake to continue. "When you're ready, just knock on this door," I said and retreated through it.

A few minutes later, Constantin opened the door without knocking. Jonathan was still asleep in the other room, and I was checking my face in the mirror. Constantin came toward me holding a long tube wrapped in light-blue tissue paper.

"Dad!" Nick yelled. "Close the door. I'm changing."

Through the open door, I caught a glimpse of him walking around in his underwear.

"Relax," Constantin said. "You have nothing she hasn't seen already." Constantin came closer. "This is for you and for Jonathan. I know it's not much, but for old times' sake, let's call it my Rembrandt."

"Oh, no," I responded, instantly guessing what he was offering. "You can't do this."

"Yes, I can. It is a family heirloom, you love art, and I want you to have it. You are like family."

Family, that word again, balance and trust, in my dictionary. I saw Constantin's face, his tall forehead, his white hair combed back, and his steely blue eyes, not a cloud on that face, not a hint of worry. Yet I knew how vulnerable he was on the inside, his son and grandchildren in this half of the world, his wife in the other. I found it remarkable that it was I who was witnessing this. Here he was—slightly awkward, yet outspoken and confident looking, almost five years after his Sinaia accord and still struggling—whereas I was at home. My mother, my father, and my siblings had gotten out of Romania, and Jonathan and my children were here.

I had made it. He hadn't.

Gently, I unwrapped the tube and set the painting on the coffee table. The dark profile of the gladiator emerged through the soot of time.

"It's beautiful," I said. "Thank you. I'll have it cleaned, and I will place it in a gilded frame, and I'll display it at home with my art collection. I have built an entire art collection now, Constantin."

Later that afternoon, after Jonathan joined us and we drank a bottle of champagne to celebrate the occasion, after the boys returned from the pool and received the small gifts Nick had brought them, and after we admired the photographs of Lydia and their children, we decided on dinner at an Italian place within walking distance. We stopped at the casino, watched a few games of craps, tried our luck at a roulette table, and lost. We crossed the strip and slowly made our way to the restaurant, near the Dunes Hotel.

"High-stakes poker is the only game worth playing," Jonathan said with a smile on his face, which I understood and resented.

I suspected Jonathan was planning to play poker that night again. To entertain our guests, I had obtained two tickets for them to a late show. "I couldn't get more than two," I told Nick when I gave him the tickets. "It's a very popular show. Jonathan and I have already seen it." I slipped him a one-hundred-dollar bill with the tickets. He tried to give it back to me, and I insisted, "Take it. This is an expensive place, and you'll need it for drinks and tips and your cab ride back. Trust me." He hesitated, and then took the money.

The restaurant was crowded and noisy. We started with mixed drinks, except for Constantin, who drank vodka straight up. There was a lot to say about the children and about the old days, and we even made a few lame jokes about Constantin's car. He told us that Grandmother, his mother, had died two years before, at home, with a cigarette in her hand. He mentioned this last detail proudly, like a badge of honor, and then he and Jonathan shared a cigarette. It had been a long time since I had seen Jonathan smoke.

The first bottle of wine we had with dinner didn't last long, and Jonathan called the waiter, a shy young man who spoke English with a heavy accent.

"Miguel." Constantin read his nametag.

"Yes," the waiter said.

"*Italiano?*"

"No, Hispanic."

"Oh, *Espania*! Beautiful. I have been to Cuba, you know?"

The waiter seemed lost.

"Cuba, Fidel Castro," Constantin insisted. He got very excited. "*Comprendes? Bombero el fuego!*" he yelled.

"Go," Jonathan said to the waiter. "Bring us another bottle."

The young man left.

"I've been to Cuba," Constantin repeated. "I really have, as a doctor, on an official exchange. I know you Americans feel this disdain toward Cuba, but it wasn't that bad. Fidel was supposed to come to our farewell dinner, and he never showed up. I remember a song they taught us over there. It went *Bumbacia, bumbacia*, or something like that."

"*Bumbacia* doesn't mean anything in Spanish," Jonathan said.

"But it does," Constantin said. He tapped his fingers on the table, to a certain rhythm in his head. "*Bumbacia, bumbacia*! Where is Igor, to sing to us when we need him?"

We left the restaurant after eleven. Constantin wobbled a little, but Nick was OK. He told us that he and Constantin would drive to the Grand Canyon in the morning, spend the night there, and come back the following evening. I thought that was a great idea, and Jonathan agreed. We hailed a cab and dropped them off at the show.

"Are you playing poker tonight?" I asked Jonathan on our ride back.

He nodded.

"Try to join us for breakfast before they leave on their trip."

The next morning, I called the front desk and asked them to locate Mr. Sommer in the casino. They called back in about twenty minutes and said Mr. Sommer was still playing. They said he apologized to his guests and wished them a safe trip. He would be back upstairs in less than two hours. I was disappointed, but I had resigned myself to Jonathan's demons.

At the breakfast table in the restaurant, Bari and Yari made their usual fuss, and Marybeth had a hard time restraining them. Constantin's face looked puffy, while Nick acted impatient.

"Relax," Constantin said. "The Grand Canyon has been there forever."

Nick was a true outdoorsman, eager to get rolling.

After they left, Marybeth took the boys to the pool, and I went upstairs. I was changing to go shopping to buy some nice gifts for Nick's children when the phone rang.

"Mrs. Sommer," the voice said, "a few minutes ago your husband was rushed to the hospital."

I clearly remember those words—*my husband*, they called Jonathan my husband.

Jonathan had collapsed at his poker game. There was froth at his mouth and a bead of blood in one of his nostrils.

The aneurysm in his brain killed him before he reached the hospital.

PART 3

Chapter 1

SHIVAH

The limo picked me up in front of the hotel. It was an area shaded by a large canopy, but the air was hot and dry. Betty Suarez, the hotel's assistant manager, waited for me, and we rode to the hospital together.

"I'm so sorry," she said when I sat next to her in the limo.

I was wearing the most somber outfit I could find. I would have liked the protection of a black hat, but among the many things I had brought with me from San Diego, I didn't have one, so my head was uncovered.

I nodded at Betty and looked away.

At the moment I was experiencing no sense of loss. The thought of Jonathan's death had never crossed my mind, and while I understood it conceptually, I couldn't accept it as real. I was responding to what was requested of me, but only on a rational level. The news hadn't touched me inside, and my reaction to his death was that I moved slower than before and with more self-awareness.

Earlier, in my suite, I had wondered whether to go to the swimming pool, find Marybeth and the boys, and tell them. I decided to wait because I didn't know what to say. "Boys, your daddy is dead." Was that what one said? Should I bring them upstairs and tell them about a man dressed in black with a sickle? Would they know what a sickle was? Would they be scared? Or should I lie and say their daddy had an emergency and we had to go back to San Diego without him?

And I didn't know what to do with Nick and Constantin. They weren't returning until the next evening, and there was no way I could reach them by telephone, but they were adults and would understand. Still, this was ruining their vacation, ending it abruptly. I almost broached the subject with Betty, but I stopped myself, realizing that my worry was misplaced, even silly.

The midmorning traffic was light. We slid by the big hotels and turned onto a freeway. The air conditioning was blasting, and after a few minutes I froze and wrapped my arms around my chest to keep myself warm.

That was what the mortuary felt like—I was sure.

A doctor and a nurse waited for us at the hospital, and we followed them into a windowless room. Jonathan was on a stretcher, his body covered by a white sheet, his head and face exposed. Somebody had cleaned his face and closed his eyes. He looked peaceful.

I lifted the sheet and touched his hand. It was cold, unresponsive.

For a second or two, I almost felt satisfied, as if I had just received the assurance I needed—this was not a demonic prank; this was real. Then pain hit, like a wall that collapsed, like a storm, like a river. My knees started to shake, and I felt the desire to wail and pull at my hair. I wanted to throw myself to the floor, roll on it, and flap my arms like an injured bird. Somehow I managed to get hold of myself and turn to the doctor. He was young, with chiseled features. He must have seen me shaking and must have noticed the blood draining from my face, because he grabbed me by my arm and steadied me.

"Do you need a moment alone?" he asked.

"No," I said.

"OK, then let's get you to sit down."

We walked through a long corridor, him supporting my arm, and we found a sofa inside a glass atrium flooded with sunlight. The brightness was painful.

The nurse held a small plastic bag she must have retrieved from somewhere. "His personal effects," she said and handed it to Betty.

"When we print the death certificate, we'll send it to the hotel," the doctor said. "And let us know what the arrangements are."

"Mr. Sommer was Jewish," Betty said.

The doctor walked away and returned with a prescription and a glass of ice water. "Stop by the pharmacy before you leave. It's Valium. I trust you're not allergic. Take one pill as soon as you can, and you'll feel a little better. But don't rush. Stay here as long as you need."

As young as he was, he seemed used to my kind of pain.

I drank a few sips of water. Betty and the nurse watched me. Then Betty gave me the plastic bag, and I opened it without thinking. Inside were Jonathan's gold watch, the room key, a few casino chips, and his wallet. I remembered he had been wearing a gold pendant around his neck, but I didn't say anything.

"I have to go," the nurse announced apologetically.

Of course she had to go. She had paperwork to finish, other deaths to attend to. Eventually they would all leave—doctor, nurse, hotel assistant manager. They would do their jobs and disappear. My friends and relatives would come and go, and my servants would stick around for as long as I paid them. They would all pretend to feel sorry for me, and some of them would, but in the end I'd be left alone, now that Jonathan had left me. It would be just me and my two little boys.

Panic rose in my body, and I felt my skin turning hot, as if the sun had burned through the glass and singed me in spite of the air conditioning. I asked for a tissue, and Betty went to get some. When she returned, she remained standing. I took a few tissues from the box and patted my neck, my chin, and my forehead.

"Take your time," she said, but I understood she was ready to go, and I stood up.

Back in my suite, I called Carlos.

"Stay where you are," Carlos said. "I'll charter a plane and come get you and the children. You'll be back in San Diego tonight. In the meantime, don't sign anything, and I'll take care of everything when I get there."

The three of them returned from the pool. Silently I watched the boys eat lunch and go for their afternoon nap. While they slept, I talked to Marybeth. She was visibly shaken. We hugged, and I cried on her shoulder.

By the time Carlos arrived, I had finished packing my suitcases, and Marybeth had gotten the children dressed and ready.

Jonathan's things were still in his closet—shirts, pants, neckties, and an evening jacket.

"I couldn't make myself touch them," I told Carlos.

The children were in the other room.

"I understand," he said. "Somebody from the hotel will take care of it. Do you want them shipped to your house or donated to charity?"

"It doesn't matter. You decide."

"I'm here for you," he said.

For the first time in my life, I perceived his presence with a measure of comfort.

"Carlos, what will I do?"

"You'll be all right. In his will, Jonathan has left almost everything to you."

His answer offended me. "I didn't know Jonathan left a will, and that's not what I meant. What will I do without Jonathan?"

"This is hard," he said. "Jonathan was my client *and* my friend, and I am shocked by his death, also. But we have to be strong—you especially. When you're ready, I'll explain Jonathan's will to you, the sooner the better. I'm his executor, and you did the right thing by calling me today. You can trust me."

Carlos was wearing his red bow tie. His dark hair was tousled, not slick as usual. A deep furrow crossed his forehead, and he seemed to have a hard time being businesslike. I understood he was hurting.

"I trust you," I said.

"Let's go home," Carlos said. "I settled with the hotel, and the limo is waiting."

Marybeth and the children left first. The bellboy loaded the suitcases on his cart. I grabbed my purse and the roll containing the painting Constantin had given me.

"What's this?" Carlos asked, pointing at the painting.

I told him.

"Is it valuable?"

"I'm not sure."

"Give it to me," he said quickly. "I'll keep it for you in my office."

"But I want it."

"I know. This is just a precaution."

⸎

In the morning Carlos brought in a woman from Beth Israel to run our household. Her name was Rachel. "Only for the next several days," he assured me. "To help keep the Jewish tradition for Jonathan."

The first thing Rachel did was run to the kitchen. Food had to be kosher. She talked to Remy and promised written directions. She asked Juan to remove all the cut flowers from the house and cover the mirrors and paintings. I told Juan I agreed, except for my bedroom. Rachel summoned Carlos and me to the library and produced a typed schedule of upcoming events, including the service and the funeral.

"Over the years, Mr. Sommer had been an active contributor to the Beth Israel Congregation of San Diego. It's a privilege to return the favor."

Her use of the word *favor* felt awkward. She was being paid for her services, I was sure. The fact that Jonathan had given money to a synagogue, any synagogue, was surprising to me, and I looked at Carlos for confirmation.

He nodded.

"We'll have notices placed in local newspapers," Rachel said. "In the *San Diego Daily Transcript*, and the *Union Tribune*, and the *San Diego Hispanos Unidos*. And *LA Times* in the Los Angeles area. Mr. Sommer was a distinguished member of our community, and hundreds will turn out for his funeral." She looked at me as if she expected me to feel pride, and continued, "*Shivah* will start tomorrow afternoon, as soon as we return from the cemetery. The rabbi will bring a Torah scroll to the house and help you say the *Kaddish* after the *Aleinu*. We'll place tall candles on windowsills where they'll burn for seven days. *The flame of God is the soul of man*, as they say in the Proverbs. With everybody paying you shivah calls, you won't have to worry about having ten people for a *minyan*. Besides, we are a reformed congregation and allow women to join. You'll decide who reads the Kaddish, but it will have to be a man, an adult man, and Jewish."

"My brother is coming from Israel," I said. "He speaks Hebrew."

"The Kaddish is in Aramaic," Rachel answered.

I wanted to say that I knew, but there was no point. "Most of my family lives in Israel," I told her. "My mother, my siblings, my grandmother, and Jonathan's sister, Leah, with her family. My sister cannot travel because she is pregnant. Eight months pregnant, and her doctor said it's too risky." I drew in a breath and went on as if in a trance. Talking was healing. "I was never too close to my sister. But my brother, Jacob, is coming, and I am close to him. And Leah is coming together with her husband. The three of them will be staying here. My father is coming also. I haven't seen my father in fifteen years, and he has never met Jonathan, but he decided to join, I guess, to provide me some comfort." I stopped and inhaled one more time. Carlos blinked a few times and rearranged his bow tie. I kept going. "My father is coming from Germany with his second wife, Laura, and Elise, my half sister. They'll be staying with us also. So besides Adina, my real sister, only my mother will not be here. Somebody had to take care of my grandmother, she told me. My grandmother's ninety. I think my mother never liked Jonathan, even though he had been so nice to her and had helped her and the rest of my family with money. And maybe it's better that she isn't coming, since I wouldn't know what to do with her and my father under the same roof." I stopped again. The blinds were drawn over the windows, and the thousand tomes in the library seemed remnants of an epoch that had disappeared. "It took this tragedy to almost bring them together," I added and burst into tears.

"Cry," Rachel said. "This is the true meaning of shivah. It gives you time to express your grief, not hide it. And it is also a celebration of life. People bring food to the house, they mourn with you, eat with you, and remember their good times with Jonathan. They will help you look to the future, my dear."

"There is no future."

Rachel left, and Carlos suggested that rather than cover the paintings with black cloths, we remove them and place them in storage.

I was too distraught to object or reject the idea.

<hr />

It must have been almost six in the evening when Nick called from Las Vegas. I was upstairs with Marybeth and the children.

"My God, Miriam," Nick said. "What a tragedy. How did it happen?"

I wanted to tell him, but I started crying, and he stopped asking questions. Marybeth took the phone and told him the funeral was tomorrow. "Yes," she said. "We understand you won't be able to make it."

Constantin asked to talk to me, and Marybeth gave me back the receiver.

"Can I be of any help?" he started. "As a friend and a doctor."

I didn't say anything.

"I'm sorry," he added. "I admired your partner."

It seemed a strange word, and I echoed, "Partner?" Then I said it myself. "Yes, he wasn't my husband."

"Now, now, what does it matter? Jonathan was the man you loved, the father of your two beautiful children. And he loved you more than anything in the world. You know it; I know it." There was a long pause, and Constantin said, "Listen, what you need to cling to right now are your children. How are they?"

"They're as good as expected."

"What did you tell them?"

"I told them their daddy was dead. What else could I tell them?"

"Did they understand?"

"I think Baruch did."

"Baruch is the older?"

"Yes, he's five years old. When I told them, he just lifted his eyes at me. I read pain in his eyes, real suffering. As for Yaron, he knows something is going on, because he doesn't want to play and only walks around with a serious little face, taking his clues from his brother."

"Talk to them about Jonathan every day," Constantin said. "Unless you do, they won't remember their father."

I couldn't stop crying, and I put down the receiver and walked out to the sunroom. The bay reflected the evening sky, water shimmering like tears of silver. Beyond the windows was the outside world, everything the same as before, the sky, the sea, and the shimmering water, the people. Tears rolled down to my chin and dripped on the carpet. Jonathan was in his casket now, of carved mahogany. It was a millionaire's casket, with silk padding and a heavy lid. As if it made any difference. I would be happier, I thought, if I could believe for at least a moment that Jonathan was in a better place, his soul living on forever; that there was something after one died, incomprehensible, magical.

I took a step back from the window and stumbled over the love seat, remembering the afternoon when Jonathan returned from his trip to Ecuador and gave me the sapphire ring. I remembered the lovemaking and the days that followed, my nervousness, and my scheming. Naïve as I was, I thought I could entice him into marrying me. *Till death do us part.* Now Jonathan would be mine forever.

I didn't believe in the afterlife, and neither did Jonathan. It was strange he had donated money to a synagogue and never told me about it. He hadn't done it to be in a better place today, of course not. He had been proudly accepting his heritage—that was the reason.

I loved Jonathan, and his death was the end, no matter what people might tell me.

A sense of loss was muffling everything around me, deep and unavoidable, with sudden bursts of intensity that caused me to double over in pain, cry, and shake with fear. And yet there were things going on all the time, normal things, daily things, telling me life was refusing to wait or stop for even a second. Carlos was right to bring Rachel to the house and have her remind me of the meaning of shivah. There were children to be fed, guests to be welcomed. Jacob would be arriving in less than an hour. Leah was arriving later—they took different flights from New York—and my father later yet, on a flight through Chicago. Somebody had arranged for all of them to be picked up at the airport.

I had not become Jonathan's wife, but I *was* the lady of the house. Nobody had lost as much as I had. We were burying Jonathan tomorrow, and this was *my funeral.*

⸎

I was alone in my bedroom when I heard the front door—Jacob, my brother, my favorite. I took a peek at myself in the mirror, my eyes reddened, my face bloated from crying, but there wasn't much I could do, and I rushed downstairs.

"Miri."

I fell into his arms.

In his early thirties, on the way to a tenured position as professor of political science at the Hebrew University in Jerusalem, he still smelled of childhood: of pine and dust and a fast-running river.

"Thank you for coming."

"Of course I came; are you kidding? Oh, Miri, I am so sorry."

"Thank you," I said. "And how was your trip? You must be exhausted."

"You know, there is a spot north of Nahariya where, if you stop on the highway, you see Lebanon to the north, Syria to the east, and the Mediterranean to the west. It took me six hours to fly here from New York. This *is* a big country."

It was his first time in America.

We moved into the day room, and I called Remy on the intercom to bring us some coffee.

"Quite a house. I'm impressed," Jacob said and started looking at the paintings that hung on the walls. "Did you pick these out?"

I sensed he was looking for something to say that for the moment had nothing to do with Jonathan. We both needed a little small talk, a few extra minutes to settle in, to get reacquainted.

"I'm glad you're getting to see the paintings," I answered. "We're taking them down tonight and sending them into storage."

"Why?"

"My lawyer said so—I think it has something to do with Jonathan's will and the inheritance."

"Get them back soon," Jacob said. "They're beautiful."

"I'll give you a tour of the house later, but first I'll show you to your room, and then I'd like you to meet Bari and Yari. It's almost their bedtime."

He nodded and announced suddenly, "I'm seeing somebody right now, a young woman from Morocco. Her name is Chantal. She has a daughter from a previous marriage."

"Mother must be delighted."

"Mother is much calmer these days. Tell me, when is Dad arriving?"

"In a few hours. Leah and Yitzhak are getting here before him."

"We were on the same plane from Israel," Jacob said. "Leah looked very distressed, and she was glad Yitzhak came with her. They squabbled all the time over his smoking. They sat in the smoking section of the plane, and I sat a few rows ahead of them and could hear her continuously nagging him to quit. He would say yes, and yes again, and then turn his back on her and light another cigarette. It was funny and also endearing, such a sweet, old couple. She did it for him, and also for herself, to take her mind off Jonathan, her brother, her last surviving blood relative, as she put it. Now she's alone in the world, except for her husband and children."

"She still has her husband."

"Yes," Jacob said. "She still has Yitzhak." He stopped, as if realizing that comparing my pain to Leah's had no purpose. "But Dad, oh, my God," he went on. "I haven't seen him in almost twenty years. And he'll be here tonight. Quite an event."

"It's Jonathan. His death is the cause of this *event*. Jacob, who would have expected it?"

"I'm so sorry," he said.

I hugged him and put my head on his shoulder. "It's difficult," I said, fighting tears.

"I met Jonathan only a few times, and I really liked him. He was always so fun and generous."

"He was a good man. I loved him." It felt comfortable having his shoulder.

Remy walked in with the coffee.

"Thank you, Remy. This is my brother, Jacob."

"Nice to meet you," said Remy. "Miss Miriam, the resemblance between the two of you is uncanny. I mean, as much as a young woman can resemble a man, if you know what I mean, and I hope I'm not overstepping."

I erased my tears with the back of my hand and smiled at Remy. "No," I said, "you're not overstepping."

After he left, I added, "Jacob, I'm alone now. And I have two little children."

"I can't wait to see them."

"I'm scared."

"You've always been my courageous sister. How old were you when you decided to leave Romania?"

"Seventeen."

"And you weren't afraid. You were going into the unknown, all by yourself, and you didn't know the word *fear*. You made it possible for all of us to follow you, and you got us all out of the country."

He wanted to make me feel better, and pride rose in my heart. "Yeah," I said. "That was easy."

"And you weren't afraid years earlier at the waterfall, when you jumped with your fists at Mathew."

My brother. He had saved my life that day at the waterfall, and yet he was giving me the credit.

We spent the next morning getting ready. The house was full, and that made it easier. I found the energy to talk to my boys, and later, with Rachel and Marybeth, we picked their clothes for the funeral. I didn't want them in black, so we chose navy-blue shorts and white button-down shirts with black bands sewn over the breast pockets. Their yarmulkes were secured with bobby pins.

"We'll have to rip small tears in these shirts after the funeral," said Rachel.

It was customary for shivah.

Juan helped Remy prepare a late brunch on the patio in the shade of our mulberry tree. The weather was good, and I thought it would be more relaxed than in the formal dining room, given that our visitors were jet-lagged and needed time in the morning.

My father came down first and sat at the head of the table.

I sat near him. "We didn't really have a chance to say much to each other last night. Dad, how are you?"

"I'm OK. But more importantly, how are you? I'm so sorry."

"Glad to see you, and mostly in pain."

"I'm sorry I never met your husband."

"He wasn't my husband."

"Then I'm sorry I never met the father of my beautiful grandchildren."

There were croissants and bagels in the middle of the table, smoked salmon, cream cheese, capers, chopped onions, scrambled eggs, and an assortment of fruit and cheeses. There were silver thermoses with tea and coffee, pitchers of orange juice, and a jug of ice water.

My father filled his plate with food and took a few sips of coffee. "This is a fantastic place," he exclaimed. "Under different circumstances I'd say we were in paradise, but, Miriam, I'll make you a promise. From now on, we'll come here often. Your children, I want them to know me."

I sensed in his voice a newly found determination. He was still a handsome man, with his thin face and bright eyes and his short graying hair, and I realized he had aged a lot since I last saw him. I remembered an old black-and-white photograph with the two of us perched on a wave breaker in Eforie on the Black Sea. That photograph was somewhere in my bedroom, and I decided to go find it.

"Hey, Dad," I said, getting up, "here's Jacob. You haven't seen each other for ages."

In the house, I ran into Leah and Yitzhak. Last night Leah had looked tired and lost. I had hugged her and cried in her arms. We had lost the same man, I thought, and understood each other's pain.

Now her face was rejuvenated, her hair combed, her clothes somber yet very becoming. Like the resemblance between Jacob and me, her resemblance to Jonathan was unmistakable. It was painful for me to look at her because of it. She was four years older than Jonathan, which meant she was over fifty. Another decade and she'd be my mother's age.

"I'll be right back," I told her. "Food is being served on the patio."

Upstairs I asked Marybeth to take the children outside to eat. I went into our bedroom to search for the photograph. Everywhere I looked, there were Jonathan's things—his hairbrushes and his linen, his slippers, his mints. I looked at framed pictures of us smiling contentedly into the cameras, picked up the sunglasses I had bought him on our last trip to the desert, opened the notebook I had given him to begin keeping a diary that he had never started, rummaged through his wallet, and tried on his heavy gold ring. It was depressing.

Here was the book I had been reading before we left for Las Vegas; I'd never finish it or want to hold it in my hands again. Here was the dress that I had worn two weeks ago when we went to our usual restaurant at the Dell. These were all things that needed to disappear. I needed to give them away, or shred them to pieces, or burn them and scatter them to the winds. Such was the photograph with my father—a heartbreaking reminder of a time and a world that would never return.

I stopped searching and sat on the bed. I took my head in my hands. I gave up.

When I went back downstairs, I saw my boys running circles around the guests. Bari stopped, took a banana from the fruit basket, peeled it, and started eating it. He left the peels in the middle of the table. Mimicking his older brother, Yari grabbed an orange and immediately dropped it to the ground. The fruit rolled under the table.

"Pick it up," Leah told him.

Yari shook his head, hesitated, and ran away. Bari ran after him.

From her seat at the table, Marybeth was silently observing the scene. My father was talking to Jacob. His second wife and his daughter, my half sister, were not there yet. Carlos and Rachel were eating.

"Bari, Yari!" Leah yelled. "Both of you! Come back here."

"Let them be," Yitzhak said and puffed on his cigarette.

My father stopped talking to Jacob and turned to Leah. She was sitting at the opposite end of the table. "They're children," my father said.

"It doesn't matter," she answered, looking grim. "We are mourning my brother."

I took a step forward and called my sons. They came. I tucked Yari's white shirt in and caressed his head. "They'll have plenty of time to miss their father," I said to no one in particular and took them inside the house.

I wished my mother were here, and the mere thought of it seemed amazing.

———— ❧ ————

People were waiting downstairs, but that's how it was—I took my time.

In my vanity mirror, I applied enough foundation to cover the dark circles under my eyes and hide the puffiness in my cheeks, and a pale lipstick to tame the redness of my lips and allow them to blend with the whiteness of my face. I brushed my hair until static caused tiny sparks to fly off my silver brush. From my dresser drawer I pulled out my panties and bra. They were black. I placed drops of Chanel on my neck, on the underside of my wrists, and on the back of my knees. The black dress I had selected was loose on me. I had lost weight in the last two days, but I had no other outfit for the occasion. The dress was simple, with a cut that softened the contour of my body and reached below my knees. Its long sleeves ended with narrow cuffs held together by little black buttons. I sat on the bed and slowly pulled on a pair of black nylon stockings, one leg, and then the next, raising my dress and stretching the material on my calves and thighs. I went to my full-length mirror and made sure that the seam at the back of my legs was straight. Stilettos were out of the question, and I settled for a pair of black shoes with low heels and small, elegant gold buckles. I considered a large pendant around my neck but changed my mind and wore the gold Star of David I had from Jonathan. It was a delicate touch, I thought, matching the gold on my shoes. I turned the sapphire ring on my finger with the stone on the inside, such that it looked like a simple wedding band. When I finished dressing, I wove my hair into a bun and covered my head with a black, wide-brimmed hat with a thin black veil covering my eyes and half my face. I stepped into the children's bedroom and realized that my boys and Marybeth were already downstairs. I left their room and approached one of the two arched staircases. The missing paintings along the walls had left ugly patches of faded paint.

As I started descending, the people waiting below fell silent. Bari and Yari followed Marybeth, my maid of honor, all dressed in black. Jacob took a step forward.

⊶∞∞⊷

Prior to leaving, Carlos asked me to step into the den for a private conversation. He was nervous and kept touching the knot of his bow tie. "There'll be a woman at the service, and later at the cemetery," he said. "A teenage boy will accompany her. They know who you are. The woman used to be Jonathan's wife. She still is, according to papers. They separated years ago, shortly after Jonathan met you, but they never divorced. The boy is her son from a previous marriage. They live in Nebraska."

I took a few steps backward and found a chair.

"Her name is Loretta," Carlos continued. "Her son's name is Victor, and he was a difficult child. He's seventeen now, a pothead who wants to drop out of high school. Jonathan had to step in several times to expunge his record with the authorities and post bail money. He tried his best to influence Victor, but it was hard from far away. Jonathan had adopted Victor, and he considered the boy's upbringing his moral obligation. This was why he hadn't divorced Loretta. He wanted to preserve his guardianship over Victor until the official age of majority."

"You mean until the age of eighteen?"

"Yes," Carlos responded.

"I didn't know any of this. Jonathan never told me."

"He wanted to *protect* you. But I thought you knew he was married."

"I heard rumors, and I hoped they were false. I confronted Jonathan twice, and he refused to tell me."

"Technically Victor is your sons' older stepbrother. At the funeral service, he and Loretta will sit in the front row with the family. They'll come to the cemetery, and perhaps to the reception, later."

"They shouldn't come to the house," I said. "I'm not sure I can handle it."

"As you wish, but she's still Jonathan's wife."

"This is my home, isn't it? That's what you told me."

"You're in pain," Carlos said. "You're grieving, but Jonathan chose you. What do you have to lose? Think about it."

Rows of folding chairs underneath a wide canopy were reserved for the family. The hole in the ground was perfectly rectangular. A mound of arid dirt was piled up on the far side, and the casket was supported by straps above it. Facing the grave, the rabbi was reading aloud. Behind the chairs, a few hundred people formed a horseshoe, heads down, swaying in the monotonous rhythm of the Hebrew prayer. I understood certain words and missed others. Seated in the front row to my right were Bari and Yari. Then came Marybeth, Carlos, and Rachel. On my left were Jacob, Yitzhak, and Leah. Bari and Yari were somber. Loretta sat next to Leah. Victor was in the second row, immediately behind her. He was tall and visibly muscular. Nobody introduced us, but I felt their presence at all times, milling around earlier, sitting a few chairs away from me now, pretending I didn't exist, ignoring me. I didn't greet them, and I didn't embarrass myself in performing what would have been a hypocritical gesture of civility. At the funeral home, I saw Loretta up close. In the room reserved for our family, we superficially brushed against each other, and I realized she was an attractive woman, much older than I, perhaps a few years younger than Leah. She was not clad in black, as I was, and I took that to signify a much lesser sorrow. When she saw Leah, they embraced. They knew each other from before—from before my time with Jonathan—and even though I understood, I felt jealous.

The rabbi stopped praying.

Four men from the cemetery stepped forward and lowered the casket slowly by the straps. When they finished, the rabbi took a handful of dirt and threw it into the grave. There was a low thud, a drumming sound like a message.

The rabbi turned and moved to the end of the front row.

"Mrs. Sommer," he said to Loretta.

The next day Carlos came to the house.

"My ex sends condolences," he said when he saw me.

"Thank you. Are you staying for dinner?"

"I'd love to, but first I'd like to talk to you about the will."

We went into Jonathan's office and closed the door. He placed his briefcase on the huge desk and sat in Jonathan's chair. I sat on the other side, facing him. My eyes fell on the framed photograph of Jonathan on horseback. He looked young in that picture, and happy. There was a cocky smile on his face—one that I knew well, that he displayed every time he did something enjoyable. I wondered if Loretta had been with him when the picture was taken. It must have been at the stable in Rancho Santa Fe. I went there once and never went back. Eventually, Jonathan sold the horses. The beautiful saddle he brought me from South America remained unused on the wooden horse in my former studio.

Carlos opened the briefcase and pulled out a sheaf of papers.

"Here," he said, handing the papers to me. "A copy of the will for you to read and keep. I have the original at the office. You might find it confusing and full of legalese, but don't worry. That's how wills have to be written. Just ask me if you have questions."

He seemed sad as he leaned back in Jonathan's chair.

"What does the will say?" I started.

"Miriam, he left everything to you—or maybe not everything, but almost. Jonathan's estate is substantial, and therein lie the potential complications. Other people might desire a piece of it—Loretta, for instance. In California the estate goes to the surviving spouse as a matter of common law, but only in case of intestacy."

"Intestacy?"

"When there is no will."

"And when there is one?"

"Then all bets are off, unless somebody contests it. The probate court determines the will's validity. Sometimes it leads to lawsuits. That's why I want to hurry. I want to go to the courthouse with the will and the death certificate as quickly as possible, and file a petition for probate. But you need to agree. And since I was the one who wrote the will for Jonathan, most likely we won't need to sign a proof of witness affidavit. I'll find out when I go there. Anyway, it's customary to do it within thirty days from..." His voice trailed for a few seconds.

I looked at Jonathan's picture again. He was handsome.

"...thirty days from the death of the testator," Carlos resumed, and I understood he hesitated to say that Jonathan was dead. "I also need to publish a notice of the probate in a local newspaper. You see, Jonathan named me as the executor. The estate will pay for my services, but the court has to agree to it, and that's part of the probate, also. Once they do, I'll have fiduciary responsibilities to the heirs."

"That's me," I said.

"That's you and your children, and Victor."

"Why Victor?"

"Jonathan created three equal trusts in his will, two for Baruch and Yaron, and the third for Victor. Actually, he created Victor's trust first, when he adopted him, and he modeled the other two after it when your children were born. Each had a starting value of two million in mutual funds and shares in Jonathan's businesses. They're more valuable now, I imagine. The rest of Jonathan's estate is willed to you, and that's quite a fortune."

I waited.

"The estate is appraised at two hundred million dollars," Carlos stated. "Less the money he had placed in the trusts, less the debt he might have and the inheritance taxes, you'll be left with a hundred and eighty, give or take a few million."

"Is this house worth that much?"

"The house is *real estate*. The *estate* includes this house and all the furniture inside it, other houses or properties Jonathan might have owned, his investments, his bank accounts, his businesses, and all his personal assets, like cars and artwork and jewelry. Now the trusts are part of the estate, but they are excluded from probate. And you are the trustee for your children, which means you'll have to administer their trusts until they reach the age of twenty-one, and I'm the trustee for Victor."

"For another four years," I said.

"Correct, in my case, but in your case it is much longer, and one day I'll have to explain to you your rights and obligations. And another thing: *your* assets are not part of Jonathan's estate, but you have to prove they are yours. For instance, the car you drive is yours if it's registered in your name and paid for with your money. Otherwise it gets thrown into the mix, and the same is true for your paintings. That's why I got them out of the house—we don't want to have to prove anything if we can avoid it."

Behind Carlos was a window that opened into the garden. Like most everywhere else in the house, the blinds were drawn. They had stayed drawn since the day we returned from Las Vegas. Daylight was being kept out, and our secrets in. A candle burned on the windowsill, its flame flickering yellow and orange. Carlos's crown of black hair was surrounded by the light of the flame, like a halo.

The governor sent a telegram offering condolences.

An article appeared in the *San Diego Business Journal* about Jonathan's businesses and his real-estate holdings. The article was impressive. The author wrote that Jonathan had been a genius of sorts, skilled at spinning straw into gold. His passing would be a great loss to the business community.

"I used to dabble in real estate," my father said.

I shrugged. It was so much like my father to have dabbled in everything.

I told Carlos I didn't know anything about Jonathan's professional life and felt overwhelmed and proud reading the praise in the newspaper. "He talked little of his work," I said. "I would have never imagined. He was modest. You were right—he sheltered me. Now I have to come out from under his wing. Whether I like it or not, I have to do it, as his heir now, and an owner of his business."

"You don't have to do anything," Carlos assured me. "That's where I come in. As soon as I get confirmed as executor, I'll meet with Jonathan's partners, sell his shares, and address his obligations in all of his businesses."

"I want to know and be part of it."

"Of course you will," answered Carlos.

During shivah, a routine settled over the house. The mornings, spent mostly around the breakfast table, were followed by my visitors taking short trips around town. Every time they left, they apologized profusely, as if afraid I would shatter to pieces in their absence, and they explained why the trip was of paramount importance to them and said that they needed to borrow one of my cars. Jacob was the only one who stayed behind. The afternoons were long and quiet. To my surprise, I was able to sleep while my children were napping, a deep sleep, like a journey to another planet.

In the evening the house came alive. People stopped by, sometimes clusters of them at once. Some came from the synagogue to express the support of the community. Many I didn't know. Marina and Tony came every day. Nelu came. Marina must have said something to him, and his presence was a pleasant surprise, given how unjustly I had severed our friendship years ago. Billy Pratt, the accountant, visited and made sure to tell me how much he had appreciated working with Jonathan and how generous Jonathan had been. Kenneth Antonio Topaz, Jonathan's partner in South America, came with his wife and four children. Constantin called a few times from Maryland, always in the late afternoon. He wanted to make sure I was OK. He had me on the speakerphone, and in the background I could hear Lydia and Nick getting their toddlers ready for bed. Lydia would come to the phone, and we would talk for several minutes. My mother called, and after telling me how sorry she was for my loss, she complained about Grandma's health. Carlos visited after finishing his work in the office almost every day. Rachel, who was at the house during the day, left promptly at five. Jacob read the Kaddish, and we ate in the formal dining room, fifteen or twenty people each time.

During meals, I managed to be the lady of the house, blocking my pain, taking care of friends and family.

Once or twice I was tempted to raise my glass and announce that Jonathan, my Jonathan, had left me a rich widow. I would have used the word *widow*. The fact that we never married didn't matter. We lived together and had children together. We had the same last name. Mr. and Mrs. Sommer—everybody knew us as such. Money was important, and it allowed me to secure the future. And since I was wealthy now, so was my family and Jonathan's family, and from now on anything they ever wanted—within reason, of course—I could and would provide for them.

I thought such thoughts and was tempted to utter them, but I knew better and kept my mouth shut. A grateful silence enveloped me.

———— ✖︎ ————

Adina's husband, Menachem, called from Israel. A princess had been born. Adina had delivered early. The baby girl was six pounds two ounces, nineteen and a half inches long. Mother and baby were resting happily at the hospital.

For an instant it felt great to welcome a new life to this world, and I hoped that even my mother was happy.

———— ✖︎ ————

On the last day of shivah, after prayer, we all went out and walked for not more than twenty minutes through the neighborhood. It was the customary way of *reconnecting* to the world outside. The sun was setting, and the evening was peaceful. There were no people in the streets, only the rare swishing of cars and the rustling of leaves. The sky was dark blue. The air was fragrant. A few white clouds floated in the wind. To the west, the ground dropped, and from certain places we could see the bay and the Coronado Bridge in the distance between the houses. Gardens were full of blooming flowers, their petals bright and delicate. As a painter, I always thought of my surroundings, of how the sky and the water and the trees were different in one place from any place else, or of how similar they really were, how vast and how never ending. How on a spring day in Bucharest in front of Constantin's house I saw nature exploding. How I saw orderly ants, a cat, and beautiful lilac trees. How I knew that the San Diego Bay reminded me of the Bay of Haifa, and how distinct they really were, continents apart. How the air could be hot or freezing cold, or humid, or dry, and I would breathe it in all the same. But if I stopped now and looked, if I thought about such things now, if I really felt the world around me, I would stop breathing. I would understand how insignificant I was, how few people cared about my pain, how Jonathan's death didn't matter, and how all of us would die soon.

I didn't stop, and that evening as we walked, none of us talked. We went down one hill, up another, and back to the house.

Rachel, who had walked with us, gave me a hug and went home.

Leah and Yitzhak went to pack their suitcases. They were leaving the next day for Israel.

My father and his family would stay two more days, and Jacob another week. I was thankful for Jacob.

I had had my reservations regarding Leah, but she was Jonathan's sister, and I was sorry to see her go. Besides me, she felt his absence the most. A few years ago they had buried Samuel. Now Jonathan was dead. I imagined her as a child playing with her brothers in war-torn Romania, hiding together from the Nazis, and surviving the deaths of their parents. Later, she left Romania for Israel. Like me, she did it alone and made a life for herself. Yitzhak looked like a college professor, more so than Jacob would ever look. He chose his words carefully, smoked a lot, and didn't move very much. He certainly didn't seem practical or energetic, the way I thought an engineer would be. Like Jacob, and my father, he hadn't shaved during shivah, and by now his face was covered by white stubble that made him look older and weaker. But he was there for Leah. Together, they had their two sons. When Jonathan was alive, I didn't feel they were family, but during the last few days, we learned to understand each other, and I hoped that my children would be close to their cousins one day.

I decided to give them a gift, something personal. I had the two Stars of David, one from Jonathan and the other from my mother. Giving her the one from her brother would be a real sacrifice. I liked it and wore it often, and I had it on the day of the funeral. I opened the drawer, took the piece from its box, and looked at it in the light. The six diamonds sparkled full of memories. The short love letter Jonathan had written to me after our second date—the only one he had ever written—was still tightly folded inside the box under the velvet lining.

We've been apart for only a few hours, but I can't wait to see you again.

…Believe me, I think of you constantly. You are around me, all the time.

Miriam, I'm happy.

I sat on my bed, trembling, and looked up at the ceiling. "Jonathan, my dear Jonathan."

Something from her brother to me, and from me to her—yes, that was the perfect gift for Leah.

For Yitzhak I selected Jonathan's cigarette holder, from his uncle in São Paulo. Jonathan had a collection of lighters, also, but the cigarette holder was a better choice. It was sterling silver engraved on the outside in an ivy-leaf pattern. Inscribed in flowery Gothic lettering on the backside of the lid was the name of the original owner, *Sommer ç U Fleků, Praha, 1837*, massive beer drinker and patriarch of all Sommers, possibly including my grandfather. Below the lid were a silver stylus and a hinged paper-thin ivory plate. On it, the notations "60,000 pesos, 120,000 pesos, and 240,000 pesos" were written in Jonathan's handwriting. The numbers held no explanation but seemed to suggest a person earning more and more money and saving. The cigarettes could be arranged underneath, kept in place by a yellowed elastic band. Yitzhak smoked Israeli Time cigarettes. I couldn't find those in San Diego, and I asked Jose to buy me a pack of Marlboro Reds, of which twelve fit inside the cigarette holder.

Yitzhak thanked me profusely.

"Leah," I said when I gave her the pendant, "I have this from Jonathan."

"And you're giving it to me? You shouldn't."

"I want you to have it and remember us."

"I will remember," she said, and she hugged me.

We both cried and promised to call each other.

Elise announced she needed a dress. She had a wedding to attend when she returned to Germany, and she thought an American dress would impress her friends. My father turned to me and asked me to go shopping with my half sister. "It would do you a world of good," he said.

I hesitated, but Jacob encouraged me as well.

It was gloomy outside, like many mornings in San Diego. By noon the fog would melt and the sun would be shining. I got dressed in a black skirt, a white blouse, and a gray jacket and pinned a gold brooch with rubies arranged like the petals of a rose on my lapel. I considered wearing a hat but changed my mind and let my hair hang loose over my shoulders. Before leaving the house, I hugged my children and assured them I would be back soon.

We drove in my old BMW convertible. It was as if somebody was trying to rub my face into the world, with the wind swirling and the scenery flying by while I made conversation with my very young half sister. The last time we met, I had been sixteen and she had been six. She didn't remember us meeting.

We parked in the underground garage at Macy's and took the escalators. Elise found a beautiful lamé dress, dark gold with gold sequins. It was cut low at the back, all the way to the waist. She had my father's slender build and long handsome features, only more delicate, and when she tried on the dress, she was radiant. Watching her, I thought of myself at her age. I had been beautiful, too, and I had felt alone in the world, like a leaf in the wind. I had been with Zvi and occasionally with my friend Daniel. I had been envious of Lydia, who seemed solid and settled. I hadn't known what I wanted to do or how to find my balance.

When I met Jonathan, I had liked him right away, but there was something unpredictable about our relationship, lighthearted. It might have been that only I had felt that way, and he had just accepted me the way I was and embraced me. He gave me stability. He gave me my children, and a sense of belonging. And all this time I had thought I was in control, when it was he who had led me with his sure hand and placed me on my trajectory—on *my own* trajectory. He had allowed me to grow and to choose my path, and only corrected when necessary. Of course he had skeletons in the closet. Show me a person who doesn't. And now Jonathan *was* dead. Now he had left me. Forever. Now I understood how much he had meant to me, how serious and talented and generous he had been, and how much I had loved him. How much I still loved him, and how life, my life, would never be the same. I would never replace him, but like my half sister, I was still young. I would go on. And I was a wealthy woman, too—God, *was* *I* wealthy!

We found a pair of stylish gold sandals that complemented the dress, gold filigree earrings, and a gold bracelet watch. When I encouraged her to take the earrings and the watch, Elise hesitated.

"Don't worry, the dress and everything else is my gift to you," I told her, and she melted like a snowflake and kissed me.

—⁂—

I embraced the idea of giving. I felt magnanimous, and Jonathan would have loved it. In my sorrow, this was important.

I decided to give my father the gold pocket watch that Jonathan had bought for himself years ago in South America. I found the old black-and-white photograph I had of my father and me on the wave breaker. The corners of the photograph were curved and yellow. I was the small skinny girl in a dark bathing suit clinging to her father. His face was young and reassuring. Behind the two of us, the sky and the surf seemed ominous.

I had a copy made and then cropped the faces from the middle of the photograph and placed them inside the pocket watch for my father.

That evening, after I put Bari and Yari to bed, we had our last dinner together. My father had some wine, and it made him nostalgic. He grabbed Jacob's hand and mine, and holding both our hands, he told us we were still his children. It was factually true, and totally unnecessary.

When I gave him the watch and he saw the cropped photograph inside, he covered his face with his hands. "I don't deserve it."

The next day Jacob and I drove them to the airport. On the way home, I panicked. The prospect of everybody leaving scared me. I begged Jacob to stay longer, knowing full well he couldn't.

—⁂—

My paintings were stashed against the wall in the farthest corner of the playroom. There were those Nelu had brought from Romania and the ones I had painted since I moved to San Diego. A folded easel stood to the side. My drawings were in a portfolio hanging from a hook. A palm tree in a dark-red ceramic pot blocked the access and the view.

Sprawled on the floor, Yari was playing with toy race cars. Even though shivah was over, he was wearing his white shirt with the black ribbon. He loved it. Marybeth had the shirt washed and pressed and its tear sewn and had given it back to him. I found it strangely endearing.

Bari was trying to climb on the wooden horse, which was too tall for him, but he was stubborn and nimble.

"You didn't send *these* paintings to storage," Jacob noticed.

"No, only the ones I had purchased. These are *my* paintings. They have no value."

"Show them to me."

I wasn't sure. The stigma of mediocrity played heavily on my memory, but my desire to have Jacob see them was strong. Like an exhibitionist, I was frightened by what I was about to do and yet compelled by a desire I could hardly withstand. I hadn't realized it until that moment, but I felt like a different person with Jonathan gone and nobody to watch over me and protect me. I had only my children to love, and I needed to be strong for them and for myself. Painting was my passion. Color was my language, light and shadow my way to feel and connect to the world inside and outside me. Which artist didn't suffer from self-doubt and bouts of depression? What did I have to lose? What more could I lose?

I lifted the stack of paintings and drawings and spread them on the floor. There were sketches, charcoal drawings, aquarelles, and oils. The old ones were in front of the bay window, the more recent ones in the middle of the room.

Bari and Yari came closer. They followed Jacob and moved gingerly between the paintings, leaning their small heads in this direction and that while looking.

"These are Mama's paintings," I said.

"They're great," Jacob said.

"Mama, I want to paint," Bari said.

I caressed his head. "These are from my O'Keeffe period," I told Jacob, pointing at the canvases in the middle of the floor.

"I like this one," Jacob said, looking at the portrait of Pani.

"Don't you think it's too...traditional?"

"No. It brings back memories."

"Do you know who Georgia O'Keeffe is?"

"I do."

"She's old now. Do you think there is a resemblance?"

"Between your work and hers?"

"Yeah, between our art, our styles."

"I don't know," Jacob said.

"Mama, I want to paint, too," Yari said, repeating after his brother.

"OK, kiddies, if you want to paint, Mommy will show you how."

I looked at Jacob and smiled. We unfolded the easel, and I pinned on it two pieces of paper. With a crayon I drew an oval on each. I drew two eyes in one of the ovals, a nose, and a pair of lips. "Jacob's head," I announced.

The boys laughed. Jacob laughed also, moved into the light that fell from the window, and stretched his neck.

"You see, he is posing," I said. "Bari, I'll get you some paints, and you finish this second drawing just like I did the first."

As soon as I opened the box of supplies, Juan came in the room.

"Miss Miriam, Mr. Veranda is here. He needs to speak to you. I let him into Mr. Sommer's office and asked him to wait there."

"The lawyer," I told Jacob.

"Go," he said. "Talk to him. We'll be OK, the three of us here."

I found Carlos in Jonathan's chair. His black briefcase was on the desk.

"Loretta's contesting the will," he said as soon as I entered. His voice was resigned.

I remained standing.

"Be ready for things to get ugly," he continued. "We'll have to work with the probate courts. Loretta is arguing that you exercised undue influence over Jonathan. She'll bring character witnesses if necessary and say he was no longer of sound mind when he wrote his last will."

"That's not true," I said.

"Of course not. But that's what she'll claim, and everything will take time now, maybe years. They might want to inventory the house. I think you have enough money to pay the staff and keep the house going, right?"

"I don't know," I said. "Jonathan and I never talked about expenses."

"Yeah, it figures. Will you still need the cook and the gardener?"

"Of course I will. I couldn't do it myself."

"Yes," Carlos said. "I'll talk to Billy, Jonathan's accountant, now yours, and we'll ensure that you have enough in the account. Once I'm confirmed as executor, I'll have to open an estate account anyhow. Loretta is not contesting me, only the fact that Jonathan left everything to you. When I receive her objections in writing, we'll get together and review them, and we'll have fifteen days to file a demurrer before the hearing."

"But everything will be OK in the end?" I asked.

"I hope so, and if not, we'll have to settle."

"Settle?"

"Yes, give Loretta a piece."

"I don't think so. That's not what Jonathan wanted."

"You don't know that, and you might not have a choice."

"If Jonathan wanted to leave her something, he would have put it in the will. And how could I have influenced Jonathan? Tell me. You and he wrote the will. I didn't even know it existed." I started pacing. "Can't you testify to this during the hearings? Can't we bring our own character witnesses, people who knew Jonathan?"

"We can and we will," Carlos replied. He loosened his bow tie. "And the burden of proof is on Loretta. But she's Jonathan's wife and has a copy of his earlier will. It's complicated."

"What earlier will?"

"The one Jonathan wrote before he separated from Loretta."

On the desk, near the briefcase, was the picture of Jonathan on horseback. I picked it up and looked at it. In it, Jonathan was smiling.

"That's right," I said, putting the picture back down. "Everybody knows they were separated."

"Not for the courts, they weren't."

"What do you mean?" I said. "She lived in Nebraska."

"Again, the fact that they separated will have to be proven."

I paced in silence. Then I stopped and asked Carlos, "Did you help Jonathan write that earlier will?"

"I didn't."

"And how do you know about it?"

"I saw it," he said. "Loretta came to my office and showed it to me."

"She came to your office? When? My God, Jonathan's body's still warm."

"Loretta has every right to do it," Carlos said. "In fact, if she hadn't contacted me, I would have called her myself."

"Why?" I asked. "I thought you were my friend."

"I am."

"No, you're not. And you listen to me. Your job is to defend Jonathan's last wishes. She has no rights and won't get anything from me, you hear? I've had enough. Enough. You can see yourself out. I have to take care of my children."

I left the room in a hurry and slammed the door behind me.

Upstairs, I found Yari crying and Jacob trying to comfort him. Yari's shirt was on the floor. His tiny naked upper body seemed golden in the late afternoon light. Bari was standing silently by the aquarium, looking guilty. Toys were spread everywhere.

"What happened?"

"Nothing, really," Jacob said, obviously relieved to see me. "He tripped and fell, and stained his shirt. Bari pushed him."

"He started it," Bari said.

"Yari," I said and hugged the small child. "Yari, my baby." I kissed his face and dried his tears. "Baby, your Mama's here." He felt warm in my arms, and he trembled. The touch of his bare skin filled me with tenderness. I needed to smother him, love him. I needed to be there for him, for both of them. "Bari," I said to his brother, "come here." The boy moved toward me, slowly. He was the older one, taking his time, showing his independence, needing me also. I hugged Bari and Yari together. The tension seemed to evaporate. That's what I needed to do—be there. They relaxed in my arms and molded themselves to my body. The anger, anxiety, and fear that had choked me while I talked to Carlos started to dissipate.

"Go see where he is," I told Jacob. "I left him alone downstairs."

He understood I was referring to Carlos.

Marybeth came in and found me and the boys on the floor drawing together. She brought a clean shirt for Yari, and we tidied the room, first the toys, and then the paintings.

"I'll go feed them dinner," she said when we finished, and she took Bari and Yari to the kitchen.

I went to my room and sat on the bed, utterly exhausted. Spending time with my children was therapeutic. They needed me, but I needed them more. They gave me purpose. They were my fountain of strength.

I clutched my head in my hands. Outside it was getting dark. I considered turning on the lights, but there were reminders of Jonathan everywhere, and I hoped they would melt away in the darkness. The wall above the dresser stood bare. Two etchings by Ianco used to hang there, him and her, in green and dark silver. I wanted my artwork back and knew I would have to be patient now, especially now, with the claim made by Loretta. Carlos would tell me. I needed to listen to his advice, and that made me angry. The calming effect of hugging my children vanished. No, calm was the wrong state of mind. I had to be angry. Angry was better than calm, or sad, or in pain, or in mourning. Angry had a sense of direction.

I heard voices next door and realized Marybeth and the children had returned from the kitchen.

"They're ready for bed," she told me. "Would you like to come and say good night to them? Tuck them in?"

I remained silent.

"Take your time," Marybeth said and closed the door behind her.

Jacob appeared in the other door, with Carlos. "Knock, knock, it's us. We came to see how you're doing."

"I'm great," I said, hoping they'd sense the sarcasm.

"May we come in?"

"Sure. The more the merrier."

They entered but stood by the door. Through semidarkness I felt Carlos's discomfort.

"Well, look around while you can. No idea how long I'll be able to keep the house." I turned on the light on my nightstand and addressed Jacob. "Carlos gave you the good news, I imagine."

"I did not," Carlos said. He flattened his shirt. "Miriam, what you and I discussed is privileged, and if you want to share with your brother, you do it."

"Yes," I said. "I'll do it."

There was a long silence.

"Let's move to the sunroom," I suggested. "The children are going to bed, and I don't want us to disturb them."

I got up, and the two followed me. I checked my face in the vanity mirror. We walked past Jonathan's huge teak armoire and through the L-shaped study attached to the bedroom. An arched doorway led to the sunroom. I lit several of the decorative candles that happened to be on the table. "Let the flame burn the soul of men," I said, certain that Carlos would remember Rachel's words. Then I added, "You can see better outside with the lights off."

"Miri, this view is magnificent," Jacob exclaimed.

Carlos looked through Jonathan's telescope, while Jacob found a pair of binoculars on the side table. The spot on the horizon where the sun set was purple. While they admired the view, I sat on the love seat and closed my eyes. Something was missing. It felt as if Carlos had something else to say on the subject we had discussed earlier, but he wouldn't do it in Jacob's presence. And it felt as if he was in fact glad not to approach the matter, and I was glad also. We avoided the elephant in the room, the topic most pressing on our minds. And it was comfortable to hear the two men speak, calmly, neutrally—my two protectors.

When I opened my eyes, Marybeth was standing in front of me with Yari's shirt in her hand.

"I put this in the wash, but the paint didn't come out. The shirt is ruined."

"Then throw it away."

"Are you sure? This is the shirt Yari wore during shivah."

"Do you think I want to keep a reminder?"

"I thought it was special."

"Jonathan's dead. Nothing is special."

"If you throw away that shirt, Rachel will be disappointed," Jacob said. There was irony in his voice, and I'm sure that he meant it as a joke, but his comment irked me.

"You know what? I don't care. I don't care at all about Rachel."

I stood up and took a few steps toward the two men. Jacob placed the binoculars down on the table.

I addressed Carlos. "Why is Rachel still here? Why is she coming back every day? Shivah's over. Send her home. Get rid of her, please, now, tomorrow. She's done coming here."

A new wave of anger filled my chest, suddenly, and I could hear it ring in my ears. The three of them seemed ridiculously composed.

"And while you're at it, get rid of these also," I screamed, and I pushed the binoculars across the table to Carlos. The candles flickered.

There was a massive silver bottle opener on one of the side chests, and I knocked it off with a swipe of my hand, sending it to the floor with the thud of a cannon. "And this," I screamed again.

I saw Jonathan's favorite bathrobe folded on a shelf above. He liked wearing it in the sunroom sometimes, I remembered. I grabbed the bathrobe and threw it at Jacob. "And this also..."

"Miriam, please calm down," my brother said.

"I'm done being calm," I snapped. "I've been calm until now, and look at what's happened. Now they're taking me to the cleaners. They want to evict us from my house, get my car and my furniture, take my children."

"Nobody's taking your children."

"Oh, yeah? Nice of them—all they want is my money!"

"Listen, we understand you're going through a grieving process. And we're here to help," Carlos said.

"*Grieving process*? Well, when you put it like that, it's clear." I trotted back into the bedroom and stopped in front of Jonathan's armoire.

The three of them followed.

I swung the doors open. "Take all this away," I screamed, ripping Jonathan's clothes off the hangers and throwing them on the floor. "Get rid of it, all of it. I don't want it."

I kept throwing shirts and jackets and pants and underwear until Marybeth came forward and grabbed me by my shoulders. I turned. She lowered her arms and immobilized mine. Her hold was firm, her touch reassuring. "Easy, now, easy," she said. "We'll get rid of all these, as you wish; no need to be upset. Let's quiet down, and let's not wake up the children. Come. Let's go sit. Let us all catch our breath for a few minutes."

I needed to be restrained, held tight, guided. My eyes met my brother's, and I saw he was worried.

"Breathe," Marybeth said, and I started breathing.

She led me to the bed and sat me down.

Silently, Jacob and Carlos left the room.

I hardly slept that night.

In the morning I decided to give Jacob my portrait of Pani as a parting gift. On the back I wrote in red ink: *To my brother, Jacob, an image from the childhood we shared, with love, Miri.* I considered getting the painting framed, but I realized it would only make it harder to carry.

When I gave it to him, he said, "What? No gold for me, and no silver?" Then he laughed. "Miri, I'll treasure this. Thank you."

His freshly shaved face looked youthful. He was leaving that evening.

Back from the airport, I put the children to bed and had dinner in the kitchen with Remy and Marybeth.

"You can trust Carlos, Miss Miriam," Marybeth told me. "He and Jonathan have been friends for many years."

It was the only time I remember her calling Jonathan by his first name.

Chapter 2

SHADOWS

After dinner, alone for the first time, I had the urge to call Leah. I wanted to tell her what Loretta had done to me, and have her share in my outrage. But in Israel it was six in the morning.

At night my sleep was agitated. Twisting and turning, I rationalized that, with every day that passed, my fear and anxiety would dull their sharp edges, and my pain would become, if not easier, then part of a new reality. In fact, Loretta was helping. Implausible as it was, there was a positive side to the fight she was provoking, to the fact that a fight loomed ahead. All my energy would be channeled in that direction, causing me to ignore the anguish I was feeling.

Poor Jonathan, he had thought he had taken care of me. But he should have known Loretta would contest the will. He could have divorced her and married me. That would have solved the problem. Now I understood why, when talking about Jonathan's will, Carlos had been worried. Jonathan had failed me and his sons—our sons—by not marrying me, and now I would have to fight the fight he had left me, with its legal, banal, and meticulous details. I had to pour my mind and my soul into it.

Jonathan's well was deep—it held plenty of water. I could split the fortune I inherited if I wanted to and still have more than enough, but I was doing this for my children. For their sake I could learn to be callous.

Or so I thought, until I talked to Carlos again and told him I was sorry for getting upset the previous evening.

"No problem; I understand," he answered. "And I have news. The probate court confirmed me as the executor of the estate. They will not inventory the house, and they agreed to use the list of items attached to the latest will for their final distribution. That means the paintings are not itemized but indicated together as artwork."

"This is good, isn't it?" I asked.

"Yes, it is, but I have bad news as well."

"Bad news?"

"Yes. This morning Leah contested the will also."

"Isn't Leah in Israel?"

"She's done it through her attorney. In fact she's using the same lawyer Loretta is using, adding her objections to Loretta's."

"They must have talked while she was over here," I exclaimed. "They met behind my back and agreed to do this."

"Evidently."

What was there to say? While pretending to mourn for her brother in my house, Leah had conspired with Loretta. She looked me in the eye every day during shivah, consoled me, and dried my tears. And all the while, she plotted and calculated. The death of her brother became an opportunity for her. And Yitzhak, with his innocent face, was a party to it, also. They took my beautiful gifts and drove in my car to their secret meetings with Loretta.

"She stabbed me in the back, and she's twisting the knife in my wound," I told Carlos.

"It's time to develop scar tissue."

Carlos explained that, according to the earlier will, Leah and Samuel were supposed to inherit about 10 percent of the estate. Then, as soon as the boys were born, Jonathan hurried to prepare the new will, and he omitted any mention of Leah to Carlos. Samuel was already dead. Jonathan and Carlos talked about it later and wanted to amend the will to include Leah, but they didn't get a chance to do it. And now Leah was taking action.

"People do nasty things for money," Carlos added.

Loretta and Jonathan had separated almost a decade ago, and Jonathan had taken good care of Victor. It was only normal that Jonathan met somebody else. What did Loretta expect him to do? Shrivel? I didn't even know why they went their separate ways, but they did, maybe because they stopped loving each other. Or was it something that Jonathan did? Or Loretta? Maybe *she* cheated on him; one can never be sure. And how about Leah, to turn against me, her own family? She could have talked to me, and I would have understood and accommodated her, but instead she had joined forces with Loretta. With Jonathan gone, my boys and I had become fair game.

"Carlos," I said in a determined voice, "I want the paintings I bought shipped to Jacob in Israel, and I know the art dealer who'll do it."

"As you wish," Carlos said. "They are yours."

Carlos went to New York to settle some of Jonathan's businesses. I didn't go. The intent was to sell Jonathan's shares, and I had nothing to offer. Besides, I wanted to stay with my children.

While Carlos was away, I familiarized myself with Jonathan's will and with the probate process. I learned the practical meaning of terms such as *forced heirship*, *domestic partner*, *intestacy*, *going concern*, and *laws of descent* or *tenancy by the entireties*. Carlos had used some of these terms when explaining things to me. The others I found in books Marina brought me from the university library. I studied the rules of administering the trusts for my children and tried to anticipate Loretta's and Leah's objections to Jonathan's will. These would be presented in bulleted format, Carlos told me, following the court's requirements. As soon as he was back, we would get them and prepare the demurrer together.

The hearing was scheduled in four weeks, and I fantasized about taking the stand, dressed all in black, sad and mesmerizing. Your honor, I would start in a voice full of dignity, the way I saw it done in *Perry Mason* reruns. From what I had heard, the judge was a stern man in his fifties. He would give me leeway in my presentation and slow me down only from time to time to allow the court stenographer to record every word of my testimony. I would speak about my childhood in Bistrița and about my passion for art and my dedication to painting during adolescence. At age seventeen, I would say, I chose freedom over comfort and immigrated to Israel, where I studied fine arts at the University of Haifa. And then I met Jonathan. A murmur would reverberate through the audience, while I would continue, choked with emotion. It was love at first sight, I would declare. He was two decades my senior, but it didn't matter. He was strong and handsome, and I took the fact that we shared the same surname as a good omen. We met on a flight to Romania. I was going there to visit my family, and he to take care of his sick brother. That fact alone told me volumes about his values and generosity. We saw each other when he visited Israel, until one day when he told me he couldn't be without me and invited me to come live with him in America. I gave up a great deal to be with him—my country and friends, the proximity to my family in Romania, my studies, and my future as an artist. He told me we couldn't get married right away, and I didn't question him. I wanted to be with him—that's all I wanted. He said he would make me happy, and he did. In the beginning in America, I was homesick and lonely. Jonathan traveled a lot. He always did. He took me with him sometimes, but not always. I understood he was his own man, a businessman, a strong person with a past and principles. It may sound strange, but loneliness was what I had to accept in order to be with him, and I decided I was willing to do it. I trusted Jonathan implicitly.

When I told him I was pregnant, Jonathan was elated. We named our first son Baruch, meaning "the blessed one" in Hebrew. Our second son, Yaron, was born two years later. I became a busy mother of two, and no, I had no idea that Jonathan had prepared a will naming me as the sole beneficiary. I had never asked for it. I had never thought of him dying or of losing the happiness we had together. He wrote the will without my knowledge, as he did many other things that had to do with business and finances.

Then I would look directly at the crowd and say that I would happily trade everything he had left me in that will for him to return from the dead and be with me and our children.

"In a few months," I told Bari and Yari at bedtime, "we will travel to Israel and visit Grandma and your uncle Jacob. The first time I met your father was in Israel. I was studying to become an artist, and your daddy was nice to me and very handsome."

"Marybeth says Daddy's in heaven," Bari uttered.

"Yes," I told him.

"She says people are happy in heaven."

"They are, but he'd rather be here with you than in heaven."

"Will he come back to see us?" asked Yari.

"People don't come back from heaven, never ever," said Bari, and he twisted his face in a manner that suggested his younger brother didn't understand simple concepts.

I decided to change the subject. "Would you like to become artists, like Mommy, and paint the way I showed you when Uncle Jacob was here?"

"No, but can we get a dog?" Bari answered.

"I want to paint," said Yari.

I felt the sadness buried inside them, but I couldn't be sure if it was indeed their sadness, or mine spilling over.

Carlos called from La Guardia. "They leaked the whole thing to the press. Have somebody run and buy *The National Expose*," he said.

"Who leaked what, and what's *The National Expose*?"

"A tabloid. It turns out Loretta has a relative who's a reporter there. She told him about you and Jonathan, and they're trying to hurt you. You'll see. Good thing Judge Russell can't stand publicity."

The article was titled "San Diego Beauty Challenged in Will Dispute." Three photos arranged in chronological order illustrated the story.

The first picture was of Jonathan and me, eight years younger, on the beach by the Savoy Hotel in Tel Aviv. I immediately recognized it as one of the two photographs Jonathan kept on his desk. I was to his right, looking at his face, the sun splashing on mine, hair flying in the morning breeze on the shore of the Mediterranean. I was holding my hat up against my white cardigan. We looked happy in that picture, content. Small waves were breaking behind us.

"The Sommers in Tel Aviv," read the caption.

"Together for the first time," I murmured, and I wondered how the publishers got hold of the picture. Had they ever sneaked in the house, into Jonathan's study, and made a copy? Had Carlos, or any of the guests, or possibly Rachel, given it to them? Could I trust anyone, and was the entire world a conspiracy?

Then I remembered Jonathan had sent a copy of that photograph to Leah, and a spark of disappointment flashed through my body.

The second picture was a close-up of me clad in black, seated in the front row at the cemetery. Through my veil, there was little to see of my face, except the pain of the moment. The caption said "Bereaved at the Funeral," and it was both off-putting and scandalous that they avoided my name, lacking, I guessed, a formal title for me.

The third picture was a snapshot of Elise and me shopping at Macy's, our faces illuminated by a sudden and juvenile delight. "Half Sisters Shopping Days after Funeral," the caption read, its implication clear. I became livid at the sight of it. Out of my continuum of sorrow following Jonathan's death, this was the moment they stole of me, this singular, unfortunate glimpse of alleged detachment: young lover frolicking in the glow of shopping. Of course she's happy. How could she not be? The old man had croaked and left everything to her in his will, just as she'd planned it.

Loretta had been feeding malicious information to the magazine; that much was clear. And somebody must have followed us and snatched the pictures at Macy's.

I rushed to a window at the front of the house and looked into the street. Our circular driveway was empty, but a black sedan was parked in front of the neighboring house. It could have been our neighbor's car or somebody else's. I tried to see if there was a person inside, but couldn't.

Back in my bedroom, I read the article. It was unusually long and detailed, and it seemed hurriedly written and often confusing, considering the relatively simple story it was trying to tell. It began with Jonathan's birth in Turda, in 1933. There were details about his childhood that only Leah could have provided. They wrote that Jonathan's father, an attorney educated in Vienna, traveled often to Cluj, Budapest, and Bucharest, leaving the responsibility of raising three little children to the women in his family. Jonathan's mother was religious and sickly. I wondered how much Jonathan remembered of his mother and why he had never told me anything about her. His brother, Samuel, had contracted polio at age three. Two paragraphs were dedicated to describing Turda, which was interesting in and of itself but irrelevant to the story. The reporter, I guessed, was trying to show he had done his research. Shortly before the war, for business reasons, Jonathan's father moved his family to Baia Mare, but following the Second Vienna Award, when Northern Transylvania fell under Hungarian control, he decided to send his children back to Turda and have them stay with his sister. The children survived the war, but the father, the mother, and the grandparents were deported to Auschwitz, where they perished.

I set the article down. Baia Mare was a place I had heard about. Gabriel had gone there to study painting. There was a famous Painting Colony there, before and after the war. When I was a teenager, Baia Mare seemed remote to me, far away in northern Romania. In fact, it was close. With my American perspective, I now realized how small Transylvania was. It was hard to fathom that, in spite of the very efficient Nazi machine, Jews in one place were left alone, while in another, only several kilometers away, they were forced onto freight trains and killed.

The writer didn't say anything about Jonathan's life on Doña Alexandra's ranch in Mexico, crucial to the origin of his fortune, which ultimately was the subject at hand. I guessed Leah didn't know much about that part of Jonathan's life and the reporter didn't bother to check. There was no mention of the Mexican woman who I believed had been Jonathan's first wife in America, but a lot was said about the love between him and Loretta.

She was originally from Nebraska, part of a large family. She got married early to her high school sweetheart, had a child, Victor, got divorced several years later, and went back to live with her parents. In 1968 she went on a business trip to California, as a representative of a communal agricultural association, and gave a speech, at the end of which Jonathan approached her with a few trivial questions. Their relationship started with that dialogue about cattle and corn and progressed with breakneck speed. He invited her to dinner, and then a movie, and before long they were in love with each other. They married a few months later, Loretta moved to California, and Jonathan purchased the mansion in Del Cerro. While they waited for the place to be renovated, they lived in La Jolla in a condo overlooking the coast.

I found this part of the article revealing and hard to read. I detected a pattern: Jonathan the charmer, the womanizer. First Consuela, and then Chiquita, and then Doña Alexandra, the Mexican wife, Loretta, and I. How many more had there been? How many had tried, thrown themselves at his feet, threatened, cajoled, cried, and moved on? How many were still waiting for him? The story he had told me about the gentleman from Guatemala who walked with a cane and was surrounded by beautiful women because he knew how to listen, well, that gentleman was Jonathan, I now understood. And I wanted to laugh and to cry.

There were details about Victor's difficulties in elementary school, and about Jonathan's devotion to him. The article did not dwell upon the fact that he wasn't the natural father.

It alleged that trouble started in the fall of 1974, when Samuel's health took a turn for the worse. Jonathan had to interrupt his business trip to Israel and go to Romania. Loretta decided to join him. They met in Bucharest in what Loretta called "one shabby suite" at the Lido hotel. It was her first and only journey to that communist country, which, in her opinion, didn't deserve a place on the map. During that visit Jonathan became silent and reserved. For months afterward Loretta tried to salvage their marriage and understand what had happened. She sweet-talked Jonathan, bought him presents, and made sure he had plenty of rest. He kept to himself, spending huge amounts of time traveling or buried alone in his study. Loretta started sleeping in another bedroom—they were in the big house by then—but Jonathan didn't seem to mind. Then the truth came to light. She overheard Jonathan talking on the phone in a language she recognized as Romanian. His voice was warm, very soft, and she knew he was speaking to another woman.

The article continued with a dialogue, obviously as related by Loretta and reproduced by the author for the sake of authenticity.

"Who was that?" Loretta asked when Jonathan finished talking on the phone.

"A business associate," Jonathan responded.

"A Romanian business associate?"

"Yes."

"Jonathan, why don't you tell me the truth?"

He did. He said he was in love with someone else. He had met her on his flight from Israel to Romania. She was young and beautiful. She was all that he wanted in a woman, and more.

Loretta was crushed. She cried. She found out who the woman was: a gold digger, a fortune hunter, a shallow beauty who masqueraded as an artist and lived well beyond her means on the posh Carmel Hill in Haifa. She decided to fight and protect Jonathan against his own weakness.

"Reconsider," she said.

"No," Jonathan said. "Without Miriam, life has no meaning."

"But, Jonathan, she's twenty years younger than you. This is such a cliché. She'll take advantage of you, suck you dry, and discard you like a sack of potatoes. I'm ready to forgive you, my love, and take you back, but I'll never give you a divorce."

"I don't need a divorce," Jonathan said. "Go back to your family in Nebraska and let me be on my own. In return, I'll buy you a nice house over there and take care of you. I'll help support Victor until he turns twenty-one. You've seen my last will and testament. When I die, if I die before you, you get everything I own, except for what I set aside for my sister and brother. Loretta, please don't fight me on this."

I threw the article to the floor. "Marybeth," I called.

She came in through the side door from the boys' bedroom.

"Take a look at this article," I said, pointing at the magazine. "Is this true, and if so, why didn't you tell me?"

She picked up the magazine and turned pale.

"What's this about, Miss Miriam?"

"Read it," I said. "*You* tell *me.*"

"Miss Miriam, I have to get Bari from preschool. Can I do this later?"

"No, read it now. It's still early."

She sat next to me on the bed.

Looking over Marybeth's shoulder, I read the article for the second time. What bothered me now were expressions like *gold digger* or *fortune hunter*, suitable for a real soap opera.

When Marybeth finished reading, she sighed.

"Well?" I said.

She looked at me with her green eyes, full of compassion. "I'm sorry you had to read this, Miss Miriam."

Her face was broad and familiar. I knew every wrinkle in that face, every twitch and grimace. I felt closer to her than to most people, yet I allowed my frustration to come out of me. "I appreciate you saying this, Marybeth," I uttered in the most cutting tone of voice I could muster. "But why didn't you tell me earlier?"

"Tell you *what*, Miss Miriam?"

"I thought we were friends. I thought we confided in each other. You're raising my children." I stopped for a few seconds. She was obviously very tense. "The only thing you've ever told me was that Jonathan was married. Actually, you didn't even go that far. You said you *thought* he was still married. No mentioning of the fact that you knew Loretta, or that she had lived in this house almost until the time I moved in, or that she had loved Jonathan."

"They fought all the time," Marybeth said. "There was madness in the house, a constant slamming of doors, threats, and yelling and screaming. She didn't love Mr. Sommer, Miss Miriam."

"For crying out loud, after all these years, why don't you stop calling me *Miss* Miriam?"

The boys were snuggling in my bed.

"Before I met your dad, he worked as a cowboy in Mexico," I told them. "He worked on a ranch that belonged to a rich lady who was much feared and respected. She had a beautiful name, Doña Alexandra. Your father was young but very smart and ambitious. Doña Alexandra liked him. Everybody liked him, and he was the boss of all the cowboys. One day they took their livestock to pasture on the other side of the ranch. It rarely rained in that area of Mexico, and the animals were hungry. The ranch was as wide as it is from our house to the ocean, and they had to cross a mountain and a ravine. You know what a ravine is, don't you?"

They didn't, so I explained and continued my story.

"At the bottom of the ravine were these boulders. A calf stumbled and fell to the ground. Most animals passed by the fallen calf, but her mother stood near her. Your dad was riding a big white horse. He dismounted and kneeled by the injured calf. 'Her leg's broken,' he said and asked another cowboy to find him two planks. They needed three men to hold down the calf while your father bandaged her leg, and while he worked, the mother cow gently nudged his shoulder. Then he told the cowboys to empty the cart they used for provisions, and he placed the calf inside on a soft layer of blankets. 'I'll take her back to the ranch and get the vet,' your dad told his men. 'I'll catch up with you later.' He rode slowly in front, a horse pulled the cart, and the mother cow followed them on the mountainous trail. That day, your father saved that young calf's life, and the mother was grateful to him. A mother doesn't abandon her babies, never, no matter what."

I looked at my children to see the effect my words had on them. Yari was watching me with big, concerned eyes, but Bari was already asleep.

On Monday I drove to Carlos's office. No car was following me. His office was in a white stone building near the Gaslamp District. The secretary escorted me into a sunny conference room that could easily seat two dozen people. There were hunting scenes on the walls, and they reminded me of the artwork I had found in the house when I first moved to California.

"Carlos will be with you in a few minutes," the secretary said. "I'm sorry for your loss. I still don't believe it. Mr. Sommer used to come here often."

I nodded and sat at the head of the table.

"My name is Belinda. Let me know if you need anything, a cup of coffee or water."

Left alone, I began thinking of this kind of life—the business world with its legal agreements and cutthroat competition, with secretaries, conference rooms, and modern city buildings. I was trying to follow in Jonathan's footsteps, not because I wanted to, but because Jonathan had left me no choice, and I felt out of place and lonely. I had been lonely before, but I had never thought I would feel so alienated after almost seven years in America.

Carlos walked into the room, wearing a gray business suit, a white shirt, and his bright red bow tie. Confidently he placed several manila folders on the desk and sat next to me.

"Miriam, I'm glad to see you. Welcome to my office."

I looked out the window. Downtown San Diego stretched below. "How was New York?" I asked.

"Fantastic. I reached agreements with three out of the four corporations Jonathan was associated with. And the fourth will be done in a week. I won't bore you with details, but financially we're doing OK, better than OK. Belinda is preparing the full report. You'll see it. But now, here's the paperwork Loretta filed with the court."

It was short—several pages in all. The beginning was full of personal information and legal terms, but the main point was the assertion that Jonathan's new will had been written under undue pressure exerted by me. Carlos and I had expected that, and now I saw that no real evidence was provided—of course not, because there was none. As Carlos put it, all was circumstantial. According to them, this was a classic case of a much older man madly in love with a young, predatory woman. The gullible man lost his mind and his decency. He forgot his previous commitments and his place in the world. Our two sons were part of the plot and contributed to the old man's biased judgment. But the existence of the old will was Loretta's proof, representing the real wishes of the deceased.

"They imply I had my two sons as a means to get to his money. I feel *diminished*," I told Carlos. "I'm not sure if I can handle this."

"You can."

"The magazine article stated Samuel was supposed to inherit a share of the fortune as well."

"I told you so, but Samuel's dead."

"Leah's not."

"Trust me, and let me draft the demurrer."

The hearing lasted less than twenty minutes. Judge Russell was a tall white man, totally bald, with a face pockmarked by acne or some childhood disease. He met us in his chambers.

Carlos warned me that Loretta's attorney, Milford Thomas, was a power-house. Leah did not come, but Loretta was there. Her eyes downcast, her lips tight, she consistently avoided looking at me.

Judge Russell was quick in addressing her and Thomas. "As you know," he said, "this testator, any testator, is allowed to write a will favoring some people, and later write a different will in favor of others, annulling the first. This is not illegal. What is illegal is to exercise undue influence on the testator in order to have the will modified. That's the subject of this hearing, and that's what you have to prove. Adultery, as appalling as it might appear to some, is also not illegal. If adultery is all you have, you're wasting my time. However, there is a lot of money at stake, and I'll give you a chance to prepare arguments and collect information. But I warn you: no character assassination. This is a court of law, not a script for a South American *tele-novela*. Settling out of court would be ideal. As I said, changing one's mind is not illegal."

I smiled. Only fools never change their minds.

"Understood," Thomas said.

"The clerk will schedule the next hearing in two months," Judge Russell said.

Living without Jonathan was like walking through virgin snow—no pathway ahead, only footsteps behind me as far as my eye could see. If the sun came out, the light would blind me. If clouds gathered in the sky, they would dump more snow and cover the tracks.

Loneliness was like snow—cold, penetrating, especially at night. My bed was huge. It was a king-size bed that had been too big even with Jonathan in it. The void next to me was a precipice, a void like black snow. I was a young woman. Sometimes my flesh was hot and I felt like I was falling for a long time. When I reached bottom, I was covered in sweat. The sheets were wrinkled and gathered under me. My nipples hurt. My stomach felt tight. I touched myself and I moaned.

The exhaustion I had experienced during shivah had disappeared, and I could no longer sleep. Often I took Bari and Yari into my bed, but that was not right. It wasn't healthy. They were growing boys who had to stand on their own.

I talked to Marybeth, and she told me more about Loretta. That woman had not been a saint. She had no taste. The things she had done to the house were horrendous. She was rude to the staff and fought with Jonathan all the time. Victor was a problem child.

Marybeth confided in me. Her former husband used to beat her. Good thing she had the strength to divorce him. Being with my children and me meant a lot to her. Like me, she had no pathway ahead.

I told her about Pani and how she had left us. How she had abandoned *me*.

"Don't judge her too harshly," Marybeth said.

"I don't. A long time ago I painted her portrait."

Through Jonathan I had found a new world and reached balance. His friends had become my friends. During shivah many had come to the house. My family had come. Now they had all left. I remained with Carlos, Marybeth, and Marina, and of the three of them, two of them worked for me.

I didn't want to suffocate Marina. I would see her two or three times a week. She had her family and her work.

"You'll come out whole at the other end," she said.

I didn't know what "the other end" represented, but her words made me feel good. Sometimes we walked around Lake Murray. There was a playground by the lake, and I took Bari and Yari along. We talked about family, about university, and about Nelu. I talked about painting again and about Georgia O'Keeffe.

Shortly after Jonathan's death, I thought I would get involved with some of his work. His footsteps were there for me. But I couldn't do it. His world, the business world, was too rigorous and all consuming. I didn't want to learn finance, catch planes early in the morning, be on a schedule, or write long reports.

When I first met Carlos, I didn't trust him. Now I depended on him. His divorce had affected him. He had changed, or maybe I thought so because I didn't have too much of a choice. Now he was our guardian.

After the hearing Carlos said, "We are doing well. I will contact a few of Jonathan's former business associates and have them deposed. I want to demonstrate how smart and independent Jonathan was. No chance for you to manipulate him. And let's find Jonathan's former wife, that Mexican woman. Looking into Jonathan's history with women might show that he knew how to handle his romantic entanglements. Of course, only if you agree."

"I do," I said, even though I didn't like the idea of having details about our private lives exposed. In my opinion the magazine article had said too much already. Privacy was important, I thought.

For several weeks I didn't know what to do with myself. Bari was in kindergarten. Marybeth took care of Yari during the day. Remy cooked. Juan tended the grounds. To paint I needed clarity and peace of mind, which for now were out of the question. I had my sewing machine brought upstairs and started designing black outfits for myself. While sewing, I let my thoughts roam freely. I feared I could be left penniless, even if the boys had their trusts. What if Carlos was wrong? What if Loretta had something up her sleeve, a sleazy detail, a witness, or a trick of the trade? I'd be lost. I had two children. No way could I ever go back to the way I used to live before Jonathan.

<hr />

The car was black and had tinted windows. Marybeth noticed it first.

"It's parked far enough away for us not to see it from the house," she said.

I went up the street to look but couldn't see anything inside. There was a eucalyptus tree growing by the sidewalk between the car and the entrance to our driveway. In the evening the car left, but it returned the next morning and parked in front of the eucalyptus tree. Two men stepped out of the car and knocked at our neighbors' doors. At the fish market, a young woman approached Remy and said she wanted to ask him a few questions about the Sommers. She offered money, but Remy refused. The third day the black car parked closer yet. A van with small windows pulled in behind the black car. It carried cameras, tripods, and recording devices. One man walked up to our front door.

I came out of the house, dressed in black. "What do you want?" I snapped.

"Would you grant us an interview?"

"No."

"Why not? The world deserves to know your side of the story."

"There's no story," I said.

A flash went off in the bushes.

I told them to go.

"There is always a second side, Miss Sommer. Don't you believe there is?" the reporter insisted.

I turned my back on him and sensed continuing flashes, like popping soap bubbles, until I entered the house.

I called Carlos. "I'm scared. They're everywhere, like the black plague."

"They're nothing of the sort. They're press."

"What do they want?"

"Gossip. Scandal makes money," Carlos said.

"Can't we do anything?"

"Maybe Judge Russell can get an injunction. That would stop them from coming onto your property, but nothing more. The street is public ground. We live in a free country, you know."

"I hate this country," I said.

Marina came to the house, and they accosted her. She walked fast.

"Press cars are parked all along the street," she announced.

"I'm so sorry," I said.

"Don't be. There is enough money at stake for the story to be fascinating. You're an instant celebrity. People eat these things up."

"What about the children?"

"They won't bother the boys. It's you they're after," Marina said.

"The boys will grow up. They'll be able to read about their mother and father in the papers."

"That's a long time away, but maybe you should drop out of sight for a while."

⎯⎯ ∞ ⎯⎯

The second article was harder to take than the first.

My father had left my mother for a younger woman, they wrote, and my mother, my brother, my sister, and I had had to move into the modest apartment of the Levinescus, my maternal grandparents. To meet increased financial obligations, my grandfather, cardiologist and member of the Communist Party, had to work long beyond retirement age. While Jewish, the family was nonobservant, and we, the children, grew up in that confusing and often arrogant emptiness brought forth by the lack of religious principles and traditions. As a result, and following in the footsteps of my father, from the young age of fourteen, I acquired the suspect reputation of being *easy*. In Bistrița, where everybody knew everybody, I was observed kissing older boys in the bleachers of the soccer stadium or on park benches. My lover and art teacher was Gabriel Gelb; I was sixteen and he twenty-three. So did I twist his mind that he, an otherwise decent young educator, agreed to sever his long-term relationship with Cecilia, a woman his own age he was planning to marry. And as if to spite the entire community, in the year that followed, the two of us kept our so-called love in full view, walking hand in hand, riding noisy motorcycles late at night, smoking, kissing in the main town square, and making out in the public library. In my craving for attention, I could be seen with my easel at the market, under the somber columns of Sugalete Row, or in the woods by the waterfall, sticking out like a sore thumb, always wearing a hat and dressed in provocative outfits designed by me or of an undetermined Western origin, unlike the drab clothes worn by most people in that era of communist utopia. Naturally, mature men swarmed around me like the pigeons around the church tower.

The article claimed that I dumped teacher Gelb and that the poor man, devastated, disappeared from town forever. I continued my careless existence like a butterfly, flying from man to man, until the day I remembered my Jewishness and, without any consideration for my family or country, decided to leave for Israel.

There were those who said I had to do it, having worn out my welcome in Bistrița.

The story skipped over the difficulties I initially faced in Israel and over my meager existence at the student hostel in Romema. It continued with me taking random art classes and residing in a charming Carmel studio apartment, more expensive than any student could ever dream of renting. For emphasis, the article included two beautiful photographs of the Haifa Bay as viewed from my window.

No wonder, the author noted, I later found residing in San Diego agreeable.

To protect the source, the author did not disclose the name of the middle-aged, married cosmetic surgeon who made my life on Carmel possible. Clearly that man was enamored with me and completely unaware of my ongoing relationship with Daniel, a man my own age, who would appear in my bedroom as soon as the surgeon would leave. And even though the surgeon was more than amenable to spending large sums of money to fulfill my latest extravagances, eventually I broke up with him. He was no match for the American millionaire I had the good fortune of meeting on a plane during one of my routine trips to see family in Romania. Amazingly, the American carried my last name, a fact that guaranteed a touch of magic.

The American was married. Together with his wife, he was raising a difficult child.

Born in Romania, Jonathan Sommer was a pillar of his community and a generous contributor to the Beth Israel Congregation of San Diego. He was in his early forties, a man at his peak, full of charm and determination. He concealed the affair from his wife, and vacillated for months, seeing me when on travel to Israel. He ensured my financial well-being, which, truth be told, for him amounted to hardly more than a trifle. With time, I understood the true worth of my latest catch and started tightening my web. When Jonathan asked me to join him on a trip to Romania to visit his brother, Samuel, I went along. Gladly.

Here is what Doru Ionescu, the head of the Romanian family that had adopted Samuel and taken care of him for three decades, had to say about me. *"She was aloof. Obviously we weren't good enough for her. Jonathan stayed with us, as he always did during his visits, while she elected to spend the night at the most expensive hotel in town. I told my wife she was trouble. And you should have seen the limousine they were riding. Boy, I knew Jonathan was a well-to-do fellow, but never before had he behaved in a manner that I would call ostentatious."*

After that trip Jonathan and Loretta separated. But they never divorced. Loretta was Catholic, and a divorce would have been unacceptable. Besides, Jonathan had promised to remain involved in Victor's life, and he wrote a will in Loretta's favor. Then he brought me over. While he traveled to Nebraska often to fulfill his familial duties, I, the new mistress of the beautiful San Diego mansion, ran the household. The first thing I did was fire the cook.

I should have seen it coming, Morris, the cook, said in his interview. *From the day she arrived, she acted mean to me, always complaining.*

Now, the article concluded, *Miriam Sommer's carefully concocted plan appears in jeopardy. Even with a will in her hands, with a record like hers, what reasonable judge would deny Loretta, the true Mrs. Sommer, a share of the inheritance?*

In all fairness and in the interest of full disclosure, the reporters of this newspaper attempted several times to interview Miriam Sommer and her staff, but our requests were denied repeatedly.

What followed was the series of photographs taken of me in front of the house on the day I went to confront the reporters. I looked skinny and desperate, like a wet crow, black clothes flapping.

I was on the phone with Carlos talking about the article when Marybeth came in.

"There is a woman asking for you downstairs."

"Who is she?" I said.

"I don't know. She's from Mexico, and she says she knew Jonathan."

"Is she a reporter?"

"I don't think so. She speaks broken English," Marybeth said.

I told Carlos about the visitor, and he asked me to be careful. "If in doubt, or if you need anything, I'm here."

"Take her to the day room and stay with her until I come," I told Marybeth. I changed into a black skirt and sweater and checked my face in the mirror.

In his room, Yari was playing with his toys.

"Mama has a guest," I told him. "Marybeth will be right back here with you."

Downstairs, I found the woman seated on the sofa with her overcoat on, and Marybeth standing by the window. There was an uncomfortable silence in the room. The woman seemed tired and possibly intimidated.

"Hello, I'm Miriam Sommer," I said and extended my hand.

She rose to her feet. "Carlota Westfalia," she said. "I know Jonathan."

"Jonathan passed away."

"I know. I heard from newspaper," she responded.

"Mrs. Westfalia, what brings you here?"

She was a midsize woman under fifty who in her youth must have been quite attractive, not like a beauty queen, but a tomboy of a girl, with quick brown eyes and curly hair. Naughty. Sexy. Now her hair was speckled gray, falling in uncombed curls over her thick collar. She was dressed in a way that seemed peculiar for San Diego: a navy-blue wool overcoat buttoned up to her neck, navy-blue pants, and a pair of brown winter boots.

She sat on the edge of the sofa and then leaned back and took a few seconds before saying, "Business. I wish business. Do you speak Spanish?"

"I don't, but we have a man here who does. Marybeth, please ask Juan to join us."

"I will," Marybeth said and turned to the woman. "Mrs. Westfalia, I don't see a car in the driveway. Did somebody give you a ride, or did you walk here from the bus station?"

"Not important," Mrs. Westfalia answered.

Marybeth shrugged.

I didn't know where the bus station was, but I imagined it was at some distance.

"Would you like anything to eat or to drink?" I asked Mrs. Westfalia.

She hesitated and then nodded. Her face was broad, with vaguely American Indian features. Her eyes and the corners of her mouth were framed by wrinkles. Her lips were thin and colorless.

"Marybeth," I said, "please ask Remy to bring us some snacks, tea, and coffee. And don't forget about Juan, and Yari's alone upstairs."

We exchanged a meaningful glance to confirm things were under control, and Marybeth departed.

Mrs. Westfalia unbuttoned her heavy overcoat, revealing a silky beige blouse and a large cross on a silver chain around her neck. She drank a cup of tea and ate several small open-faced ham sandwiches Remy brought us on a platter.

When Juan came in, Mrs. Westfalia started talking, and Juan translated.

She had arrived the other night from Mexico City and had spent the night in Tijuana, where her cousin lived. In the morning she caught the bus to San Diego. A reporter had contacted her earlier about Jonathan's death. Loretta knew of her and her cousin because years ago they had met in Mexico City. Jonathan used to send her money. Sometimes the cousin would come to San Diego and get it. Jonathan helped her because he was generous, not because he had to. They had been good friends in their youth, long before either of them had married. God, she still remembered the first night she laid eyes on Jonathan, a handsome young man, sleeping in a hammock behind the servants' quarters on Doña Alexandra's ranch, under the summer stars.

"What were you doing on the ranch?" I asked her.

Juan translated.

"I was still in high school. In the evenings and on weekends I helped my mother with the vegetables. Maya Alvarez was my mother's name."

"So Westfalia is your married name?"

"Yes, I got married after I ran away from the ranch. My husband was German, and we met in Mexico City. We have a son and a daughter, but he left me."

"Wait," I said. "You ran away from the ranch?"

"Yes."

"And your name is Carlota? Do you have any other names?"

"The people on the ranch called me Chiquita."

"My goodness."

"I loved him," she said. "When I realized he and Doña Alexandra had fallen for each other, it was time for me to go. He had always been nice to me, such a gentleman, and he had never touched me or kissed me. Not even when I asked him to," she added, smiling.

"Your father was Juarez," I said.

"Yes."

"He suspected Jonathan."

"My father was a stubborn Mexican man."

"Chiquita, this all happened twenty-five years ago."

"I was sorry to hear Jonathan is dead."

"Thank you. You said you had business to discuss."

"Loretta told the reporter she suspected Jonathan was my son's father, and the newspaper offered me money to say that."

"But it's not true?"

"It isn't. I left the ranch in 1955, and my son, Albert, was born in 1958. He is twenty-six today."

"What does Albert do?"

"He's a mechanic and works for the railroads."

"And your daughter?"

"She's married. She's with her two little children at home. We can all use money. It's never enough."

"How much money did the people from the newspaper offer you?"

"Two thousand American dollars. That's a lot for us."

"Two thousand dollars to tell a lie."

"Loretta thinks it isn't a lie," Chiquita said.

"Give me a few minutes."

I left her with Juan and went to call Carlos. The things people did. I was touched and uneasy at the same time.

"Feed her and put her up for the night," Carlos said after I told him the story. "We'll send her to Tijuana tomorrow. Tonight I'll stop by the house and have her sign an affidavit never to disclose anything about Jonathan to any newspaper unless she clears it with us first. And let's offer her money, more than the press. Say five grand."

"Ten grand," I said.

"Tell us about Daddy," Bari said.

The boys were in their pajamas.

"Let me think. OK, here we go."

They jumped on their beds, ready to listen.

"You know, when I was a student, I had very little money," I said.

"Until you met Daddy," Bari said.

"Sometimes I would go to the beach in the evening to look at the sea. Walking on the beach was fun. The water was deep blue, green, and black. The sun was setting, reflecting on the surface of the water and creating a shiny ribbon of gold. There were seagulls flying overhead. What I liked the most were the boats bobbing on the waves, some close, others all the way at the horizon. Some were sailboats, but most were motorboats, moving quickly, flying on the water and leaving a trail of white foam behind. I would look at those boats and try to imagine the freedom the people riding in them were enjoying. I could almost see myself in one of those boats, facing the wind, letting my hair fly, or leaning overboard to touch the water with my open hand. When the sun descended below the horizon, the evening breeze would make me cold. I would shiver and leave the beach. Getting a boat was too expensive, and I couldn't afford it, but I could dream about it. Then I met your dad, and I told him how much I liked the sea."

"And he bought a boat," Yari guessed.

"He didn't buy me one, but he rented a yacht for us. It had two decks, sleeping cabins, a bathroom, a changing room, and a dining room. It had a young captain, two mates, and a cook."

"Like Remy," Bari said.

"Just like Remy. I remember when we left in the early afternoon. The heat was oppressive, but on the boat we felt the cool breath of the sea. The water parted ahead of us with a soft swish, the wind caught in our faces. I was dressed in white, and my hat had a string that tied under my chin. The wind was strong, and I had to hold the hat on my head with my hand. Your dad laughed at me and said I should take it off, but I have very light skin, and the sun can burn right through me and cause freckles to appear on my nose and my cheeks. The boat was rocking near the shore. As we gained speed and went farther out to sea, the water seemed to become calmer, or I got used to it, and the rocking became pleasant, comforting, reminding me of when I was a baby and my mother rocked me to sleep. The farther we went, the better I felt, and it was on that boat that I knew I could follow your dad anywhere and be happy with him. It was just the two of us and the sea, the sky, the wind, the parting water, and the seagulls. On the way back we had dinner on the lower deck, and your dad played beautiful music on the tape player. By the time we reached the marina, it was late, and most other boats were in for the night. Our boat was the biggest and most majestic of all."

"What's majestic?" Bari asked.

"*Majestic*," I said, "is for kings and queens. You know how you say 'your majesty' to a prince, like in *Cinderella*?"

I called Lydia and told her how outraged and embarrassed I felt over the articles in the magazine. I was so upset I could barely talk.

"Don't worry; it will be all right in the end," she said, trying to comfort me. "Take a deep breath. I don't understand these things, but I know you're fair and generous, and you will settle."

"I don't know what I'll do. It seems like the whole world is against me. The other day, this woman, Chiquita, showed up. I don't know why she came. I mean, I do, but people come out of the woodwork all the time to lay claim against me. As if it's not hard enough that Jonathan died. And I have all his businesses to worry about. And the fight over the inheritance. I hate it, and I feel overwhelmed. You know, when I think about our life in Israel, I remember how frugal but simple it was. Now my mother and grandmother are in Israel, and Jacob, and Adina with her new baby girl. Lydia, where did I go wrong?"

"Nowhere," Lydia said. "You have two beautiful children, and you need to think about them."

I called Jacob in Jerusalem and talked to him about the articles.

"Marina has a good point," he said. "Why put up with all this? Get the hell out of there."

"Easy for you to say, but I live here. My children are here, there are legal issues to settle, and I would need to talk to Carlos about it."

"He'll contact you if he needs you, and you can always return for the hearing."

"That's several months away."

"Even better. Go to Switzerland for the summer, south, on the border with Italy. It's beautiful. Take the children with you, and Marybeth. You can afford it. Remember when I had that conference in Geneva? I passed through Lugano. You'll love it. Talk to Dad; that's one of the things he does for a living. He'll find you a nice villa for rent."

I felt my brother's excitement.

"I'll think about it," I said.

Then I paused and added, "Jacob, I want to ask you a favor. I'm making arrangements to send the artwork that I have in storage to you for safekeeping. I'll send you the receipts and everything, and when the whole thing is over, I'll take them back. They'll be insured, about fifty in all, paintings only. Art dealers will bring them over to you several at a time. Some are very expensive."

"Expensive things leave a trail," he said.

"It's all above board, and you don't have to worry. But you know, if I cannot paint, at least I want to know that my beautiful art collection that means so much to me is in a place I can trust. I'm hurt right now, and I have no idea where I'll end up hiding once this thing is over."

Carlos and I met a few times to plan our strategy, and we identified people from my past who could be good character witnesses. I was worried about the allegations in the tabloid, while Carlos dismissed those as garbage. He tried to focus on people who understood me and my character, my true relationship with Jonathan, and that the accusation that I had unduly influenced his will was false. While I talked, Carlos took notes in longhand on a yellow legal notepad, and several times he asked Belinda to join us and type my statements. I told him—them—about my life, about how we met, and what I knew about Jonathan's life in Mexico. We spoke about events that had shaped me, the moments when I had needed courage and strength, and those when I had felt alone and vulnerable. I said that the only person who could have provided information to *The National Expose* about Zvi Rave was Mrs. Shames. But, I commented, Mrs. Shames liked me, and I liked her, and I was sure she had been tricked into it or hadn't understood the implications. We talked about Nick and Lydia, and about Constantin, and about the way all of them had been nice and such good friends to me and to Jonathan.

"Constantin had decided to immigrate to America," I told them. "This was a long process, and Nick was writing letters to Senators Dole and Rockefeller to help their chances. But all of them, all of these people, would be positive witnesses," I assured them.

We talked about Nelu and came up with a plan to have the paintings sent to Jacob.

The sessions proved therapeutic. Mostly I stayed calm and businesslike, but once I lost control and got angry.

"Jonathan left me all alone," I said.

Carlos was listening carefully. We were in his office, seated side by side on a narrow sofa facing the tall windows in front of his desk. Belinda was near us at a portable typing desk. A second lawyer, Carlos's assistant, was present. His name was Reggie Whitewater. It was in the middle of the day, the bright daylight making me squint.

"He left all of us," Carlos answered.

"For me he was everything," I said.

Belinda stopped typing.

I took a small handkerchief from my purse and squeezed it. "I have to fend for myself and my two little children."

"He left you a fortune," Reggie said. It wasn't his place to comment.

"I don't need his fortune. He left me alone. He *betrayed* me."

Carlos looked down, uncomfortable. "It wasn't his fault he died," he uttered.

"He should have married Miriam," said Belinda suddenly. We stared at her as she rested her fingers on the keys.

"Carlos," I said, "I am tired. I've decided to take the children and go away for a while. I've decided to disappear." I started crying. "I rented a villa in Lugano," I added.

"Go," Carlos said. "Staying in touch won't be a problem, but I will miss you."

His handsome face looked sincere.

Chapter 3

ICE CREAM IN LUGANO

The villa my father found for us near Lugano was a few miles west of the Italian border, separated from the lake by a perfect row of tall cypresses, with a small stony beach, a boat shed, and a private pier. Remy, who traveled to inspect the premises ahead of the family, had the current owner outfit the kitchen with a professional gas stove. The villa itself dated from the middle of the nineteenth century, when it belonged to a family of Russian aristocrats. The living areas were remodeled and tastefully furnished, while the pier, the shed, and the Mediterranean garden reflected the imprint of time with a tinge of romantic neglect.

There were five bedrooms on the second floor, the master bedroom equipped with a marble bathroom. I found the arrangement ideal, placed the children and Marybeth in two bedrooms closest to my own, and left the other two for overnight guests.

The living room downstairs provided stunning views of the lake, while other windows in the house opened toward the mountains. A porch outfitted with woven raffia furniture wrapped around the lake side of the villa.

Remy organized his living quarters in a converted stone barn on the property.

We rented two cars, a Land Rover for shopping and family trips, and a black Mercedes Benz, mostly for myself and for special occasions. Downtown Lugano was a two-minute drive or a twenty-minute walk away on Strada di Gandria, following the lakeshore.

I liked Switzerland. It was what I had always imagined America to be before I moved to San Diego—clean, functional, naturally beautiful, and orderly. I liked the well-dressed people in the streets and the fact that I could walk almost anywhere. I liked the fresh produce in the supermarkets and the small, elegant boutiques.

We arrived on a summer day when the air was so clear that even the mental fog and jet lag of the overnight flight across the Atlantic dissipated. The deep blue and gray lake reflected the mountains covered in lush green vegetation. The streets were narrow, sidewalks wide, and most buildings displayed intricate sculpted stone and wrought-iron facades and red-shingled roofs. Clusters of flowers were everywhere. It rained in the afternoon. After seven years in San Diego, not only the children, but I, too, wondered at the miracle of that afternoon summer storm, when the sky turned black in a matter of minutes and torrents of rain came pouring down, washing everything, huge droplets splashing on pavements, foaming against the tiles on our patio, bubbles bursting, pools forming in our crushed-stone driveway, little branches, petals, and leaves flying everywhere. When the rain stopped, we opened the windows. In rushed the fresh air, cool and imbued with the fragrance of lake, oleander, and pine.

I didn't sleep well the first night, but after several nights of jet lag and bad dreams, I started finding some much-needed rest. The children seemed happy. We began each day with a renewed level of eagerness, as if big adventures awaited us, and even though the loss of Jonathan still pained my heart, and the fight for the inheritance occupied my mind constantly, there was no question that the change had done all of us good.

Marina and her son Bobby came to visit. We spent the week exploring Lugano and the nearby areas. We strolled through Piazza della Riforma and Parco Civico, admired the Cattedrale di San Lorenzo and walked through the village of Gandria, and took the funiculars up Monte Brè and Monte San Salvatore, where we climbed on the roof of an old church and marveled at the spectacular views of the lake and mountains. Remy spoiled us with outstanding local dishes, which we enjoyed on our porch in the evenings.

My father visited next, by himself. I drove Dad around Lugano, pointing out some of the sites again, my knowledge of my new temporary home proudly displayed. He seemed less interested in being a tourist and happier spending time with his grandchildren. He took the boys fishing. As they dug for worms in our garden, I voiced my disgust for the squirming creatures, and he laughed and said it built character. It was so typical Father.

I had never been to Italy, and he suggested the two of us take a short trip to Rome over the weekend. I worried about being away from my children, but he convinced me to go, and somehow we found ourselves on a plane Friday night and spent two full days and two evenings in that miraculous city. Being with Father made me feel younger, like the little girl I had been years ago when we still lived together. It was the first time since Jonathan's death that I felt really excited, and I even discarded my black uniform for casual and comfortable dresses and slacks. We visited the Sistine Chapel and St. Peter's Basilica, the Colosseum, the Pantheon, the Trevi Fountain, and many of the other famous churches and squares. Bowing to our Romanian roots, we made sure to see Trajan's Column and its bas-reliefs immortalizing the occupation of Dacia by the Romans in the first century, and on Sunday afternoon prior to dining in Trastevere, we went to see the statue of the Capitoline Wolf at the Palazzo dei Conservatori on the Campidoglio.

Copies of the various depositions Carlos was working on came by fax delivered to Canton of Ticino. Remy drove into town to get them, since most arrived in the early afternoon while my children were napping. Belinda had typed explanatory notes describing the circumstance for each interview and the effort that went into it. As Carlos explained, the depositions had limited legal value, but they contributed a great deal toward rebuilding my good image after the damage caused by the magazine articles.

The first deposition was from Mrs. Shames. Carlos had asked Ben Pinkas to take it. Mrs. Shames had just moved to a retirement home at kibbutz Dalia. A journalist from *The National Expose* had interviewed her previously. When

Pinkas spoke to her, she was warm and friendly. Her joints were swollen, and she moved slowly, but her mind was sharp as a tack.

Below is the transcript.

Name: Rosalie Shames
Place and year of birth: Poland, 1906
Place of interview: Kibbutz Dalia, Israel
Relationship to Miriam Sommer: Landlady

Miriam Sommer, yes, I call her Miri. She started renting from me in 1974. She was a girl then, barely twenty-one or twenty-two years old. I know because I checked my records when I talked to the newspaper. In 1975 she went to America to get married but continued renting for several years. That's the kind of tenant I like—they send money, but they're not there to make any difficulties. Not that Miri had ever caused me a problem. She hadn't. She was polite and kept her place clean. Quiet. She was like a little princess. Sometimes I would talk to her and give her advice: Go out there and find somebody because it's hard for young women. A boyfriend, you know, like I would tell my daughters. She listened, and she seemed to agree with me, always with a smile on her face.

Once she came back from America for several months to get her visa resolved. You should have seen her then. She looked more mature, more sure of herself, and she had a beautiful car. We even went on a day trip together.

I say this because when she came over the first time to check out the place, you know, in 1974, she was very shy. She came with a man, a doctor. They weren't holding hands or anything, and I thought he was her uncle. They looked at the apartment together, but only he spoke, and he was the one to pay in advance and cosign her papers. He was older than her and spoke Hebrew much better. It was clear he had been in the country for a while. I later learned he was from South Africa and she from Romania. I myself am from Poland, and I got here during the Mandate. When I came, there was nothing. Today you look around and see highways and buildings everywhere.

So I told the American reporter about the doctor. I gave his name, Zvi Rave, because I found it in my records. He said the magazine would run a story about Miri's husband, who had died suddenly and had been an important man who deserved the attention. Miri had two children, they said; quite a tragedy. I didn't accept their money, and I answered all their questions.

Then my daughter bought a copy of the American magazine and translated the article for me. It was a few days before I moved to this place, and I got very upset to see how bad people are and how they lie and fling dirt at each other. Believe me, I cried in frustration.

You know, I was the landlady in that building, and part of what I did was observe people. I constantly watched them coming and going. I rarely left. Zvi Rave used to come a few times a month, maybe, and only in the afternoons and the evenings. Then he stopped. And he never spent the night, and they never went out.

Miri wouldn't admit it, but I know she was lonely. She went to the university, where she studied photography, and sometimes she went for a walk with her camera. Besides one or two friends, she didn't have anybody. Once a year she went back to see her family in Romania. I remember I even thought that Zvi, whoever he was, could have been a little more mindful of her age and more generous. He could have taken her out from time to time and shown her around. We have restaurants, movie theaters. But he didn't.

Such a beautiful girl Miri was. She needed to live a little.

A day later I received another fax with the depositions that Reggie had taken in Romania. Nelu accompanied him, to guide him and translate. Everywhere they went children surrounded their car. "*Chunga, chunga,*" they yelled. Good thing Nelu was there to tell Reggie that what the children wanted was chewing gum. The locals were wishing for American blue jeans, specifically Lees or Levis, those brands more important than American-style freedom and democracy. Nevertheless, given the grim living conditions, Reggie was impressed by how open and friendly the Romanians were.

They approached Constantin cautiously, so as not to create any problems for him for talking to foreign visitors.

"No worries," Constantin assured them. "I stopped working, and I resigned my party membership and my teaching post. What are they going to do to me? I'm an old man. The sooner we leave the country, the sooner they'll grab my apartment and give it to one of their cronies. That's how things work around here."

Name: Constantin Bardu

Place and year of birth: Kishinev (Romania at time of birth, currently territory of the Soviet Union), 1923

Place of interview: Bucharest, Romania

Relationship to Miriam Sommer: Friend of the family

Miriam and Jonathan have been to my house twice. They were pleasant, straightforward, and generous, and I liked them a lot. That's why I offered and eventually provided Samuel Sommer with medical expertise. I'm a doctor. I help people. That's what I do.

In the United States, when I visited my son, I had the opportunity to see them again. We met in Las Vegas, the evening before Jonathan died. As a doctor I can tell you he was a man in full control of himself, healthy and strong, a man's man. He died of an aneurysm. That is difficult to predict and can happen at any time. The assertion that he was moonstruck in the last months of his life and that Miriam could have manipulated him into changing his will is absurd. If he rewrote the will in her favor, it was because he loved her. Ask any of his recent business associates, and I am sure they will agree.

Nick and I wanted to go to San Diego for the funeral, but we simply couldn't afford it, and I'm not ashamed to admit it. Besides, Nick had to return to work.

In Bistrița, Reggie and Nelu located Miss Diddieny. She had a studio in a development of apartment buildings built in the 1960s near the Youth Concert Hall. Gabriel had performed there once. Miss Diddieny was still single and still working. Her photograph was included. The original must have been in color, but what came through the fax machine was faded black and white. I could see she had aged and remained slim and bony. Her brown hair seemed to have turned gray.

Name: Flora Diddieny

Place and year of birth: Romania, 1933

Place of interview: Bistrița, Romania

Relationship to Miriam Sommer: Family friend

I met Miriam after her parents divorced and her mother moved into her parents' apartment.

What can I tell you? I watched her grow and become a beautiful and resourceful young woman. We lost contact after she left Romania, but the Miriam Sommer I know was not a person to marry an old man for his money.

On her way home from school, she stopped and visited me. I enjoyed that. I lived in a one-room apartment, much smaller than the one I have now, at Sugalete, across the street from the Evangelical church. Sometimes Miriam would get there before me. She knew where I kept the spare key, and she would enter the old room, sit on the wide windowsill, and draw what she saw outside: the church, the statues, the park, and the people. Her talent was obvious. At that early age she drew with a perfect sense of proportion. Her portraits had distinct features and were recognizable. And another detail—she was fascinated with my emergency medical kit. She'd take it out of my drawer, arrange it on the desk, and draw its components separately and together—gauze, Band-Aid, tweezers, scalpel—again and again, in amazing minutia, as if to memorize each and make it her own. It was shortly after the accident she had at the waterfall, when she tore a gash in her leg and almost bled to death. I think playing with that medical kit was her way of making peace with her near-death experience.

One day she drew an imaginary market scene in front of the church. It was so good that I convinced Dr. Levinescu, her grandfather, to hire an art tutor for her. We contacted Gabriel Gelb, who taught art at the high school. Her drawings, and later her paintings, improved. She was dedicated, spending time all throughout Bistriţa with her easel, painting anything and everything she saw.

I had no doubt she'd become an accomplished artist, and I was proud for the role I had played in helping her discover her life calling. By age seventeen she stopped taking lessons from Gabriel, and soon after she left for Israel.

She returned once or twice to visit her mother, but that's all that I know.

Miss Diddieny didn't mention my romantic involvement with Gabriel or the fact that she had helped me procure birth control pills. But the pills were still illegal in Romania, and Miss Diddieny wouldn't be the one to expose our secret.

At the end of the interview, she volunteered to take Reggie and Nelu to see the house where I grew up. They walked past Sugalete Row and the Evangelical church. When they reached my former house, behind the carriage gate the red wooden entrance door was unlocked. Nelu pushed it in, and the three of them entered the dark foyer and stopped at the base of the marble stairway to look at the stone bust of the young maiden. The skylight above was still cracked. A family lived upstairs, but when they knocked at the door, nobody answered. The gate to the backyard was chained.

I should take the kids to visit Bistriţa when they get older, I thought, with a bittersweet feeling in my heart, after reading these side notes by Belinda.

Next Reggie and Nelu found our former neighbor, Ileana, who lived in the same development as Miss Diddieny.

Name: Ileana Petrescu
Place and year of birth: Romania, 1935
Place of interview: Bistriţa, Romania
Relationship to Miriam Sommer: Neighbor

I've known Miriam since she was a child, before she moved in with her grandparents. She used to visit them and stop to see me. She was very sweet. I lived with Tokachi in the former stable in their backyard. Times were tough, but we were young, and every time Miriam came by, we did something fun. I remember we made mustaches out of the silk of freshly picked corn ears.

Later—I don't remember exactly when—Miriam started drawing and painting. I would say she was good. She'd come down to see us and had us both pose for her. As Tokachi put it, that girl had what it took.

Tokachi had never been a loving person, and in the end I left him. As far as I know, he's somewhere in Hungary, Balaton area, I think.

To this day I'm still alone. It's not easy for women, and that's why I understand what Miriam is going through. She was a nice girl, but such is life; what can I say?

While in Bistriţa, Reggie and Nelu looked through the records at City Hall and found the death certificate of Mr. Moisil.

I had expected another good reference from him, but that kind old man who had brightened Grandfather's afternoons with chess games, talked about Russian chess masters, and consumed copious amounts of Russian tea and sugar cookies had left our world.

They also tracked down Mathew. He was a veterinary doctor, married and living on a farm south of town. His specialty was large animals. After talking to him, Reggie determined there was no valuable information to be derived from an actual deposition, but he included a photograph and a statement. I immediately recognized Mathew's crop of blond hair and his Adonis look that drove schoolgirls to fight over him, now marred by a wrinkled forehead.

"I was a teenager, of course, and I behaved like a jerk," he said in his statement, referring to my accident by the waterfall.

Nelu and Reggie contacted Cecilia. She was a teacher at the high school I had attended and remembered me well. She thought Gabriel lived in Western Europe, perhaps in Switzerland, but she didn't care to know.

A surprise contained in the package was the deposition from Elena, Pani's cousin, who was still in Vama, that little town in northern Moldova near the border with the Soviet Union. Traveling to Vama took a full day.

Name: Elena Sabot (née Stakarovski)
Place and year of birth: Poland (Galicia), 1928
Place of interview: Vama, Romania
Relationship to Miriam Sommer: Varvara (Pani) Stakarovski's cousin

I don't know Miriam, but I feel like I'm related to her.

We found Varvara in 1969, twenty-five years after we retreated from Poland and got separated. She was happy to come live with us, but she missed the Levins, or the Levinescus, as they called themselves after the communists took over. And of all of them, she missed Miriam the most.

I don't know if you know that the Levins had taken Varvara off the streets after the war and literally saved her life. She worked for them and slept in the kitchen, but they surrounded her with kindness and treated her like family. They called her Pani, which means madam in Polish.

I'm married, and I have my husband's family and our children here, but Varvara had nobody after the war. When she came here, she helped a lot in the house. She was a great cook—the best. And she liked to eat. The older she got, the more she ate, and we wanted to stop her because she had diabetes, but it wasn't easy. She would eat and eat, as long as food was lying around. All in all, she was happy here, I hope, but it was hard for her.

She had never loved a man. She had never married and never finished high school. And she was so big.

Sometimes the two of us would walk to the river—Moldova River, you know—or to the Egg Museum and talk about Miriam, about how smart she was, how beautiful and educated, how she understood art, and what a great artist she was. Miriam was the daughter Varvara never had. She would have liked to see her again and dreamed about going on a trip to Bistriţa, but that was too far away.

In Bucharest, on their way back home, Reggie and Nelu looked for Claudia and uncovered that she had married a Cuban and now lived in Havana, clearly outside of their reach.

Another fax came from Pinkas. He had met Peter, my friend from my car trips through Israel.

Name: Peter Horowitz
Place and year of birth: USA, 1952
Place of interview: Haifa, Israel
Relationship to Miriam Sommer: Acquaintance

I met Miriam through Judith and Michael, who took art classes together with her at the University of Haifa. Miriam moved to the States, while Judith and Michael continued their studies and got married. Then Miriam returned to resolve a visa issue and dropped by the university to look for her friends. I happened to be there, and that's how we met. I'm still at the university, studying for my PhD and working as a teaching assistant.

Miriam had a large station wagon and was looking for people to travel with her and explore the country. The three of us jumped in right away. I was smitten with her.

I'm from Pittsburgh originally, from Shadyside. Now I live in Neve Sha'anan. Miriam's Hebrew was rusty, and we spoke English when we were alone. She had a wonderful accent, if you know what I mean. I'm single, and I meet many women, but not many like her. She was beautiful and moved with much grace. She was generous, too. The four of us drove to Masada, to Galilee, and to other places. She never asked us for gas money, not even once.

At Sachne I took Miriam swimming, and we held hands in the water. She was white like a marble statue and very attractive. It's been years, but I'll never forget. I felt encouraged that afternoon and asked her to dinner. She said she was married, which, of course, didn't matter to me. But it mattered to her. She brought me to my senses in a firm and delicate way. No woman had ever rejected me so sensibly, and it was clear to me she had said no to many other men in her past.

I'm sorry if she's going through a difficult time, and please let me know if there is anything I could do to help.

Carlos was right. All these depositions and snippets from my past didn't advance our legal case, but they helped restore my confidence. It was money well spent.

After reading the depositions, I walked through the streets of Lugano as if I was floating. Life seemed normal again. I hugged my children. Marybeth discovered a *Konditorei* near Stazione di Lugano, and we went there for ice cream and fun. Remy drove us to the farmers' market in his Rover. For Yari, we found a summer program for three and four-year-olds. Bari started taking horseback riding lessons. Jonathan would have been very proud of him. In Parco Civico we were caught in a downpour. The trees offered little protection. Marybeth picked up Yari, I held Bari's hand, and we ran to the car. We laughed. The afternoon air was warm, and we got soaked to the skin. At home I saw that my black sandals were ruined. We dried the children and changed them, and I told Marybeth I'd go back into town and get myself a new pair.

I didn't want to parallel park, so I found a multilevel garage and took the escalator to the street. After the storm, the air smelled good. Rainwater dripped from gutters and accumulated along the curb. Pedestrians were everywhere. Cars passed on the wet pavement, raising a fine mist.

It wasn't the first time I was alone in Lugano, but I felt liberated. How wonderful that all those people in Romania and Israel had good things to say about me. I was thankful to them, and I loved them for it. They made me nostalgic and oddly happy. Thinking of them—Ileana and Diddieny and Mrs. Shames and Peter and Pani's cousin and even Mathew—made me proud.

They said I was beautiful and showed promise, and I hoped they were right. Perhaps I really had a gift. Like Georgia O'Keeffe, what I needed was peace.

My old friends, all of them, had grown, matured, and changed. Some of them had moved away, and some had died.

I was sad to hear the news about Pani. I imagined telling her about Jonathan, bringing Bari and Yari along and enjoying the surprise on her face. Spoiling her with gifts. Your memory is with me forever, I'd say. She'd hug me. We'd cry. We would ride to the Egg Museum in my limousine and admire the hand-painted Easter eggs. But now it was too late. In a way, she had died young, I mean, much younger than Mr. Moisil, and I was sorry he had died as well—my grandfather's friend.

Then there were those people who had left the country, Gabriel and Claudia, Tokachi even, all over the world. Things were bad in Romania, and people were leaving in droves. But to go live in Cuba, my God!

Too bad they didn't find Gabriel Gelb. If he had settled in Switzerland, he could be in this town. He could be vacationing here or come here on business. His train could be pulling just now into the station.

If all those people were good to me, I could be good, also. If they were kind, I could be kind.

The shoe store was on the other side of the street. I waited for the light to turn green and then crossed.

The saleslady greeted me. She was young, maybe my age, neatly coifed. I lifted the veil off my face and showed her the sandals I liked on the rack. She nodded. It was a small store, a boutique, and I was the only customer.

While she was gone, I thought about Rome. In Rome I had told Father I was enjoying myself for the first time since Jonathan died. I liked the streets, the imprint of ancient history, the art, and the crowds. I liked distances that were short.

"Walking," I said to my father, "is moving at a human pace. Cars are too fast."

"Kiddo," he said, "you have Europe in your DNA."

"Yeah, but I like America, too."

"America's not a different country or continent. America's another planet," my father said.

In Rome, we had gone to see the Capitoline Wolf. As incredible as that myth was, with a she-wolf who suckled two little boys, it was only after Romulus killed his twin brother, Remus, that he succeeded in building Rome. Achievement required sacrifice. I remembered the replica of the statue in Bucharest, standing in Romana Square as a symbol of Romania's Latin heritage and then being moved to a more obscure location so as not to overshadow the Soviet influence.

The saleslady returned balancing five cardboard boxes in her hands. I tried on pairs of sandals one after the other. There was a full-length mirror on a column in the middle of the room. I looked in the mirror, removed the veil altogether, folded it, and placed it in my purse.

"Sorry for your loss," the saleslady said.

"Thank you," I said.

I bought two pairs of sandals and left the store.

When I first met Jonathan, our relationship had been light and playful. I had been eager for friendship and love, but how could I have known? *A white veil, a black veil?*

Things change all the time, and they're never what they appear to be.

I looked up. The wind had blown the clouds away, and the sky was light blue. Our love had matured much more slowly than the change in weather, and now I knew without a doubt that Jonathan had been my true love. That day I understood that people change and that building a life together requires sacrifice. Why wait for others to show goodness when I could go first? I didn't have to fight Loretta, or Leah, or Doru Ionescu. I could forego a part of my money, be generous and kind.

Jonathan would want that.

Outside the shoe store, I saw a man walking ahead of me. Two women were in between us. The man was slender, Gabriel's height, and he carried a black guitar case. The garage was two and a half blocks away on the other side of the street. The man walked in that direction. When he got to the corner, the light was green. From where I was, I could see he wore glasses. Gabriel had glasses as well. When I arrived at the crossing, the light turned red. The man was walking quickly on the other side toward the garage. The distance between us was growing. There were no cars in the street, but people waited for the light to turn. This was Switzerland—one didn't cross against a red light. On my shoulder I had my purse, and I held the bag with the two shoeboxes in my hand. The bag was bulky. When the light turned, I started to run. It was silly of me. The man couldn't possibly be Gabriel. I had learned from the report he might live in Switzerland, I had thought about him, and now I was seeing him in the streets. Switzerland was a big country, and Gabriel could be anywhere. I ran the full block and then slowed down. The man was less than ten yards away. And if he did turn out to be Gabriel, then what? Would I give him a hug? Would he play his guitar for me? The man walked fast, and I kept pace with him. I started sweating. The shopping bag was hitting my knees, and the top button of my blouse came undone.

We entered the garage. He got on the escalator and stopped, waiting to be taken to the upper floors.

I stopped on the escalator a few steps below him.

"Gabriel," I said, but my voice was too weak. I needed to breathe. "Gabriel, is that you?" I said louder in English.

He stepped off the escalator on the second floor, turned, and asked me, "Are you talking to me?"

"I'm sorry," I said. "I mistook you for somebody else."

Carlos called. "They caved."

At first I didn't know what he meant.

He explained that he had received a message from Milford Thomas that they wanted to talk. They wanted to settle out of court and proposed a 50-50 split, but that was just the beginning. Carlos could get 70-30 or even 80-20, and the 20 would cover Loretta, Leah, and Doru Ionescu as well.

"Listen, Miriam," Carlos said. "There is something else. I have a client I need to meet next week in Paris, and I could stop and visit you. I would love to see you and explain face to face."

The next day I received another fax containing a deposition from Mona Kurt, Doña Alexandra's daughter; some information about other people from South America, obtained by Kenneth Antonio Topaz; and a deposition from Lydia.

NO PORTRAIT IN THE GILDED FRAME

Name: Maria (Mona) Kurt (née Martinez de Salina)
Place and year of birth: Oaxaca, Mexico, 1932
Place of interview: New York, USA
Relationship to Jonathan Sommer: Former associate

After my father died, first my brother, Felix, and then I moved to the United States. People blamed us for leaving our mother behind. Others said it was her own doing.

My mother was a stern woman, and my father did not know how to handle her. She wasn't happy in her marriage, but she wouldn't admit it, and she took her frustration out on us. She was very proud. People who knew her say I'm like her.

Because of her, neither Felix nor I wanted to live on the ranch. If my mother suffered when we left, she didn't show it.

In 1956 Jonathan wrote to us that our mother was dying and asked us to come. Felix didn't want to go. He worked on Wall Street and found an excuse to avoid the trip. I was studying at the Conservatory in Baltimore. I felt remorseful and went.

Jonathan met me at the airport in Oaxaca. He was young, much younger than I had expected, considerate, and good looking. I spent a week on the ranch, and when he drove me back to the airport, I think we both felt an unexpected bond between us.

Mother died less than a month later. To our surprise, in her will she left Jonathan one-third of the ranch. When Felix and I inquired, we found out that Jonathan had been her lover. He pleaded with us to leave the money in the business, but Felix was angry and wouldn't hear of it.

I, myself, went through a range of emotions. I shared in my brother's discomfort and wondered how a young man my age could honestly fall in love with a widow twenty-five years older. Yet I was content my mother had found some happiness in the end, a fact that exonerated me (us) in a way, and I left my money in the ranch. To keep things going, Jonathan had to borrow and buy my brother out. Several years later Jonathan sold the ranch and paid me the original sum and my part of the profit, which represented a huge amount. He made me a wealthy woman.

He visited Baltimore once, years later, and we met. He told me about my mother, and I understood he had loved her a lot. There was this magic again between us, but we knew it was to no end.

I'm sorry he died.

Mona's deposition was followed by a short note about her marriage to one Andrew Kurt, and about their children. They now lived in a suburb of New York.

Kenneth Antonio Topaz learned that Jonathan's uncle from São Paulo, Martin Sommer, the doctor, had died. His three children, who were alive and married, had only a sketchy recollection of Jonathan that did not merit being recorded at all.

Kenneth tried locating Consuela and failed.

Lydia's deposition was long and flattering, as I would have expected from a good old friend. The one thing that pleased me a lot was her recollection of seeing me for the first time on the plane that took both of us from Romania to Israel. She was already inside, surrounded by her family, so I didn't see her when I came down the aisle and walked past her. She recognized me later at the university, but mentioned it only briefly to me.

The way Miriam looked that day, Lydia stated in her deposition, *I was convinced she was an American movie star. I thought that once we landed in Israel, she'd be picked up by a limousine and taken straight to the Ritz.*

I remembered the moment I boarded the plane, on November 7, 1972, almost to the day three years before meeting Jonathan. I was wearing an ankle-length flowing brown skirt, a chocolate-brown cashmere sweater, and a long white wool overcoat that enhanced my figure. My black straight hair reached to the middle of my back. I knew that my clothes cut a sharp contrast with the dull and practical travel attire of the time, and I was aware that everybody was watching me. I carried one hatbox from my grandmother and one rectangular box of chocolates from Jacob in one hand, my sunglasses, the boarding pass, the passport, and an Italian leather purse in the other. I had just said good-bye to my family and was suddenly alone, for the first time in my life, on a plane traveling into the unknown. I was scared, but I didn't want to show it. In retrospect, Lydia could have realized I was no American actress simply by spotting my passport—a drab brown passport issued to people without citizenship. But she didn't see it or she didn't think about it, thus locking within herself that idealized image of me forever. And now, so many years later, when she finally shared that memory with me, she helped me again to rebuild my trust in myself, for the way I appeared to her, then and now, was important to me.

———— ✇ ————

I drove my Mercedes to Stazione di Lugano, parked near the century-old building, and went inside. Carlos was arriving by train from Lucerne and staying for the weekend at Barony Le Pergole on Via Violetta, a few minutes by car from our villa. It was noontime. We had been in Switzerland for six weeks, and I realized I was happy to see him. And he was bringing news, good news, I hoped.

Dressed in an elegant suit, white shirt, and red bow tie, he stood out in the crowd of summer travelers. A lawyer coming to see his most important client, wanting to look impressive. In one hand he carried his indispensable black briefcase, in the other, a small leather suitcase. When he saw me, he put it down and waved to me.

"Miriam," he said. "Nice to see you."

"Same here." As we hugged, his cheek brushed mine, and I detected a vague smell of dust and aftershave lotion. "Are you tired?"

"A little," he said.

"I'll take you to the hotel to check in. Then you can come to the villa, and we'll have lunch. Remy's cooking."

"I have a better idea. Drop me off at the hotel, and I'll pick up you and Marybeth and the kids at three in the afternoon. Wait for me on your pier."

"On the pier?" I said.

"Yes," he said. "I have a surprise for you."

———— ✇ ————

Carlos had chartered a 128-foot white motor yacht and crew for a few hours. Bari and Yari proudly wore life vests. Everything on board was modern and sparkling. On the upper bridge, a lounge area had doors that opened out to a full-width aft deck with chaise lounges and sun pads. A table was set with snacks, desserts, fruit juices, white wine, and champagne. The owner's suite had a private office area. Several guest cabins with well-appointed living spaces occupied the levels below. Steep exterior stairs led to them.

The children went berserk. They ran up and down the stairs and entered all cabins and lay in all beds. They liked the high-tech bathrooms the best. They went to the front of the yacht and, holding on to the railing, they watched the sharp bow parting the waters. Once safely on our way, the captain called them into the cockpit and let them hold the wheel. They hollered, sat on lounge chairs for a few seconds, and ran again. They gobbled down their snacks. Marybeth went everywhere with them. She sighed, rolled her eyes, and clasped her hands, but she was excited, too.

When I was alone with Carlos, we talked about Jonathan's will. We had already agreed to meet and review details the next day, but I found it hard to avoid the subject.

"What do you think made them come to us with a suggestion to settle?" I asked.

"My demurrer, but mostly the depositions from Jonathan's business associates," Carlos said. "I didn't send them to you, but I sent them to Milford. He's a smart lawyer; he knows. These business people we deposed all agree Jonathan was a man at the top of his game, determined, impossible to manipulate. And they themselves are well respected, with connections and money and stature."

I looked at the water. It was perfectly calm. I had seen it every day from the shore, but here, in the middle of the lake, the gleaming surface borrowed the gray and the blue of the sky, and the green of the trees, and the black of the rocks and the mountains, while deep under it stayed indifferent and cool.

"Then why should we agree?" I asked. "I dislike Loretta. Why put millions on the table for her?" I had already decided I would agree to a settlement, but I wanted to be like the water of the lake, deep and keeping things to myself.

Carlos filled two champagne flutes.

"Because we don't know what Judge Russell might decide, and if Milford loses, they are likely to appeal, and this could drag on and on, for two years or longer. Do you want to wait? Do you want more gossip in the papers, more people from the past to lay claim to Jonathan's fortune? Haven't you suffered enough? Put the millions on the table to work for you," he said and handed me the champagne.

I took a sip. The breeze blew my hat off.

Carlos laughed. "Why are you still in black?"

"I think I'll keep dressing in black for a year. It's an old custom. That's the least I can do."

"It becomes you," he said.

I looked away. The lake was narrow and long. With every turn we took, we saw new scenery, forests, small towns, mountain peaks. There were birds in the sky.

"Thank you for a perfect afternoon," I said.

"I'm glad you're enjoying it."

"The boys are enjoying it also, and the yacht is...*majestic*."

Music was coming through the loudspeakers.

Carlos poured more champagne, and we clinked glasses.

"The sooner I reach a deal for you, the sooner you'll return to the States. This is quite an incentive," he said.

"Listen to the music," I said.

"I mean it."

"I'm not returning." The words escaped from deep inside me. I didn't know I would utter them. They floated into the air and mixed with the song. The song didn't matter. I realized I had thought that thought, but I had never dared say it aloud.

Carlos loosened his bow tie.

"I think I want to move back to Israel," I continued. "I've been hurt, and I want to isolate myself from the past and from all the people who tried tearing me apart. I want to hide for a while. I think I'll keep the house in San Diego but live in Israel and see how I feel. I want to forget."

"I think you wanted to do this all along. That's why you had your paintings sent there. You would like to start painting again, wouldn't you?"

"Very much."

The song ended.

"You're not religious," he said.

"I'm not, but of late I think Israel might be where I belong. Where my children belong. I have family there, you know. And we want a dog."

"You have good friends in San Diego," he said.

The sun was still in the sky, but there was a pale moon also, on the other side, and clouds were moving toward it.

"You're Catholic, right?" I asked.

"I am."

"God has many faces. When I lived in Romania, I dreaded Christmas and Easter. I felt I was the outsider during the holidays, as if I didn't belong. Kind of the way I feel in the States during the Super Bowl." I laughed at my own comparison.

"I could teach you football," he said, and he grabbed the railing, facing the lake. "In the very beginning, I didn't like you too much." He turned and looked at me. "I thought you were out for his money, but slowly my feelings changed."

"I didn't like you in the beginning either," I said. "People change all the time and learn from their losses."

"Will I be able to visit you in Israel?"

"If you want to, of course."

"Miriam, you and I, do you think we stand a chance?"

Clouds covered half of the moon.

"It's too early," I said.

EPILOGUE

(From the *Savion Flier's Monthly Supplement*, November, 1982)

An anonymous buyer has finally purchased the famed Rembrandt Estate in the exclusive Tel Aviv suburb of Savion. The property used to belong to businessman Albert Silverstein, who was rumored to have decorated the first floor of the main house with over fifty valuable oil paintings, including an original Rembrandt—thus the name of the estate. After the death of Silverstein four and a half years ago, his adult children, who all live abroad, waged a prolonged legal battle over the inheritance, which eventually resulted in the placement of the property into the hands of a select real-estate broker from West Germany. The paintings might have been part of the purchase.

Recently the wealthy inhabitants of Savion have observed a beautiful young woman and two little boys taking residence on the Rembrandt Estate. So far, the young woman has kept to herself. She has made no attempts to meet the neighbors and has not been seen in the presence of men, if one discounts the two occasions when she appeared with a middle-aged male companion who was wearing a white shirt and red bow tie.

During her walks through the quiet streets of Savion, the woman is sometimes accompanied by her boys and their nanny, and other times she is alone with her white husky. She is always clad in black, from her soft low-heel shoes to the diaphanous veil that drapes over her face and most of her long charcoal hair.

It is rumored that she is a connoisseur of fine art and that while studying at the University of Haifa, she enjoyed the attention of many admirers. Later she married an older, wealthy American who died and left her and the two little boys a fabulous fortune.

During the long days of summer, people of all walks of life travel from Tel Aviv to Savion to catch a glimpse of this captivating and elusive new celebrity.

ACKNOWLEDGEMENT

I am grateful to the people who generously gave their time, feedback and advice in the process of writing this book:

My friends Marianna Roman, Dr. Michael Finkenthal, Sarah Herman, and my daughter Nira Duvan, read the first draft of the novel and provided valuable input.

My friend Rebecca Garcia patiently performed the first complete edit of the manuscript and spent countless hours with me debating and discussing characterization and plot.

Throughout the four years it took to write the novel, the members of the Baltimore Novel Workshop—Lucy Hoopes, Clark Riley, Sandy Kelman, Karol Edlund, Judy Tanner, and Judy Rousuck—reviewed the chapter by chapter progress of the story during our biweekly meetings. They gave me written and verbal comments, always kind, encouraging, and to the point.

My son and daughter in law, Daniel and Denise Duvan, who live in San Diego, showed me around town helping me paint it in words.

My wife Viorica, my most critical reader and trusted editor, was always at my side while writing the novel and throughout the times and places described in *No Portrait in the Gilded Frame*.

AUTHOR BIOGRAPHY

Tudor Alexander was born in Bucharest in 1950 and moved to the United States in 1977. He holds a master's degree from the Polytechnic Institute of Bucharest and an MBA from the University of Connecticut. He lives in Maryland with his wife, Viorica, and has two adult children.

Alexander started writing in high school, publishing many short stories in literary magazines. After the 1989 Romanian revolution, he began contributing to a Romanian weekly publication. He published several novels and short story collections in Romania, including *The Runners*, *Smoke*, *Planet New York*, *One Morning and One Afternoon*, and *The Visitor*.

Planet New York is available on Amazon in English.

Alexander writes in both Romanian and English. His books feature immigrants yearning to adapt to their new surroundings and escape their past. Often, the characters are people who, like him, took a leap of faith to find political and intellectual freedom.

Made in the USA
Lexington, KY
22 August 2016